## PRAISE FOR

# CAUGHT U

"Fresh, engaging, and incredibly sexy! Be prepared to have a bucket of ice cubes handy to cool you down! It's lip-biting good!"

—*Under the Covers Book Blog*

"Amazing from the very first page. It is definitely one of the best books I have read." —*Night Owl Reviews* (5 stars, Top Pick)

"A very steamy and satisfying read." —*Fiction Vixen*

"*Caught Up in You* is Roni Loren's best book to date. An angsty backstory made beautiful by a hero who doesn't know how perfect he is. Don't miss this Ranch treat!"

—Carly Phillips, *New York Times* bestselling author

# NOT UNTIL YOU

"Loren takes readers on a wild, sexy ride!" —*Fresh Fiction*

# FALL INTO YOU

"4½ Stars! Steamy, occasionally shocking, and relentlessly intense, this book isn't for the faint of heart. But with fiery, emotional characters and their blisteringly passionate relationship, it is also one that isn't easily forgotten." —*RT Book Reviews*

*continued . . .*

"Fast-paced and riveting with clever plot twists. Loren writes vivid descriptions, and *Fall Into You* is a hot erotic romance."

—*USA Today*

"This is quickly becoming one of my favorite erotic romance series . . . It's hot, it's sexy, full of alpha dominant goodness, and a thrill of a story."

—*Under the Covers Book Blog*

"*Fall Into You* is an erotic romance with heart and serious heat, one that I could not put down."

—*Romance Novel News*

## Melt Into You

**RITA finalist for Best Contemporary Single Title Romance**

"Quite a ride. The story is heartfelt and pulls you into the relationships with the characters. *Melt Into You* takes the traditional version of romance and twists it so that the idea of three individuals in a relationship seems perfectly right."

—*RT Book Reviews*

"I can't say enough about this book. It really gave me everything that I want in a romance. It's edgy, entertaining, emotional, and romantic. It's just beautifully written. The sex scenes are sizzling hot. The BDSM scenes are accurate and descriptive. The plot line is like a roller-coaster ride. It's full of ups and downs and moments where you can't take any more and your tummy is in knots, but when you hit the last page, you say, let's ride it again."

—*Guilty Pleasures Book Reviews*

"This one is deeply emotional, gut-wrenching at times, and sexy as sin."

—*Romance Novel News*

"Roni Loren's books are masterful, story-driven, sensual, and very erotic . . . definitely one of my have-to-get-as-soon-as-possible series!"
—*Under the Covers Book Blog*

"Loren does an incredible job portraying the BDSM lifestyle in a sexy and romantic way . . . Loren should definitely be put on the must-read list."
—*Bookpushers*

## CRASH INTO YOU

"Loren writes delicious, dark, sensual prose . . . Multidimensional characters, a very complicated relationship, and suspense combine to make *Crash Into You* unique and emotional—an impressive debut from Loren."
—*USA Today*

"Revved up and red-hot sexy, Roni Loren delivers a riveting romance!"
—Lorelei James, *New York Times* bestselling author of the Blacktop Cowboys and Rough Riders series

"Hot and romantic, with an edge of suspense that will keep you entertained."
—Shayla Black, *USA Today* bestselling author of *Ours to Love*

"A sexy, sizzling tale that is sure to have readers begging for more! I can't wait for Roni Loren's next tantalizing story!"
—Jo Davis, author of *Hot Pursuit*

"This steamy, sexy yet emotionally gripping story has the right touch of humor and love to keep readers coming back for a second round."
—Julie Cross, author of the Tempest novels

*Titles by Roni Loren*

CRASH INTO YOU
MELT INTO YOU
FALL INTO YOU
CAUGHT UP IN YOU
NEED YOU TONIGHT

*Not Until You*

PART I: NOT UNTIL YOU DARE
PART II: NOT UNTIL YOU RISK
PART III: NOT UNTIL YOU CRAVE
PART IV: NOT UNTIL YOU TRUST
PART V: NOT UNTIL YOU BEG
PART VI: NOT UNTIL YOU SURRENDER
PART VII: NOT UNTIL YOU BELIEVE
PART VIII: NOT UNTIL YOU LOVE

*Specials*

STILL INTO YOU

# Need You Tonight

RONI LOREN

HEAT | NEW YORK

THE BERKLEY PUBLISHING GROUP
Published by the Penguin Group
Penguin Group (USA) LLC
375 Hudson Street, New York, New York 10014

USA • Canada • UK • Ireland • Australia • New Zealand • India • South Africa • China

penguin.com

A Penguin Random House Company

This book is an original publication of The Berkley Publishing Group.



Library of Congress Cataloging-in-Publication Data

Loren, Roni.
Need you tonight / Roni Loren.
pages cm
ISBN 978-0-425-26856-8
I. Title.
PS3612.O764N44 2014
813'.6—dc23
2013044622

PUBLISHING HISTORY
Heat trade paperback edition / March 2014

PRINTED IN THE UNITED STATES OF AMERICA

10 9 8 7 6 5 4 3 2 1

Cover photograph © Photokin/Shutterstock
Cover design by Rita Frangie.

To my husband, my family, and my readers.
Without your support, I would just be that weird girl
who spends way too much time thinking
about imaginary people.

# Need You Tonight

# PROLOGUE

*Someone's naked ass is on my imported marble countertops.* That was Tessa's first thought when she walked into her kitchen that warm Tuesday afternoon. Not, *Why is Doug home this early?* Or, *Why does he have his pants around his ankles?* And most definitely not *Why is my best friend moaning like an injured cat?* Nope. Tessa's brain couldn't absorb those things just yet. Instead all she could think about was how there was a butt cheek sliding along the spot where she'd chopped strawberries for breakfast.

The two occupants in the kitchen didn't even notice they were no longer alone, apparently too caught up in their counter defiling to bother. God, were they *that* oblivious and swept up in passion? It's not like she'd been particularly quiet walking in. And she'd slept with the man who'd dropped trou in this little tableau for the last thirteen years. She knew he didn't inspire losing yourself to the moment. But maybe he saved his good tricks for Tuesday afternoons when he fucked the woman Tessa would've trusted her life with before today.

Tessa cleared her throat, attempting to draw their attention, but all that greeted her was the sound of Doug telling that *lying bitch* how hot she was. Rage washed through Tessa in a slow, powerful roll, boiling up and over until she was shaking with it. She calmly set down her purse next to the fruit bowl and wrapped her hand around a large navel orange. Without pausing to reflect, she lifted the fruit and launched it right at her husband's head.

It went whizzing past him without notice, sailing into the living room, but she couldn't stop herself now. She picked up another and hurled it even harder. This one hit him right on the ear with a fat thud.

"*What the fuck?*" Doug's hand went up to his ear, and he swiveled his head her way. "Shit."

The traitor on the counter opened her eyes then, her gaze going wide.

But Tessa kept throwing. Oranges, apples, a grapefruit that landed with satisfying impact. It was as if some other force had possessed her. Fruit whizzed across the kitchen, pelting the both of them as they scrambled to get up and pull their clothes around themselves.

"Ow, Tessa, stop it! What the fuck is wrong with you?" Doug roared as he yanked at his pants with one hand while trying to fend off flying fruit with the other.

"What is wrong with *me*? *Me?!*" Tessa shouted, knowing she sounded like a lunatic but unable to stop herself.

"Tessa, honey," Marilyn said, hands out in front of her, blouse still hanging open. "Let's just calm down, okay?"

Tessa pinned her former best friend with a glare. "Did you just *dare* speak to me?"

"Marilyn, sweetheart," Doug said softly, putting a hand on her elbow and blocking her from Tessa with his body. "Why don't you get out of here? I'll deal with her."

*Sweetheart? Deal* with her? Loud, crashing bells were going off in Tessa's head. She was glad the knife block was out of reach because she wasn't sure she could trust herself in that moment.

Marilyn nodded after a quick, worried glance at Tessa then hurried through the living room toward the sliding glass doors that led to the pool area and a backyard exit. Apparently, she knew better than to try to walk by Tessa to get to the front door. Wise move. Because Tessa was ready to throw down Jerry Springer style.

With a tired sigh, Doug turned back to Tessa, his fly still unbuttoned and his dick still half-mast behind the material. The bastard hadn't even lost his erection. In fact, he looked more annoyed that he'd been interrupted than ashamed of what he'd done. Tessa's fist balled. "You lying, cheating asshole."

He pulled on his dress shirt and looked around at the carnage of busted fruit on the floor. "Call the maid and have her come in early to clean this up. It'll draw ants if it sits too long. I've got to get back to my office."

Tessa blinked, almost too stunned to speak. "*That's* what you have to say for yourself?"

"You don't want to hear what I have to say." He adjusted his cuffs like it was any other day of getting ready for work and not like the whole foundation of their marriage had shattered beneath them.

"Oh, no. I really do," she said, seething.

His mouth curled in condescension. "Fine. You want to hear that I need something on the side? That you don't satisfy all of my needs?"

"Your *needs*?" If she'd had another piece of citrus to throw, she would've reached for it then. How many nights had she put all she had into pleasing him even when he hadn't put half the effort toward her? How many times had she donned expensive lingerie trying to catch his eye? She'd been willing to do *anything* for him. She'd loved him.

And he'd been screwing around on her the whole time. With her *best friend*. The thought almost doubled her over. She reached out and grabbed the edge of the counter.

"Look, you're upset. I get it. But, Tessa, it's just sex. I don't love them, and I'm not going to leave you for any of them. They're not a threat to you."

"You have the nerve to talk to me about love right now?" she asked, her throat trying to close. *Them*. So it was more than Marilyn. She wondered if Marilyn knew she was just the tramp in the Tuesday slot on his calendar. "You're disgusting."

His lips curved back into that patronizing smirk he was so good at. "And you're boring in bed and my intellectual inferior, but I've learned to live with it. At least you're nice to look at now that you've gotten your gym routine back on course."

The hateful words knocked the breath right out of her. Doug had said mean things to her before in the heat of the moment. They'd been together since high school, so of course they'd had their fights. He could be critical beyond reason, always watching that she didn't eat too many calories or go outdoors without makeup or say the wrong thing in public. She'd tolerated it because she knew how concerned about image he was in his role as the great Pastor Barrett of the Living Light mega-church. And she'd comforted herself with those moments when he was sweet and indulgent with her behind closed doors. He had the capacity to make her feel like a princess. And even though those times had grown few and far between over the last few years, she'd had no idea his opinion of her had sunk so low. *Boring in bed. Inferior. Stupid.*

God, is that what he told the women he cheated on her with? *My wife isn't too bright, and she's clueless in the sack.*

She grabbed her purse, her stomach threatening to toss up all its contents. She couldn't stand here for another second and look at his smarmy face, smell the scent of sex in the air. "Go to hell,

Doug. I hope you're happy with your college-educated whores. Now you won't have to worry about me getting in the way."

He scoffed. "Come on, Tessa. Stop being melodramatic. You're not going to *divorce* me. Your life and everything in it exists because of me. Leave and it all goes away. You're going to give up all this just because I like a novel fuck every now and then? Please. You wouldn't even know how to survive without a man taking care of you." He grabbed his wallet and flipped a piece a plastic her way. "Here, take the credit card. Go punish me by buying something useless and extravagant—you're good at that—and we'll move on."

The credit card landed at her feet, and she had the urge to spear its platinum face with the heel of her Jimmy Choo pump. He was right. If she left him, every bit of her lifestyle would disappear in a poof. From the clothes on her back to the oranges she'd hurled—all of it was funded by him. There'd be no way to prove his affair in court, not with the legal demons he could afford to hire. And she'd signed a prenup. She'd be left with a pittance of alimony. All the comfort and security she'd worked toward her whole life would be gone. She'd be back where she started all those years ago—a nobody with nothing.

Alone. With no money of her own and only a high-school education to her name.

She bent and picked up the card from the floor, turning it in her fingers before dropping it in her purse.

Doug smiled, satisfied. Victorious.

Without another word, she turned on her heels and calmly walked back out to her Mercedes. When she made it into town, she bought the two most extravagant things she could think of.

The services of an attorney.

And a plane ticket home.

It'd be the last of Doug Barrett's money she'd ever spend.

# ONE

"Hold up. Why are you buying condoms?" Tessa snatched the box of Trojans from Sam's fingertips and held them up like Exhibit A. "You said this was an emergency stop."

Sam sent her an innocent look, one that Tessa had seen her use rather effectively on both sets of foster parents she'd shared with Sam. "What? I'm out. And we may need them."

"You may need condoms," Tessa repeated. "For a *cooking* class."

Sam grabbed another box from the rack. "*We* may need them. I'll get some for you, too. You never know who we might meet."

Tessa groaned and looked up at the buzzing fluorescent lights of the drugstore. Sam's ability to look for dating opportunities around every corner never failed to amaze Tessa. "We're not going to meet anyone. It's a cooking class. It's going to be married couples, women, and gay men."

Which is exactly why Tessa had agreed to go. After months of Sam trying to drag her out to bars or clubs on Friday nights to get her over that "dickwad ex-husband," finally her friend had come up with something that didn't make Tessa's stomach turn and her body break out into a cold sweat. But now, as she took in Sam's snug skirt and high heels, Tessa's dread was growing. She'd thought Sam had simply chosen to dress up because the class was being held at one of the swankiest restaurants in Dallas. But now the puzzle pieces were locking together into a new picture.

"Straight men like to cook, too," Sam pointed out as she strolled away from the prophylactics aisle toward the cosmetics section. "Particularly when it's a Perfect Match meet-up event."

Tessa's shoe squeaked on the floor as she halted midstride. "Sam, you better be screwing with me."

Sam grabbed a lip gloss off a rack and held the colored cap next to Tessa's mouth, frowned, then picked up a different color. "I'm not screwing with you. I'm *helping* you. My friend is the receptionist at the local Perfect Match office. She offered to sneak us onto the list because the event wasn't full. How could I pass it up? It was like fate tapping my shoulder. You want to scratch items off your list. This will accomplish that and maybe get you a date as a bonus. Two for the price of one."

"Learning to cook is on my list. Dating is not. Dating is actually diametrically opposed to the whole spirit of the list."

"Diametrically? Wow, someone's getting *A*s in her night classes." Sam gave her a teasing smile and dropped the lip gloss into her handbasket. "And if I'm not mistaken, one of the items you have on that sacred to-do list of yours is to tackle being 'boring in bed.' How exactly do you plan to fix that one without actually coming into contact with the opposite sex?"

A guy perusing greeting cards across the aisle gave them a sideways glance and smirked. Tessa's face heated. "Could you at least try to keep your voice down while discussing my sex life?"

"*What* sex life?" Sam replied, not bothering to lower her voice. "This is exactly why we're going tonight. You need to loosen up. Be open to a world of infinite possibilities. And by possibilities, I mean hot men."

"Ugh." She should've never let Sam see her stupid list. It'd been something she'd written down in those first few weeks after she'd left Doug and her life in Atlanta. She'd landed in Dallas with no plan, no place to stay, no job. All she'd had was her suitcase and a head filled with all the critical things Doug had said to her over the course of their marriage and that final day in the kitchen.

He'd said she was nothing without him.

And as she'd sat in Sam's guest room one night, trying to put together a resume to apply for jobs and feeling sorry for herself, she'd realized the bastard had been right on some level. Since she'd met Doug in high school, her entire existence had been centered on being who he wanted her to be. Being what *everyone* wanted her to be. For Doug, it was the doting girlfriend. For her classmates, it was the bubbly, popular cheerleader. For her foster parents, it was the girl who never broke the rules and went to church with them every Sunday.

She'd been a master chameleon without ever realizing it. It'd kept her from being moved to yet another home. It'd kept her safe from the vicious bullying in high school. It'd given her a way to secure a future with a man who would take care of her. She'd never be that little girl left alone and scared again.

Only the whole plan had been built out of Popsicle sticks. She'd counted on someone else for her happiness and security. A fatal mistake. How had she ever let herself be so stupid as to trust someone again? Her mother had said she'd always be there and look how that had turned out. Trust was for suckers.

As Tessa had stared at that blinking cursor, she'd made a decision. Never would she let herself depend on anyone else again. She would survive on her own. She'd done it for years as a kid. She could do it now. And she wouldn't just make it through, she'd transform. Thrive. She'd vowed that by the end of the year, a resume of her life would no longer be a stark blank page. She would take those insults Doug had hurled at her and use them as fuel, not only to find a job but to tackle every facet of her life. She'd prove that she was more than the trophy wife she'd let herself become.

But that plan had not included dating. Sex, maybe. Eventually. She didn't plan to enter the convent and abstain for the rest of her life. But dating and any emotional entanglements would only send her sliding backward. "Sam, I'm not ready to date. You know that."

Sam sighed and linked her arm with Tessa's, leading her to the register. "So come for the food and cooking lesson then. The whole point of these meet-ups is that it's a no pressure environment. And we're getting sangria and a fancy meal *for free*. How long has it been since you've had a chance to eat at a restaurant that doesn't serve food wrapped in greasy paper?"

Tessa groaned. "Don't remind me."

One of the main reasons she was interested in cooking classes in the first place was because she missed the delicious meals Doug's housekeeper used to prepare for them and all the gourmet restaurants she and Doug had gone to regularly. If she had to eat another bowl of canned soup, she might stab herself with the spoon. But she didn't have the income to fund nice restaurants anymore. So if she wanted to eat something that wasn't frozen or canned, she was going to have to learn how to cook it herself.

Sam swiped her credit card and took her bag from the cashier. "Exactly. Barcelona is one of the hottest restaurants around. This is your chance for a major treat. The only sacrifice is that you'll have to make small talk with a stranger who happens to have a penis. Big deal."

Tessa sighed, her ability to fight against Sam's hopeful gaze crumbling. Sam had good intentions, even if they were misguided. And really, what was a little awkward small talk with someone Tessa would never see again when there was free sangria to be had? "You're lucky I'm a sucker for tapas."

Sam's face broke into a grin, and she pulled out the lip gloss to give it to Tessa. "Gloss up, babe. Let's go cook some shrimp and break some hearts."

---

When Tessa walked through the doors of Barcelona, it was like walking through a portal to a world she wasn't a native of anymore. Soft Spanish music played, the scent of exotic spices drifted through the air, and the saffron-colored walls flickered with the dancing light of candlelit tables. Every detail screamed trendy elegance and money. As did most of the guests sitting at the tables. She could almost see her old self sitting among them, glass in hand, diamonds sparkling at her throat, her husband sitting across from her telling her about the latest plan he was working on. Anyone looking at them would've been envious.

But seeing the image in her mind's eye now showed a picture that was warped and tarnished. An illusion. The conversation would've been one-sided because Tessa had never understood Doug's business speak. The diamond choker around her neck would've probably been a guilt gift he'd given her after one of his affairs. And the glass would've been filled with sparkling water instead of wine because Doug didn't allow drinking for either of them in public.

She didn't miss this world.

And she didn't miss that woman.

"Hello, ladies, do you have a reservation?" the host asked.

Sam stepped forward. "We're here for the cooking class."

"Ah, yes," he said, his smile welcoming. "Follow me. You'll be in the banquet room."

The host led them through the main dining area and then through a short hallway and another set of doors. The banquet room looked much like the other side of the restaurant, but the lights weren't as low and there were tables set up around the perimeter with cooking equipment and little bowls of ingredients.

In the center of the room, there were smaller, more intimate tables where they'd presumably eat their meal after learning how to prepare it. Pitchers of sangria gleamed ruby red on each table. A number of people were already sitting at the small tables, mingling and drinking. The tinkling sounds of nervous, first-date laughter mixed in with the music.

Tessa's stomach did a flip, and she almost turned to leave. Sam put a hand on Tessa's arm, as if reading her unspoken intention, and guided her forward. "Don't chicken out now."

A man with a clipboard near the entrance grinned brightly. "Welcome to the meet-up ladies. I'm Jim, your event liaison for the night. Names?"

"I'm Samantha Dunbar, and this is Tessa McAllen."

Jim scanned the clipboard, nodding. "Ms. Dunbar, your perfect match is Cory Heath, table five. He's already here if you'd like to head over and say hi. We're letting everyone chat and enjoy their drinks for a few minutes before the class starts. Break the ice, you know?"

"Sure," Sam said, peeking over at the salt and pepper-haired guy at table five, scanning him from head to loafer. "Sounds good."

But Tessa's brain snagged. "Wait a second. I thought we were mingling with everyone?"

Jim smiled. "Oh, no, ma'am. Perfect Match is full service. We took the profile you sent us and matched you up with someone compatible for the evening. No use wasting time on people you have nothing in common with, right?"

"The *profile* I sent in?" Tessa asked, shooting daggers at Sam.

Sam sent her a please-don't-kill-me look and gave Tessa's hand a squeeze. "Just try to have a good time, okay? I promise, it's no big deal. It'll be fun."

With that, Sam hurried off toward her "perfect match." Tessa had to fight hard not to lose it right there. Not only was she going to have to manage a date with a stranger, but said stranger would be under the impression that they'd been matched together. And God only knew what Sam had put in Tessa's profile. Probably that she enjoyed long walks on the beach, tantric sex, and belly dancing.

Jim was scanning his list again, and Tessa smoothed the front of her dress. She hadn't thought to put much effort into her outfit tonight. This was supposed to be a cooking class after all. So she'd stayed in the pale pink blouse and black skirt she'd worn to work. But now she felt plain and out of place. Everyone else had put on their A-game ensemble for date night.

God, why was she even worrying about it? *This isn't a real date.* She'd been trained by Doug to look her best at all times because you never knew who you'd run into, and sometimes that old urge was hard to shake. But she wasn't here to impress anyone. She was here to drink sangria and to learn how to cook. That's it.

The door opened behind her as more people came in.

"Ms. McAllen?" Jim asked, a small frown curving his thin lips as he lifted his gaze from the clipboard. "Do you have your confirmation number with you? You're not showing on my list."

"My what?" She automatically put her hand on her purse but knew she had nothing of the sort in there. "No. My friend set all this up for us both."

"Hmm." Jim tapped his pencil on the clipboard. "Well, I'm not showing you on here, which means we don't have confirmation of your payment. If you'd like to pay the fee now, we can let you stay for the class. Then if you find your confirmation, we'll refund you. But since you weren't on the list, we won't have a match set up for you. You'd be staying for the cooking portion only unless we have any other walk-ins."

No match? That sounded like a fantastic idea. She'd never been so happy to be left off a guest list. "How much is it?"

"Two hundred dollars."

A gasp escaped her lips. *Two hundred dollars?* She should've expected it at a place like this, but the number still caught her off guard. And it was a number she couldn't fund. "I'm sorry. I'll have to find out what happened to my original fee and do this another time. Maybe I can talk to my friend and see if she has the information."

He smiled kindly, but she saw the instant dismissal in his eyes. He knew she was bailing because she didn't have the money. He knew she didn't belong there. "Of course."

Shame tried to edge in, heating her cheeks. But she swallowed it back. She would not get teary over missing some stupid cooking class. She took a step to head toward Sam's table, hoping that even though they were technically party crashers, her friend had some magical confirmation number. But before she could move forward, a warm hand touched her elbow.

"I'll cover the fee."

She stiffened at the touch, but the rich timbre of the man's voice rolled over Tessa like sun-heated ocean water, making her want to close her eyes and soak in it, stay there a while. She turned around, her gaze going up, up, up, and finally colliding with clear blue eyes, a face made for Greek sculpture, and lips . . . God, his lips. She couldn't imagine those had ever been used for anything but sex and sin.

She wanted to bite them.

As that image flitted through her mind, any shot she had at a normal, polite response evaporated into mist.

"I'd hate for you to miss one of the best meals of your life because of a computer glitch," the man said with a ghost of a smile.

Tessa simply stared back like she hadn't understood the language he spoke. The way he held her gaze had her thoughts scattering and her brain reaching for some memory she couldn't quite grab ahold of. She shook her head, breaking the gaze and trying to clear her head. *No. Get it together, Tessa.* This stranger was offering to pay two-hundred dollars for her to eat. She knew how that worked. She'd played that game before. "Really, that's very kind of you to offer. But I'll just come back another time."

He pulled his wallet from his pocket, pulled two crisp bills from it, and handed it to Jim. "I insist. And it's no problem. I'm sure they'll pay me back when they find your original reservation."

Tessa shook her head again, even though her mind was already fast-forwarding and picturing how decadent it would be to sit and sip sangrias with this stranger. But she couldn't fall into her old habits and let him pay her way. It didn't matter that he was gorgeous or that he didn't seem to mind or that he was wearing a watch that said two-hundred dollars was insignificant for him. "I'm sorry. I can't take your money."

Before the stranger could protest, she moved past him and the few people waiting behind them to head for the door. She needed to get out—now. She knew it was ridiculous, but she had the sudden urge to cry, to scream, to pound on something. All she'd wanted tonight was to relax and have a fun girl's night with Sam. Instead, she'd been reminded of the life she used to have, how feeble her bank account was now, and how fucked up she was when it came to men.

She moved through the hallway that led back to the main dining room in a rush, hoping to reach the parking lot before the tears broke free, but a hand touched her shoulder. "Hey, hold up."

The quiet command of his voice and the gentleness of the touch had her slowing her step before she could think better of it. She closed her eyes, took a breath, and turned around, speech prepared. But when she saw the genuine concern on his face, her words got stuck in her throat.

He tucked his hands in his pockets, the move pulling his black dress shirt snug across what looked to be long, lean muscles beneath. His eyes scanned hers. "Are you okay? I didn't mean to chase you off."

She put her hand to her too-hot forehead, trying to catch her breath and center herself. "I'm sorry. It wasn't you. I'm fine. This night just isn't working out like I thought it would."

"Expected to meet your perfect match?"

She made a sound that was some mixture of a snort, a sob, and a laugh. "Ha. Hardly. What a joke that is. A perfect match."

His mouth lifted at the corner, his blue eyes dancing in the flickering light of the wall sconces. "Come on, you don't think there's the perfect someone out there for everyone? Someone who's meant to fit only with you? All the movies say so."

"Movies sell us a bill of goods," she said flatly. All that mystical aligning of stars was such bullshit. People got into relationships for what it could do for them. When the benefit ran out, they moved on. She'd seen that proven over and over again.

"Uh-huh," he said, his tone teasing. "So you're telling me you paid two-hundred dollars to attend something you don't buy into?"

"I didn't pay," she admitted. "A friend told me she'd get me on the list. And I—I wanted to learn to cook and to taste the food."

He glanced back at the closed door and chuckled. "Ooh, a party crasher. How scandalous."

His low laugh was like a gust of summer air across her nerve endings, reminding her of someone long ago. Someone she hadn't had to be a chameleon for. She found herself smiling, her dour mood lifting. "That's me. A scandal a minute. And now I'm causing more. I'm sure your perfect match date is anxiously awaiting you inside."

"Nah, I'm not sold on a perfect match, either. But instant attraction . . ." He stepped closer and the air in the room thickened and warmed. "That I subscribe to. So, Ms. Party Crasher, answer me one question. Are you leaving because you were opposed to the money or me?"

She blinked, caught off guard by the question and his nearness. "What?"

"You came here tonight to take a class and have a nice meal. I was happy to help you do that. So, did you turn down my offer because you think the money comes with strings or is it because you're opposed to spending the evening with me?"

"I—" She wet her lips. The way he'd said *spend the evening with me* had her mind conjuring pictures of him braced over her, his blond hair mussed, his eyes burning through her, and that sensual mouth whispering dirty, filthy things in her ear. Her thighs clenched, and she tried to come up with something to say that wasn't, *God, you're beautiful, please push me up against this wall and make me forget my name.* "I can't accept the money."

That answer seemed to please him. "And me?"

She couldn't tell if it was the warm, smoky spices from the restaurant mixing in, but even the scent of him was exotic and dangerous, tempting. She wanted to bury her face in the open collar of his shirt and inhale. And possibly lick. No, scratch the *possibly* on that, tasting would definitely need to be involved. All her resolve disintegrated in the space between breaths. "I'm not opposed."

He reached out and pushed a stray lock of hair away from her face, the simple brush of fingers like lightning rods touching her skin. "So if I promised you I wouldn't pay a dime for the rest of the evening, would you agree to spend it with me?"

She swallowed hard, the notion almost too much for her psyche to absorb. She knew what he was offering wasn't simply dinner and a chat. There was a ripple of heat beneath each uttered word, a promise. Her body was on board with this plan, whether her good sense agreed or not. Already, she could feel the flush of arousal tightening her nipples and making her panties cling. She hadn't been touched by anyone since Doug, and her experiences with him had always been underwhelming. Just being close to this mystery man made everything inside her feel hot and alive. But it'd be stupid and reckless to say yes. She'd never had a one-night stand. She didn't even know if she was capable of it. Plus, what if she really *was* boring in bed?

She'd told herself that Doug had thrown that out there just to hurt her, but what if there was some truth to it? Her sexual history was nearly nil since she'd gotten married so young. What if she hopped in bed with this guy and was completely out of her league?

"I can't leave. I'm my friend's ride," she said, her voice thready and breathless from him being so close.

His smile was slow, sexy. "I never said we had to leave."

She closed her eyes, his mere presence overwhelming her system and making her heart pound in her throat. "What do you mean?"

His breath brushed her ear. "Take my hand, and I'll show you."

A shiver worked its way down her neck and along her skin. Every nerve ending screamed for his touch, all the years of pent-up frustration surging to the surface and demanding relief. She needed this escape, this release. She needed to feel like a woman again.

When she looked up at him finally, the pure confidence and interest shining there in his eyes had her nerves smoothing. She knew in that moment that this man would never allow her to be boring in bed. This was a man who got what he wanted. A man who wouldn't be afraid to tell her exactly what to do, how he liked it, and how he was going to have her.

Suddenly, she wasn't so interested in sangria anymore.

Or sitting in the car alone to have a good cry.

She reached out and let her hand slide into his.

Maybe she'd scratch something off her list tonight after all.

# TWO

After settling her at the bar, Tessa's mystery date ordered her a sangria.

"Hey, you said you weren't going to spend any money," she reminded him. Not that she was opposed to a guy buying her a drink, but she was holding him to his word.

"On the house, ma'am," the bartender offered as he slid the fruity concoction her way.

Tessa lifted an eyebrow at her date. "Are you the house?"

The corner of his mouth twitched into a boyish expression that almost looked out of place on his Nordic features. "Something like that. Will you excuse me for a few minutes while I get us a table?"

"That's fine." She lifted her drink in mock salute and sipped, the rich taste like an elixir for her nerves. God, she'd missed good wine. "I'll keep this lonely drink company."

"Lucky for the drink." He looked to the bartender. "Make sure the lady has whatever she likes."

"Yes, sir," the bartender said with a quick nod as he poured drinks for other guests.

Before he could turn to leave, she reached for his shirtsleeve, a sudden thought hitting her. "Wait, I don't even know your name."

His smile was easy, pleased. "I know. Yet, you said yes anyway."

She bristled. Well, hell, what did he mean by that? That she was some trampy chick that didn't even worry about names before she let some stranger seduce her in a hallway? She frowned, her own internal answer surprising her. Shit. *Did* she care about his name? This wasn't a real date. It wasn't get-to-know-you-to-see-if-we're-meant-to-be time. They both understood what this was. His name, what he did for a living, where he lived—did any of that matter tonight?

No. It didn't. In fact, maybe it'd be easier if she didn't know all that much about him. That'd make it easier to keep this casual and fun. No risk.

"Call me Van," he said smoothly.

"Van," she repeated. She got the distinct impression that was some sort of nickname. He wasn't offering his last, and she wasn't asking. And if he was going to use a semi-faux name, so could she. "Contessa."

That was the name on her birth certificate, so it wasn't a lie. But she hadn't used the pretentious-sounding thing since elementary school and had legally changed it to Tessa a few years back. However, it was the perfect fit for her night off from her real life. Tonight she wasn't going to be the recovering trophy wife trying to scrape her way through this new life. Tonight she was going to be a carefree woman who'd scored a fling with a man so freaking gorgeous, he looked like he could've walked off a movie set. And she refused to feel bad or guilty about it. She deserved this indulgence, dammit.

"Contessa." Van said her name as if he were rolling it around on his tongue and tasting the flavor of it. He took her hand and brought it to his mouth, kissing the top of it while holding her gaze. "Pleasure to meet you."

She swallowed hard as a hot shiver chased up her arm and down her spine. Man, he was good. Good enough that she should probably be running the other way. Men that smooth and good-looking were dangerous. But hell if she could bring herself to move. Or speak.

"Stay put, Contessa. I'll be back in a moment."

He released her hand, leaving her tongue-tied, and headed toward the main dining room. Tessa turned back to the bar to gather herself. She wrapped her palms around her glass to steady her shaking hands. The bartender gave her a quick glance and a barely concealed smirk. Jesus, she must look like some swooning twit. But this wasn't even close to a fair fight. It'd been so long since she'd had a man lay his charm on her, and certainly never one with as much presence as Van.

Looking back, she realized Doug had never had to truly charm or court her. He'd won her with over-the-top flattery, pretty words, and expensive gifts. Things her inexperience had mistaken for love. He hadn't had to work any harder than that. He'd been handsome and popular. A jock. The perfect match to her cheerleader. And he'd made her promises she was starved for—promises of security, permanence, and safety. A home she would never have to leave.

What a fucking joke it had all been. He'd wanted a wife for window-dressing. Maybe he'd loved her at some point, or thought he had, but obviously anything that had been there had quickly faded, especially after they'd tried to have kids and failed. She'd been stupid to believe marriage would give her some sort of insta-family, some place in the world. Marriage was a sham sold by fairy tales and movies. Of all her married friends, how many had made it past that ten-year mark? Probably not even half. And the ones who were still together, how many were fooling around behind their spouse's back like Doug was?

She finished her drink and ordered a second.

No, this was better. She had her eyes wide open now. No starry-eyed love or misplaced trust mucking up the waters. Tonight she'd probably sleep with Van. Tomorrow, he wouldn't call her. And she wouldn't be waiting for him to do so. No expectations or obligations. No need for lies and pretenses.

In fact, the faux name was going to be her first and last fib of the night. If they were going to have a date, she was going to be one-hundred-percent honest and completely herself. Not the version she thought he wanted to see. She was done with all those bullshit games she'd played for so long. If that screwed things up, then so be it. He didn't deserve to see her naked if that was the case.

A warm hand pressed against her lower back, startling her off her internal soapbox.

"I'm ready for you now."

She wet her lips and set her drink down. The way he'd said it—*I'm ready for you* instead of *Are you ready?*—had made something flutter inside her. Nerves. Anticipation. She wasn't sure, but the feeling was far from unpleasant. She turned to face him, letting him help her off the stool. "Where to?"

He offered her his crooked arm. "Follow me."

They walked through the dining room, turning a few heads. She didn't doubt the glances were for Van and not her. Something about the man called for attention. Not just his height and good looks, but some regal air that enveloped him. She scanned the room as they walked, looking for empty tables, but the place was packed. When they reached the back of the restaurant, Van led her away from the dining room and toward a door down a small hallway.

"Where are we going?"

"Up," he said, pulling the door open for her and guiding her forward.

A set of stairs greeted her along with a chain that had a Closed sign hanging from it. She peeked back over her shoulder. "I don't think we're supposed to go up here."

He leaned past her and unhooked the chain. "I promise they won't kick us out."

So he worked here apparently. Maybe he was the general manager or one of the owners. That last one was a distinct possibility. The man definitely strolled around like he owned the place. But she had a feeling he walked around *every* place like that. Without voicing her questions, she headed up the stairs. When she reached the door at the top, Van stepped past her and pushed the door open.

She sucked in a breath at the unexpected gust of cool air and the view on the other side. A rooftop deck spread out before them, complete with quaint little tables and a vine-covered pergola laced with twinkle lights overhead. On the far end, there was a long, rustic table with candles and a full outdoor stove and grill.

"Wow, this is beautiful."

"Yeah, it's my favorite spot in the restaurant. But we don't use it during the winter months except for the occasional party."

"Or for a random woman you pilfer from an online dating event."

He grinned. "Exactly. But I think it's warm enough tonight to not be a problem."

"So we're going to make some poor waiter traipse up here to serve us food?"

"Nah," Van said, taking her hand and leading her forward. "You came here to learn how to cook. So we won't need any staff."

As they got closer to the long table, she saw there were little bowls of ingredients on the far end like they'd had at the event. She glanced over at him. "*You're* going to teach me to cook?"

He cocked his head, looking playfully offended. "What? You don't think I can cook?"

She let her perusal of him travel from the top of his head down the front of his black dress shirt and gray trousers to the tips of his clearly expensive shoes. "You don't look like you spend a lot of time in a kitchen."

"And you don't look like a woman who'd spend her evening crashing a date meet-up. But looks can be deceiving, right?" He let go of her hand with a smirk, unbuttoned his cuffs, and rolled his sleeves up his forearms.

For some reason, the simple movement fascinated her, like she was watching his urbane shell being peeled back and revealing the real man beneath. She pulled her attention away from those big, capable hands. "So what kind of woman do I look like then?"

He gave her a similar head-to-toe assessment then met her gaze. "One who doesn't usually break the rules or take a risk."

She scoffed. "Oh, really?"

His smile was knowing as he grabbed a knife and cutting board from the counter then placed a wedge of white cheese on it. "Am I wrong?"

"I'm up here with you, aren't I?" she said, challenging him.

He moved the knife as if marking a point in her favor on an invisible scoreboard. "Touché."

Following his lead, she grabbed a loaf of crusty bread and another knife to start slicing it. "So you admit you're a risk?"

Before she could cut into the bread, he laid his hand on hers, stilling her movements. "Don't use that knife. You need a serrated one for that kind of bread."

She glanced down at his hand on hers, the warmth of his touch a little too welcome. "Oh, right."

He replaced the knife with one that had a jagged edge. "And I'm no more of a risk than going to the dating event and sitting with a stranger."

"So this is a date?"

He took one of the slices of bread, placed a piece of cheese atop it, and then held it in front of her lips. She opened her mouth and let him feed her a bite of bread and cheese. He was so close now, she could see the flecks of green mixing with the blue in his eyes. Somehow he managed to both intimidate and cajole in one simple look. "It's whatever you want it to be, Contessa."

The salty cheese hit her taste buds, and she had to remind herself to chew, to breathe.

"Good?" he asked.

She nodded, though the movement felt stiff. "Manchego. One of my favorites."

He lifted an eyebrow. "A woman who knows her gourmet cheeses but doesn't know how to use a bread knife? Interesting."

She was tempted to refute that claim, tell him it was a lucky guess, but she stopped herself. No more lying.

"I don't want this to be a date," she blurted out.

His forehead creased. "What?"

"I don't want this to be a date," she repeated. "Dates suck. It's two people telling each other what they think the other person wants to hear and hoping they get it right. It's a farce."

He leaned back against the table as if giving her space to voice her opinion. "Okay, so what would you like this to be?"

"Let's make this an un-date. No fronts, no lies, and no ridiculous promises to call the next day. You didn't invite me up here because you think I could be some perfect match for your future. And I didn't come up here for that either."

He'd been watching her with equal parts amusement and intrigue, but now a flicker of something else edged in, something that made her insides flip over. "So what did you come up here for, Contessa?"

Well, here it was, her opportunity to put her money where her mouth was and be blatantly honest. He was probably going to run, but so be it if he did. "A year ago, I walked in on my husband cheating with my best friend. Instead of even pretending to be sorry, he proceeded to give me a long list of my faults and told me to get used to his affairs."

Sharp disapproval flashed over Van's features.

But she didn't let his reaction stop her. She needed to lay it all out there. "I left him, my life blew up, and now I'm putting the pieces back in place. I'm not looking to date anyone. I'm not looking for love or even a boyfriend. I came up here tonight because I haven't felt desire in a long time, and you made me feel that in the hallway."

"Contessa—"

She took a deep breath. "I came up here to use you, Van. To *be* used. I need a night off from . . . all of it."

The shift in his expression was enough to have any remaining words shriveling in her throat. All traces of his sympathy over her story had vanished and in its place, unadulterated lust took root. "Text your friend and tell her you've found a ride. I'll have your keys sent down to her."

The command in his voice rippled through her. "But I—"

He pushed off the table and stood in front of her, cupping her chin. "You told me your reasons, now do you want to hear mine? I brought you up here because from the moment you walked into the restaurant tonight, I couldn't take my eyes off of you. I would've sat through a cooking class about dishes *I* created just to be next to you. Let me give you your night off."

She was jittery in his grasp, her body literally vibrating with the need for him to touch her more. "But the cooking class still has two hours left. We could—"

He pressed a finger against his lips. "I promise I'll need more than two hours. I haven't even given you your first lesson yet."

Her heart was thumping and blood was roaring through her veins, heating all the best spots. She couldn't do this, right? She didn't even know this guy. Considering a quickie with him had been risky enough. But sending her ride home and spending the whole night with him was a whole different story. "I can't go home with you."

He leaned down and brushed his lips along her jaw, his blond hair falling forward and tickling her cheek. "We don't have to go anywhere but here."

Even the simple touch had her ready to groan aloud, her body starved for this kind of night. This kind of man. How long had it been since she'd felt so desired, so utterly seduced? Maybe never. Somehow, Van made it all feel so easy, so natural. Like saying no would be a preposterous notion. Even though it was the most logical answer.

But that logic angel sitting on her shoulder didn't seem to have much fight to her tonight. No, instead there was another altogether deviant voice whispering in her ear. *Stop denying yourself. You need this. You've earned an indulgence. A woman should not live by vibrator alone.*

She took a long, shuddering breath, letting the temptation take her under. "I'll text her."

"Good girl," Van said, the words she'd normally find patronizing like a hot caress against her. "I'll make sure it's worth the trouble."

After Tessa had sent the text and gotten one back from Sam, complete with about twelve exclamation points following her *OMG*, Van left for a few minutes to bring her keys down. And he must have brought them in person because Sam sent another text shortly afterward.

HOLY shit, girl. U've hit the hookup lottery. Enjoy the condoms!

Tessa was still laughing when Van came through the doorway. He smiled. "What's so funny?"

"My friend approves of you."

He gave her a roguish grin. "I'm charming that way."

"And she thinks you're hot," she said matter-of-factly. "That goes a long way with Sam."

He laughed, not bothering to deflect the assessment of his hotness, and crossed his arms. "And what do you think?"

She lifted her chin, jaunty. "I think I don't like cocky guys."

He stepped in front of her chair and braced his hands on the table behind her, caging her in. His expression held playful challenge when he leaned in her space. "Liar."

She raised her eyebrows. "How would you know?"

"Because you didn't wait a whole year only to waste a night with some guy who's unsure of himself." He put his lips next to her ear, his voice turning dark and ripe with promise. "I may be cocky, but I'm not going to fumble around. I'm not going to lie back and wait for you to take the lead. I'm going to feed you the best meal of your life. Bite by bite. Then I'm going to fuck you. And I promise, when you wake up tomorrow, you won't remember the food."

# THREE

*Sweet baby Jesus.* Tessa had no idea what to say to Van's illicit promise, so she didn't even attempt to respond. But she could feel heat traveling through her like an electric current, turning on switches she didn't even know existed. She closed her eyes and pulled in a deep breath, but that only made it worse because she got a lungful of his spicy scent.

Van pushed off the table he'd braced his hands on and straightened. "Still want to have dinner with me?"

She lifted her gaze to him. He'd made his intentions clear, and he was giving her an out. This was her chance to go back to the safety of her apartment where there would be no handsome strangers making her feel vulnerable and off-balance, where there would be no risk of her embarrassing herself, and no dreaded walk of shame to face in the morning. But as she stared back at him, she knew she'd suffer one thing if she walked away now. Regret.

Because no man had ever caused such a visceral response in her or inspired such primal need. And she knew instinctively that he wasn't writing checks he couldn't sign. He was promising her the sex of her life, and she had no doubt he could provide it. And maybe it was base and wanton to simply want this man to take her over and use her for their mutual pleasure, but dammit, she couldn't think of anything she needed more right now than to let go like that.

"I'm very hungry," she said finally.

His eyes lit with satisfaction. "Well, far be it from me to deny you a meal." He extended his hand. "Come on, I still owe you a little Cooking 101 lesson."

She took his hand and let him lead her to the stove, feeling as if she'd crossed some portal she couldn't walk back through, like if she turned around now, there'd only be mirrored glass to tap. They both knew what tonight was about now. No pretenses. But apparently, he was still going to hold to his promise of teaching her how to cook. He grabbed a bottle of olive oil and a bowl of what looked to be nuts and set them on the tiled counter. He picked up one of the nuts and lifted it to her lips. Dutifully, she opened her mouth and let him slide it in. He took his time pulling his fingers back, letting them casually brush her lips.

"These are blanched almonds," he explained, his tone soft in the quiet night. "They won't have much flavor yet since we haven't toasted or salted them. But I want you to get an idea of what they taste like before. It's an important step. Taste your ingredients and your cooking throughout the process so you can adjust seasonings as you go."

She crunched the mostly tasteless almond and swallowed, trying to concentrate on the lesson and not the way his deep voice was seeping inside her and dialing up her internal thermostat. *Focus.* "Why are they blanched?"

"It provides a better surface for the seasonings and they look nicer in a bowl. We serve these on every table with the manchego." He turned on the burner beneath a small skillet on the stove then handed her the bottle of olive oil. "We'll need about three tablespoons of oil."

She scanned the utensils on the counter. "I need a measuring spoon."

He smiled. "Don't have any of those up here, but it doesn't have to be perfect. Cooking is a lot about feel and developing your instincts. Trusting yourself. A tablespoon is roughly one swirl around the pan. Do three of those."

Though she was a little nervous she'd somehow manage to screw up the simplest of recipes, she followed his instructions and poured the oil into the pan. "Is that enough?"

"Yep, now wait for the oil to shimmer a little and then you can dump the almonds in. Extra virgin olive oil has a low smoke point. It can burn or catch fire quicker than other oils, so don't use it on too high of a heat and put your ingredients in before it starts smoking."

She felt like she was the one with the low smoke point. A few more touches and heated glances from him and she was sure she'd catch flame, too.

When the oil started to glisten and slide easily around the pan, he gave her a little nod, and she poured the almonds in. He stepped behind her, put a hand to her waist, and reached around to give the nuts a quick stir with a wooden spoon to coat them. The smell of fruity olive oil filled her nose, but all she could think about was Van pressed against her back. He was so much bigger than she was—not in the bulky way like Doug had been—but tall and lean and honed. It made her feel petite and feminine in his hold.

She swallowed past the sudden dryness in her throat. "Now what?"

"Now we wait for them to get fragrant and golden." He set the spoon down and turned her around in his arms, shifting the two of them away from the hot stove. "And we taste."

He picked up the olive oil again and drizzled some on his fingers. She watched in fascination as some dripped to the ground like green-gold raindrops.

"People usually think of Italy for olive oil, but Spain produces some of the finest stuff out there. Good enough to sip like wine." He lifted his hand to her mouth then ran slick fingers over her lips. "Or to kiss off of a beautiful woman."

Before she had time to react, he lowered his head and captured her mouth in a slow, coaxing kiss. The fruity oil slid over their lips and mixed with the lingering flavor of sangria and something distinctly him. Her hands went to his chest, her fingers curling into his shirt. His lips were even more decadent than she'd imagined—soft and sexy and commanding. A vivid appetizer to what she suspected was going to be a very lavish meal. And it'd been so long since she'd been kissed—even longer since it'd been done with passion—that she found it hard to control her starved response. She craved more, needed it.

When he moved to pull back, she said his name like a plea.

Needing no further encouragement, he banded his arm around her waist as he kissed her again and backed her into the table without breaking their connection. Before she could lever herself upward, he lifted her onto the table and deepened the kiss. Their tongues touched and sparks seems to flare out along her nerve endings. She groaned into his mouth, overwhelmed by the all-encompassing response to such a simple act. Somehow Van had transported her back to her high-school days where everything was new and an openmouthed kiss was as erotic an experience as she could imagine.

She slid her arms around his neck and gave herself over completely, opening to him and surrendering to the moment. When he laid her back onto the table and unfastened the top button of her blouse, she was too far gone to worry about anything. She didn't care that they were out in the open and anyone could walk in. She didn't care that they were outdoors and only protected from the view of people on the street by a row of potted trees. And she forgot to worry whether or not she was in over her head.

Van finally broke the kiss to drag in a breath and worked a few more buttons to get her shirt fully open. His gaze traced over her simple lace bra with ravenous heat. "We're going to burn the almonds."

"I don't care," she said, slipping her shirt off.

With one swift movement, he reached over and turned off the burner, then he was back over her, holding the bottle of olive oil above her. "Take off your bra, Contessa. I need to taste you."

She did as she was told with fumbling fingers and tossed the scrap of fabric aside. As soon as she lay back against the table, the drizzle of oil hit her skin, sliding over her nipples and down her belly. She closed her eyes and moaned softly, the sensual feel of the liquid against her conjuring images of Van taking himself in his hand and marking her skin with his release.

His hands trailed up and over her ribs, bringing oil with it, then he cupped her breasts, sliding his fingers over slippery skin and making her arch with need. He pinched her nipple between lubricated fingers. The desperate sound she made bordered on embarrassing. "Van, please."

He let out a soft curse. "Baby, I want to take my time with you. But God, I can feel how near the edge you are already, and it's driving me to the brink. I'll never make it through a meal."

"That makes two of us."

He groaned and bent over her, taking her nipple in his mouth. The combination of the warming oil and his talented tongue had her back bowing up. Lord, she'd forgotten how lovely foreplay could be. Doug had been all about the end game, convinced that because he was well-endowed, that'd be enough for any woman.

But size only went so far and getting to orgasm had always taken work on her part, a concerted effort. But right now, she felt like one stroke between her thighs and she'd go off.

His hand went to the hem of her skirt, slipping beneath it and gliding along her thigh with well-oiled fingers. She reached for him, her hands acting on their own volition, and gripped his thick hair, holding him against her breast and silently begging him to move his hand higher up her thigh.

He slipped free from her grip and lifted his head. "Just lie back, baby, and put your hands above your head. I'll take care of you."

She did as she was told and followed him with her eyes as he grabbed her blouse and wrapped it around her wrists. "What are you doing?"

"Exactly what I want," he said simply, as if that were explanation enough. "I have a bit of a thing for control. You okay with that?"

A ripple of apprehension went through her. "I'm not sure. What do you mean?"

His lips curved. "Ever done anything kinky before, Contessa?"

She thought back to the time she'd bought risqué lingerie and a set of handcuffs to surprise Doug. He'd wrinkled his nose in disgust and told her to throw that crap out. "No."

"How come?" he asked as he traced his fingers along the delicate skin of her forearms.

God, why the questions? Couldn't they just get to it? She didn't want to rehash those embarrassing memories.

"Because it's for girls who try too hard," she blurted, remembering how ridiculous Doug had made her feel as she stood there in that corset and heels. *If I wanted to sleep with a cheap whore, I'd hire one, Tessa. Take that shit off.*

Van came back into view, his eyes meeting hers, amusement touching his lips. "Is that right? Well, I hope I can change your mind on that one because you look very, very sexy stretched out and bound. But if you're not on board, I'll release your hands."

Somehow the sincerity in his voice and the heated look on his face had her guards falling away. She found herself wanting to comply, wanting to be sexy for him. "It's okay. I'll try it."

"Thank you."

He leaned over and took her mouth in a languorous kiss, dipping his tongue deep and giving her another preview of just how skilled he was with his mouth. A moan caught in the back of her throat, and her hips lifted off the table involuntarily as need built low and fast. Lord, could she come from a kiss? Her body was begging for that to be true. It had been so long. But even though no orgasm came, by the time he pulled back, she was sure her muscles had liquefied and her bones had disintegrated.

He nipped her bottom lip. "Move your hands from this spot, and I'll stop what I'm doing. Understand?"

She nodded quickly, ready to agree to anything if it meant he was going to touch her again. "Yes."

The pleasure that flickered over his features at her acquiescence was its own reward. He walked back to the end of the table and gathered her skirt up her thighs, revealing her pink cotton panties—panties that were now damp and clinging. He ran the tip of his finger down her crease, rubbing the wet cotton against her most needy parts.

*Oh, God.*

"Look how pretty and wet you are for me already." He outlined her clit with his fingertip using enough pressure to make her arch but not enough to send her over. "Do you need to come, baby?"

She gasped as his finger moved inside her, still covered with the fabric of her panties. The slight abrasiveness of the cotton only ratcheted up her sensitivity further. "God, yes."

He moved his finger with gentle undulations. "It's too bad that olive oil is bad for condoms. Otherwise, I could get you off with a few simple strokes of my hand."

She whimpered. God, how could he tease her like this? Couldn't he see she was about to lose it? She went to reach for him, but as soon as she moved her bound arms, he stopped the stimulation. She let out a sound of frustration. "Van, please."

"Put your hands back where they're supposed to be and maybe you'll get what you want."

The calmly uttered command almost undid her. She should've been rankled by his bossiness. He didn't know her or have the right to order her to do anything. But for some reason, she found herself complying and burning even hotter.

When the backs of her hands landed on the table, Van yanked her panties down and off. "Good girl. Spread your knees for me."

Feeling a blush work its way up her body at the vulnerability of her position, she did as she was told. Her eyes fixed on the vine-covered pergola above them and the twinkle lights, and she tried to breathe. If she didn't calm down, she would come as soon as his mouth touched her skin and she wanted to enjoy this.

"So fucking sexy, baby," Van said gruffly as he looked down at her. "I'll take this as an amuse-bouche any day of the week. The food can wait."

He locked his arms under her knees and pulled her to the end of the table, then lowered himself between her thighs. He draped her legs over his shoulders, and Tessa went liquid. That sinful mouth was against her in the next moment, and her entire body contracted with pleasure. His slid his hands under her bottom and lifted her closer, opening her with his tongue and kissing her pussy with the same single-minded focus he'd had with their kiss.

She writhed in his hold, her eyes wanting to roll back in her head at the sheer decadence of his tongue. But he wasn't letting her wriggle away. Whether she could handle it or not, she knew he was going to get exactly what he wanted. And what he wanted was for her to fall apart. This wasn't a tentative warm up or prelude. It was an annihilation of her control. His slick hands kneaded her ass as he feasted on her, the rough handling stimulating hot spots she hadn't even been aware were there. The whole combination was hurtling her toward oblivion without brakes.

Her fists curled into her palms, the binding around her wrists tightening as she flexed. And a sudden shot of nerves went through her. "Van, I'm going to come. People will *hear*."

Because there was no way she was going to be able to keep quiet.

In the span of two seconds, Van lifted away from her and reached for something from one of the bowls behind her. "Open and bite down."

Her eyes widened, but she did what he said. He tucked a fat orange wedge between her lips, then was back in position like he'd never paused. His tongue glided over her center then he sucked her clit between his lips and tugged. She shattered. Her back lifted off the table and she bit down hard on the orange, the juice squirting into her mouth and dripping down the corners of her lips as she cried out. Van dug his fingers into her ass to hold her in place and his mouth dipped precariously lower, teasing a forbidden place that had never felt a man's touch much less his tongue. Light broke behind her eyes, splintering into color, and she groaned low and deep.

Her orgasm climbed another step higher instead of relenting, and the orange fell from her mouth. She began to pant, trying to bank her noises, and her body shook with the force of a release that felt like it'd been building for months. "I can't, I can't . . ."

Van was over her before her next breath. He clamped his hand over her mouth, his eyes dark with desire. "Just let it have you, baby. I don't give a damn who hears you. But I'll help keep you quiet if you want me to."

She nodded. He moved his hand away from her mouth and

yanked his shirt tails from his pants, wiping the olive oil on it, then he pulled a foil packet from his back pocket. He ripped the condom wrapper open with his teeth and undid his pants.

"Give me one more, beautiful. I know you have it in you."

With that, he positioned himself at her entrance and pushed inside. A gasp escaped her, the feel of him stretching her an exquisite shock to her system. Her body resisted despite her slickness—the feeling almost foreign again. But the edge of discomfort was the most decadent kind of pain. She wrapped her legs around his hips, trying to open herself fully. She needed all of him. Right. Now.

"Lord, baby, you're gripping me so hard," he groaned. "Am I hurting you?"

"Yes," she said breathlessly. "A good hurt."

The wicked gleam that flared in his eyes had her thoughts emptying.

"Mmm, my favorite kind." He rocked forward, his eyes closing as his fingers dug into her hips, and he buried himself deep. His body shuddered along with hers, the remnants of her orgasm still sending aftershocks through her. "Oh, fuck, yes. You're so hot around me. I can feel your pussy trying to milk my cock."

She bit her lip, the dirty talk an unfamiliar experience but not an unwelcome one. To hear such a seemingly sophisticated man talk so coarsely did something to her, made her feel like she was seeing the primal version behind the curtain. "You have a filthy mouth, Van."

"And you fucking love it," he said, leaning down and licking the sticky orange juice at the corner of her mouth, as he thrust into her again. "You blush, but your eyes go hot. You're not craving polite."

She gasped as he angled just right inside her. "I don't know what I crave."

"Yes, you do." He rocked into her harder and with more speed.

"You said it yourself. You want to use and be used. Come again for me, baby. Use my cock. Let me feel you break apart beneath me."

He braced one hand next to her head and tucked the other between them, stroking her clit with every thrust of his hips. Her lids fluttered shut as the tide of sensation built to a breaking point.

"Eyes on me, gorgeous. I want you to see who's fucking you. And I want to watch you go under."

She forced her gaze upward, the intensity of his stare burning through her. His dark blond hair had fallen forward and the twinkle lights sparkled above him, a fierce lion with a gilded mane. Then he smiled. And she lost it. The cry that roared up her vocal cords would've been loud enough to be heard at the restaurant downstairs, but he levered down and kissed her, capturing the desperate sound before it escaped. She poured everything she had into that kiss as her body went molten around him.

He pressed his palm against her bound wrists, pinning her to the table and pumping into her hard enough to rattle the bowls behind her. Her orgasm rolled through her in powerful, crushing waves and he tore away from the kiss, his groan of pleasure raking over her senses as he sunk deep and spilled inside her.

"Fuck, baby," he said, letting his forehead meet hers, his chest rising and falling with panted breaths. "So much for the slow and easy evening I had imagined. I promise I at least planned to feed you first."

She laughed beneath him, overcome with some weird combination of euphoria and the bizarreness of the whole situation. Here she was lying naked on a restaurant table with a perfect stranger slathered in olive oil and orange juice and drifting down from the best orgasm of her life. Who was this woman?

He chuckled along with her and reached up to untie her hands. "We're a mess."

"But my skin is now exceptionally moisturized, and I smell *amazing*," she said, grinning.

"Indeed it is." He pressed an openmouthed kiss to her sticky neck and inhaled. "And yes, you do. Citrus and sex, let's bottle that."

Her stomach flipped at the words. Citrus and sex were what her kitchen had smelled like after she'd found Doug. She'd thought she'd never be able to smell orange juice again without thinking of that horrible day. But Van had rewired her associations in a few mind-blowing moments. Now she wanted to roll around in that scent. "We'll make millions."

"No doubt." Van gave her another quick kiss then eased out of her. He turned to discreetly strip off the condom and zipped up before looking back in her direction. "Remind me next time to not take no for an answer on bringing you back to my place. At least there I'd have a shower and towels to offer you."

She rolled her wrists and then pushed up on her elbows, offering him a smile, but knowing there would be no next time. That'd been their agreement, her one condition. Tonight could only be an escape. A fantasy.

She couldn't handle any more than that.

Especially with a guy who could make her feel like this. One who could make her feel this wanted and sexy, this . . . special. She knew she was definitely not the latter for him. Van was way too smooth and confident—a seducer. She doubted his bed was ever cold.

He was a playboy.

He was a temptation she couldn't afford.

# FOUR

Kade Vandergriff smiled when he heard soft snores coming from his left. Oh, how quickly a shitty day had morphed into an amazing evening. When he'd headed out tonight for location visits, all his frustration from a completely useless session with his attorney about their seemingly winless case had come along with him. It probably would've been wise to go home afterward to let himself settle down. But he hadn't been able to stomach the thought of pacing the halls of his big, empty house for the night. The silence and space would've made him crazy.

So he'd driven into Dallas to visit his restaurants, hoping to channel all the crap from the day into a productive evening. But after only a few hours into his drop-in visits, his frustration hadn't gone away but had instead morphed into nebulous, growing anger. By the time he'd arrived at Barcelona and discovered three of their most popular dishes had been eighty-sixed because of the manager's oversight, Kade had been on the verge of a Gordon Ramsay moment.

But then Contessa had walked into the restaurant, chatting

with her friend and looking like she wanted to be anywhere but there. Kade had stopped midsentence in his lecture to his manager and had forgotten why he was so damn pissed. He'd left his manager without another word and followed Contessa into the dating event, having no idea why he felt so compelled to follow her or what he was going to do once he got to her. But when her name hadn't been on the list, he'd jumped at the opportunity to step in. A few minutes into their time upstairs, she'd made him forget every crappy thing that had happened that day. He'd gotten lost in the moment, lost in her.

He glanced over at his dozing companion. Contessa had curled up on one of the sofas in the bar to wait while he picked up the last of the food and dishes they'd used on their rooftop "un-date," but exhaustion had apparently gotten the better of her. Or maybe it was the six-course meal, the three glasses of sangria, and the two bouts of amazing sex. Even he was feeling weary on his feet, and staying up until three A.M. was not a rare occurrence with his schedule.

Not for the first time, he wished they were back at his place where he could strip her down and tuck her into his bed for the night. Wake her up with his tongue between her thighs because damn the woman was sexy when she came. It was like each time it happened, she was surprised, like she didn't think herself capable of that passionate of a response. And for some reason, she thought she wouldn't like kink yet had responded to his commands with beautiful capitulation. Which, of course, only made him want to find out just how out of her mind he could drive her. They'd only scratched the surface tonight.

But he had a feeling he wasn't going to get another chance. She'd laid it all out up front, refreshing but brutal in her honesty. She'd wanted an escape tonight. She'd wanted to use him for that, and he'd been happy to oblige. Hell, the one-night fantasy had become his specialty lately. Not that he was complaining. He'd enjoyed playing the third in a few scenes with his friends' submissives at The Ranch, the private BDSM resort he belonged to. And he'd had his fair share of casual encounters over the past few years with kinky women, as well as vanilla ones. Fun nights. Exciting flings. Wild adventures.

But in the end, the result was always the same. After the initial rush, he lost interest. Since his divorce, even women who'd been open to considering moving the relationship to a more intense level—the level he desperately craved—he couldn't seem to muster up the desire. Too often, it felt like those women were simply agreeing to his flavor of kink because of all the fringe benefits. He'd been down that road. Nothing like finding out the girlfriend you're tying up and flogging actually hates pain and all things kink and is only taking it because she wants you to buy her that Coach purse or bring her on that trip to Maui.

But even the women who hadn't been motivated for the wrong reasons had lost his interest in a month or two. The lifestyles reporter at the local paper had taken to calling him the Time Share Bachelor because his relationships had ended on such a predictable schedule. He never strayed, but he never stayed either. Sometimes he wondered if his divorce had rewired him to only be capable of the temporary. So perhaps it was best for all involved that Contessa walked away from him tonight. Clean. Easy. No attachments or regrets. Everyone could look golden in a one-night stand. A flawless fantasy night for both their memory banks.

Kade sighed as he carried an armful of bowls into the kitchen to rinse them out, unable to shake his desire for more time with Contessa despite his perfectly valid internal arguments. They'd spent hours together. He'd taken her twice. It should be enough. Plus, she was vanilla for God's sake. This wasn't like meeting some girl at The Ranch where he could imagine all the dirty things they could try out and mutually enjoy. Contessa, despite her little glimmers of bravado, had a shyness about her, like she was almost awkward about sex. When he'd pinned her hands above her head, her eyes had gone as wide as a virgin's on prom night. She may've been married, but clearly her husband hadn't given her any more than the basics.

A damn tragedy, that. Because the kind of eager responsiveness she'd shown upstairs proved the woman was built for pleasure, starved for it. And everything in his body was giving a battle cry to be the man to feed her. But there was no way in hell he was going to chase her for the chance. He didn't chase. Period. He'd spent too many years when he was a kid doing that crap, and it only got you humiliated. Chasing. Pining. Fantasizing about girls he couldn't have. Only to be turned down so she could go be with the jerk who treated her like shit.

Never again. He'd learned. Girls who wanted to be chased, wanted to be in control of you. And control is one thing he'd never relinquish again.

"Need any help?"

Kade looked up from dumping the last of the food into the trash bin, finding Contessa wearing a sleepy-eyed half smile. He shook his head, his whirling thoughts calming at the sight of her. "Nah, it's been a while since I've been on clean-up duty in a kitchen, but I haven't forgotten how to do it."

"So are you a chef?" she asked.

He smiled, amused that she hadn't bothered to ask his position up until this point. It was a nice change of pace. Most women knew his whole resume before ever saying word one to him. "I went to culinary school, so technically, yes, I could be a chef. But that isn't my current position. I own this place."

And many, many others. But he didn't need to volunteer that at this point. He kind of liked her not knowing the whole restaurant mogul aspect of his career. No matter what, it changed how people interacted with him once they knew.

"Wow, impressive," she said, though she sounded more wary than impressed. "So you were totally cheating when you said you wouldn't have to pay for anything. Technically, you're paying for everything, down to the electricity keeping this light on."

He grinned. "Are you going to convict me on a technicality?"

"Totally."

He sighed. "Tough jury. Well, I have handcuffs in the car. Let me finish cleaning up and then you can take me in."

She laughed. "Somehow I don't think you're kidding about having handcuffs."

He sent her a sly grin but went back to rinsing off the last of the dishes. Actually, he didn't have any in the car, but at home . . . At home he had enough restraints to bind her in a hundred ways and never repeat a method. "A gentleman never reveals his secrets."

She went quiet for a while after that, and he began to regret the off-the-cuff comment. The girl had just gotten out of a marriage where her husband was keeping the biggest secret of all, and here he was joking about secrets.

He wiped his hands on a towel and turned to her. "Sorry, I didn't mean, with your husband—"

"Oh, no." She shook her head, cutting off his apology. "You're fine. Truly, I wasn't even thinking about the situation with my ex. Just about our agreement for total honesty."

Total honesty. Like not even giving her his real first name or the scope of his job. He was doing stellar on that all around. But she was looking so pensive that he couldn't help but walk over to her. He put his hands on her arms, rubbing the chill bumps there. "What's on your mind?"

Her gaze slid to the right and down as if there was something eminently more interesting on the floor. "I'm trying to fight the urge to ask you a supremely embarrassing question, but one that I need an honest answer to."

Uh-oh. That sounded like a no-win trap if ever there was one. But what was he supposed to say to that? "Well, since you've already declared that we're not going to see each other after tonight, I'd say you probably have nothing to lose by asking."

She took a deep breath, her teeth pressing into her bottom lip, and her gaze still locked on anything but him. "When I caught my husband cheating. He told me it was partly my fault, which I know is bullshit."

"Total bullshit," Kade agreed.

"But he said I was boring in bed," she rushed on. "And I can't help but wonder if maybe—"

"That fucker."

Her attention snapped upward, surprise in her eyes.

He cupped her face in his hands. "Baby, I don't know much about you. I don't know your last name or what you do for a living. I don't know if you take cream in your coffee or if you prefer tea. But I can tell you one thing for sure. There is nothing *boring* about you. Tonight was amazing. *You* were amazing. And if that idiot ex-husband of yours didn't know what to do with a gorgeous woman and all that passion you have brewing right beneath the surface, then that's on him."

All the tension sagged out of her, and she closed her eyes, nodding in his hands. "Thank you."

The soft response and her obvious relief nearly undid him. What kind of asshole made a vibrant woman like this doubt herself? He half wished her ex was here right now. Kade would let the guy watch as Kade took Contessa right in front of him, let him watch how glorious she was when given pleasure by a man who knew what he was doing.

"Don't give his words another thought," he said, kissing her forehead and wishing he could swipe the memory from her mind with the gesture.

"I know I shouldn't, but it's hard not to let doubt creep in. When you approached me tonight, I almost chickened out because I thought I might embarrass myself. I'm not that experienced. I married him so young and—"

"Contessa," he said, frustration edging his words. "Stop."

She blinked up at him, apparently taken aback at his change in tone.

He lowered his hands from her face, fighting the sudden urge to turn her over his knee and spank her for even giving that jerk another second of thought. "Stop doubting yourself. Inexperience does not mean boring. Boring is a woman who isn't present with you in the moment. Boring is a woman who lies there and doesn't participate or who isn't open to trying new things. Boring is an attitude, *not* a lack of skill or experience. If you've got the desire, the rest can be learned. Taught."

All it took was a good teacher and a willing student. And right now, he was feeling quite professorial.

"You think?" she said, looking unconvinced.

"Baby, nothing is sexier than a woman who wants to learn." He moved forward, backing her into the wall, loving the little gasp she made when his burgeoning erection pressed against her. "In fact, it's my biggest turn-on, showing a woman exactly what to do to please me."

She wet her lips, her nerves visible right there at the surface. "Sounds like kind of a selfish way of looking at it. How to please *you*."

He chuckled and slid his hand down along her hip. "Yes, but pleasing me reaps so many rewards. I always repay with interest."

When he snuck his hand beneath her skirt and upward, she tilted her head back against the wall and groaned. "What would you teach me?"

He smiled with promise. She'd left her panties off since they'd been ruined earlier, and his fingers easily found what they were seeking. "The list is long, baby. It'd definitely take more than one night. I'm a kinky fucker."

"Van," she gasped, as he curled his fingers inside her, sliding deep into the slick heat.

"Want to be my student?" He pressed his thumb against her clit, rubbing in slow, tight circles. "I promise lots of one-on-one attention."

"Oh, God." She rocked against his hand almost as if she was trying to resist the urge but couldn't stop the movement. Her voice went breathy. "I can't—I can't get involved. With anyone."

The words sounded like a plea instead of a statement. She was so close to the edge already, even after her orgasms from earlier. God, he loved how hot she ran. Her arousal coated his hand, her sweet scent filling the sterile kitchen. "I'm not asking you to date me, baby. I'm not good at that anyway. I'm offering to show you what you're capable of, to teach you what you want to learn. To have fun."

Her fingers twisted in his hair as she rocketed toward release with her eyes squeezed shut and her head lolling from side to side against the wall. "Van!"

"Come for me," he said, his voice going gritty with his own need to see her explode again. "Fuck my hand and take what you know I can give you."

Her shout was sharp and desperate as she shattered in orgasm, the sound winding through the kitchen and empty restaurant. She called his name in a pleading prayer and melted against the wall like butter on hot cast iron.

He pressed his forehead to hers, breathing deeply with his own desire pounding through his veins. God, she was something to behold when she let go. No fucking way was he going to let her get away with only tonight. He needed more of this.

More of her.

When her writhing had turned to gentle swaying, he slipped

his hand from beneath her skirt and brought his fingers to his mouth. Her eyes fluttered open in time to see him savor her taste and suck his fingers clean. Her lips parted slightly, and her barely concealed shock made him want her even more. Innocence and passion—her mix of it was a potent drug to his system.

"Kiss me," he said, a gentle command and challenge.

After only the briefest hesitation, she closed the distance between them and brought her mouth to his. He took her lips in a languid kiss, knowing she'd be able to taste her tart flavor on his tongue. He would convince her right here and now with actions and not words that she shouldn't walk away yet, that she needed to explore this as much as he did. He would make her crave more. But right as he was deepening the kiss and pulling her against him, an acrid scent tickled his nose. He dismissed it for a moment, too wrapped up in the feel of Contessa in his arms, but soon the smell was too strong to ignore. He pulled back, alarm bells starting to ding through the growing fog of desire in his head.

"What's wrong?" she asked.

"Do you smell that?" He let her go and peered over his shoulder toward the kitchen.

She sniffed. "Smells burnt."

He shook his head. That wasn't a burnt smell. It was a *burning* smell. He strode toward the appliances, checking to see if an oven or stove had been left on or if a greasy towel had been left somewhere and ignited. But nothing seemed amiss. His staff was well-trained to check and double check everything for safety before closing up each night. But the smell was growing stronger.

"Van!"

He turned. Contessa pointed at the door that led out to the side hallway and exit. Dark black smoke was creeping beneath. Dread rushed through him. He closed the distance between the two of them in three long strides, grabbing her purse from the countertop and shoving it at her. "We need to get out of here. Now!"

She let him hustle her toward the door that led to the dining room, but when they swung the door open, a rush of hot, acrid smoke blew right in their faces. His eyes and throat burned with it, and Contessa started coughing beside him. "Van."

"Get down low," he barked, keeping a hold of her elbow. Heat shimmered in the air as they crouched down and heard the first roar of flame and crack of wood. The sound seemed to be coming from the main dining area, though it was impossible to see anything in the smoke. "Stay with me. Don't let go. I'm going to get us to a back exit."

Contessa was coughing hard now, unable to respond. Shit. He needed to get them out fast before she took in too much smoke. And why the fuck weren't the sprinklers going off? Luckily, he knew the layout of this restaurant better than his own house. It was one he'd designed himself. It'd been his first baby, the one he loved the most. And now it was burning. Crawling on their hands and knees, he led Contessa through the banquet room and to an emergency exit. He hopped to his feet and shoved the door open with his hip, a wave of cool night air swooping in as he dragged her outside and into the back alley.

"Baby, talk to me," he demanded, his heart hammering in his chest.

She'd stopped coughing and had gone heavy in his arms. He hauled her up and off her feet and carried her away from the building. Sirens wailed in the background as he laid her out on the grass in front of the flower shop across the street. Her cheeks were black with soot and her eyes were shut, but he could see her chest still rising and falling.

"Contessa, come on, baby, take a few deep breaths for me." He tugged off his shirt and ran to a water fountain to soak the fabric. Then he hurried back to her side, his lungs still burning, and wiped the soot away from her face with the cool cloth. "Come on, sweetheart. You're scaring me."

She coughed, a loud hacking sound, but it was one of the sweetest Kade had ever heard.

He rolled her onto her side. "That's it. Get that shit out."

A fire truck sped to a halt in the street and men poured out, two heading Kade's way and the rest going for the building. The young firefighter hustled over and knelt next to Contessa, while the other flagged down an EMS crew that pulled up behind the fire truck.

"Ma'am, we're here to help you," the first one said, as he started checking her over.

"She took in too much smoke," Kade said in a rush. "We got out quickly, but there was so much smoke so fast."

"Was there anyone else in the building?"

"No."

The EMTs were already hurrying over with equipment and oxygen. She was going to be all right. Help was here.

Kade sank back onto the grass, relief enveloping him. *Thank God.*

In the background, flames licked up the side of his restaurant, engulfing and devouring his favorite location. But he couldn't find it in himself to care at the moment. Contessa was going to be okay. The restaurant was just wood and metal and could be replaced.

"Sir, do you know this woman?" the EMT asked. "Or if she has any medical conditions or allergies I should be aware of before we take her in?"

Contessa tried to speak but she started coughing again and they put an oxygen mask over her face. She pointed to her purse. Kade grabbed for it and pulled out her wallet to dig for information. He found a medical card. "She's allergic to penicillin and codeine."

"And what's her name?" the EMT asked, not even looking at Kade.

"It's Con—" But he stopped himself when his eyes landed on the name listed on the card, his throat trying to close. "It's Tessa McAllen."

"Thank you."

But Kade didn't even hear him. Or notice another medic who came over to check and see if he needed any help. All Kade could hear were his own words repeating in his head. *It's Tessa McAllen.*

*Tessa McAllen.*

*Tess . . .*

Everything inside him knotted—longing mixed up with a paradoxical dose of pure bitterness. For a moment, he was transported back years to a version of himself he'd tried to forget existed, to a night he'd tried to obliterate from his psyche.

"Sir, you can ride with us to the hospital or follow us there if you feel okay to drive."

"I c-c-can drive." *What the hell?* He nearly slapped his hand over his mouth, the stuttered word like the sound of breaking glass to his ears. He hadn't flubbed a word in over a decade. He rolled his shoulders, shaking off the reappearance of the old tic.

The medic adjusted the oxygen mask on Tessa's face. "Looks like she's going to be fine since you both got out so quickly. But we want to get her checked out and run a few tests to be sure."

Kade nodded absently as he stared down at Tessa. Her hair was blonde now and she was curvier, softer in the best possible way. But, of course, all those years would've changed things. Nothing about him resembled the boy she'd known back then either, not even his name.

She was still as beautiful as he remembered, though. And based on some of the things she'd said tonight, probably just as unattainable.

The only difference was maybe this time he could actually do something about it if he wanted to. The question was—did he want to? Last time he'd taken a risk on Tessa McAllen, his life had blown up and disintegrated around him. He didn't need that kind of drama in his life again or a regular reminder of what he most hoped to forget.

But as he watched Tessa get loaded into the back of the ambulance, he knew there was no way he could step back and let her walk out of his life a second time. She'd said that she only wanted tonight. She'd said this was a one-time thing.

Kaden Fowler would've turned and gone home. That boy had been used to hearing *no*.

But Kade Vandergriff didn't even know what the word sounded like.

# FIVE

*1996*

Kaden Fowler sat in a shaded spot with his back against the grimy brick wall of Henley High's recreation building, hoping to blend into it. The rest of the junior and senior class were either still inside the cafeteria eating or were gathered in small groups around the main yard, claiming their piece of concrete or grass and trying to impress each other.

Kaden never did either here—try to impress *or* eat. After one too many *fatass* and *oink-oink* comments in junior high, he'd learned to fill up at breakfast and then wait until dinner to eat again. Even after he'd shot up six inches over the last year and was more bulk than chub now, the jerkoffs who'd teased him then wouldn't fail to remind him of his former fat-kid status. Once branded as such, it never went away. And if they didn't pick on that, they'd go after his other obvious weakness—his stutter.

He pulled the latest Stephen King novel and his Walkman out of his backpack, putting the headphones over his ears, and turned to the place he'd marked in the book. But before the guitars could even kick in on Metallica's "Until It Sleeps," a lilting laugh cut through the music and carried his gaze up and across the yard. The minute his eyes landed on her, his stomach tightened into a fist of familiar longing.

Tessa McAllen twirled around, showing off some cheerleading move to her gaggle of friends. Her light brown hair fanned out around her, and the little spin made her skirt flit up a bit, revealing a golden swath of upper thigh and the edge of what looked to be pink panties.

Pink panties. *Fuck. Me.*

Kaden grimaced and shifted his weight, willing his body not to respond to the sight. And putting extra effort into forcing his mind not to draw in the rest of the picture of what was beneath her skirt. God, he'd imagined that so many times it probably qualified as some diagnosable mental illness. And if he let his thoughts go there now, he may as well drop out of school and go on the lamb. Because sporting a boner in the fucking schoolyard would be an unredeemable humiliation to come back from.

After she finished her demonstration, her boyfriend, Doug, slid his arm around her and gave her a discreet pat on the ass. Kaden wanted to break every bone in that fucker's hand. It'd take care of two things at once—without that hand Doug couldn't touch Tessa like that *and* he wouldn't be able to throw a damn football again until the season was over. His daddy's money couldn't buy that back for him. Boo-hoo. The king would be ousted.

The morbid thought made Kaden smile.

"Hey, what the fuck are you grinning at, asshole?"

Doug's loudmouth best friend, Quincy, had been hanging in the group with Tessa. But now the guy's focus was solidly on him. Kaden barely resisted flipping the dude off and looked back down at his book, pretending the music was too loud for him to hear.

But, of course, the idiot couldn't let it go. He ambled over, the group trailing behind him like a pack of dogs following a scent—in this case, the scent of potential drama and humiliation, the most enticing of all here at school.

Quincy peered down at Kaden, his bug eyes making him look like a pissed off pug. He kicked the front of Kaden's Doc Martens. "Hey, I'm talking to you, K-K-Kaden."

A few of them laughed at the old joke. Tessa didn't. She had this cute little frown line between her brows that he wished he could reach over and smooth with his thumb. He didn't think that'd be appreciated though. So instead, he shoved his book in his bag and stood, not saying a word. He'd worked hard to beat his childhood stutter, but when he was nervous, it came back like a fucking horror movie villain who wouldn't die. So he'd learned to keep his mouth shut when at all possible.

Not that he was nervous about shit-for-brains Quincy, but Tessa . . . Well, he'd probably forget how to speak the English language if he tried to say anything to her. Once he was up on his feet, he was looking down at Quincy. God bless that unexpected six inches of height. At least something had gone right this year.

"So what's the smile for, big boy?" Quincy asked, dialing up the menace in his voice, but backing up an inch. "You wouldn't be looking at Douggie's pretty girlfriend would you?"

Heat rushed upward, and Kaden prayed it wouldn't make it to his face. "N-n-no."

*Fuck!* Why did his body have to rebel on him at the worst goddamned moments? Blushing and stuttering. He should just hand over his balls now.

"N-n-no?" Quincy teased.

"We all see how you look at her," Doug said, stepping next to Quincy.

"Guys, stop it, okay?" Tessa said, her gaze darting away from Kaden's. "Leave him alone. The bell's about to ring."

"No, babe," Doug said with that smarmy, I'm-better-than-you

tone that seemed to be his default. "I need to look out for you. I don't want some freak staring you down and thinking God knows what. You see the kind of books he's always carrying, how he dresses. Sick fuck."

Her jaw clenched. "He doesn't look at me like anything."

That was a lie. He did. But he wasn't thinking *sick* thoughts. Well . . . depended on one's definition of sick he supposed. "Why would y-you care if I look at her? Threatened?"

Quincy snorted, and Doug gave Kaden a curled-lip once-over. "By a fucking fag with long hair and thrift store clothes? Hardly."

Kaden smirked. "Well, if I'm a f-f-fag, then you have nothing to worry about. And maybe I'm l-l-looking at her because I feel bad for her. She has to deal with your sorry ass."

With that, Kaden shoved past Quincy and made his way through the group. If they were smart, they'd let him go. Because he worked hard to stay out of trouble. Dealing with his stepdad any time he stepped out of line was more trouble than it was worth. But if those pricks laid their hands on him, he'd fight back. And though he probably wouldn't win since he didn't push weights every afternoon like those guys, he was feeling mean enough to fight dirty and inflict some damage before they took him down. Part of him hoped they'd try.

He walked to the main doors without looking back. No one came after him.

Maybe those douchebags had a few brain cells left after all.

---

Tessa looked toward the far end of the library then back down to the note Mrs. Rombach had given her after Tessa had earned her third *D* in English. "You've gotta be freaking kidding me."

"Can I help you find something, Tessa?"

Tessa turned to find the librarian, Ms. Solis, sending her a pleasant smile from behind her fortress of a desk. "Um, Mrs. Rombach wants me to sign up for tutoring in English."

The woman's smile turned a tad sympathetic—*oh my, the poor cheerleader who got the looks but not the brains.* That's what she was probably thinking. Tessa had seen that look before. She wanted to correct her, wanted to tell the librarian that she had *A*s in math. But all this poetry and Shakespeare crap just didn't make sense. How was she supposed to understand stories in a language that didn't even resemble her version of English?

"She's matched you up with Kaden Fowler, dear," Ms. Solis said, pointing toward the tutoring room in the back of the library. The walls of the room were clear glass and soundproof, so there was no mistaking the shaggy blond head bent over a book. "And don't worry. I know he's a little quiet, but that Kaden is sharp as a tack. Goes through at least three books on his own a week."

Tessa forced her face to form some version of a smile. "Is there someone else available? I mean, not that I doubt Kaden's skills or whatever, but I don't think he likes me very much."

"I'm sure that's not the case," she said, a little glint in her dark eyes. "Just give it a chance. If you feel he's not the right tutor for you, you can talk to Mrs. Rombach."

Well, crap. Mrs. Rombach was *not* her biggest fan. She had a feeling the woman had some sort of vendetta against the cheer squad and would simply fail her if she complained about which tutor she'd been assigned. Plus, if word got back to her foster parents that she was making waves, everything could go to hell. The *D*s were going to be hard enough to explain.

With a heavy sigh, Tessa hefted her schoolbag higher on her shoulder and headed toward the back, determined not to make this a big deal. She tapped on the door before swinging it open, and Kaden lifted his head. The *oh-shit* expression on his face probably mirrored the one she'd worn when she'd walked into the library a few minutes ago.

"Uh, c-c-can I help you with something?"

She winced inwardly at his slight stutter, remembering how horrible Doug and Quincy had teased him a few days ago at lunch. Kaden hadn't helped his situation, though, when he'd insulted Doug in front of the group. Her boyfriend was mostly harmless. Quincy usually was the one who got Doug pulled into stupid crap. But Doug wasn't going to let someone like Kaden call him sorry and let it go. And he'd certainly shit a biscuit if he knew she was spending time with the enemy.

Which is why she needed to come up with a plan. Fast.

"Okay, so, yeah, I need your help." She set her bag on the table and glanced over her shoulder. Doug would be at football practice by now, but that didn't mean one of their other friends wouldn't wander into the library for something. A lot of the after-school clubs met in here.

"With?" Kaden prompted.

She pulled out her latest essay test and flattened it on the table. "I'm failing English, and you're my new tutor."

"Y-y-you're the girl who needs help in English?" He scraped a hand through his too-long hair, cursing under his breath.

"Yes. Me. And look, I know you don't like me. And I'm really sorry for the other day. Those guys can be jerks sometimes."

"Sometimes?"

"It's mostly Quincy," she said, peeking over her shoulder again.

"Sure it is." He nodded toward the glass partition with a smirk. "What are you looking for? Afraid someone will see you in here with the s-s-sick fuck?"

She gave a dramatic sigh and sank into a chair. This was not going at all how she'd planned. She hoped she could smile and sweetness her way through this. She wasn't unaware of the effect she had on guys. God hadn't given her much. Useless mother. Dead father. A crapton of foster homes. And not enough skills to know what the hell Hamlet was about. But he had given her a way with boys.

Unfortunately, this boy seemed immune, so she was going to have to give it to him straight.

"Listen, Kaden. Hate me all you want, but they pay you to tutor and right now, I'm the girl who needs help. But I don't want to cause crap for either of us."

"Meaning?" he asked, sounding bored.

"Meaning if Doug or any of my friends sees us together, he's going to make your life hell. And I'm going to get an earful of shit."

He lifted an eyebrow.

"What?" she asked, the simple look making her feel self-conscious.

"N-n-nothing. Just never heard you swear before."

She winced. Truth was, she'd developed a potty mouth at her last home placement. Her foster sister, Sam, had been quite colorful in her speech. But Tessa had learned to curb it when she moved in with the Ericsons. Her foster parents were super strict and would kick her out if they had any clue how much of a delinquent she was capable of being. And there was no way she was giving them up. They'd been the closest to having a real family as she'd ever had.

"So do we need to do this here?" she asked, ignoring his comment and tightening her ponytail.

"The tutoring? No. I just have to sign off that you showed up and for how long."

"Great. Do you have somewhere else we could go?"

"You mean, where we can hide?"

She huffed. "Come on, Kaden. I'm not trying to be a bitch, but you know how it is."

His shoulders sagged like he'd had a sack of sand thrown across them, but he nodded and tucked his books in his bag. "It's a small t-t-town, Tessa. Where are we gonna go?"

She chewed her thumbnail and peered over her shoulder again. They definitely couldn't go to the coffee shop or the park, even the McDonald's had other kids hanging there all the time. And her place was not an option. Boys couldn't come over when her parents weren't home, period, no matter what the purpose. "What about your house?"

He paused in loading up his backpack and looked at her like she'd suggested he get them a rocket to the moon. "You want to come to my *house*? Your boyfriend would gather a lynch mob if he found out we were hanging out alone like that."

She shrugged. "He'd be pissed. But it's not like he'd get the wrong idea, I mean . . ."

The slight wince he gave was almost imperceptible but she felt like shit the minute she realized how it'd sounded. Like he was no threat. Like she was so far out of his league that there was no possible way anyone would worry about them alone together.

"Kaden, I didn't mean that—"

He looped his backpack over his shoulder as he stretched out to his full, impressive height. The smirk was in place again but there was a sad note in his blue eyes. "Save your apology. You don't need to play that nicey-nice, everybody-needs-to-like-me game with me. I know who we both are. And I know where we stand. Let's go."

The comment was like a swift slap right across her cheek, knocking off the bright face she put out in the world. In just a few brief minutes, Kaden Fowler had called bullshit on her. She hurried after him as he made his way out the side door and into the parking lot. She did a quick scan to make sure no one was around. "You don't know what you're talking about. I don't *need* people to like me. They just do."

He sniffed and dug his keys out of his ripped up jeans.

"Okay, so maybe *you* don't."

"And that b-b-bothers the shit out of you."

She quickened her step, trying to keep up with his long, easy strides. "It does not."

But it totally did. It was suddenly driving her crazy. Why didn't he like her? She'd never personally done anything mean to him. She couldn't be held responsible for Doug and his friends.

Kaden stopped next to a beat-up Dodge Challenger and turned to her. "I live over on Dunlop Road. You can follow me. At a reasonable distance, of course, so no one links us t-t-together."

She gritted her teeth. "Fine."

She turned on her heel to stalk to her car, but he called her name before she could take a step. She looked back to find him leaning against the top of his car, staring out toward the football field instead of turning in her direction.

"It's totally bothering you, isn't it?"

She groaned. "Shut up. Point taken."

He smiled but there was no humor in it. He opened his door to climb into his car, but before he closed it, his eyes met hers. "Don't worry, princess. Your record is still perfect. My problem isn't that I don't like you. It's that I like you too much."

And with that, he slammed his door and shut her out.

# SIX

Tessa cupped her hand over the mouthpiece of her phone, hoping no one in the office would hear her conversation. "Doug, I better have read this email wrong."

Her ex-husband made a dismissive grunt. "Having trouble reading now? Maybe I should've used smaller words."

*Fucking bastard.* Tessa gripped her phone, trying to keep her seething response from slipping out. Last thing she needed was for her current boss to send a complaint to the temp agency for an unhinged receptionist yelling at her ex-husband in front of the whole office. "Look, I get that we hate each other. Whatever. But are you really so heartless that you'll let innocent kids suffer just to get back at me?"

He sniffed. "Always so dramatic. This is merely a business decision and nothing else. That charity was your pet project, not mine, and it's a cash sieve."

"It's called nonprofit for a reason, Doug." *Jackass.*

"If it's such a worthy cause, you should be able to find other donors. I'm done keeping it afloat with my church's money. I told the congregation to pick a new charity to focus on this year."

"Doug, please, don't do this." She hated the plea in her voice, but all she could think about were the kids at Bluebonnet Place who would lose services and the employees who'd lose their jobs. She'd started the project five years ago when Doug had told her she should get more involved in his church's outreach activities to look good to the congregation. She'd had no desire to put on more of a show at church than she already did, so she'd asked for seed money to start a charity instead. Looking back over her years with Doug, it was the one thing she could be proud of. Even though it was her ex's money that had funded it, she'd poured her guts into the project, determined to help foster kids who were aging out of the system. She was all too familiar with how it felt to be staring down eighteen with no family behind you, few job skills, and limited funds to better your education.

But now the whole thing was going to be drained dry and abandoned if the cash wasn't there to support it. After the divorce, she'd given the lion's share of her divorce settlement money to Bluebonnet. God knows she'd had no desire to live off Doug's handouts for another second and wanted to put them to good use. But even with that donation, she knew the charity only had enough cash to make it to the end of the year.

"Tessa, if you had thought this through better, you wouldn't have left me in the first place and wouldn't have to worry about this, so don't try to lay some guilt trip on me. This is your doing. Your decision."

She ran a hand through her hair, gripping a few strands tight against her scalp, trying to keep her composure while her mind was screaming, *You self-centered piece of shit. You cheated! You! I didn't do this.*

"Doug, you know I'm not going to be able to get this much money in time to keep it going. Can't you wait to pull funding in six months? We can make a big to-do of how you're contributing despite our differences and give you all the credit. The press will love it." She loathed her supplicating tone but knew that's what got him off—beating her down and winning.

He snorted. "The *press*? You mean the same press you spilled lies to after the divorce? You know how much of my congregation I've lost because of the shit you spread about me? I'm still repairing that damage."

"I only told them the truth. I can't help how they relayed it. And I had to do something after you put rumors out there that I was some pill-popping tramp who strayed on you."

"Right. Because you were an angel. Gabriel was just lying about you meeting him mornings in the guest house. I should've known then and let you have someone on the side to degrade yourself with. You always did like to slum it."

Her nails dug into her palm. That story again. She knew damn well Doug had either paid her former personal trainer money or blackmailed him to go to the press and fabricate some story about her. It had to have been something big because before that, Gabriel had been a friend to her, keeping her company and making her laugh during those often lonely days. The guy was probably going to graduate school on a full ride now, courtesy of her ex-husband.

"Good-bye, Doug."

"Hold on," he said, right as she was about to pull the phone from her ear. "I do have one way I *may* consider giving you the funds you need."

Her gut knotted at his tone, but she forced herself to stay on the phone. She knew whatever he was going to propose would be something she didn't like, but she was willing to do a lot to keep those kids at Bluebonnet from losing funding. "And what's that?"

She could almost feel his viper grin over the phone. "I would need you to *beg*, darling. Get on those pretty knees and tell me how you can't get through without me. That I was right. Then, you'd need to go to the press, admit to your affair with Gabriel and your emotional problems, and tell them that I was a good husband who took care of you."

Her lunch almost came up at the image, the bitter taste burning the back of her throat. "Fuck you."

He laughed. "I'll take that as you considering the option. Try it your way first if you'd like. I'm sure raising a few hundred grand on your own between those dead-end jobs you're doing will be easy as pie. You know where to find me when that flops."

The dial tone buzzed in her ear—harsh and final. Round three thousand and four to the snake. It seemed like every time she went to battle with Doug, he ended up with the last word and the smile. She hung up the phone and rubbed a hand over her face, all the starch draining out of her.

"Everything okay, Vanessa?"

She looked up. It was on the tip of her tongue to correct the guy on her name, but frankly, she didn't remember his either. She'd gone on so many assignments for the temp agency in the past few months that they were all starting to blend together. "I'm fine. What can I help you with?"

He dropped a small voice recorder on her desk. "I've dictated a report that I'd like you to type up for me. I'll need it before I leave today."

"Sure. I'll get right to it," she said with practiced enthusiasm even though she'd never typed from dictation before.

After a quick nod, he strode off and she tucked the earbuds into her ears without hitting Play. The office hummed around her as she sat there at her borrowed desk, watching people moving back and forth with their tasks, chatting with co-workers and catching up from the weekend. No one had asked her how her weekend had been. No one cared. She was a stranger. No one knew that she'd had the best sex of her life on Friday night and had passed out from a fire. No one knew that she'd slipped out of the hospital before Van could get there because she couldn't trust herself to turn him down. No one knew that her ex-husband had just ripped one final rug out from under her. And no one knew that the fate of an entire charity and at least a hundred kids was now resting on her very unqualified shoulders.

She was simply the temp filling in for a beloved co-worker who was on maternity leave.

Part of her relished the anonymity of it. She'd hated the spotlight she'd been under in her marriage as the TV pastor's wife. But sometimes she couldn't help feeling the loneliness of it now. Besides Sam, she had no one here. No roots. No friends. Not even co-workers she could get to know. She'd hoped to find a more permanent job by now, but the market was tough for entry-level positions and though she was taking night classes, she didn't have the fancy experience to put on a resume yet.

Hell, maybe she should've just stayed with Doug. They could've lived their separate lives in the same house and pretended to still be together in public. She'd known couples who'd done that. She could've put all her effort into charity work and not had to worry about if she'd have enough money for the gas bill or if that noise outside at night was some criminal in her not-so-desirable neighborhood trying to break in.

But then she'd have to look at Doug's smug face every day. *I told you so. I told you that you couldn't survive on your own.*

*Screw that.* She shook her head, disgusted that'd she'd even entertained the thought. Another day in that house with Doug and she'd probably be sitting in a jail for attempted murder. Her life now may not be posh or flashy, but at least she could wake up every day knowing that everything she had was hers and hers alone. No one was paying her way. No one owned her.

She'd figure out some way to help her charity. Even if it meant she'd have to go door-to-door to ask for donations. She would not fail those kids. And she'd be damned if she'd give her ex-husband the satisfaction of seeing her beg.

With renewed resolve, she turned toward her computer, hit the Play button on the voice recorder, and started typing.

---

"You know, I'm not some crazed stalker," Kade said, tucking his hands in the pockets of his slacks and trying to look as harmless as possible.

Sam, the raven-haired girl he'd given Tessa's keys to on Friday night leaned against the doorway and arched her pierced brow. "Which is exactly what a crazed stalker would say."

He smirked. "Good point. Can you at least tell me how I can get in touch with Tessa?"

"How did you even find me, stalker guy?" she asked, a glint in her eyes.

He could tell she was enjoying torturing him and not truly threatened by his unexpected visit. Somehow he doubted this girl was afraid of much. She was cute as a pixie but he sensed she was all scrappy badass beneath that sweet smile. He pulled a piece of paper from his pocket. "Your name and address were on the event list."

"You stole private documents? Now you're admitting to your criminal behavior. That is the first step to recovery."

Damn, maybe this girl was a dominatrix on the side because she wasn't giving him an inch. "Look, Sam, I know you're going to be loyal and protective of your friend. I respect that. But after the fire, they took Tessa to the hospital, and I got held up by the police. By the time I got there, she was gone. I'd like to make sure that she's okay. And when the fire broke out, we were in the middle of a conversation I'd like to finish."

She sighed. "Yeah, I've got a feeling what kind of conversation you're talking about. But listen, she's fine. No permanent damage from the fire. And as for the other thing, she left before talking to you for a reason. She's not looking to start up something with anyone. You were just a checkbox on her list, a one-time thing. Be glad. Isn't that every guy's dream? No strings or obligation to call the next day."

He started to respond to the question but then his mind snagged on the other part. "Wait, what do you mean, I was a checkbox on her list?"

She groaned and put her hand to the door, swinging it toward him. "Good-bye, stalker guy."

"Sam—" But the door was already clicking shut.

*Fuck.*

Sam wasn't going to budge. Plan B time. He headed down the hallway of the apartment building and pulled his phone from his pocket. As usual, his assistant, Maile, answered on the first ring. "What's up, boss?"

"Are you at your desk?"

"Chained to it, as always. I work for a slave driver, you know."

He snorted. "My sympathies. Whatever you're working on right now, put it on the side. I need you to dig up as much information as you can find on a woman named Tessa McAllen, birthdate October third, same year as me."

How he still remembered Tessa's birthday was a wonder, but it was there, seared on his brain like some permanent brand.

"What is this regarding? Is she a new business contact?" Maile asked, slipping into professional mode.

"No, this is a personal matter. Any information you find should remain confidential."

There was a pause on the other line. "Wait, is this about the fire? The police were here this afternoon, looking to talk to you again. Boss, no offense, but you shouldn't be doing your own investigating. If someone—"

"This isn't about that." Not directly at least. A detective had called him earlier today to inform him that they now suspected arson instead of an accidental fire. Kade knew they'd be searching for Tessa to get a statement, and he'd at least like to warn her before she got dragged into it. But, of course, if he said he was only seeking her out for that reason, he'd be a damn liar. "I need this information ASAP. I'll be back in the office this afternoon."

"You got it," Maile said, hanging up without a good-bye. He loved that the woman was pure, no-frills efficiency. He had no doubt she was already on task before the phone settled in its cradle. He'd probably know when Tessa's first baby tooth fell out by the end of the day.

And sure enough, a few hours later, Kade was sitting at his desk with a pile of printed documents in front of him. Maile pointed at the stack, indicating the colored sticky tabs she'd added to certain pages. "I labeled basic stats with green. But the gist is she doesn't live far from here, has been working for a temp agency, and has no family in the area. Also, no criminal record."

"Okay."

"Work history's labeled with blue. Not much info there. Though, she is the founder of a local charity. Gossip has the yellow tabs. Lots of that available."

"Gossip?" he asked, glancing up from the top page, which held Tessa's address and a newspaper photo of her in a party dress.

Maile pushed her black bob behind her ears and frowned. "Apparently, she was married to a pastor of one of those big time mega-churches in Atlanta up until a year ago. Pretty high-profile guy, Sunday sermons were broadcast on regional television, that kind of thing. The divorce made the society pages since they were a prominent couple in the area. Looks like things got nasty. Each accused the other of infidelity. She didn't say much more than that publicly but the husband had lots to say. He accused her of being a pill popper, a gold digger, a cheater, and said she shirked her godly and *wifely* duties . . ."

"Wifely duties? What the fuck?"

"That's what I'm saying. That line alone made me want to find this guy so I could kick him in his junk. Nothing was substantiated from what I can tell. And apparently this Marilyn Wallace, the reporter who penned most of the negative stories, used to be Tessa's close friend, so that's pretty interesting that she'd turn on her so quickly. My guess is she had some added motivation to write up the stories. But regardless, it looks like the society pages ate the shit up. The pastor's reputation got dinged pretty good. People left his church, and he almost lost the TV slot. But looks like after some damage control, he was able to hold on to his contract and convince his congregation to give him the benefit of the doubt. She wasn't so lucky. The press labeled her the washed up, pampered ice princess and called it a Cinderella story gone bad. Apparently, she didn't come from money."

*No. She didn't come from anything,* Kade thought, an old sadness welling up. And he knew beyond a doubt that Tessa would have never popped pills. Tess's birthmother had abandoned her because of drugs. In high school, Tess hadn't even liked taking over-the-counter medicine, so that part was definitely bullshit and lies. He skimmed through a few of the documents. "Who was the guy?"

Maile flipped through the pages on her steno pad. "Um, something Barrett. Hold up, I wrote it down."

But Kade already knew the rest of the answer, a bitter, icy cold moving through him. "Douglas Barrett."

"Yeah, that's it," she said.

Kade sat back in his chair, feeling like a truck had rolled right over him. Douglas Barrett. It'd been a name he'd tried to block out of his memory completely, one that dragged him back to years he never wanted to revisit. *Doug fucking Barrett.* God, Tessa had gone through with it. She'd married that sociopath anyway. And had stayed with him all those years. She'd known what Doug had done that night—well, enough of what he'd done—and had still given herself to him.

For the security. The money.

Things Kade hadn't been able to offer her.

"Boss, you okay?" Maile asked, her brows pinched together. "You don't look so great."

He rubbed his eyes and took a long, deep breath, doing his best to shove the past back to where it belonged. He was beyond all that. He would not let one drop of that leak in. All he was interested in was learning more about who Tess was now. "I'm all right. Anything else I should know?"

Maile pulled a paper from the bottom of the pile and slid it his way. "Last year, her charity applied to be the sponsored organization for our annual Dine and Donate event. We didn't select them since we were focusing on homelessness last year. But they're on the consideration list for this year since we're planning to choose a charity focused on children."

He perused the application in front of him. It'd been filled out by the director of Bluebonnet Place but under the founder column was Tessa's married name. Even seeing Doug's last name sitting next to hers made his stomach want to heave. But an idea was already forming in his head, lifting his mood a bit. "Are we close to selecting an organization yet?"

Maile sighed. "No, with Evelyn on medical leave, we don't have anyone heading up things right now. I think PR is looking to hire someone from the outside to handle it."

Kade smiled and pushed the application back toward Maile. "Please call the charity director and tell her we're considering the organization, but that I insist on meeting with the founder to find out more about their work first."

Maile narrowed her eyes, evaluating him like his grandmother did that first night he'd shown up on her doorstep. "Kade Vandergriff."

"What?" he asked, feigning innocence.

"You have that scheming look on your face. What are you up to?"

"Me? I'm just trying to get more involved in my company's charitable contributions."

Maile shook her head and looked to the ceiling. "Lord, help us all. Kade's got his eye on a woman."

"Aww, you know you're the only girl for me, Mai," he teased as she rose from her chair.

She glanced back over her shoulder and stuck out her tongue. "Eww boys, gross."

He chuckled. "I don't blame you. I've seen your girlfriend. I wouldn't leave her for me, either."

She smirked. "So who is this Tessa McAllen to you, really?"

He leaned forward, bracing his forearms on his desk and looking at the photo of Tessa again. "Guess we're about to find out."

# SEVEN

"You should come with me," Tessa said, anxiously flipping through the brochures and paperwork the director had handed over to her. "You'll be so much better at this than me."

Iris gave her a warm smile and folded her hands on top of the desk, that stern grandmotherly vibe wafting off of her. "Ms. McAllen, his assistant was very specific. Mr. Vandergriff wants to meet with the founder, not me. And no one is more passionate about this place than you are. You're going to do great. In fact, I still don't understand why you don't take a position here. I'd happily step down to assistant director since I'm only a few years from retirement. This is your baby."

Tessa tucked the papers in her bag, her palms sweaty already. This was exactly why she hadn't appointed herself director when she moved back. Just because she had founded the charity didn't mean she was qualified to run it. She had a high school education and a resume that could barely fill half a page. *Hi, can I take your order?* was much closer to her skillset than this. Doug hadn't even let her near the financials of Bluebonnet because he said it would take too long for him to teach her what she was looking at.

How the hell was she supposed to meet with the CEO of some giant company and sound even halfway intelligent? Especially with the pressure of knowing how much was riding on this. Getting selected could mean the answer to her prayers for keeping Bluebonnet open. But if she flubbed it, the hard-working woman sitting in front of her would be out of a job and all those kids she'd passed on her way in would be out of services.

No. She wasn't going to let that happen. She took a steadying breath. "Okay, yes, I can do this."

"Of course you can, dear." Iris's dark hand covered Tessa's pale, shaking one, giving it a squeeze. "And if this opportunity doesn't work out, there will be more. I've been sending letters to lots of potential donors. Something will come through. You've created a good thing here. Others will see that and want to help."

Tessa nodded, trying to absorb some of the older woman's confidence and shake off the veil of guilt that tried to envelop her at Iris's assertion. Yes, Tessa had created good things here by coming up with the concept and providing the funds via her ex-husband. But the day-to-day miracles belonged to the woman behind the desk and the rest of the staff. The pictures lining the walls were of kids with employees and volunteers who were in the trenches here day to day. The only photos of Tessa were one from opening day when she'd cut the ribbon they'd tied around the building and another at an awards ceremony. In the grand scheme of it all, Tessa's role was remote and minor at best—the face of the charity but not the backbone. That fact hadn't bothered her before, but now it dug into her gut like a burr, sticking there and reminding her of its presence with every breath.

She so didn't deserve to be the person representing the charity to some bigwig donor today, but it looked like there was no way around it. And maybe, if by some miracle she could pull this off, it would help make up a little for her hands-off approach the last few years.

She gathered all of her documents and stood. "Thank you, Iris, for the pep talk and for everything you do here. I can't tell you how much I appreciate the way you put your soul into this place."

Iris rose from behind her desk and came around to give Tessa a hug. The move made Tessa stiffen with surprise, but soon she found herself returning the gesture. Iris pulled back and patted Tessa's cheek. "It's my pleasure, dear. And we're glad to have you here in town with us now. That man was no good for you."

Tessa laughed, caught off guard by the woman's candor. Usually, she was the consummate professional, never uttering an unkind word toward anyone, except maybe the occasional *bless his heart*. "I couldn't agree with you more."

"Now, go get us that money, girl," Iris said with a grin. "And don't you be a stranger around here. This is your home as much as it is ours."

"Yes, ma'am," Tessa said, feeling an old twinge at the word *home*. That simple word had always been such a fleeting concept in her life. Any time she thought she had fledgling roots starting to dig in, the sand shifted beneath her again and the rain washed them away. And here once more, life was trying to pull something else out from beneath her.

No, not life this time. *Doug*.

The bolt of anger that flashed through her at the thought had her shoulders pulling back and her chin tipping up. No freaking way was she letting him win.

No matter what she had to do, she was going to get this money.

She gave Iris a quick good-bye and headed to her car with renewed resolve. Watch out, Mr. CEO, because Tessa McAllen wasn't taking no for an answer today.

---

Tessa's confidence flagged slightly when she arrived downtown and stared up at the gleaming building that held Vandergriff Industries, but she didn't have time to let all the insecurities rush back in. Her appointment was in less than fifteen minutes, and being late was not an option. She hurried to the bank of elevators and punched the button for the twenty-second floor. On the ride up, she read over the bullet points she'd typed into her phone and practiced her spiel in her head.

*Fake it 'til you make it.* The little tome Sam had offered kept replaying in her mind. If Tessa acted like she was confident and well-informed, people would believe it. That was the theory at least. And she *was* well-informed about the charity. Confident? Well, that'd require the faking part.

When she reached the office of Kade Vandergriff, a serious-faced Asian woman lifted a hand in greeting from behind her desk but was on the phone. She motioned for Tessa to have a seat and that she'd be a minute. Tessa sat in one of the cushy chairs along the wall and fought the urge to gnaw on her thumbnail—a childhood habit that liked to resurface at the worst times. Waiting rooms had never been happy places for her. Child services. Principals' offices. Therapy sessions. Police stations. Waiting rooms usually meant bad news.

The woman put the phone in its cradle and came around the desk to greet Tessa. "You must be Ms. McAllen."

Tessa stood and put out her hand. "Yes."

"I'm Maile, Mr. Vandergriff's assistant." She shook Tessa's hand and gave her an almost undetectable once-over, her eyebrow lifting slightly as if she was surprised by what she found. Maybe she'd been expecting an older woman, someone more distinguished to be the founder of a charity.

"Nice to meet you."

Maile smiled, and it changed her whole face, bringing effortless beauty to the surface. "Same. I'll let Mr. Vandergriff know you're here. He should only be a minute."

"Thank you."

Maile slipped back behind her desk and lifted the phone again while punching a button. "Ms. McAllen is here to see you." She gave a quick nod. "Yes, sir. I'll send her in."

Tessa gripped her documents close to her chest, butterflies the size of velociraptors crashing around in her stomach.

"You can go on in," Maile said, indicating the door behind her.

Tessa thanked her and took a deep breath, then headed toward the door, letting her I'm-totally-calm-and-confident mask slip into place. She'd practiced that facade with every new school she'd started, every new family she'd been placed with. Don't let anyone see fear. The knob turned with ease in her hand, and she pushed the door open.

But the face that greeted her on the other side had all her plans tumbling into a free fall like a plane with broken wings. She could almost hear the whine of wind rushing past her ears. *Mayday, mayday! Boom! Crash!*

Van, no, Mr. *Van*dergriff, smiled and stood. "Hi, Tessa, why don't you shut that door behind you and come on in?"

She blinked, realizing she'd frozen there in the doorway like some slack-jawed sculpture. She cleared her throat, her skin flushing from foot to crown. "Right, of course."

She shut the door and somehow found her way across his very large, very posh office and stopped in front of his desk. The vision of him standing there in his expensive pinstripe suit with the view of downtown Dallas framed behind him in the large corner-office windows was almost too much to take in all at once. He'd exuded confidence on Friday night, but this version of him almost made her tip backward in her heels with the force of his presence. He took the papers from her grasp and set them on the desk, then took her hand between his. "I'm so happy to see you again and to see that you're all right after the other night. You are okay, right?"

"Uh, yeah." She stared at him, lost for a moment in that penetrative blue gaze, the memory of that night stirring both arousal and embarrassment. She'd been so wanton with him . . . and way too honest. This man hadn't just seen her naked, she'd told him things that you only tell your closest friends—or people who you thought you'd never see again. "You gave me a fake name."

She cringed at her accusatory tone. Damn, that wasn't what she'd meant to say.

He released her hand, amusement flashing through his eyes as he motioned for her to take a seat. "No, I gave you a nickname I occasionally use. And you weren't totally forthcoming on the name bit either, *Tessa*, so maybe we should call it even."

She sat down, ready to explain, but as the present moment finally settled in around her, it hit her that though she was reeling, he didn't seem at all surprised to see *her* there. "You knew it was me who was coming today."

He gave an enigmatic smile. "We have a lot to talk about."

She glanced down at her stack of brochures, suddenly remembering why she'd come there today. *Oh, God*. How in the hell was she supposed to pitch her children's charity to a guy who'd licked olive oil and orange juice off her boobs? She wanted to put her face in her hands and die right there. That would be easier than suffering through this conversation. "I don't even know where to start. This . . . I wasn't expecting . . ."

"Tessa," he said, cutting off her rambling with a firm but kind voice. "Don't be embarrassed. We're both adults, and everything is fine. How about we get this business stuff done first? Then we can tackle anything else afterward."

She rolled her lips inward and nodded, doing her best to regain her composure. "Sounds good."

He leaned back in his chair and hooked an ankle over his knee, as if settling in to evaluate her, but he started talking before she could begin her speech. "First, let me explain a little about our event so you know what we're looking at. Every year, Vandergriff Industries gathers the top restaurants in the city, not just the ones we own, to participate in a large, upscale wine and food event called Dine and Donate. Each restaurant who participates sends a team to man a booth that sells appetizers and cocktails to attendees. We try to have at least thirty restaurants participate so that people have a variety of cuisines to sample. We also book local bands to play throughout the day and then usually a well-known act to headline the night. All proceeds go to the selected charity for that year."

"Wow, sounds like a major undertaking," she said, already imagining how much money something that large scale must bring in for the lucky charity.

"It is," he agreed. "And we've been very successful with it over the last few years, which is why so many charities solicit us now."

She wet her lips, nerves creeping back in as she pictured a line of worthy charities wrapping around the building, hoping to be the chosen one.

"And we wish we could select them all, but the biggest impact comes from choosing the one each year where we can really make a significant difference."

"Right."

"So," he said, leaning forward and putting his forearms on the desk, "tell me why being selected would make a significant difference to *your* charity."

His laser gaze pinned her to the spot, and it felt like her tongue dried out and shrunk to half its size. She fiddled with opening the brochure in front of her while trying to find her voice. "Well, I brought—"

His hand landed over hers, stilling her nervous movements. "No, don't read to me about it. *Tell* me, Tessa."

She looked up, her heart doing a discordant drumroll against her ribs. This was her chance, *Bluebonnet's* only chance to survive right now. All those people and kids were counting on her. She couldn't freeze up like a frightened mouse or screw this up because she happened to be intimidated by/attracted to/left speechless by this man. She nodded and he released her hand.

"Bluebonnet Place is a charity focused on helping older children in foster care develop life and work skills so that when they age out of the system, they have a foundation to stand on. We assign them mentors who help them with college applications and with applying for financial aid. We assist them in getting jobs during high school to gain work experience and skills. And we provide a place where they can come after school if they need a break from their household or the group home or the streets."

Kade nodded, seeming as if he was listening with every ounce of his attention. It was both unnerving and confidence building.

She cleared her throat, encouraged by his interest, and began to share the statistics of how many kids aged out of the system and what their likely outcomes were without support. The grim numbers made her stomach twist, but she continued on, her passion for the cause starting to rise to the surface and speed up her words.

Kade took a few notes and appeared appropriately concerned by some of the more dire statistics.

"And I know that we're small and still relatively new," she continued, "But—"

Kade held up a hand, halting her. "Don't start apologizing and undermining everything you just said."

She bit her lip, swallowing back her instinct to spout disclaimers. "Okay."

"It sounds like an amazing cause, Tessa. Truly. I'm impressed that you put such a thoughtful organization together."

"Thank you." Her heart was like a Boombox rattling her ribcage, and her palms had gone sticky with sweat against the arms of the chair.

"And it would be an honor to have Bluebonnet Place as the featured charity at our event."

*Ohmigod, ohmigod, ohmigod.* It was like everything was happening in slow motion, like a dream.

"However . . ."

Her breathing stopped, the awful word clanging in her ears.

"There would be some conditions," he finished.

The air whooshed out of her in a gust. Conditions. Not a *no.* Conditions! She could handle that. Heck, she couldn't imagine anything that would stop her from saying yes. Anything would be better than crawling on her hands and knees and begging her asshole ex-husband for help. She grabbed her pen and flipped her steno pad to a fresh page. "What do you have in mind?"

"Evelyn, our point person who is usually in charge of the event, is on medical leave."

"Okay." She made a note.

"And I know that you're currently working for a temp agency, is that correct?"

She frowned, unsure what that had to do with anything and how he knew the information in the first place. "I am."

He tugged open one of his desk drawers and pulled out a folder. His eyes met hers. "I need you to quit and come to work for me."

# EIGHT

Tessa tilted her head, the words not quite registering. "Wait, you want me to what?"

"In order for this to happen, I'll need you to quit the temp agency and take over the event this year as coordinator," Kade said, his tone no-nonsense.

She stared at him, wondering if he'd knocked his head on something or maybe had gotten sauced on his lunch break. Clearly, he was talking crazy.

"We'd, of course, pay you a fair salary since the position will be full time for the next few months." He slid a document her way, pointing to a salary number that would take her at least two years of temp work to make. "You'll have a small office in the PR department and access to one of their assistants if you need administrative help."

"Van, I mean, Mr. Vandergriff—" she said, panic rooting in her chest and spreading outward. He was being *serious*?

"Please, call me Kade."

"Kade," she said, her eyes lifting from the document before her.

All the things he'd said about the event swam through her brain, forming a whirlpool of *there's no fucking way* protests—thirty restaurants, booking bands, getting a headliner . . . "I appreciate the offer, but you don't understand. I'm not qualified to—"

"Of course you are," he said, his tone not leaving room for argument. "No one will be more passionate about swaying people to participate. I received a copy of your resume from the temp service. You have the basic office skills you need to stay organized, and the admin can help with the little details. Your main focus will be on garnering participants and planning the event. You listed event planning in your Other Skills section on the resume."

*Shit.* Once again she was reminded why lying was such a bad idea. She'd added that at Sam's suggestion to fluff up the resume. And sure, Tessa had planned big parties before, but only at her home, nothing for anyone who was paying her to get it right. "Those events were personal ones. Nothing official. I don't think I'm capable of taking on—"

"This is the condition, Tessa. Nonnegotiable. I have complete faith that you can do this. If you can't get the donors lined up, your charity is the one that suffers. And I know you won't let that happen."

Her lungs felt like they'd been flattened with a rolling pin. She tried to pull in a breath. There was no way she could take this on. It'd be an utter failure. The highest-level job she'd ever held was the one she had now, and that was only one step above being ticket taker at the local theater. But if she turned it down, Bluebonnet Place wouldn't get the money at all. She'd walked in promising herself she'd do whatever it took to get this chance and now that promise was coming home to roost like a big, fat, squawking hen.

"Do you accept my condition, Tessa?" Kade asked, all business.

Did she accept? As if she had any choice. Nerves moved over her skin like static. What if she completely embarrassed herself?

What if donors laughed in her face? She rubbed her hands along the arms of the chair, trying to get them to stop shaking.

"I guess I do. I'm not sure why you would want me to—" Another worry sparked in the hollows of her chest, cutting off her train of thought. "Wait, tell me you're not doing this because of what happened between us Friday night."

She'd die if this was some handout because she hadn't had money that night, or worse, if it was some after-sex payoff. Bang the CEO, get a job.

He smiled. "Rest assured. I'm not doing this because of Friday night."

She nodded, hearing the sincerity and taking comfort in that. *Thank God.* "Okay."

He pulled out another sheet of paper and slid it on top of the other. "I'm doing *this* because of Friday night."

She peered down at the new document with dread. "What is it?"

"This says that you will report directly to the head of the PR department, not to me, and that I have no say-so in your employment status and no authority to terminate you in the future."

"I don't understand. Why does that matter?" she asked, scanning the page but not really understanding why it was necessary.

He reached out and put a finger beneath her chin, lifting her face toward his. "Because when you're in my bed again, I don't want you worrying about business getting mixed with pleasure."

Her ribs pulled tight, her spine going ramrod straight. "Excuse me?"

He lowered his hand but not his uncompromising gaze. "I told you on Friday. One night was not enough."

"And I told you that's all I had to give," she said, the words barely making it past her constricted throat. "Is this a condition of the deal?"

His lips curved with hot promise. "Of course not. I plan on pursuing you whether you take the job or not."

"Kade," she protested, goose bumps breaking over her skin at the thought of him touching her again. But *bad idea* didn't even begin to describe what getting involved with him would be, especially now. "I can't, we can't . . ."

He stood and walked around the desk, sliding into the spot in front of her. The look he gave her when he perched on the edge of the desk and peered down stripped her to the studs. "Tell me you haven't thought about Friday night."

Her gaze dropped to her hands. God, of course she had, about a thousand times since she'd left him. *I can teach you things.* His naughty words had reverberated through her every night when she'd lay in bed alone. "It doesn't matter if I have or haven't."

"Of course it does. In fact, right now, that's all that matters to me," he said, his voice like warmed honey sliding over her. "Put me on your list, Tessa."

Her attention snapped upward. *List?* "What? How do you know about—?"

"Your friend, Sam, let it slip when I tried to find you to see if you were okay," he said, as if it was totally normal that he'd sought out her best friend to track her down.

Humiliation washed through Tessa, and she made a mental note to kill her best friend. *Headstone: Samantha Dunbar, death by TMI.*

"So what item did I check off for you?"

She put a hand to her forehead. *Jesus. This is not happening.* "We are so not talking about this."

"Oh, we so are." He nudged her with his knee, his whole demeanor switching to playful mode. "I'm dying to know. Was it seduce a stranger?"

She snorted. "Hello, *you* seduced *me.* I was minding my own business, thank you very much."

He grinned. "Okay, I'll grant you that. So, let's see, was it, have a one-night stand? Do something kinky?"

She groaned. "You're not going to give up, are you?"

"Nope."

"Fine, my list has things on it I want to improve. One of them was what my ex said to me about being bad in bed."

Kade's expression instantly darkened. "Your ex obviously had no idea what to do with you."

"Probably not."

"No probably about it." Kade hooked both his ankles around the legs of her chair and dragged her and the chair forward until she was braced between his knees. He laid his hands over hers on the arms of the chair and leaned into her space, his expression full of temptation and illicit intention. "*I* do know what to do with you, *to* you. Give me a chance to show you, Tessa."

She stared back at him, captured in the spell he was weaving around them, her body warring with her common sense. Everything about Kade called to her—his voice, his smile, the way he looked at her as if she were the most decadent meal of his life. He was temptation wrapped up in an unfairly sexy package, like a tropical vacation to her midwinter life.

"You don't understand. My life is all kinds of complicated right now. I'm juggling so much already—a new town, night school, trying to find a career, my list. And now with this job it's going to increase a hundred fold. I don't have the ability to add one more potentially complicated thing."

His gaze softened. "It doesn't have to be complicated. In fact, I can make it exceptionally uncomplicated."

"Sex is always complicated," she replied, but there was no punch in her protest.

"No, sex is *complex*. Relationships are complicated. Friday night was as simple and straightforward as it gets."

She lifted an eyebrow. "You call that simple? That was like a three-ring circus compared to my former sex life."

"This further proves how neglected and sheltered you've been," he said, his tone full of graveness but humor crinkling the corners of his eyes. "I can show you complex. Complex, kinky, deviant. Pick your poison."

She smiled, remembering his words from the other night. *I'm a kinky fucker.* "Sounds like I'd need to create a whole new page of the list to cover all that."

He leaned back to grab something on his desk and then reached for her hand. Before she could figure out what he was doing, he stamped the top of her hand.

She glanced down to see his signature in blue on her skin. "What's this?"

"My full endorsement of that idea. Make a new list. Put me on it."

She laughed. "You're weird, Kade Vandergriff."

"So I've been told. But for the sake of my fragile ego, let's label that as charming instead."

She shook her head, unsure what to think of this quirky man. One minute he could intimidate her right out of her clothes, the next he could make her feel like she was hanging out with someone she'd known forever. When she'd walked into this office and had seen him sitting behind his big desk in a big office with his finely cut designer suit, she'd had a hard time not dropping him into the same box as Doug. Wealthy, arrogant, and powerful. A guy who spent his life looking down at everyone around him from atop some self-righteous golden pulpit and only taking an interest in someone if it could serve his own plans or image. But as the conversation went on, she was realizing Kade had a completely different vibe, one that seemed out of place considering his station in life. And it was making her want to know more.

"I don't know what to say to all this," she said honestly.

"*Yes.* That's the word you're looking for, I believe. And look, I get that you're unsure because I've thrown a lot at you today. But let's make this as simple as can be. I'm asking you to spend another evening with me. No strings or expectations. Just another night to relax, explore, and enjoy each other. Preferably without fire and life-threatening smoke inhalation involved. If afterward you don't want to get together again, that's your call. I would never hold that against you."

The tune he was singing was a pied piper's song to her system. *Relax, explore, and enjoy.* She didn't even know what relaxing felt like anymore. Friday night with him had been the closest she'd gotten to that state in as long as she could remember. But she sensed there was fine print hiding in his words. He was saying she could walk away, but he wasn't expecting her to. That easy confidence unnerved her. But she couldn't make herself close off the option just yet. "What exactly would you want to check off my list?"

His thumbs traced over her knuckles as he watched her with careful eyes. "What experiences or fantasies do you have knocking around in that head of yours?"

Being under his heavy gaze was like being chained to the chair. It made her realize how little her ex-husband had *really* looked at her. That kind of rapt attention was potent. But she didn't know how to answer Kade's question. Sure, she had some fantasies. Who didn't? But there was no way she had the guts to say them aloud. She'd mentioned a few to Doug once, and he'd looked at her like she'd lost her mind. No way was she risking that embarrassment again. "I don't even know. I didn't have room to think outside the box in my previous relationship. Doug had . . . issues about those things."

"Issues?" He asked leaning back and giving her a little space.

She shifted in her chair, uncomfortable with sharing this much but somehow unable to shut up. Kade's focus on her was like feeding her truth serum. Maybe she'd contracted Sam's TMI disease. "He expected his wife to have the proper image—conservative, God-fearing, a lady. A Southern belle for his congregation to adore and admire. But it wasn't just a public role. That expectation applied in and out of the bedroom."

A sour expression crossed Kade's features. "Meanwhile, he's screwing around on you."

"Yep." Saying it aloud sounded even more depressing than knowing it. Her entire sexual history centered around a man who, after the first few years, had barely been interested in her beyond taking her out to be on his arm for photo-ops and church services. He took care of her in the sense of buying her nice clothes and giving her anything monetary she needed, but the little spark she'd thought they had between them had died a quick death after they'd married.

From the start, he'd liked the idea of Tessa being a *lady*, proper and sweet and respectable. Even in high school before he'd started pursuing the business of religion, he'd wanted to preserve her virginity until they were married. Back then, it'd seemed chivalrous and romantic, but she hadn't realized where that motivation had come from. And once they had wed, sure, they'd had sex, but it had always been in the most traditional sense possible—in the dark, in bed, missionary style. Anything else was deemed trashy. *I don't want to fuck my wife, Tessa. I want to make love to her.*

And Tessa had gone along with it, feeling guilty for even craving anything different. He'd made her wonder if her desires were somehow some defect from her "white trash" genes. But she'd eventually understood where Doug's logic had come from. His mother had developed a colorful reputation of bed-hopping with wealthy men after her divorce from his dad. And when Doug was a freshman, a sex tape of his mother and a local congressman had been leaked to the press, complete with the details of all the sordid acts they'd done together. Tessa knew the scandal had torn Doug to pieces, causing him to switch schools and miss most of that year. When he'd finally told Tess about it after they'd been dating a while, he'd vomited after.

And she'd felt awful that he'd had to go through that. But it hadn't meant she'd stopped hoping that he'd be able to come to terms with that and loosen up a little. That things would get better. But of course, they hadn't. Instead, he'd apparently chosen to *fuck* other women who were not his wife to fill in the gaps. She got to be the expensive, untouched china in the display case while the other women served more base needs.

Kade wouldn't put her in the china case. He wanted her like she was Friday night—lustful and bold and dirty. He didn't want to polish and display her; he wanted to unhinge her.

And maybe that's exactly what she needed.

"What if you pick what happens instead?" she said on a surge of bravery. "I would've never been brave enough to plan out what happened Friday night. The fun was in the, I don't know . . ."

"In the lack of control," he said simply. "You liked that I took over."

She smoothed her lipstick, considering his theory and realizing he was dead-on right. As soon as he'd stopped her in the hallway, the barrage of worries and *what ifs* had fallen away and she'd been happy to let the tide that was Kade Vandergriff sweep her onto a new beach. And once they'd gotten upstairs, she hadn't had to think or worry about who would make a move or if it would be awkward or if she did something wrong. He'd taken care of it all, taken care of *her*. She'd just followed his lead and instructions and enjoyed.

The realization niggled at her. She'd spent too much of her life letting someone "take care of her." She didn't want to be that girl always looking to let some guy handle things. But when it came to sex, she was out of her depth. Having him guide her was a big part of the appeal. She just had to be sure that control didn't bleed into anything else.

"I guess that was a big part of it," she admitted. "It felt more comfortable to let you take the lead."

A pleased smile replaced his serious expression and as if no longer able to keep from touching her, he took her hands and pulled her to her feet, caging her between his knees. "Well, lucky for both of us, my favorite thing of all is taking charge, so I'm more than happy to oblige that wish. You give me the okay, and you won't have to worry about another thing. All you'll have to do is show up and be mine for the night."

That last part sent her mind racing down bunny trails she hadn't even known were there in her psyche, images of what being his for the night would mean. "Are you going to make me wear a Princess Leia costume and chain me in your garage or something?"

He slid his hands onto her waist. "Wicked girl, now you're just talking dirty to turn me on."

She rolled her eyes, but the way he was looking at her had her body waking up in all the important places.

"I need to hear you say yes, Tessa. I want you. Once wasn't enough. And I know you feel the same way." When she opened her mouth to respond, he tugged her even closer, lowering his voice. "In fact, I'd bet the net worth of this company that you're wet beneath this prim skirt right now, imagining all the things I could do to you. It's taking all my self-control not to slide it up and feel for myself."

Heat washed over her skin, like opening an oven and feeling the blast of it. Instinctively, she pressed her thighs together and averted her eyes, knowing he was right and hating that she was so freaking transparent.

He captured her jaw with gentle fingers and turned her head to face him. "Don't be ashamed of that, own it. We're two grown people who are attracted to each other. That's something to celebrate and enjoy, not feel guilt over. Fuck being a 'proper lady'—whatever the hell that's supposed to mean—and be a woman who takes what she needs and deserves without apology."

The fervor of his words hit her on some level deep beneath the layers of the person she put out into the world. That permission to grab onto what she really wanted or needed had never been presented to her like that before. Her life was full of how she could accommodate others, fit into the proper cardboard cutouts of their lives so she'd have a place, each foster home a new script to follow. And even when she'd become an adult, she'd simply signed onto another role with Doug—a paper doll with pretty costumes.

"I'm not sure I even know how to do that."

"Then let me show you. One more night, Tessa. That's all I'm asking."

She took a deep, spine-straightening breath, resolve crystallizing inside her. On the exhale, calmness bled through her. Good or bad, her decision was made. "How do you want to do this?"

The satisfaction that illuminated his smile was almost reward enough. He leaned in and touched his lips to hers, a soft, cajoling kiss that had slow, rolling awareness building in her. "Can you trust me?"

She closed her eyes, her entire being melting from the simple contact of his lips against hers. Trust? Ha. She didn't have any of that to give. But she'd asked him to take control so she found herself nodding anyway. "Okay."

"Good. Give me your address and phone number." He handed her a stack of sticky notes. "Let's get together tomorrow night. If I keep you in here much longer, my assistant will be wondering why this interview is taking so long."

"Where are we going to go?" she asked as she jotted down her information on the paper. "I'd prefer to keep this private since I'll be working here now."

He smiled and molded her body flush against his, her hands and the stack of sticky notes caught between them. God, he was so solid, so . . . *guh.* Her knees wanted to buckle beneath her just so he could hold her up. "That's where the trust part comes in, beautiful."

"Oh." It was all she could manage to say with him pressed so close, his hardening erection imprinting on her hip.

"Now, go tell Maile that you're hired and need to fill out a new employee packet."

She grimaced and pressed her forehead to his, his instructions reminding her of just how screwed up of a situation this was. "This is so very, very wrong."

He grinned, the boyish expression changing his face into something much less intimidating but no less attractive. "Ah, but that's part of what makes it so damn fun."

"You're bad."

"You have no idea." He released her and grabbed the stamp again. Before she could figure out what he was doing, he hiked up her skirt, exposing her black underwear.

"Kade!"

"Hush." He crouched down and traced a line along the edge of her panties, pulling them down ever so slightly. Electric pulses of warmth shot through her, every ounce of her being zeroing in on that single touch. But instead of dipping his hand lower and relieving the tension building there, he pressed the stamp to the spot right below her navel. "There we go. All mine for now."

Her mouth fell open as she saw his name in blue on her skin. "You did not just *stamp* my girl parts, Kade Vandergriff."

He laughed as he stood and tugged her skirt back down. "No, I stamped *you*. All the parts are mine through tomorrow night. Now stop dawdling and get to work, Ms. McAllen. I'll pick you up at seven tomorrow."

She shook her head and stuck the sticky note with her address and phone number to the lapel of his jacket. If he got to brand her, then she got to brand him back. "A chill just went down the spine of every HR manager within a fifty mile radius."

He laughed and lifted the signed document from his desk,

holding it up. "Not true. I have no power over you, remember? At least not when it comes to work."

"And outside of work?"

With an expression she couldn't quite pin down, he turned back toward his desk. "See you soon, Tessa."

# NINE

"Hold up, you hired someone to head up the fundraiser without even consulting me? Dude, *not* cool."

Kade turned the volume down on his car's speakerphone, deserving any wrath his younger stepbrother, Gibson, wanted to throw his way but not needing to hear it in full stereo. "Look, I know, but I have good reason. And yes, she's inexperienced but I know she's going to work her ass off."

There was a long pause. "I'm waiting for this good reason. I don't have time to babysit someone."

Kade sighed and turned into the driveway. "Hey, I'm here, we'll finish this inside. Do I need to wear a hazmat suit?"

"Nah, I'm not contagious anymore. But you may want to wear a helmet 'cause I'm kind of feeling like I want to punch you right now."

Kade sniffed and cut off the ignition, ending the call. He grabbed a paper sack from the passenger seat and climbed out of his car. Gibson's golden lab, Sasha, gave a happy bark from the front window when she saw Kade striding up the walk. He gave her a little wave and pulled out his key, but Gibson opened the door before Kade could get it into the lock. Sasha charged past Gib with excited whines and greeted Kade, stopping just shy of tackling him to the ground.

Kade grinned and gave her head a scratch. "Hey, pretty girl."

The dog bounced on her front legs and appeared ready to launch herself at him again, but Gibson grabbed her collar. "Sorry. I haven't been able to take her on her walks the last few days. She's stir crazy and sick of me."

"Can't blame her there," Kade said, giving his brother a once-over. Gibson's normal uniform of Armani suits sans neckties had been replaced with wrinkled pajama bottoms and an old Pearl Jam T-shirt. And his dark curly hair was going in three different directions. "You look like you've been at an all-night kegger then passed out in the yard."

"I wish," he said, heading into the kitchen. "At least then I would've probably gotten drunk and laid. Strep throat was much less fun. Want a beer?"

"You got Diet Coke?"

Gib gave him that look that said diet soda was a chick's drink, but pulled one from the fridge and tossed it Kade's way. Kade caught it with his free hand and set the bag he'd been carrying on the counter.

"What's that?"

"I brought you Avgolemono soup from that place by the office, figured that'd be better than chicken noodle from a can."

Gib's face brightened as he leaned over and opened up the bag, peering in. "Aw, hell yeah. That's the good stuff right there. I'm telling you, you need to buy that concept. There are far too few Greek places around here."

"Don't worry, a Mediterranean concept is next on my list." He slid onto one of the barstools on the other side of the counter. Sasha settled at his feet as if waiting for her own takeout to be handed over. "And go ahead and eat. It's still hot."

Gib looked up, eyes narrowing as he pulled out the container of egg-lemon soup. "Don't think this absolves you from hiring someone in my department while I was out. Start talking."

Kade shook his head, amused by this hard-ass version of his little brother. Growing up, Gibson had always been the meek one. Hell, the poor kid hadn't had much choice. After Kade had left home, Gib's father—Kade's stepfather—had moved on to Gibson as the next easy target and had escalated from verbal beat-downs to real ones. The thought still made Kade's blood go cold. He'd never thought that bastard would rail on one of his own kids.

Kade opened his soda and took a swig as Gib hopped up on the opposite counter and eyeballed him. "The woman I hired is the founder of the charity we'll be sponsoring. She's very dedicated to the cause."

"Okay . . ." Gibson said, then took a bite of soup, keeping his eyes on Kade.

"And I told her the position was only temporary at this point. Though, obviously, if she does a great job and Evelyn is unable to come back, feel free to keep her on."

"Sounds like a big *if* on the great job part," he mumbled between bites. "So why her? What's with this rush to hire? I'm going to be back in the office tomorrow. You could've waited for me to interview her."

Kade blew out a breath, figuring he just needed to lay it out there and deal with the consequences. "Because it's Tessa McAllen."

"Tessa McAllen." Gibson's dark brows dipped low, like he was trying to access an old file in his brain. Kade could almost see when the light bulb clicked. Gib's spoon dropped into the bowl. "Wait, *the* Tess? From high school?"

"The very one."

Gibson put his bowl aside and slid from atop the counter. "Jesus, Kade."

"She's divorced and is trying to get back on her feet. Her heart is in the right place with this charity, and I think she can do the job."

"And you think you can get her in bed," he said flatly.

Kade's jaw clenched.

"Goddammit, man. You saddled me with this girl because you want to get her naked? You could've done that without the song and dance." He flattened his hands against the counter in front of Kade, scowling. "Look, I know she was like the forbidden fruit for you back then, the girl you couldn't have. Hell, I get it. I wanted her, too. But come on."

"You *what*?"

Gibson shrugged like it was no big deal. "I was two years younger but I wasn't freaking blind. That girl was *hot*. Every time she walked across the quad in those little skirts, I had to stop whatever I was doing to watch. That chick had legs for days."

Kade's fingers gripped his bottle hard enough to make the plastic crinkle.

"And I know you think y'all had something between you two. But after everything went down, she never came back around, Kade. She never asked why you didn't come back to school or where you'd gone. She stayed with that prick of a boyfriend and went on like nothing had happened. She was hot, but she was a stone cold, self-serving bitch."

"Hey," Kade said, anger surging at the accusation. "She didn't have a lot of choices. You don't know anything about what her life was like. There was a lot of pressure on her, and I couldn't give her what she needed. Not back then."

"Bullshit, bro. There's always a choice. Did you know that after you left, rumors started that you had tried to rape her that night and dickhead rescued her?"

Kade looked away. He'd heard a version of that story from his mother when she'd called to check on him a few weeks later. But he'd been living with his dad by then and too numb about everything that had happened to care.

"And Tessa didn't say a damn thing to dispel it," Gib said, disgust in his voice. "I had to go to school hearing people calling my brother a pervert and a freak. Even after your class graduated, I had people giving me the side eye like I was some sort of criminal."

"I'm sorry you had to deal with that," Kade said, wishing he could've shielded his brother from more than that after he'd had to leave town. Maybe if he hadn't been so fucked in the head over it all, he could've gone back and not only protected Gibson but told Tessa the real truth about that night. He could've saved her a lot of heartache, but he'd run far and fast and had forced himself to forget about that previous life. "The whole situation was twisted and fucked up. Tessa was caught in the middle and did what she had to do to protect herself. She's not what you think. Trust me. I need you to give her a fresh chance. It's been a long time. We've all grown up and moved on."

Gibson leaned against the wall, crossing his arms. "I thought we had, but here you are, looking like you're chasing after her again. Tell me the truth. Is this just about helping her out?"

He could lie to his brother, but it'd be pointless. Gib was too smart not to figure it out the first time he saw Tessa and Kade in the same room. "No. I'm sleeping with her."

"Fuck. Of course you are." He leaned his head back, looking to the ceiling as if it held better answers. "And now she's willing because instead of some punk kid from Dunlop Road, you're *the* Kade Vandergriff."

"It's not like that. In fact, I had to persuade her into a second date. She didn't know who I was when we slept together. She found out about my job when I called her in for the interview. And she still doesn't know I used to be Kaden Fowler."

Gibson stared at him like Kade had lost his mind. "She doesn't *know*?"

He sighed. "There hasn't been a good opportunity yet. And I wanted her to get to know me as I am now, not by who I used to be."

"And what happens when she finds out you fucked her under false pretenses?"

"Well, technically, I didn't realize who she was either at the time." He rolled his bottle cap between his fingers.

"And what about that you're a dom?"

He groaned. "I don't think I need to drop that bomb on her any time soon. At least not officially. I told her I like being in charge and that I'm kinky. She's intrigued by all of that, but she's also as jumpy as a squirrel after her divorce. I have a feeling Doug wasn't just verbally abusive but a controlling fuck—and not the fun kind of control. God knows what she went through in her marriage. I need to tread carefully."

"And here we go again," Gibson said. "My brother tortures himself by going after a vanilla girl who's going to be freaked out by how you are. Why waste your time, man? You sure you're not a masochist? You should just drop this whole thing, and I'll sign you up for a session with Fabienne at The Ranch. She can beat this stupid notion out of you."

Kade sniffed. "No thanks, I'll leave that to you. I'm sure those paid sessions are very fulfilling."

Gib's expression darkened. Even though Kade was well aware of why Gibson went to The Ranch, the BDSM resort they both belonged to, neither of them usually acknowledged it aloud. He had a feeling his brother wasn't as comfortable as he pretended to be with his conflicting proclivities.

But Gib shrugged, seeming to shake off the comment. "Hey, it's better than getting knotted up in some relationship then realizing too late that your girl's not into what you're into. You've been down that road. Don't do that to yourself again."

"This isn't a relationship." *Yet.* "Tessa isn't in the market for something serious," he added, the reminder of his past mistakes like a mallet to the chest. He refused to liken this situation to that one. He and Angie hadn't worked because he'd changed the rules of the game two years into their marriage. He'd never enter into another commitment without the woman knowing his very deepest kinks.

"*She* doesn't want anything serious. And what about you?"

"Does it matter?"

"Fucking brilliant," he said with a shake of the head. "You're already getting tangled up, aren't you? This girl is under your skin again."

Kade slid off the barstool and stood, knowing his brother's concerns were coming from the right place. Gib knew all too well the consequences Kade had had to deal with after his failed marriage. And he knew what was at stake now. But he was growing tired of the interrogation. He couldn't explain what it was about Tessa to his brother. He couldn't even explain it to himself. He just knew that when he was around her, his *mine* gene activated. More than a decade may have passed, but that automatic reaction hadn't changed. It was probably something he simply needed to work out of his system because he'd been thwarted the first time around. But regardless, it wasn't something he could ignore. "I'm just having a good time with her."

"Bullshit. Let's not pretend I don't know the kind of setup you really want with a woman—that's anything but just having a good time. And you never go into anything without a plan, so don't feed me that line, either. What are you going to do?"

Kade pulled his phone from his pocket and checked the time, unwilling to risk being late for his plans with Tessa, then looked back to his brother, meeting his gaze with grave determination. "You really want to know?"

"Yes."

"Fine. Tonight, I'm going to introduce her to kink, fuck her until she can't remember another guy ever existed, and make her wish she'd chosen me all those years ago. Is that what you want to hear? Then I'm going to use what I didn't have then to sweep her off her goddamned feet so that she agrees to another night and another."

Gibson scoffed. "Un-freaking-believable. So that's what this is about, huh? Your ego and proving you can get the unattainable chick from your past?"

Kade's molars ground against each other. That wasn't it at all. Gib didn't get it.

His brother stepped forward and clapped him on the shoulder. "A few minutes ago I felt sorry for you. But now I just feel sorry for her, bro. Because I've seen you in this mode at work. You think you know what you want, but as soon as you conquer her and have her wanting you back, you'll be done with her. Acquisition accomplished, move on to the next restaurant chain. The only reason this girl is still interesting to you is because she's the challenge you never won. And Kade Vandergriff always wins."

Despite Kade's attempt to ignore his brother's pop psych analysis, the accusation was burrowing right beneath his skin, seeking purchase. Though, he *didn't* always win. Maybe in business, but not where it really mattered. If that were the case, he wouldn't have an unused bedroom decorated in pink and purple daisies at his house. "Fuck you, Gib."

Gib huffed with laughter for a moment then as if the air was taken from his lungs, he went stone cold silent. A strange expression crossed his face as he lifted his eyes. "Hey, wait a second. What if . . ."

Uh-oh. Kade didn't like the sound of that. "What if, what?"

Gibson's eyes were bright now, a sure sign that bad shit was about to commence. "This could actually be the perfect solution."

"What the hell are you talking about?"

"Didn't your lawyer tell you that anything that made you appear settled and stable would help your case?"

Kade crossed his arms, wary. "What does that have to do with anything?"

"Tessa is attractive." He raised one finger as if counting off something. "And she is in charge of a charity for kids. Why did she get divorced?"

"Doug cheated."

Gib pointed at him as if he'd gotten an answer right on a game show. "Ha! Perfect. A victim on top of all of that. And you who rarely publicly dates anyone anymore already has them chomping at the bit. You couldn't paint it better. The media would . . . Eat. That. Shit. Up. The Time Share Bachelor reconnects with his old love. Golden."

"Gib . . ." Kade warned, the threads of what Gib was spewing starting to weave together in a recognizable pattern. The PR person in Gibson was at full throttle and zooming down a dangerous road.

"What? I'm serious. You want more than clandestine sex with Tessa. Don't fucking pretend you don't. I know you. So why not use that while you can? What better way to convince the court and your ex than to have proof in the damn newspaper? Then after the case, whatever happens, happens."

He gave his brother a look that he hoped conveyed the level of his contempt for the idea. "Are you serious right now? You want me to use Tessa to *fake* a fucking relationship to win in court?"

"No," he said, excitement still buoying his voice. "Don't fake it. Have it. You want to anyway. Just don't do it in your normal behind closed doors style. Of course, keep the kinky stuff out of the press if y'all go there, but bring her out to places, parade her around a bit. They won't be able to tie her to anything sordid. You can say you left all that alternative lifestyle stuff in your past."

"You're insane." But the crazy idea was sneaking into the crevices of Kade's mind and infiltrating his thoughts. Yes, he wanted Tessa. Long-term? He had no idea. He didn't know if she would even be open to his lifestyle. Plus, his track record with long-term since his marriage sucked. Gib hadn't been off base on what he'd said about Kade's history. He could think a woman was the best thing in the world, believe that he wanted something more with her. But the minute she said she loved him or wanted something serious, it was like all his interest deflated. He'd feel smothered and trapped and would already be fast-forwarding through the familiar life cycle in his mind: marriage, kids, disillusionment, hate, divorce. Just the thought of going through that again would send him into panic mode. He'd shut the relationship down before the girl knew what had happened.

But regardless of his pattern, he knew he needed Tessa for longer than a few nights. And there was *nothing* in life he wanted more than to be able to see his daughter again for more than a few supervised hours a month. There wasn't much he wouldn't do to make that happen. And Gibson was right about the press. Tessa was built to be a media darling. Beautiful, charitable, a survivor of an awful childhood and recovering from a bad marriage. Plus, it wouldn't look rushed because they'd known each other as teens.

Gibson nodded while he watched Kade. "See, *see*, I'm starting to make sense, right?"

"I would never admit to that. But even if you were, you're railroading way ahead. I barely got Tessa to agree to see me a second time. She doesn't want anything to do with a relationship. And when she finds out who I really am . . . I don't know how she's going to react to that."

Gib gave him a *come-on-now* look. "Dude, you're Kade-fucking-Vandergriff now, not that kid she used to know. Women at The Ranch fall over themselves trying to get you to look their way. Change her mind. Woo her."

"Did you seriously just advise me to *woo*? Is that your professional PR opinion or your brotherly one?"

"Shut the fuck up."

Kade groaned and ran a hand over his face. "I can't do that. I don't want to hurt her, man. She's been through enough. I know I'm interested in her right now, but I can't give any guarantees. You know how I am."

Gibson shrugged. "She let you fall in love with her all those years ago and bailed. Turnabout's fair play as far as I see it. And unless she never plans to date again, it's not like she's going to be safe from heartbreak. It's part of the deal. You're going in with good intentions. That's all anyone can ask."

"Look, I appreciate your concern, but I'm not looking for relationship *or* legal advice. All I came here for was to ask you to treat Tessa well as an employee and not to bring the past into it."

Gibson lifted his hands palms out, determination still hovering at the edges of his expression. "You know I'm here for whatever you need. And of course I'll treat her professionally. Well, unless at any point you ask me not to."

Kade bristled. His brother knew he had a penchant for threesomes, and he could imagine Tessa going out of her mind under the overwhelming attention of two determined men. But he'd promised Tess the personal stuff wouldn't muddy the work stuff. She needed to know her boss was only her boss. His protective instincts rose up like a beast inside him. "Don't go there. Don't even flirt."

Gibson grinned wide, making him look like the incorrigible teenager he used to be. "Oh, you've got it bad. Fine. I'll look and not touch. You're the worst boss ever, by the way. But don't shoot down my idea about the public relationship yet. Give it some thought. If you're going to try to be with her anyway, what's the harm?"

Kade let out a frustrated breath. His brother could annoy the shit out of him and this idea was nutso, but he knew Gib was well-intentioned. He knew how heartbreaking it was for Kade to be reduced to cameo appearances in his daughter's life. He grabbed his keys. "Fine, I'll think about it, but right now I need to go. You gonna be in the office on Monday?"

"Yep, I'll be there with bells on. Apparently, I've got a new employee to train."

*Training.* Yes, that was on Kade's agenda, too. Just not quite the same kind.

Hopefully, Tessa would be open to both of their lessons.

Because Kade was definitely ready to teach.

But first he was going to have to come clean and tell her who he was and hope to hell she didn't run in the opposite direction.

*Kaden Fowler, come on down.*

# TEN

Tessa had no idea what to wear on her date when she had no idea what said date involved. What if she wore jeans and he showed up in a suit or she wore a dress and he wanted to go hiking or something? But before she could deliberate much more, her cell buzzed. She grabbed it from her dresser and read the text message.

> Will be there in half an hour. Wear a casual dress or skirt and bring a sweater or jacket. See you soon. -K

The message was simple and to the point, but her skin tingled with heat as if he'd told her to show up naked. God, it wasn't even fair how easily he affected her. It was as if all her teenage hormones were reappearing after a decade-long nap. She wasn't the type to get swoony and fluttery over guys. Tessa had never had that sensation around Doug. She'd cared for him and had enjoyed the attention he'd given her, but he hadn't made her stomach twist and dip.

But Kade could inspire that with one stupid text message. What had gotten into her? She used to hate when Doug told her what to wear. Why was this any different? Maybe her silly reaction was just the result of a lethal combination of Kade's good looks and a practiced charm that could melt the panties off any woman in a ten-mile radius. He was *that* guy. The guy who could get any woman in his bed, but who never really showed anyone what lay beneath all that flash and urbanity.

Normally, it'd be the guy she'd steer farthest away from, the heartbreaker. But in this case, that type of man may be exactly what she needed. The perfect one-night stand—or two-night stand as the case may be. She needed fun in her life, an adventure. Like she'd told him that night at the restaurant. She wanted to use him and be used. Maybe it wasn't ladylike or proper to want that, but she was nothing if not intensely practical. They both had needs the other could fill tonight.

As long as she kept that in perspective, she needn't worry about the rest of it. She slipped into a casual flowered dress and tossed a white cardigan over it, then went into the bathroom to finish her makeup. After she was done, she locked up her little rental house and sat on the porch swing to wait. The evening had a touch of coolness to it but the breeze soothed her still feverish skin. Maybe by the time Kade arrived she wouldn't look like some blushing virgin waiting to go to the sock hop.

Her phone rang, lighting up the inner pocket of her purse. She pulled it out and groaned when she saw the name blinking on the screen. The last thing she wanted to do was answer, but she knew if she didn't, he'd call all night and interrupt her date. She lifted the phone to her ear. "Hello."

"Where did you store my grandfather's gold watch?" Doug barked, not bothering with a greeting. "You didn't take it, did you?"

She took a breath, forcing her teeth to unclench. "Hello, Doug, how are you? Yes, this is a bad time actually. Thanks for asking."

"Don't be smart, Tessa. Just tell me where it is."

"I have no idea. You never gave it to me. You showed it to me and then I didn't see it again." She stood, the swing squeaking from her hasty dismount, and started to pace the length of the porch. How had she tolerated this man for all those years? How had she not seen how cruel and hateful he'd become? She didn't want to think about what that said about her.

"That's crap. I know I gave it to you to put in storage," Doug said, breaking her from her morose thoughts.

"Doug," she said, trying to keep her tone even as she continued to pace the warped, wooden boards creaking beneath her feet. "I can't deal with this right now. I have a date and am about to walk out. Maybe check the lockbox in the guest bedroom downstairs."

"I already—" But he didn't finish the initial thought. "You have a *date*?"

She almost laughed at the incredulity in his voice. Half of her wanted to say—*Yes, with a ridiculously sexy man who made me come more times in one night than you did for most of our marriage.* "Yes, last I checked, I was no longer married and free to do that."

He sniffed. "Already on the prowl, huh? How much money does he have? Because I know you're not spreading your legs for some guy who can't afford your Prada habit."

"Go to hell."

He cursed back at her, his voice getting louder as he gained steam, and now she could hear the slight slur of alcohol lacing it. Fun. She'd learned early with Doug that his asshole gene amplified when under the influence of his evening scotch. "Come on, tell me. Millionaire? Billionaire? I know that's what gets you wet. Not big cocks, but big bank accounts."

The ugly words made her want to gag. "You're disgusting. Don't you dare talk—"

But before she could finish her threat, the phone was plucked from her hand. She spun around to find Kade. Anger shimmered off him like heat waves rising off the road.

"Kade, I—"

Kade held up a hand to halt her and put the phone to his ear, a murderous look in his eyes. "Hello, Doug."

Tessa could hear her ex-husband's booming voice come through the phone with crystal clarity in the quiet evening. "Who the fuck is this?"

She closed her eyes, dying of humiliation. The last thing she needed was for Kade to get pulled into her ugly divorce shit. "Kade, please, don't."

But Kade gave her a stern I've-got-this look. "Doug, this is the guy who isn't going to allow you to disrespect Tessa. Do not call this number or bother her again. Talk to her through her lawyer. And if you ever dare speak to her again the way you just did or attempt to bully her, I will personally fly to wherever you are and shove your tongue down your throat. Do we have an understanding?"

His tone was calm as water on a windless day, but the icy ferocity behind the words rocked Tessa back on her heels. She braced herself for the explosion from Doug. No one talked to him that way.

"Who the fuck do you think you are?" Doug shouted into the phone. "She's my goddamned wife."

"No, she's your *ex*-wife," Kade reminded him, the utter stoicism in his voice probably driving Doug to the brink.

"Oh, so you're the date, huh?" Doug challenged, his snide tone obvious. "Hope your bank account is big, friend, because that bitch only has one reason to *date* anyone."

Tessa tried to reach for the phone, mortified at the exchange, but Kade stepped back. Cold fury had settled in those blue eyes. "This conversation is over. Your communication with Tessa is over. Contact her again, and you and I will have a problem."

He laughed. "You think I'm afraid of you?"

Kade's grim smile sent a chill through her. "You should be."

With that, Kade ended the call and handed back her phone. She took it, trying to keep hot tears at bay. Embarrassment was like a living, breathing entity holding her in its claws. "Kade . . ."

"Get rid of this phone and number. I'll get you a corporate-issued one tomorrow. You don't need him having access to you like that." The words were clipped, the residual anger from the call still clear in the tight set of his jaw and shoulders.

She stared down at the phone like it was a rattlesnake that had bitten her. "I'm so sorry you had to hear that, that he—"

"Hey," he said, closing the distance between them and sliding warm palms to her upper arms. The hard edges of his expression softened and melted away as he looked down at her. From ruthless to kind and considerate in two seconds flat. "No apologies for things that aren't your fault. I heard what he said to you. He's an abusive asshole who gets off by tearing you down. Don't give him his thrills anymore. Cut him off."

"He's not going to stop calling. He'll get the new number."

"And you charge him with harassment if he does. He has no right to abuse you like that."

She blew out a breath. "It's not really abuse. It's just how he is. He's angry about what happened with the divorce. He thought I'd—"

"Tessa," he said, cutting her off with that firm voice of his. "It's *abuse*. He hits and cuts you with words for his own enjoyment. He tears you down and makes you feel worthless. That can be more damaging than a punch. Believe me, I know."

She stared up at him, seeing a flicker of old pain in his eyes. But she couldn't quite wrap her mind around the idea of Doug being abusive. She'd seen abuse. Before her mom had disappeared for good, Tessa had watched her mom's boyfriend knock her around. She'd sworn she'd never let a man do that to her. She would not become her mother. But here she was, feeling like shit over what some guy had said to her even when she knew the accusations weren't true.

"This is definitely not how I wanted our evening to start," she said finally. "Now you know why I wanted to keep things to one night. My life is messy."

His hands coasted up her arms to cup her shoulders, his gaze capturing hers and holding it. "You think I care about your asshole ex-husband?"

She looked away. "You don't understand. Doug can cause lots of trouble when he wants to. I'm glad you didn't tell him your name. Finding ways to humiliate people who he thinks have wronged him is a favorite pastime of his."

Kade's expression darkened for a moment, but as quickly as the shift was there, it was gone. "Baby, I'm about as scared of him as I am of a yapping puppy."

She pressed her lips together. He didn't get it. She'd learned early to not cross Doug. The man was like a dog with a bone when he perceived a slight by someone. He'd do everything he could to take that person down a notch.

"Tell me what's going through that head of yours."

The gentleness in his voice and the heat of his palms against her face nearly unraveled her. She swallowed back the emotion that wanted to show itself. "I came here to get a fresh start. But every time I feel like I'm catching my stride, my past rears up and bites me. God, those things he was saying on the phone . . . I can't even imagine what you think."

*Hope you have a big bank account.* Doug's words to Kade rang in her head, and she wanted to fold in on herself. Kade probably had gold diggers fawning after him all the time. Now she'd look like another trying to cash in.

Kade didn't say anything for a long time. But when she looked up, expecting to find judgment on his face, she found determination there instead. "I *chose* to get involved. And what I think is that your ex is a piece of shit and a bully."

"I'm not what he says I am," she whispered, her throat tightening with the embarrassment of it all—memory and a little guilt. Because part of her knew those gold-digging claims weren't entirely baseless. Sure, when she'd married Doug, she'd cared for him, maybe even thought she loved him at some point. But when things started to go bad, she hadn't tried to leave. She'd put up with his jibes and coldness because it was too scary to consider being on her own. She'd ignored the signs of deception—the way he never wanted her in his home office, the late night calls, the password locked computer and cell phone. If she had really looked, the clues that he was hiding something were there.

But the routine of her life, the posh luxury of her days had blinded her. Seeing him for what he was would've meant losing the only security she'd ever had, would've taken her admitting that she was there for the money, that her life, her friends, and the love she'd thought she'd found were a bedazzled pile of bullshit. So she'd refused to see it. Convinced herself she was content. She'd drowned herself in her shallow lifestyle. If she hadn't caught him cheating, she'd probably still be wasting away her days shopping and lunching with women who were fucking her husband behind her back.

Thinking of that version of herself made her stomach roll and pitch.

"Baby, I know you're not what he says you are. I'm the one chasing *you* down for another date, remember?" He smirked. "If you were a gold digger, you'd be the worst one *ever*."

She laughed, quickly swiping at her eyes. "Maybe I'm just an evil genius at playing hard to get."

"The truth comes out!"

She peered up at him. "So you still want to do this tonight?"

He hooked an arm around her waist and gathered her against

him. "I've thought of little else since last Friday night. Now I have a nice, warm car waiting for us. Are you going to stop dawdling and get in with me, or am I going to have to throw you over my shoulder, Neanderthal style?"

She lifted a brow and scanned over his perfectly pressed charcoal slacks and pale pink shirt. Every inch of him screamed money and urbanity. "I'm not sure you could pull off Neanderthal."

"Mmm, that's where you're wrong, beautiful," he said, cupping the back of her neck and running his thumb along the hollow of her throat. "Don't let the wrapping paper fool you. My thoughts when I'm around you are about as caveman as it gets. In fact, it's taking everything I have not to strip you down right here and take you against your front door until that wrinkle of worry in your forehead disappears and you can't even remember that phone call."

A little gasp passed her lips, and her body went on high alert.

"So are you going to get in the car or do you need me to carry you?"

Her gaze darted to the darkened street and yellow porch lights. "Let's not give the neighbors anything to talk about."

He slowly backed her into her door anyway. Her shoulders hit the wood and a shiver radiated outward, tightening her nipples and awakening things much lower. He kissed the curve of her neck, shielding her from the street with his body, and his hands crept down over her backside, gathering her skirt in his fingers.

"Kade," she whispered, teetering on the edge of letting him do whatever he wanted even though anyone could step outside and see them.

"Shh, Tess. You wanted me to take control tonight. Let me." He hiked her dress up higher in the back, teasing the bottom edge of her panties with his fingertips. "Take these off. You won't need them."

She let out a little squeak when he tugged at the elastic and pulled her panties down over her ass. The skirt slid down to cover her bare skin as he worked her underwear further down. They were stretched over her mid-thighs when a car turned onto the street. Headlights flashed over them and she froze. She tried to reach for her panties, but Kade captured her arms against her sides.

"They'll see," she whispered.

Kade lifted his head and brushed his mouth against hers. "They'll see a guy with his date. They can't see anything else. I wouldn't risk embarrassing you. It's important that you know that."

Her gaze flicked up to his, questioning.

"I like pushing boundaries, Tessa. It's how I'm built, and I think it's what you crave, too. But you have to trust that I have your back. I won't do anything to embarrass you or risk your safety."

The gravity with which he made the declaration had her heart hammering against the walls of her chest. He'd said he wanted to have kinky fun with her tonight, but she really had no idea what that entailed. The definition of kinky was so broad and her experience so slight, that she was getting the distinct impression she'd signed on for something more than whip cream and fuzzy handcuffs.

But hell if she could find it in her to stop things here. Despite the warning bells dinging a chorus in her head, she was wild with curiosity. What was this man about? What put that dark glint in his eyes? And what in God's name was he going to do to her?

"I'm not so good with trust," she said, trying to keep her voice steady as he ran teasing fingers over the bottom curve of her ass.

"I don't blame you. All I ask is that you try and let me show you I'm worthy of it."

His hands roamed, and she closed her eyes, her body already revving for him to take it further. Maybe they didn't need to go out at all. She had a perfectly comfortable bed right on the other side of the door. "I'll try."

"Let your panties fall to the ground, then."

The command sent a zing of forbidden thrill through her, and she wiggled, working her underwear down her legs as discreetly as possible. When they hit the floorboards and she stepped out of them, Kade bent and swept them up with swift precision. He tucked them in his pocket. "Very good."

She drew her bottom lip between her teeth as the cool night air swirled up her dress and kissed all the tender damp parts beneath. "Do you want to go inside?"

He took her hand and backed up a step, tugging her with him. "And ruin all the anticipation? Of course not. I'm here to take you out."

"But—" She glanced down at her fluttering skirt, feeling as if the whole world could tell there was nothing beneath.

He brought his hand to her mouth and pressed a kiss to it. "Trust."

She forced the knot in her throat down and nodded. "Okay."

But as she followed him down the porch stairs and to his car, she knew he was asking for more than she was capable of giving. She didn't even trust herself. How could she trust him?

# ELEVEN

Kade gripped the steering wheel as he guided the car south, leaving the city behind them. He should've been enjoying the car ride. He had a beautiful, panty-less woman next to him. But Tessa had no idea how much anger was still bubbling in his veins. He was sick with it. When he'd walked up to her and heard that disgusting excuse for a human, Doug Barrett, talking to Tessa like she was some dog, Kade had wanted to reach through the phone, grab the guy by his thick neck, and strangle him.

Even Barrett's voice still made everything turn to icy rage inside him. He thought he'd blocked that smarmy voice from his head, but as soon as Kade had put the phone to his ear, he'd been transported back in time. He'd wanted to let everything he'd ever wanted to say to Doug from all those years ago pour out. But this wasn't about the past. This was about protecting Tessa.

And there was no way he was going to stand by and let Doug tear her down like that. Tessa had protested that it wasn't really abuse. *Bull-fucking-shit.* Kade had experienced the wrath of words from his stepfather, that systematic breakdown of every sense of your confidence and self-worth. That could damage more than fists. Knowing that Tessa had shirked it off as "how Doug is" made Kade want to tie her down and flog some sense into her. He recognized the irony of that urge, but it didn't prevent it from coming to the surface.

"Where are we going?" Tessa asked, breaking him from his stream of thought and reminding him that he shouldn't be thinking about anyone but her right now.

He glanced over at her, the orange of the streetlights streaking across her face as they merged onto the highway. In the darkness of the car, he could almost see her as she was all those years ago. Young. Lost. Surrounded by people but alone. Like he'd been. Maybe they hadn't changed as much as he'd thought. "Not too far."

She turned back toward the window, the suburbs now blurring into the darkness. "I grew up not far from here."

*Me, too.* But he couldn't tell her that yet. "Is that what made you come back to Dallas after the divorce?"

She peeked over at him with a small smile. "Yes and no. I came here because I knew I could count on Sam to give me a place to crash for a while. And honestly, I was a little freaked out at the thought of living alone. I'd never done that. But I didn't know if I would stay. I don't have any family here or anything. But once I was back, I felt . . . better. Like I was supposed to be here, so I eventually got my own place. Sounds kind of ridiculous, right?"

"Nah, I think there's always something comforting about the town where you grew up. Even if the years you spent there weren't the happiest ones, it's like a place seeps into your blood. I've seen some beautiful cities in the world, but nothing feels quite like home."

"So you grew up in Dallas, then?"

He pulled onto a barely there side road. If its location hadn't been seared into his muscle memory, he would've never been able to find it in the dark. "No, T-t-tess. I grew up right outside it. Just like you."

He gritted his teeth at the verbal tic. God, was driving down this road with Tessa like driving back in time? First Doug, now this. Was all his old shit going to rise up and take him under? But the way he stuttered *Tess* seemed to register with her, and she pulled in a breath. Her focus darted from his face to the tree-choked dirt road. If she was harboring any fears about him being a sociopath or something, now would be when she would freak out. Dark road. Alone with some stranger. But instead she braced her hands on the dashboard and leaned forward, squinting at the clearing in front of them as if to verify she was seeing it for real.

"Kade, how do you know about . . ." Even in the dark he could see her pulse thumping hard at her throat. "*Kade.*"

She turned to him then, her gaze roving over him—every feature, every nuance. He could almost hear it all snap into place for her, like elastic popping her memory into action. He pulled the car into a spot between the trees and cut the engine, bracing for her reaction.

"*Kaden?*" she whispered, so many emotions crossing her face he couldn't pick a dominant one.

And at that simple question, all the confidence he carried around with him day to day fell away. He felt awkward and tense and unsure. "Hey, Tess."

*1996*

"Where the heck is this place? I seriously feel like we're about to star in a teen slasher movie," Tessa said as branches started to poke at her from the open window. She reached out to roll up the window.

Kaden grinned. "B-b-better hope you're a v-v-virgin then. That's the only ones who survive crazed killers in the woods."

Her jaw fell open and she shoved him in the arm. She could

already feel the blush heating her face. "Ohmigod, I cannot believe you just said that."

He shrugged, but his grin remained in place leaving him looking as unapologetic as possible. "What? I didn't ask y-y-you if *you* were a virgin. Just reciting the rules of h-h-horror."

She harrumphed and crossed her arms over her chest, secretly enjoying that she and Kaden had developed some weird sort of bond over the last few weeks where they could talk about anything. Not being friends in "real life" seemed to open up the honesty gates. "You know, you haven't stuttered all afternoon. And now you start talking about virginity and you're all tongue-tied. You're trying to tease me but making yourself nervous, so joke's on you."

He glanced her way as he cut the engine. "And you're beet red."

"So." She pulled her compact out of her purse and hurriedly dusted her nose with powder, trying to cover up her flushed state.

"So, we're even. And now I know I'll be safe studying out here. Chainsaw guy will go after you first. You're prime bait and m-m-much prettier."

She straightened at that and snapped her compact shut. "You did *not* just call me the sacrificial slut."

He laughed as he pushed open his door and climbed out. She scrambled to follow him. But by the time she got out of the car, he was already making his way to a little cabin that sat at the edge of a clearing of trees. She hitched her book bag over her shoulder and hurried to catch up.

"I'll have you know, Mr. Jump to Conclusions, that I would be safe as a lamb in those movies. Just because you think you know—"

He turned abruptly, surprising her and causing her to stumble into him. He grabbed her arm, keeping her upright, and nailed her to the spot with his gaze. "*Good.*"

"What?"

"I'm glad you haven't. That prick doesn't deserve that from y-y-you. Wait for b-b-better."

Her lips pressed together, and she shrugged her arm from his hold. "I hate when you do that. You don't even know him. If you did, you'd know that it was his decision to wait because of his religion. He's being a gentleman."

Something hateful flashed through Kaden's blue eyes, but instead of saying what he was thinking, he turned away to head toward the cabin again.

"Oh, no, don't hold back now, Kaden." She stalked after him. "Say what you were about to. I can take it."

"No. It d-d-doesn't matter." He unlocked the big padlock that was securing the cabin and shoved the door open with a loud creak. The rickety wood banged against the wall.

She followed him in, dropping her bag by the door and then kicking it closed behind her. Dread was curling in her like smoke. She probably didn't need to hear whatever it was that he had to say, but she couldn't stop herself from demanding to know. "Tell me."

He whirled around and tossed his school bag onto a worn brown leather couch. "If you think Doug's a gentleman, then he's an even better liar than I thought."

She crossed her arms, prepared to argue, but Kaden wasn't finished.

"He's feeding you a line of b-bullshit because it's what you want to hear. You don't see past the preppy, golden boy mask. None of you do. *Oh, look he can throw a ball and drives a BMW and is soooo dreamy*," he said, using a mocking girly voice. "I'm in the locker room with these dudes. There's nothing golden about any of them. You know what they talked about last week—including your gentlemanly boyfriend? How many b-b-blow jobs they scored at Tyler Brogan's house party. Apparently, Delia Johnson from Harmoor High has the brightest and longest-lasting lipstick. Hard to wash off."

Everything inside Tessa went cold. She'd missed that party because her foster parents gave her a ridiculous ten o'clock curfew. But Doug had said it had turned out to be lame anyway. "It's just talk. Doug's friends—"

Kaden scoffed. "Right. His friends. He's the knight in shining armor amongst all the assholes he hangs around with. Sure. You g-g-go on believing that."

"You don't understand," she said, hearing the feeble protest in her voice. "We haven't slept together because Doug's been the one to keep things that way. I've never told him no. If he wanted . . . any of that, he could've had it. From me."

Kaden's expression darkened, and he crossed the room. He stopped just short of her personal space, pushing his too long hair behind his ears and looking down at her with pleading eyes. "Don't, Tess. There's better out there. W-w-wait for that."

Her throat constricted, an unfamiliar feeling welling in her. Usually when she looked at Kaden, she had a number of urges—to cut his hair shorter, to put him in clothes that didn't make him look like such an outsider, to make him take a breath so he wouldn't stumble on his words. But right now, she had a hard time focusing on all the things she wanted to change about him. In fact, in this moment, she kind of didn't want to change one single thing—particularly the way he was looking at her.

"Kaden . . ." It was all she could say. She couldn't remember the rest of her intended reply.

But saying his name broke the spell. He shook his head and turned away. "This is my stepdad's hunting cabin. He never uses it anymore, so no one will see us here. And this will be quieter than trying to study with Gibson and my stepdad lurking around. Get your chapter questions out for the next test. We should have an hour or so before it gets too dark out here."

She swallowed hard, her heart pounding in her ears. This was getting dangerous. She wasn't supposed to be thinking anything about Kaden or wishing that he hadn't walked away. He was the exact kind of guy she could never let herself be interested in. Her foster dad would take one look at Kaden with his long hair and black clothes and declare him a devil worshipper or something. But even knowing that, she couldn't help the next question that fell from her mouth. "Did you wait for someone special?"

The question was loud in the dead silent cabin. Kaden's back was to her, but she didn't miss the way he stiffened. Finally, he sighed and sank onto the couch, his expression resigned when he looked up. "We both know I'm going to be safe from serial k-k-killers for a long time."

"Kaden," she said, frowning at his bitter tone and sitting in the chair across from him. "You're going to find—"

"D-d-don't." He moved his attention to pulling his books out of his bag. "Let's not play that game. We're sitting in a cabin in the middle of the freaking woods because you can't even be seen with me in public without risking your sparkly Ms. Popularity status getting revoked. No matter w-w-what I do, no one in that school will ever see me as anything other than the former fat kid with the stuttering problem. That label's been applied with super glue and you know it."

"It's so stupid," she said, twisting the silver promise ring Doug had given her round and round on her finger. "No one looks past the surface. At my last school, I wasn't *this*. It was a private school with kids from families with stupid wealth. I'm talking the kind of money that would make Doug's dad look middle class. All the cliques had been together since nursery school. When people found out I was a foster kid, I was viewed as the freak. Rumors went around that I'd been sexually abused. So, of course, that got translated into everyone saying I must be easy because I had issues. The family that was fostering me decided those rumors must be true since I started hanging out with the smoking behind the bleachers crowd, and they ended my placement because I was a bad influence on their younger children. Tessa McAllen, the very first virgin slut at your service."

He stared at her a little wide-eyed. "Seriously?"

She pulled her ponytail tighter, surprised she was even admitting all this. She'd never told anyone about her life before here. "When I moved in with the Ericsons, I decided to become someone totally different so I wouldn't get moved again. They wanted an obedient, church-going good girl. And so I am."

"Even if that's not who you really are?"

She shrugged. "I don't even know what parts of me are real anymore. But life has been a lot easier since I came here, so I don't plan on going back to the other version."

"The v-v-version that would've hung out with someone like me."

She sighed at his snide tone. "I *am* hanging out with you."

"No, Tess, I'm tutoring you while we hide from your friends. There's a b-b-big difference."

"You make me sound like such a shallow bitch."

He lifted an eyebrow as if to say *if the shoe fits.*

"You just don't get it. In a year, you'll get to go to college where all this popularity crap won't matter."

"And so will you."

"No. I won't. My grades aren't strong enough to get a scholarship, and when I turn eighteen, my time with the Ericsons is done. There is no college fund waiting for me."

A wrinkle appeared between his eyebrows. "What do you mean your time is done?"

She pulled her legs onto the chair, tucking them underneath her. "They foster hard-to-place older kids. As soon as I graduate, they'll foster someone else. I'll get a little financial aid from the state, but not enough to manage anything more than community college while working a full-time job."

Kaden looked stricken at this revelation. And she supposed someone like him, the honor student who would have scholarship offers stacking up from everywhere, probably hadn't considered the possibility that not everyone gets to go off to a big college. "Is that what your plan is?"

She looked down at her hands. "Sort of. Doug's going to go to Georgia Tech. He said I can follow him there and . . . stay with him. I wouldn't have to worry about the money stuff then. I could take some classes there."

There was a long stretch of silence then a groan.

"*Motherfucker,*" Kaden said, standing up. "That's it, isn't it? The reason you stay with him. His goddamned money."

Defensiveness surged through her, bringing her to her feet to face him. "No. I love him." Possibly. Maybe.

Kaden stepped around the coffee table in two swift movements and was in front of her in a flash. "Bull. Shit."

She reared up like he'd slapped her. "You don't know anything about how I feel."

"No, b-b-but I'm about to f-f-find out."

The increase in stuttering should've tipped her off to what he was about to do, but she was completely unprepared for it. Kaden's hands cupped her face and tilted it upward. He stared at her for a second, maybe giving her a chance to stop him, but she couldn't form a thought. Then his mouth was against hers.

She lifted her palms to his thrift store Doors T-shirt, intending to push him away. But instead, as he moved his lips over hers, she found her fingers curling into the worn material and holding onto it like a life raft. Despite his grip on her, the kiss wasn't demanding or aggressive. And it wasn't sloppy like Doug's. It was soft and sweet and . . . perfect.

His hands dropped to her waist and drew her closer. All thoughts fell away, her whole being suspended in the moment. There was nothing outside of this. No worries about the future or friends or temporary families. Just hands and lips and feeling. Only when his tongue moved against hers and her body went hot did reality come reeling back into place. She stepped back in a rush, his T-shirt slipping from her fingers.

"Stop," she gasped. "We can't."

"Tess—" The yearning on Kaden's face almost did her in.

But this was wrong. So wrong. She had a boyfriend. And Kaden was . . . who he was. And if anyone ever found out . . . *Oh, God, oh, God, oh, God.* "I need you to take me home."

"Tessa, p-p-please, wait, let's talk."

She grabbed her book bag with jerky movements, her hands shaking, and turned to head to the door. "I need to go."

"I'm sorry. I didn't m-m-mean—"

She whirled around, fiery emotion bubbling over the top of the lid she was trying to keep closed. "No? What did you m-m-mean, then, huh? Jesus, what were you *thinking*?"

His jaw tightened, and she instantly regretted her hateful mocking.

"Kaden—"

But he didn't wait for her apology. He yanked his bag off the couch, hauled it over his shoulder, and strode past her, saying on the way, "At least now we know you're not just pretending to be like them."

# TWELVE

Tessa stared at the cabin she hadn't seen in over a decade, then dragged her attention back to the man next to her. The vulnerability in Kade's eyes was such a direct contrast to the confidence that had bled from him the moment she'd met him in his restaurant. And in that glimmer of a moment, she could see the younger version of him in the lopsided set of his mouth, the stark honesty in his eyes. Everything was more refined now. Polished. The angles of his face had emerged from the roundness of youth and hardened into masculine edges. The stringy long hair had been cut into windswept stylishness. And any traces of his former stutter had disappeared. But when she really looked underneath all of that, she could still see the boy she used to know.

The boy she'd hurt.

And the man she'd slept with.

Her stomach did a somersault as all of that information crashed together in her head.

"You knew who I was and *lied*?" she asked, rewinding to the night in the restaurant. God, had this all been some revenge scheme to pay her back?

"Tess—"

*Tess.* He was the only one she'd ever let call her that. The car felt stifling all of a sudden, and she pushed her door open to climb out.

He followed suit, coming around the front of the car to stand in front of her. "I swear. I didn't know, not at first. I didn't realize it until the EMT needed your medical information and I saw your name."

"Why didn't you *say* something?"

"I would've if you hadn't left the hospital before I got there."

"Oh, don't give me that. You knew the other day in your office," she said, squaring off with him. "You could've let me know between offering me a job I don't deserve and signing me up to be your fuck buddy tonight."

Displeasure clouded his features. "You're not my fuck buddy. Don't ever refer to yourself as that again. And I didn't say anything because I needed you to know me as I am now. I didn't want that loser Kaden Fowler tainting the picture."

Her spine stiffened. "Hey, how's about I don't call myself your fuck buddy and you don't call yourself a loser. Kaden Fowler was the best boy I knew back then."

He scoffed. "Right. Which is why you walked away from him that night to be with the guy who beat up and humiliated that same boy. And why you went on to let people think the worst of me."

Tears pricked her eyes, the horrible memories rushing in like a stampede of ugly buffalo. She wrapped her arms around herself and shook her head. "You told me to go."

"And so you did."

Yes, she had. Even knowing that Doug would probably hit Kade, she'd walked away and left them there. She wouldn't defend herself on that. She'd been scared back then, lost and confused. But she'd never forgiven herself for what had happened. She and

Kaden had been on a sinking ship and she'd saved herself. She hadn't even thrown him a rope.

"I'm sorry," she said in a choked whisper. If this was supposed to be some sort of punishment, she deserved every bit of it. He was probably here to tell her that the job was a fake, that her charity really wasn't going to get help, and that he'd only pretended interest in her to get revenge. "Say whatever you want to say to me. I've earned it. I was stupid and a selfish coward."

Kade's hard expression melted away, and he moved into her space, cupping her shoulders. "Hey, look at me."

She forced her teary gaze upward.

"Don't cry, Tess." He brushed thumbs across her cheeks. "I'm not here to make you atone for something that happened back then. You did what you had to do. If you had taken a stand on my behalf, they would've pounced on you like wolves, torn you to bits like they did with me. I see now that I had nothing to really offer you back then. It was stupid teenage bravado to think I could compete and fix it for you. You needed concrete security not a wing and a prayer, and Doug had the money to give you that."

She shook her head. "Kade—"

"I buried Kaden Fowler and what happened that night long ago. Really. My life changed after that. For the better."

Tears slipped by. "How? After that night, you were just . . . gone. I heard you were hurt, that they found you—"

"I had to get out of there," Kade said, cutting her off like he couldn't bear to hear the rest of the sentence. "I needed to get away from that school. Away from my asshole stepdad. Away from Doug and his friends. And away from seeing you every day. I couldn't handle it all. When my mom found out I was planning to leave, she dropped a bomb on me that she knew who my real father was and gave me an address in Dallas. I showed up on the doorstep of a man who hadn't even known I'd existed and he took me in."

She blinked at him. "Oh my God."

"Walt Vandergriff changed my life and made me the man I am now. So, no, I didn't bring you here to punish you. I brought you here because I needed to tell you the truth, and I wanted to remind you how much fun we had together when we didn't have to worry about other people watching."

She made some sort of laugh-sniffle sound, overwhelmed by all this information and the memories. "You mean like the time you kissed me, and I acted like a total snot?"

He smiled and glanced toward the darkened door of the cabin as if seeing the ghosts of their younger selves. "But you came back for your next tutoring session and apologized, groveled even. I enjoyed that a lot, by the way."

She sniffed—not from the crying this time.

"I'd decided to leave you be at that point. Keep it a tutoring thing only. But three sessions later, you brought in a *B* plus on your term paper. You were so excited and proud of yourself, and you hugged me. *Really* hugged me. Like I meant something to you."

She glanced downward, remembering the day she'd been overwhelmed with joy over her grade. One second, she and Kade had been in a laughing embrace, the next he'd given her a look that had zipped right down to her toes. She'd backed away, scared that if she didn't, she'd ruin everything with Doug right then and there.

"I saw how you looked at me that day. *You* wanted to kiss *me*. And even when you didn't, I knew I hadn't been wrong about that kiss we'd had." Kade's eyes glimmered with mischief in the moonlight. "That was a great day. Worst case of blue balls *ever*, but a great day."

She smacked his chest and laughed. "Hey, I was trying to be a good girl."

"Thank God you've moved on from *that* awful phase," he teased, sliding his hands downward and molding his palms over her backside. "I much prefer wild and liberated Tessa who lets me lick olive oil off her naked body and agrees to let me have my deviant way with her."

She pressed her forehead to his shoulder. "Oh my God, I can't believe we're here again."

He kissed the top of her head. "Mmm, but this will be much more fun than deciphering British poetry. Promise."

The image stirred all kinds of decadent possibilities in her head. She'd been fantasizing about Kade since the first night she'd been with him. But now it all had an added layer. A few sexy nights with some suave stranger had been risky enough. A few sexy nights with someone she used to care about was far more dangerous. Especially when she'd be working at his company for the next few months. She'd turned her back on Kaden all those years ago, but it hadn't been because she didn't have feelings for him.

She let out a breath, and he pulled back a bit. "What's wrong, my little overthinker?"

She tilted her face to his. "This changes things and scares me. I need to know what you want from this. Is this really about one more night?"

The smile that lifted his lips was a wry one. "I told you. Kaden Fowler is gone. I'm not some lovesick kid. Everything I told you before this still stands. I want to have fun with you—whatever that turns out to look like. The only reason I'm rehashing our past is because you deserved to know who I was. I needed to get this out in the open and bury it for good so that we can move on."

She rubbed her lips together, considering him. He'd given her a nonanswer about the one-night thing, but part of her was okay with that. If he really just wanted to have fun, maybe this could be a good solution for her. No pressure. A friend with benefits—someone who she already knew and trusted on some level. No one else would have to know. They'd always been better behind locked doors anyway. "I can't believe I finally slept with Kaden Fowler."

He dragged her body against him, the heat of him bleeding through the thin fabric of her dress. "No, you didn't. You slept with Kade Vandergriff. And I think it's time I remind you of the difference."

Her pulse picked up speed, and she peeked at the cabin. "Your family still owns this place?"

"No. But I do."

She didn't have it in her to question why he'd keep the place. She didn't want to know. "Is that right?"

The wickedness that glittered in his eyes sent her body into melt mode. "Yep. And I'm thinking the old place needs an exorcism. Wipe away old memories with new ones."

The breeze swirled around them, snaking up her legs and making her all too aware that her panties were no longer there. "Good plan."

With that, he released her and she instantly missed the warmth. His gaze tracked down the length of her. "But first, lose the dress and anything beneath. All I want you wearing are those shoes."

Her bottom lip dropped, and she peered out at the darkened woods. "Are you kidding? We're outside."

"And alone," he said, clearly unmoved by her protest. "You agreed to let me be in charge tonight. I would like to see you wearing nothing but moonlight."

"And if I say no?" she asked, both unnerved and completely intrigued by the sensual command in his voice, the utter confidence in his stance. He looked like some fallen angel intent on dragging her over to the dark side. That part of him had always been there. Even when he hadn't had the confidence, he'd always represented everything that threatened her carefully taped together existence.

Kade tipped his head toward her as if to concede the point. "Yes, let's talk about that. Do you know what a safe word is?"

"Uh, not really." There was lingo involved in this? She was so very out of her league.

"Like I told you, I enjoy games of control. And I will push you, but you have the right to stop things. If something is too much, you tell me. You always have permission to say so. But if you need something to stop immediately or you're truly frightened or hurting, you use your safe word. It's the emergency parachute cord. Not to be used lightly."

Oh yeah, she was totally in over her head. And maybe if this had only been the stranger Kade Vandergriff telling her this, she might have chickened out. Heck, she was alone in the woods with this powerful man with no one around to save her if she needed help. If she'd been watching this in a movie, she'd be screaming at the imbecilic woman to steal his keys and book it out of there. But knowing it was Kaden had her battered trust wanting to rise up and rally. He wouldn't hurt her. He'd had the chance and good reason to do that back when everything went down in high school, and he'd kept her secrets anyway. "What word should I use?"

"The most common one is *red*. Like a stoplight."

She nodded. "Okay. Red."

"Take off your dress," he said again, but this time the words had soft edges. "You're safe with me."

The promise smoothed the last ripples of worry moving through her. *Safe.* After pulling in a deep breath, she tugged off her cardigan and then reached behind her to unzip the dress and unhook her bra. The clothes fell to the leaves at her feet, and she stepped out of the puddle of fabric. The trees rustled around them and the soft song of night things filled the air, but all she could focus on was the sound of her own quickening breaths. She was naked. In the middle of the woods. The number of times she'd had sex with the lights on could be counted on two hands, and now she was standing bare in the moonlight.

Kade's gaze moved over her like a physical touch. Anywhere his focus landed, her body tightened in response. But self-consciousness ate at her. Yes, he'd seen her naked already but it hadn't been like this. And now she knew that he was very aware of what she used to look like. Her teenage body had been thin and athletic, firm. Standing here left her acutely aware of how much had softened and rounded. Doug had reminded her regularly of how her body had changed. Her arms instinctively moved to cover her chest.

"Don't you dare," Kade said, the words like bullets in the quiet. "Let me look at you."

She lowered her hands to her side with marked effort, but her cheeks heated with embarrassment.

He took a step closer. "You are so goddamned beautiful, Tess. "

She deflected the comment with a shake of her head. "You're good at flattery."

His eyes narrowed with censure. "Is that what you think? You think I'm someone to feed you stories. Unzip my pants."

"What?"

"I think you heard me."

The shift in his demeanor had her springing into action. With fumbling fingers, she reached for the fly of his pants and unfastened them. Before she could pull away, he grabbed her wrist and tucked her hand inside. His erection pushed hot against her palm, making her fingers instinctively curl around it and her sex clench in response.

"Do you feel that?" he asked, wrapping his hand over hers. "You think I'm not enjoying the view, that I'm giving you empty words to make you feel better?"

The weight of him in her hand had her thoughts fragmenting.

She closed her eyes. "We both know I'm not a sixteen-year-old, bounce-quarters-off-her-belly cheerleader anymore."

"No, you're not. And I thought you were pretty in high school, Tess, but the woman in front of me makes that girl pale in comparison."

She huffed a sound of disbelief, unable to stop herself.

His hand tightened around hers. "From the moment you walked into my restaurant, I couldn't stop watching you and imagining what you'd feel like against me. I'm not easy on a woman. Some size four twig would break under what I enjoy. Your body is built for the things I crave."

He moved her hand away from him and guided her fingers to the curls between her thighs. His fingers intertwined with hers and stroked over her clit with slow, deliberate motion, his thick warm fingertips alternating with her cold ones. The sensation had her biting her lip and tilting her head back. "Kade . . ."

"So if you insult your body again or try to hide it from me, I'll turn you over my knee and redden that pretty round ass of yours. Understand?" He pressed his fingers inside her and she gasped both at the feel of it and the threat.

"You'd sp-spank me?" she asked, having trouble grabbing onto words as he pumped his fingers inside her with slow precision.

He chuckled softly against her ear. "Now who's the stutterer?"

"Cocky bastard," she whispered, no ire behind it.

"Yes, and a kinky one—spanking included."

She lowered her forehead to rest on his shoulder, needing him for balance. His admission had her blood moving faster, fear of the unknown warring with ravenous curiosity. "*How* kinky?"

He cupped the back of her head with his free hand and touched his lips to her ear. "So kinky that there's probably not a fantasy you can tell me that I'm not willing to make happen for you. And a thousand filthier ones that you haven't even considered yet that I can introduce you to."

*Guh.* Her belly dropped to her toes and a hefty dose of *oh-God-YES* dumped into her bloodstream. Fantasies. Lord, she'd harbored many over the years, illicit images weaved late at night while reading naughty romance novels and lying awake next to her uninterested husband. Secret desires filed away in the darkest recesses of her psyche and never spoken aloud. Things Doug would've called her a slut for even considering.

Kade must've noticed her reaction because she could hear the smile in his voice at his next words. "The question is . . . where do we start?"

# THIRTEEN

Kade could feel the shudder go through Tessa's body at his words, and he had to hold back the groan of satisfaction. There were nerves there, anticipation. Her pulse was beating hard at her throat. But he didn't sense fear in her. He knew he was coming on strong by making her strip out here. She wasn't his submissive. She probably wouldn't even know what that meant. But he needed to do something to push her boundaries to see how she'd react. He had no intentions of letting this be their last night together, but he had to make sure she wasn't turned off or freaked out with how he liked things. Because he could make a lot of accommodations, but smothering his dominance wasn't an option. He'd tried in the past, trying to convince himself it was something he could take or leave. Epic fail.

But now he could breathe a bit. Tessa had protested out of surprise at first, but as soon as he'd assured her he'd keep her safe, she'd complied. And when he'd mentioned fantasies, she'd gone so hot and wet that he'd damn near spread her out on the hood of the car for a taste. But it was way too chilly for a Whitesnake video reenactment. He needed to get her inside.

He pulled a strip of silk from his back pocket. "Lift your head. I'm going to blindfold you."

She raised her head, her gaze startled, but she didn't move away when he fastened the black strip over her eyes. She reached out and gripped his biceps. "I feel like I'm going to fall."

"Shh, take a breath. The first few seconds can be disorienting, especially in unfamiliar surroundings, but trust that I have you and won't let you hurt yourself." He moved to her side and grasped her elbow. "Now walk."

Tentatively, she put one foot out in front of her and tapped as if to make sure a trap door wasn't going to open up. Kade bit back a smile. Soon, he hoped to have her trusting him so much that she'd sprint ahead blindfolded if he told her to. But he knew that'd take time and he still didn't know if she'd agree to see him for more than a two-night stand, so he let her do her little herky-jerky steps forward while he kept her steady. When he guided her inside the cabin, he made sure she was holding onto the door frame, and then stepped back a moment to soak in the sight of her. The cabin was still dark and the moon backlit her form, highlighting every curve in silver.

Never in his life could he have imagined that the girl he'd so lusted over—maybe even thought he loved at one point—would be beautifully naked, waiting for his command, in the same place she'd spurned him after he'd tried to kiss her so long ago. It was a gift he wouldn't take for granted. If a teenage Kaden Fowler had hopped into Doc Brown's DeLorean to visit the future, he would've never made it back because this vision would've made his brain implode.

Tessa reached out to find the other side of the doorframe. "Where are you?"

"Just looking at you, Tess," he said, taking her hand again and leading her all the way inside. He pulled open the curtains to let some moonlight flood in. "And wondering how best to rechristen this cabin."

"I have a few ideas," she said, a shy undercurrent in her voice.

"Tell me."

She rubbed her lips together. He got the impression that she wasn't someone who was used to voicing her needs or fantasies. That would change quickly if he had anything to do with it. He wanted to know every sordid thought that had ever gotten her hot. But to her credit, despite her obvious qualms, she answered him. "When we used to come here, even after I'd promised myself that I'd only think of you as a friend, I'd catch you watching me with this look that . . . I don't know . . . it was so intense. I remember wondering what you would do to me if I gave you the green light. And even though I knew it was wrong, part of me was desperate to know. I'd lie in bed at night and imagine me saying yes to you, imagining what your hands would feel like on me. I'd . . . touch myself and imagine it was you doing it."

*Christ.* The words were painting a picture straight out of his teenage spank bank. How many times had he gone home with the same thoughts? Tess saying yes, Tess choosing him, Tess being his. He was surprised he hadn't developed a chafing problem with as much as he was jerking off that year. "I would've given you whatever you wanted."

She squeezed his hand. "I know. I used you as my emotional crutch. You were more my boyfriend than Doug was after a while, but I wouldn't grant you the right to act as such. You got the tough stuff without the fun benefits. So maybe the best way to rechristen this cabin is to right that wrong. You have all the green lights you want now. Take what I wish I would've given you back then."

"Tess," he said, pulling her against him, an ache in his gut . . . and decidedly lower. "Are you giving me your virginity?"

She gave him a heartbreakingly sweet smile. "Second time's a charm."

He pulled off her blindfold at that, needing to see her eyes. "I wouldn't have known what to do with you back then. But I would've done my best to make it good for you."

"I know," she whispered, her gaze a little wistful.

"If we hadn't had consequences back then and we were back here for a study session, what would you have done?"

She tugged his hand and led him toward the couch. The furniture had changed, but the arrangement was the same, like stepping back in time, the vortex sucking him through the portal. When they reached the couch, she guided him to sit. Though he wasn't used to being directed to do anything, in this situation, he was more than happy to oblige. The woman had definite intent in her eyes, and he loved a woman on a mission.

"You always sat in this corner with your knee hiked up," she said, her voice timid in the dark. "And I couldn't help but . . . look. And when some moment would pass between us, you'd grab one of the throw pillows and put it over your lap to prop your book up. I knew why you did that. You weren't always quick enough, so I saw your reaction to me."

He chuckled, remembering the embarrassment of his defiant hormones. "I was a seventeen-year-old virgin. The thing had a hair trigger around you."

She looked down at him, her teeth dragging over her bottom lip. As if on cue, Kade could feel his cock hardening. "One of my fantasies back then was to take the pillow away and ask if I could touch you. I'd heard my friends talking about the things they did with their boyfriends. I wanted to know how that would be with you."

His breath left him for a moment. If she'd asked that back then, he probably would've proven that death by spontaneous combustion existed. Boom. Done. Here lies Kaden Fowler.

She lowered herself to the ground, settling herself between his spread knees. Her gaze tracked down to his erection. "Can I touch you, Kade?"

He groaned at the soft plea in her words and pulled his belt all the way out. "Show me exactly what you wanted to do."

She wet her lips and hell if his dick didn't flex toward her at the sight. She reached out with pink painted fingernails flashing in the moonlight and tugged down his unfastened pants to his thighs along with his boxer briefs. The cool air of the cabin swirled over him, sending goose bumps along his skin. After getting his pants down past his knees, she took him in her hand, and the softness of her touch nearly pulled another groan from him.

She glanced up at him, all big eyes and long lashes. "Tell me how you like it. I wouldn't have known then, but I'm not much better off now."

Kade ran a hand over her head. Usually, he made a point to be with experienced women. They knew what they were doing and were more comfortable with his brand of sexuality. Plus, nothing was hotter than a woman who absolutely owned her desires without apology. But he couldn't help but be endeared by Tess's unsure approach. It called to the dominant in him, made him want to tutor her all over again but in things far more base than Shakespeare. He threaded his fingers into her hair, the strands like silk around his knuckles, and guided her forward. "Take my cock in your mouth, beautiful. And keep your eyes on me, I want to watch you as you suck me."

She shuddered in his grip, her eyes going a little wide at first then dreamy as she obeyed his command and lowered her head. Her gaze stayed on his as her glossed lips parted and slid over the crown. His toes flexed in his shoes at the feel of her tongue tentatively flicking along the bottom side of his shaft.

"Fuck," he muttered, his teenage ghost possessing him for a moment and stealing his normally unshakeable restraint. He grasped the base of his cock, taming the urge to rush, and guided her down further. "That's right. You can't do anything wrong, baby. That feels amazing."

Apparently buoyed by the encouragement, she grew more bold with her tongue and hands. Before long, she was working him over with steady determination and enthusiasm, bathing him in slow, decadent heat and making his eyes want to roll back in his head. But he wasn't going to look away from her and break the connection.

Her gaze stayed fixed on his even though he could tell it was a struggle to maintain the intense eye contact. He could see the insecurity there, the exposed vulnerability. The man she'd trusted had hurt her more deeply than she was letting on. There was a kicked puppy vibe that hadn't been there when he'd known her before. She'd always had cracks in the veneer. Even by high school, she'd lived a harder life than anyone should be expected to. But this was different. It was almost as if she was just waiting for him to tell her that she was bad at this, that it wasn't doing anything for him. It'd been the same when he'd offered her the job—the knee jerk lack of confidence. She couldn't see her own strength. It made him want to gather her into his arms and rewind all those years they'd been apart. Change the course.

But before his mind could run away with him, Tessa's hand slid beneath him, cupping his balls, and her lips kissed the fingers he still had around the base of his cock as she took him deep. Sparkling threads of pleasure raced up his spine. He tilted his head back with an expelled breath, finally breaking the eye contact. "Jesus, baby, you're better at this than you think. Touch me wherever you want."

She seemed to appreciate the compliment and used her free hand to follow the slick path back up as she moved toward the tip again. He peeked down through hooded lids as she licked at the head with long strokes. The move nearly undid him because in that moment, he got the real sense that she wasn't just doing this to make him feel good. She was thoroughly enjoying the exploration.

"You're like a kid with a new toy," he teased. "Trying to see how many noises you can get me to make?"

She gave him a pleased little grin. "Three groans and a few sighs so far, if I'm not mistaken. I like that I can do that to you."

"Mmm, someone likes her own slice of power," he said, knowing the dominant in him should probably mind but only getting more turned on by the thought. He'd always preferred submissives who were naturally sweet and yielding. But the idea of Tessa trying to wrest a bit of the power and challenging him made his blood race and his cock harder. Maybe he wouldn't mind that kicked puppy showing some teeth.

She kept her hand on him, stroking slow and steady, but looked up at him. "You made me lose it the other night. I want to do the same for you."

"Think you can make me come, Tess?" he challenged, fingering one of her blonde locks. "I'm pretty good at holding out these days, especially when I put my mind to it."

A little break in confidence flickered over her face but then she tilted her head. "What do I get if I can make you?"

"Besides a dose of protein?" he teased.

She sniffed.

His mouth curved. More challenge and fire trying to break through her surface. He so wanted to see what happened if it did. "You get to give the next command. Whatever you'd like me to do to you, I'll be game."

"And if you win?" she asked.

"Another date. In public."

Wariness moved over her expression, but she nodded. Agreement made. "Can you move closer to the edge of the couch? I need your pants further down."

"Whatever you need," he said, in a tone that he hoped conveyed utter confidence even though he wasn't so sure. Tessa's continued stroking already had his blood burning, and he couldn't remember ever seeing anything quite as sexy at his feet than a naked Tessa McAllen.

He scooted to the edge of the couch, and she tugged his pants down to his ankles. She moved closer and spread his knees wider, then she was lowering her head again. The moment her hot, wet mouth enveloped him, he knew he'd made a sucker's bet, but couldn't find it in himself to care. What she'd done tentatively the first time bloomed into full assertiveness, her mouth and tongue working him to within an inch of his control. Her fingernails scored lightly over the tender skin of his testicles and his teeth ground against each other. Sweat broke out on his lip.

He grabbed the edge of the couch cushions, trying to focus. Control over his own release was usually easy for him. He fed off the anticipation and the delayed gratification for him and his submissive. That usually created the biggest payoff for both. But Tess was lobbing grenades at his defenses. When her fingers crept lower, beneath his scrotum and to the sensitive skin of his perineum, he let out a strangled grunt that revealed how badly he was tanking in this challenge.

As if sensing victory, Tess took his cock as deep as she could and then circled his back entrance with the tip of her finger, moving her tongue in the same motion along his length. Her touch was still unsure, as if she'd never tried that before but thought it could be a good idea, and the innocence of it pulled the ripcord on his control. His back arched at that and white split his vision. He moaned her name and gripped her head in his hands, holding her hard as he pumped his hips and emptied inside her.

She made her own sound of pleasure as he came and that only made his utter defeat in this challenge all the more worth it. He held onto her for long seconds after he was finished, enjoying the feel of softening in her mouth. When he finally had the energy to lift his head and slide free, he found Tess looking up at him with stunned wonder.

The unexpected expression had him smiling. "Don't look so surprised. I think you hustled me with you saying you didn't know how to do this."

She licked her lips. "I've never done half of that stuff. I just . . . I followed your reactions. And you let me . . ."

"What, baby?" he said, leaning forward and cupping her face.

"Touch you however I wanted. I'm not really used to that. Doug would've—" She cringed. "Sorry."

He frowned. "It's okay. Say what you need to get off your chest. I don't want him between us. He's been there long enough."

She looked down, as if regretting bringing it up. "He had this weird thing about keeping me like this sweet, proper thing. I'm sure it's some fucked up stuff from how things worked out with his mom. But if I ever tried anything, you know, out of the ordinary, he'd get disgusted with me. Tell me that stuff was for sluts, whores, trash, whatever."

"I'm guessing those words weren't terms of endearment in his book."

She snorted. "Are they ever?"

He pushed her hair behind her ears and lifted her face to him. "In my world, yes, sometimes they are. In the circles I move in, a woman owning her desires is not only accepted, it's fucking celebrated. I don't want you to be some overgrown virgin princess for me. If you have a desire, let's try it. If you crave a certain fantasy, let's make it happen—even if that means more than just me providing it for you. And I promise you, if I called you my dirty little slut, it'd be a compliment."

She shook her head in his hands. "I can't even fathom that."

"Own what you want, Tess. No judgment here." He leaned forward and kissed the top of her head. "In fact, start now. You won the bet. Tell me what you want me to do to you."

The words sounded foreign rolling off his tongue, but he'd

stand on his fucking head and sing the national anthem if it'd help her stop questioning herself.

Tess stared up at him, chewing her lip. He expected her to ask him to return the favor and go down on her, which he was more than looking forward to. He could already taste her sexy tartness on his tongue. But there was a devilish curiosity blooming in those eyes that had him holding his breath.

She leaned back on her calves as if she needed space to make her request, and her gaze flicked down to his lap then back up to him. "Is, uh, that spanking thing only for punishment?"

His breath whooshed out of him in one big rush. He had no idea what he'd done in a former life to grant him this gift tonight, but he wasn't going to question it. "Baby, it can be whatever we want it to be."

Her lips rolled inward, her nerves rising to the surface, but she nodded. "Okay. I want to try that. Will it hurt?"

His smile was slow. "Only for a minute."

# FOURTEEN

Tessa's heart was about to burst from her chest and take a holiday. She'd put it through too much in the last week. But she refused to let her nerves take over. Kade was offering her the chance to try things she'd never done before without worry of critique or judgment. He wanted her to be dirty. And the idea was damn liberating. When she'd gone down on him and ventured into what she dubbed in her mind as the forbidden zone of touching, she'd been braced for Kade to recoil or tell her to stop. But when he didn't, she realized Kade would've probably let her do whatever she wanted. Doug would've shoved her away with some ugly name and would've asked if she thought he wanted to be touched like a fag.

And now she'd asked Kade if he would spank her. The request sounded ridiculous in her head. She was a grown woman for God's sake. But when he'd mentioned the possibility outside, it'd sparked something in her and now that curiosity was gnawing at her. Kade stood, tugged his pants back on, and looped his belt to hang around his neck. "I know you won the bet, but are you okay with me doing this my way?"

She'd remained on her knees, so she had to crane her neck to look up at him. The belt sent a glimmer of worry through her, but she took comfort in knowing she still had that safe word if she needed it. "Well, since I have no idea what I'm doing, I think that's probably a good idea."

His eyes lifted at the corner briefly, an almost smile, but then his jaw set in determination. "Good. The couch is too low. Stand up and come with me."

She pushed herself up from the floor and followed him into the small dining area. He pulled out a chair, the legs scraping along the wood floor with an ominous grind. Then he sat down with spread knees and leveled a gaze at her, looking like a prince taking his throne. The room seemed to shrink around him in supplication. She felt the urge to make herself smaller, too. Plus, the fact that he was fully clothed and she didn't even have her shoes on anymore made her feel more like a servant girl being brought before the royalty for some crime. Guards dragging her in, chains around her ankles, her clothes stripped off as they planted her at his feet. That image wasn't altogether unpleasant.

"What are you smiling about?" he asked, lifting a brow.

She put her hand to her mouth. Was she smiling? What the hell was wrong with her? That's it, her trips to the used bookstore were a liability. She was definitely reading too many old school bodice ripper novels. She shook her head in a *never mind* gesture.

"Tell me."

The softness of his tone didn't undermine the iron in the command. A little shiver worked down her neck and spread outward. "It's nothing. I've just been reading too many historical novels lately and had a silly image pop into my head of you being some prince and me being dragged into court as a captive. Ridiculous, I know."

The heat that flared in his eyes would've shown up on a thermal camera. "You'd make a lovely slave girl, Tessa. Maybe we'll have to try that some time."

She tried to wet her lips, but her tongue had gone dry, and she barely managed to eke out her reply. "Too bad you lost the bet and we don't get another date."

The corner of his mouth lifted and the sheer confidence of it nearly knocked her down. "Over my knees, Tessa. Now."

And in that moment, she knew then that he'd won anyway. That look said it all—when I'm done with you tonight, you'll be begging me for another night. The quicksand that was Kade Vandergriff had engulfed her ankles and now he was going to pull her right under. But she couldn't stop herself from walking to him and letting him drape her over his lap. She braced her fingertips on the floorboards, her hair sweeping down to curtain her.

The clink of the belt had her stiffening and lifting, but he pressed a soothing hand to her back and eased her down again. "Hands behind your back."

With no small amount of trepidation, she raised her arms behind her. Kade gripped her wrists and wound the leather belt around them then cinched the belt tight. The move put her off balance and made her even more vulnerable, something she didn't think possible. "Kade."

"Shh," he said, running a finger beneath the belt and checking how tight it was. "My way, remember. I won't let you fall."

She pulled a deep breath into her lungs, held it, and released it, trying to calm herself.

"Are you scared, baby?"

"A little."

"Good." His palm caressed over her backside, raising goose bumps on her skin, and tracked lower. He tapped her thigh. "Open wider for me."

She did as she was told, the commands falling right into the slave girl fantasy she'd conjured. She was at his mercy. It probably shouldn't turn her on, but already her body was melting like ice on hot pavement. Kade's fingers moved along her spread sex and easily slid inside, the state of her arousal embarrassingly apparent. Her body clamped around him, and she couldn't stop a whimper from escaping.

"God, baby, you're so hot and wet. You're going to get me hard all over again just thinking about how your pussy would feel around me."

She shuddered in his hold. Normally, the word *pussy* would make her cringe. It sounded so crude, but somehow the way he said it made it sound reverent. Like it was some mysterious wonder of nature to be worshipped.

There was soft laughter from above her. "I love how when I say dirty things to you, your skin turns the sexiest shade of pink. I can't wait to see how it's going to look red."

Before she could process what he was saying, a hard smack landed on the left side of her ass. She yelped at the sharpness of the sting, the unexpected pain. *Sonofabitch.* She'd asked if it was going to hurt, but it'd been almost in jest. She'd hadn't really expected it to be painful. Wasn't spanking like a play thing? A pretend game where it was more about the role play than the actual hitting? But when another stinging swat hit her right side, she realized quickly there was nothing faux about this. It freaking *hurt.*

"Kade," she protested. "I'm not sure . . ."

"Breathe through it, Tess. Trust me," Kade said, without any sympathy in his voice. "You have a safe word, but I suggest you give me a minute before you tap out."

*Trust me.* That seemed to be a recurring theme with him. And though she wasn't quite there yet, she managed to say okay. She was determined not to pull the plug too early. The pain wasn't fun, but it wasn't unbearable. She'd just hoped this would be more of an enjoyable thing than a painful one. So much for this being a reward for winning.

Kade's hand came down again and hit the back of her thigh.

Holy hell. That was even worse than on her butt. She reared up, but he kept her against his lap with his free arm. "Stay still."

"I'm trying," she said through gritted teeth.

That spurred him on more, and she regretted talking. His hand smacked her other thigh then went on a rapid trip across her ass again. *Smack. Smack. Smack.* Her body began to sweat and hum with restless energy. Her thoughts blurred around the edges. The pain was turning into something else, numb at first, then a weird buzzing sensation—like having one too many shots of alcohol. She tried to say Kade's name because the feeling was so disorienting and unfamiliar, but the word wouldn't come out. Then he landed a blow right against her sex. A million nerve endings gathered at the point of impact and exploded into currents of sensation, rippling out like a backdraft. A cry tore from her throat and everything went burning hot and needy inside her. Skin that had stung was now tingling and aching for more. Her heels came off the ground, her body offering itself to Kade.

"That's it, beautiful," Kade said, running a warm hand over her tightening skin. "Let it kick in and enjoy the buzz."

He spanked her again and she moaned, shameless at this point. Her body was throbbing and desperate for release in a flash, the soft fabric of his pants rubbing against her clit and adding to the mix. From pain to near bliss in mere minutes. "Kade, please."

"You want to come, Tessa?" he said, gravel in his voice, as if he were riding his edge, too.

"Yes," she said, squirming against his lap, seeking more contact. She was right there on the brink but needed more. She needed him. But she doubted he was ready for round two yet. "Please."

Instead of reaching beneath her to touch her like she expected, Kade slid her off his lap and onto her knees. Frustration flooded her at the delay. What was he doing? He stood and shoved the chair out of the way, then he hooked her beneath her armpits and lifted her to her feet.

She struggled to stay steady with her arms still bound and her head rushing from being upside down one minute and right-side up the next. She braced her hip against the edge of the table. "What are you doing?"

He unbuttoned his pants and shoved them down, pulling something out of the pocket before he straightened. "Come 'ere. I'm not done with you yet."

She glanced down, finding him fully aroused again, and her stomach clenched low and tight. Oh, thank you, God. Kade tore open the little foil packet with his teeth and rolled the condom on.

Without another word, he was helping her climb onto the table. He grasped her hips and positioned her over him. The tip of his cock teased along her entrance, drawing shivers from her as she looked down to where their bodies met, fascinated by the vision.

"You like watching," he said, though his voice was so gritty she could tell it was costing him something to delay the moment. "You want to watch my cock disappear inside of you?"

If she hadn't already been flushed from everything else, she would've gone crimson. But instead of watching him slide in, she looked up and met his gaze right as he lowered her down and entered her. The satisfaction that crossed his face as he seated himself deep was far more erotic than anything she could've seen by looking down. Her muscles tightened around him, the invasion blissful after so much buildup. "Man, that feels good."

"Back at ya, beautiful," he said, giving her a quick but potent kiss. "Now, fuck me, Tess. I won't let you fall."

He braced a hand on her waist to keep her steady and then tucked the other between their bodies, giving her clit a teasing stroke. It was like the starter gun going off. She rocked her hips, lifting off him then gliding back down in one fluid, toe-curling motion. The stretch of her body around him was almost too delicious to bear, mixed in with the still tingling heat of her backside. Everything felt alive, vibrating. Kade strummed her hot button again, this time with more intent. An ocean-like roar filled her ears. "Oh, God."

"Take what you need, baby," Kade said, watching her with rapt attention. "I want to watch you break open."

She didn't need any further encouragement. She plunged down on him and tilted her hips to rub her clit against his fingers with each thrust. Sensation snaked over her skin like lava flows, everything going hot and sweaty and achy. Kade whispered dirty things to her about how fucking hot she looked, about how he couldn't wait to taste every part of her again, about how sexy she'd been with his handprints on her ass. Before long, she'd lost all sense of decency and was riding him with singular focus.

"Come for me, Tess," he said, his voice no longer cajoling but commanding.

Stars filled the space behind her eyelids and the building mass of tension inside her unraveled in one spine-melting explosion. She tilted her head back and moaned his name, almost losing her balance. But as promised, he didn't let her fall. He held onto her as she came hard and long, sensations crashing over her one after another, and then soon his own sounds of pleasure were melding with hers.

When she didn't think her body could bear another second of holding itself up, she tipped forward and landed against his chest. He wrapped his arm around her and lay back on the table, cradling her to him as their labored breathing struggled to return to normal.

Minutes passed without either saying anything. Her hands flexed behind her back, her fingers aching to touch him, to unbutton that shirt and have her cheek against the man beneath, to explore. But she'd have to wait another day for that.

She closed her eyes. Another day.

"Cocky bastard," she muttered.

"Hey," he said, reaching behind her to unfasten the belt. "What was that for?"

She stretched her wrists once they were free and pushed herself up and off of him. "You win."

He lifted his brows, feigning innocence, as he unbuttoned his shirt and handed it to her. "Whatever could you mean?"

She tucked herself into the too long sleeves and wrapped the shirt around herself. "You have me thinking about a next time. What are you trying to do to me, Kade Vandergriff?"

He smiled and pulled on his pants, the quick sound of the zipper like punctuation marking the end of their night. "Just trying to see you again. Is that so bad?"

She looked to the ceiling, the thought both tempting and terrifying all in one. "Yes."

He closed the space between them and wrapped his arms around her waist. "All these years, and you're still shooting me down. A guy could develop a complex."

She sighed. "It's not that. Being with you is . . ." *Intense. Overwhelming. Addictive.* "Great. But you know this is complicated. I'm working for you now. Plus, you're who you are, and I'm the former trophy wife. Think how that would be perceived if we were seen in public. And I don't want to even think about what would happen when Doug got wind of it, especially when he figured out it was *you*."

Kade's expression turned hard. "That asshole couldn't do a damn thing."

She shook her head. "You don't understand. I think part of him still thinks I'm going to come back. You heard him on the phone tonight. He's not going to let it go if I start dating someone as high-profile as you. I don't want to bring drama into your life."

Kade's hands coasted up her back in a soothing motion, but his jaw twitched with old anger. "He can't get to you or me anymore, Tess. Yes, he has power and money. But so do I, and I have more of it. He can't touch me now, and I definitely won't let him mess with you. He'll regret it if he tries."

His words were resolute, but anxiety rolled around in her stomach.

"In fact," he said, leading her to the couch to sit down. "This could be the ultimate fuck you to him. Show him and the world that you're not broken and in hiding after all those accusations he threw out to the press. You've moved on with your life."

She sent him a smirk. "Now you're just waving Eden apples at me. The thought of putting him in his place like that . . ."

It was almost too delicious to contemplate.

His eyes were pale but bright in the moonlight. "So why not go for it? I know you're scared of what people will think, but fuck them. And fuck Doug. You and I spent almost a year hiding in this cabin because we were worried about what people would say. I'm done with that shit."

Her throat tightened at the fervent words. "I'm not ready to date anyone, Kade. I have enough going on. I'm a freaking mess right now."

"No," he said, utter conviction rumbling through the word. "You are not a mess. You're adopting his labels for you. You got a divorce, started fresh on your own with none of his money, and are about to start a job that you're passionate about. That woman is not a mess. That woman is someone who deserves to get what she wants. And whether you'll admit it right now or not, you want *this*. You want what happened tonight and more of it. I'm not asking you to be my girlfriend. I'm asking you to let me give you the experiences you're craving. Give yourself permission to have that with me."

She looked down, folding back the cuffs of his shirt to give her hands something to do. Factions were warring in her mind with daggers and arrows, tearing at each other's arguments.

"It's not about permission. This stuff is scary, Kade. This may be standard fare for you. But for me, it's like falling deeper down the rabbit hole every time." She glanced toward the dining table, replaying what had happened there in her mind. "I don't even know who this person is. This girl who's stripping in the middle of the woods and asking to be spanked."

"Tess, maybe it's *you*. The woman you could've been if Doug hadn't made you feel wrong for your desires. Have you considered that?"

God, so much had changed, yet in many ways nothing really had. Kaden Fowler was still saying shit that made her question everything in her neat little world. She shook her head and groaned, putting her hands over her face. "Aren't you supposed to be trying to get rid of me? You've gotten in my pants, now you can move on to your CEO groupies?"

He took her wrists in a gentle grip and lowered her hands from her face, a devilish little smile touching his lips. "Groupies? Come on, now. And newsflash: I've never been one to do the normal thing."

Wasn't that the damn truth. She huffed. "Freak."

He laughed and grasped the lapels of her shirt, pulling her onto his lap. "Yes, I am. And I'm starting to suspect that you are, too."

"God, you say that like it's a good thing."

"It *is*, Tess. Come on, be honest. Are you ready to go back to how things were before that night at the restaurant? Was a little spanking all that was on your sexual adventure list?"

She rolled her lips inward and nodded solemnly.

"Liar." He teased. "This is the girl who didn't want to be boring in bed. The girl who reads books about princes taking advantage of their pretty slave girls. I'm giving you the chance to try all the things that you've thought about when you're alone in the dark."

She closed her eyes, her body stirring to attention again. "Kade . . ."

"Let me show you how fun pushing boundaries can be," he said, tucking her hair behind her ear. "We can be discreet. No one at work needs to know we're seeing each other, and the press only cares who I bring to high-profile events. This can just be about you and me and dropping those rules you've had to follow all your life."

She stared at him, knowing that she should walk away right now. This was Kaden. Not some random hot guy she'd decided to hook up with. This was someone who could get to her, make her feel things, want things. And that was something she couldn't let happen. Regardless of the boy Kade used to be, the man he was now had all the warning signs. Too smooth. Too rich. Too good-looking. And single by choice.

How many women had he done the seduction thing with? How many had he talked dirty to? How many had gotten hearts in their eyes only to be dropped for the next?

But even knowing the risk, she couldn't bring herself to form the words she was supposed to. When had she ever done something this out there? This daring? The thought of Kade guiding her through fantasies she barely had the nerve to admit she harbored was like being presented the most decadent piece of chocolate cake and someone asking if she wanted a bite.

"What do you say?" Kade asked, his gaze not wavering from hers.

She took a deep breath and leaned her forehead against his, letting the honest truth fall from her mouth. "You're kind of hard to say no to, Kade Vandergriff."

"Yeah?" he said, a hint of schoolboy hope in his voice.

"Yeah. As long as we keep it out of the public eye."

He pulled back and pressed a kiss to her lips. "I can work with that. For now."

*For now.*

The words reverberated in her ears like the aftermath of a ringing bell. But before she could think too hard on it, his eyes narrowed, like he was considering something intently.

"What?" she asked, disconcerted by that evaluating stare.

She shifted off his lap and back to the couch to find some solid ground.

"What you said earlier about the prince and the captive . . . were you making a joke or is that a fantasy you find appealing?"

She put her hand to her forehead, feeling silly. "Kade, come on, don't tease me—"

"No, I'm not, I'm serious. I want to know. This is going to be about exploring your desires. I need to know where they lie."

She shook her head. "It's just a silly thing I said."

"But does it turn you on?" he asked, giving her a look like this was the most important question in the universe. "Does the idea of playing my captive or slave appeal to you?"

Did it turn her on? When the image had crossed her mind, her body had gone hot and liquid even though she'd felt ridiculous thinking about it. "Yes. I guess the taboo factor of it all. It's so . . . everything we're not supposed to want. Like the opposite of politically correct. I'm sure most women would find it kind of enticing on some level."

He gave her a pointed look. "No, not all women, Tess."

She blinked, the words stinging. "So you're saying there's something wrong with me?"

His lips curled upward. "Not saying that at all. Quite the opposite in fact."

"Oh?" she said softly.

"Yes. I think this is all going to work out just fine. All it's going to require from you is a little trust and an open mind. I'll take care of everything else." He grabbed her hand and lifted it to his mouth. "Say good-bye to the proper Southern belle, Tess. There's no place for her in my world."

Tessa swallowed hard. She was in so much damn trouble.

# FIFTEEN

Tessa sat on the floor of her living room with colored file folders spread around her in piles and her new company-issued MacBook perched on her lap. She picked up a green folder and flipped it open to pull the information she needed to enter into her spreadsheet.

"Didn't you work all day?" Sam asked from her spot on the couch. "I think it's time you take a break and tell me about Hot Stalker Guy."

Tess sent Sam a quelling look. "I'm still getting trained on a bunch of things at the office during the day and then have those night classes twice a week. It hasn't left me a lot of time to work on stuff for the actual event. I need to organize the list of potential restaurants and donors together so I can start making calls next week. And can you please stop calling Kade stalker guy?"

"Hey, the man tracked you down," she said with a shrug. "He comes by the nickname honestly. Plus, I'm in desperate need of juicy stories. My Perfect Match dude crashed and burned last night. Distract me from my shattered heart."

Tessa smirked at Sam, who was happily embroidering hot pink skulls on a pair of knee socks for her friend's roller derby team. "You look truly heartbroken. What happened?"

"I found out he hates dogs. *Hates.* Can you believe that? We saw a stray on the road, and I wanted to catch him so I could bring him to the shelter. Cory freaked out. Like God forbid he get dog hair in his new Dodge Durango. When I realized he was serious, I got out of the car and told him he could leave. I can't be with someone who would leave a stray on the highway. *I* used to be a stray on the highway."

Tessa shook her head. "So he just left you there on the road?"

"Yeah, he did. Bastard. But I wouldn't have gotten back in the car anyway." She glanced up with a smile. "In other news, I have a dog."

Tessa laughed. "Oh, no."

"It's fine. I could use the company now that you moved out, anyway. But stop trying to distract me. I need to know what's up with this Kade dude? So you're like dating?"

"No," Tessa said, typing a name into her spreadsheet and trying to stay focused. "I told him that's off limits. We're just . . ."

"Screwing like mad?" Sam offered, voice hopeful. "Fucking like rock stars?"

Tessa snorted but smiled despite herself. "You're awful."

She lifted a brow, indicating the question stood.

"Fine. Yes. He's on a mission to show me the kinky side of life, and I'm letting him. Let's call it tackling a subcategory of the list."

Sam's eyes went big, and she pulled her knees under her. "Seriously? Like giving you some course in deviant sex?"

"I guess you could say that. He used to be my tutor in high school, so I guess we're kind of in those roles again."

"That is *so hot*," Sam declared. "I love it. Does he tell you what's going to happen? Like hey, tonight we're going to tackle public sex or tomorrow we're going to have a threesome?"

Her face heated, and she had to choke back the urge to giggle like a teenager. "*Sam.*"

Tessa was used to Sam saying whatever came into her head, but having her best friend itemize sexual fantasies for consideration had her feeling awkward in a whole new way. She was still getting used to even admitting she *had* fantasies.

"What? Those two should definitely be on your list," Sam said with a knowing nod. "Knowing other people could see you can be exciting. And threesomes, oh my God, some of the hottest nights I've ever had."

Tessa shut her laptop with a snap. There was no way she could concentrate on work after *that* admission. "You've been in a threesome?"

Sam had never been a prude, but Tessa knew that despite Sam's apparent alternativeness, she still had pretty traditional ideas about love and relationships.

Sam set her embroidery in her lap. "Once in college with two guys and a few years ago with a guy and his girlfriend."

Tessa had to work to keep her lower jaw from falling open. "And you never *told* me this?"

She frowned. "Don't be so surprised. I couldn't tell you a lot of stuff. You were with Doug—a guy who preached every Sunday on TV about hell and damnation with you smiling in the pews. I didn't know how much of that was an act and how much was really you. And any time I brought up sex stuff, you kind of clammed up. I thought I might be offending you or whatever."

"Offending me? Seriously?"

Sam gave a little shrug. "Well, you know, not that there's anything wrong with it, but you've always been exceptionally vanilla, chica. I didn't want to freak you out."

Tessa stared at her, a little stunned—and slightly offended. Vanilla sounded so . . . bland. Boring. But really, when it came to her sex life, wasn't that exactly what she'd been before Kade walked back into her life? "And you're not vanilla?"

Sam's eyebrow ring twitched, which meant she was trying not to smile. "Let's just say I'm still exploring what works for me. You're take cooking and accounting classes. I'm taking bondage and dominance classes. We all have our own lists."

Tessa set her computer on the floor and climbed into her cushy love seat, work forgotten, totally fascinated now. "You're taking *dominance* classes?"

Sam feigned an innocent look. "I may or may not enjoy tying men up and making them beg. This may also be another reason Cory left me on the road. I think I scared him when I suggested rope last night."

A laugh burst from Tessa. "Oh my God, you are such a sneaky bitch for keeping all this from me. Here I am, thinking I'm a freak for letting Kade boss me around in bed and meanwhile, you're doing the reverse."

Her eyes lit. "Ooh, he bosses you around in bed? Is he a dominant?"

"This is not the point," Tessa said, jabbing a finger in her direction. "You're not supposed to keep this stuff from your best friend. And I don't even know what that means. Is that a thing? Being a dominant?"

Sam nodded seriously. "It's totally a thing."

Tessa put her hands over her eyes and leaned back against the chair. "God, even more proof I have no freaking idea what I'm doing."

Sam laughed and plopped down beside her, putting an arm around her. "Aww, don't worry. If he's dominant and good at it, all you need to do is learn how to trust him and say yes, and he'll take care of the rest. You get the easy part."

She lifted her head. "This feels far from easy."

"That's because you're still fighting with that old version of yourself. Let her go. There's no one around to judge you now. No one to decide if you're doing the nice girl thing or not. No caseworkers, no foster parents, and no dickhead ex-husband to make you feel like shit. Embrace the freedom of being a woman who can do whatever or whoever the fuck she wants. Because it's fun. Because it feels good. Because you answer to no one but you."

She leaned into Sam and smiled. "Next you're going to tell me to take off my bra and light a match."

Sam snorted. "Too much? I can get a little out of control with my girl power speeches, especially after a few glasses of wine."

"Nah, it was perfect," Tessa said, feeling lighter than she had all week.

"So when's your next date, or should I say, lesson?"

"Tomorrow night."

Sam shifted on the love seat to face her. "Do you know what y'all are doing?"

Tessa bit her lip and shook her head. "Nope. But whatever it is, I guess I'll be saying yes."

And for the first time in her life, she didn't feel at all guilty about what kind of girl that made her. Because right now, that was exactly the kind of woman she wanted to be.

"Good," Sam said, then wagged a finger at her. "Now get back to work, slacker. You've got high-level important shit to do."

"That is my official job description," she said solemnly.

"And I expect full kinktastic details this weekend."

"You'll have to get me drunk."

"Done!"

Tessa smiled, warmth moving through her. She had a best friend to count on. A sexy man to spend time with. And a job that meant something. Who was this girl? And whose life was she living?

Maybe her list was working after all.

Tessa leaned over and scanned the endless numbers on the documents she'd printed out and spread across her desk. One of the big-deal potential donors she'd called today had wanted to know more detailed information about her charity and their financial situation before he made a commitment. She'd flubbed her explanation, stumbled on her words, and exposed how little hard financial data she knew. She'd come off looking like an idiot. And predictably, the man had made up an excuse and said he wasn't able to donate this year. Thousands of dollars down the tube.

The failure had been like a fat fist punching right through the confidence she'd been feeling the night before. In that moment, still hearing the disgust in the man's voice at her lack of expertise ringing in her ear, she'd wanted to quit, to find someone who could do this job without screwing it up completely. The charity was going to go under because she was an uneducated dingbat pretending she was smart enough to have a big important job. She was kidding no one.

But right when she was on the verge of full breakdown, she'd pictured Doug's smiling face, the I-told-you-so in his eyes. That had been enough to staunch the tears that had wanted to come. And instead of having her pity party, she'd left for an early lunch break and had headed over to Bluebonnet Place to have sandwiches with the staff. They'd welcomed her with enthusiasm and had ended up brainstorming with her to help come up with ideas of how to get the kids involved in the Dine and Donate event. They'd decided that artwork and crafts would be fun. Each child could put together something to display at the event and possibly sell.

It'd been a productive visit and one that had made her feel like a real part of that team for the first time ever. That was all she'd needed to reinvigorate her. She'd left with a stack of financial documents, determined to learn everything she could about the business she'd started. But now her head was hurting and her eyes were blurring. She'd taken accounting classes over the past year and knew the basics of a P and L statement, but there were things that didn't add up in these. And for the life of her, she couldn't figure out what she was doing wrong. Gibson had suggested she talk to someone in accounting if she wanted any help, and it looked like she may have to do that because the numbers were not making sense. Based on the donations, Bluebonnet shouldn't be struggling so much to stay afloat. But clearly, she was missing something or reading it wrong.

Tessa's office phone rang, startling her from the notes she was making. She grabbed the phone and pressed the wrong button at first.

"Tess?" Kade's voice boomed through her small office.

"Hold on, you're on speaker." Her fingers hovered above the keypad, as she tried to figure out what to press. These phones had so many buttons, she was afraid she might launch a missile or something if she pressed the wrong one.

"It's the blue one," Kade offered.

"Right." She hit the button and put the receiver to her ear. "Sorry. I'm still figuring out things here."

"No worries, you'll get the hang of it," Kade said, his good nature so vastly different from the bosses she'd worked with lately. "Did you get my package?"

She glanced down at the manila envelope that had arrived an hour ago. The words *Confidential, Hold for Mr. Vandergriff* scrawled across it. "Yes."

"Did you open it?"

"No, I've been really buried this afternoon. Plus, it said Confidential."

"Good girl." She could hear the pleased smile in his voice. "I like that you follow instructions. It's going to serve you well with what we're doing."

She wet her lips and glanced toward her open door, knowing anyone could be listening. "Yes, sir."

"I'm taking you out tonight. I have a friend who's performing at a little bar in Fort Worth and a few people I know are going. I'm not usually into country music, but he's pretty good. Should be fun."

A little flutter of panic went through her, and she lowered her voice. "We had agreed to keep things private."

"I need you to trust that I'm not going to break that promise. These are close friends of mine who will have no trouble being discreet. They're a safe group for us to be around. And the bar is off the beaten path."

She took a deep breath and nodded. "Okay, but I thought this was all about fantasy. This sounds like a date."

"Appearances can be deceiving. When you can, lock your door and open the envelope. I want you to wear what's in there for me tonight. Understand?"

Her eyes moved back to the ominous package. "Okay."

"I'll pick you up at your place. Be ready."

Ha. Ready. As if she could ever truly be ready for Kade. But after the day she'd had, he could be the perfect remedy. Fantasy. Sex. And Kade. She was starting to get addicted to the combination. A dangerous cocktail, that. One she should probably put aside for something less potent. But like any good drink, she always wanted one more sip.

"I'll be there."

# SIXTEEN

When Tessa walked out her front door for their night together, it took Kade everything he had not to walk her right back inside and strip off that little black wrap dress she was wearing. The way she shivered in the breeze when she stepped onto the porch told him she'd followed his instructions, and it was killing him knowing what she was wearing underneath but not being able to see everything in its full glory. She gave him a nervous smile. "Hey."

"You look beautiful, Tess," he said, letting his gaze trace over her. Her nipples hardened beneath the material of her dress as his attention moved over them.

She glanced downward. "God, I feel like I'm naked, like everyone's going to know."

He ran his knuckles gently over one of the peaks, and her breath caught. The quarter cup bra he'd given her only offered support beneath to keep her breasts lifted, to give the illusion of a bra, but there was nothing covering her nipples and the tops of her breasts. The soft material of her dress would constantly be rubbing and teasing her sensitive skin. And anytime he brushed against her, he'd be stimulating her. "No one will know but me."

"I'm going to be blushing my face off."

He chuckled and pulled her against him, running his hand along her backside. "The bar will be dark. Are you wearing the panties, too?"

"Yes," she said, a little breathless. "Though I'm not sure of the point when there's a slit right down the center of them. I could've just gone without."

He smiled, his body heating at the image of those lacy crotchless panties beneath her dress. "I like how you think, but you'll see. That lace is going to rub up against you and the wetter you get, the more it's going to drive you crazy."

"You're an evil man, Kade Vandergriff."

"You're just figuring this out?" he teased. "Now, get in the car. I don't want to be late for the show."

Especially when Tessa was going to be a part of it.

Though, his lovely date didn't know it yet.

---

The bar looked innocuous enough. A typical honky-tonk in the older part of Fort Worth. The crowd appeared to be a good mix—couples, women on girl's night out, and a few good ol' boys looking for two-step partners. It wasn't anywhere she'd expect Kade to take her. When they'd been in high school, he'd been the anti-cowboy, preferring loud rock music and black clothes. He'd teased her endlessly about the posters of hot country singers she had pinned to her wall. But she had to admit that even though she could tell his dark jeans, plaid shirt, and boots were one hundred percent designer, he was pulling off the look pretty damn well tonight.

She bumped her hip against his as they were waiting to get in. "You forgot your hat, hoss."

He glanced down at her and smirked. "I'm trying to blend in and be discreet for you. But let's not get crazy now."

She laughed. Blend in? That was a joke. She wasn't sure Kade could blend in anywhere these days. He was that kind of guy who walked into a room and pulled attention to him like a magnetic force. But she appreciated the effort.

Kade paid the cover charge and guided her into the darkened bar. A woman was already on the stage, singing, but the music wasn't so loud that they wouldn't be able to hear each other. Kade kept a possessive hand splayed along her lower back as he craned his neck to look over the crowd—not that he had to do much craning at his height. Soon he smiled and lifted his other hand in a wave. "There they are. Come on."

They made their way through the crowd to a table where a pretty brunette was sitting between two unfairly handsome guys and laughing at something. One of the guys, a tall Hispanic man, grinned and stood when he saw her and Kade standing there. "Hey there, stranger."

Kade shook the guy's hand and clapped him on the back in that half-hug thing men do. "Hey, Andre." Kade nodded at the blond man and the woman he had his arm around. "Jace. Evan. Good to see y'all."

The girl, Evan, smiled, and Jace stuck out his hand to shake Kade's as well. "Vandergriff."

Kade pulled out one of the empty chairs for Tessa. "Everyone, this is my friend, Tessa."

Greetings were exchanged all around and Tessa carefully took her seat, all too aware of the barely there panties moving against her. Tessa didn't know what fantasy they were supposed to be fulfilling tonight, but if it was trying to keep your composure while your body slowly burned into a heap of ashes from barely there stimulation, Kade was nailing it.

Kade ordered both their drinks and laid his arm across the back of her chair. "Thanks for holding seats for us."

"Not a problem," Jace said, a mirror of Kade's pose. "Did those items you needed work out?"

Kade gave a ghost of a smile. "Perfectly. Thanks for sending them over. Though Tess hasn't let me see them yet, so I'll have to give you a final report later."

Tessa straightened like she'd been pinched when she realized what they were talking about. *"Kade."*

He smirked. "It's all right, gorgeous. Jace owns Wicked, a boutique for lingerie and erotic toys. I ordered everything from there. We're not going to shock him."

She had to be ten shades of crimson by the time it sunk in that the stranger across the table knew exactly what she was wearing beneath her dress.

Evan frowned at Jace then gave Kade a matching look. "Stop. You two are embarrassing her."

"Hey," Jace said, giving her an unapologetic half-smile. "*I* was trying to be discreet. Yell at Vandergriff."

Kade simply smiled. And Tessa realized he was doing this on purpose. He was pushing her boundaries, exposing her in a public way to see how she reacted.

Evan rolled her eyes and muttered something about boys and their mindfucks. But then she sent Tessa a kind smile. "You really don't need to be embarrassed. If it makes you feel better, these guys have me in chained nipple clamps beneath this outfit, and Jace has Andre locked into something called the seven gates of hell. Feel free to use your imagination on that one."

Andre lifted his beer in salute and smirked. "Lucky me. Evil bastard."

Tessa's lips parted, completely at a loss on what to say to that.

Kade chuckled and gave her shoulder a squeeze. "Tess, meet

my kinky friends. I could try to explain their relationship, but let's just leave it at they're shit-faced in love with each other and have unlimited access to a sex shop. So like I said, we're not going to shock them."

She glanced at Kade then back to their company. Evan was leaning into Jace, and Jace's arm was stretched over the back of Andre's chair, his fingers touching Andre's shoulder. They were *all* together? That was a lot to wrap her mind around, especially when Evan looked like a perfectly normal woman. Tessa would've never looked at her on the street and thought, kinky chick who'd wear nipple clamps and be in a relationship with two men. And she definitely would've never guessed Andre and Jace were anything but one hundred percent straight. They reeked that man's man alpha vibe.

But maybe that's exactly why Kade had chosen to introduce her to these friends. He was trying to show her that her preconceived notions about what was good or bad or proper or not were just that—preconceived and not based on the real world.

She took a long sip from her glass of wine. "Thanks, Evan. I guess I'm not quite used to being so open about these things."

She grinned. "Believe me, I understand. I had to get over that quick with these two. You look up *exhibitionist* on Google, and I'm sure it will have their photos. But I know it can feel really awkward at first. Just know that no one here is judging anybody."

Evan's warmth was like balm to her nerves. "Thanks for that." She sent Andre a sympathetic look. "And at least I'm not wearing something with the word *hell* in the title."

Jace grinned wide and glanced at Andre with a flash of dark intention in his green eyes. "Don't worry, I promise I always make the torture worth it for these two."

Tessa shivered at the sexy threat in Jace's voice, even though it wasn't directed at her, and watched as Jace leaned in to kiss Evan with unashamed sensuality. Even though it was probably rude, she stared at the display. She couldn't help letting her mind drift down that path of what it must be like for Evan to be in the center of the storm with these two. Tessa had a feeling the woman wanted for nothing in all the ways that counted.

In her peripheral vision, she caught Kade looking down at her, studying her intently instead of watching his friends. She dragged her gaze away from their companions, and peeked up at him. "What?"

His tone was knowing as he leaned close to her ear. "Just watching your thoughts cross your face and seeing your body go hot in the process. You like watching them, don't you? Are you imagining what they look like in bed with each other?"

"Kade," she pleaded, hoping to God his friends couldn't hear what he was whispering to her. She closed her eyes, the back of her neck burning.

"I've seen them, you know," he said, his voice like a caress. "They don't mind being watched."

*Oh, God.* She couldn't respond. Her teeth pressed so hard against each other her jaw hurt.

Kade smiled against her neck and kissed her there. "Show's about to start, gorgeous."

She had no idea if there was double meaning in that, but the lights went down and the next singer was announced. She took a shaky breath, trying to calm herself. Everyone turned their chairs to face the stage. An impossibly broad-shouldered man sauntered onto the stage with a guitar strapped across his massive chest. He ran a hand through his wavy, dark hair before he stepped up to the mic and gave the audience an *aw shucks* grin when they whooped and hollered for him.

"Well, thank ya," he said, a deep Houston twang lacing his words. "I'm Colby Wilkes, and I appreciate y'all coming out tonight. I hope y'all enjoy the show."

He sat down on the stool set up in front of the mic stand, and

Tessa found herself wondering how the thing was going to hold up the linebacker of a guy. She leaned over to Kade. "Is that your friend?"

"Yep. One of my best friends. The only guy who can get me to listen to country music."

She smirked. "Music snob."

He nodded toward the stage as Colby began to strum his guitar and sing a number with a smooth, soulful beat. "He kind of looks like one of the dudes you used to have pinned to your wall."

She peered back toward the stage at Colby. He really was nice to look at. Big and brawny but with kind eyes and a voice that was deep enough to make her chest vibrate when he hit the low notes. He was the type she'd have been drawn to in high school—the athlete, the cowboy, the rugged guy. But now, though she could still appreciate a good-looking guy no matter what the type, she found herself far more attracted to the tall, Nordic refinement Kade had grown into. A man who could wear a suit so well she wanted to fall to her knees and thank God for whoever decided men needed to wear those to the office.

"He does," she said simply.

Kade seemed pleased with her response and draped his arm around her to settle in and watch the show. Jace, Evan, and Andre did the same, but she didn't miss the not so casual touches among them. The hand sliding over a knee, the whispered words to each other. At one point, Andre pulled Evan into his lap and Evan's pale complexion went decidedly more pink. When Tessa surreptitiously leaned forward, too curious not to look, she could see Andre pinching the fabric of Evan's dress right above her belly. It took Tessa a second to realize what was happening, but then she remembered what Evan had on beneath. Andre had to be tugging the chain that was hooked to whatever was attached to her nipples. When Andre gave a harder pull and Evan's head lolled back, her lips parted.

Tessa felt an answering twinge in her own breasts. Her nipples beaded against the fabric of her dress. Kade glanced over at her.

Had she made a noise? Some indication of how fast her heart was beating. His gaze drifted downward, and she followed his line of sight when he smiled. Her nipples were prominently pebbled against her dress, their state obvious since there was no bra holding them in check. He squared his body to block her from the main part of the bar and ran the back of his hand along the front of her dress. Her sex clenched when he grazed her breasts.

She closed her eyes. "You're going to kill me."

Amusement lit his eyes and he pressed a soft kiss to her mouth. His fingers circled her wrist, and he moved her hand beneath the table to his lap. The hard length of him filled her palm. "Does it help to know I'm equally tortured?"

"A little." He leaned back from the kiss and she lifted her wine glass with her free hand, trying to look nonchalant as she breathed through the rush of need. Kade placed her hand back in her own lap and gave her thigh a squeeze. *Not yet*, his movements whispered. *But soon.*

She forced herself to refocus her attention to Colby and the music. She had no idea what Kade planned for tonight but was determined not to ruin things worrying over the possibilities.

Trust. In order for this to work, she had to trust him.

She could always use her safe word if it was too much.

But by the time the show ended, with the combination of her barely there undergarments; Kade's caresses; Jace, Andre, and Evan's interactions; and Colby's deep, sexy voice drifting around them, she knew she would have a hard time saying no to anything. Her body was begging for more than the soft brush of cotton against it, and her panties were so wet, she was afraid to stand up for fear of having a telltale spot on her dress.

Colby left the stage and Tessa took a long pull off her second glass of wine. Kade sent her a wicked smile and trailed his fingers along the back of her neck. "Enjoying yourself?"

"I'm thinking really not nice words about you right now."

He laughed. "Good, I'd hate for you to be thinking polite ones."

A chair scraped across the floor, drawing her attention, and the man who'd been on stage a few minutes earlier joined them.

"Well, would you look at that. They'll let any riffraff in here these days." Colby turned his chair backward and parked it at the end of their table, straddling it. "What'd y'all think of the show?"

"All right," Jace said with a shrug.

"Passable," Andre offered.

"I may be slightly traumatized," Kade concluded.

"Fuckers." Colby grinned and tipped back a beer. "With friends like these . . ."

Evan rolled her eyes. "I thought it was great."

"Well, thank you, sweetheart," Colby said, all charm and dimples.

"That's only because she came by the third song," Jace added.

Evan looked chagrined at that, and she gave Jace a backhanded smack on the arm. "Let's just announce it to everyone."

Colby's lips curved. "It's all right. My voice has that effect on women. And Jace needs all the help he can get."

Jace gave Colby a one-finger salute, but there was humor in his eyes. Tessa didn't know what to think of this strange group. They were obviously kinky and more sexually open than she'd ever seen any group of people be. But she could tell it was so much more than that. There was a comfortable affection and trust there. A vibe that spoke of deep, abiding friendship and respect. She couldn't imagine being surrounded by a group like that.

Colby's focus swung her way, landing on her with a full weighty examination. "And how 'bout you, darlin'? Enjoy the show or do you share your man's shitty taste in music?"

Her man. That sounded so foreign in her ears. She cleared her throat and set her wine glass down. "It was fantastic. You sound like Josh Turner, but your songs have that old school country vibe to them. It doesn't sound like country trying to be pop. I love that."

His smile went broad. "Well, lookie here. Vandergriff's got himself a woman who's not only beautiful but vastly superior to him in intelligence and musical taste."

Kade sniffed. "Tessa, meet my soon-to-be-former best friend, Colby Wilkes."

Colby didn't hold out his hand to shake hers, but gave her a nod and a smile. "Good to meet ya. And I'm glad y'all made it out tonight. I was about to go to Kade's house and personally serenade him with my new stuff if he didn't make it to a show soon."

Kade laughed. "Thank God I didn't have to go through that."

"So," Colby said, tapping his palms on the table. "Y'all ready to get out of here? The night's still young. And I've got a fully stocked bar at the house and a heated pool."

"Hell, yeah," Jace said, pulling out a couple of bills from his wallet and tossing them on the table. "I'm game. How 'bout you two?"

Everyone looked to Kade and Tessa with questions in their eyes. And Tessa had the distinct feeling there was way more being left unsaid than said. Kade slipped his arm around her and gave her a pointed look that reached inside her and sent everything aquiver. "I'm not sure. Are you game, Tess?"

Her throat went dry, despite her recent sip of wine, and her stomach dropped to her toes. But she wasn't breaking her promise to herself that she'd made with Sam. *Just say yes.*

She said yes.

# SEVENTEEN

Colby's house was in a pleasant, quiet neighborhood and was situated at the end of a cul-de-sac. A nice place but nothing outrageous. The kind of house you'd see as the backdrop for some family sitcom. Nothing that would indicate the people walking inside weren't simply another group of friends getting together for a couple of drinks and some conversation on a Friday night. It was a scene that had played out regularly in her old life. Neighbors drinking poolside, sharing gossip, and trading stories.

But when this group settled poolside with margaritas, Tessa knew that it was going to be far from a normal get together. For one thing, Colby was checking the temperature of the pool. And she knew she wasn't the only one who hadn't brought a bathing suit. Kade stretched out behind her on the lounge chair and wrapped his arms around her. "How's the drink?"

"Weak," she said, her voice coming out softer than expected. "But tasty."

"Yeah, that's on purpose. You've already had two glasses of wine. Any decisions you make with me tonight need to be made sober."

Across the pool from them, Evan, Jace, and Andre had pulled together a few loungers, making a space large enough for the three of them. Jace was playfully kissing Evan on her neck and Andre was peeling his shirt off. Colby had walked to a panel on the wall of the house and was turning on music. Tessa swallowed past the knot of nerves that was building in her throat. "Decisions?"

Kade pressed a kiss behind her ear, sending goose bumps down her side. "Yes. Lots to choose from the fantasy list tonight."

She gripped her drink tightly, the sweat of the glass dripping onto her lap, as she watched Jace reach out and flick one of Andre's nipple rings. Colby walked by them, giving them a glance as he made his way to the edge of the pool. "I'm guessing being a voyeur is one of the options."

"Yes," Kade said, his touch growing bolder as he coasted fingers along her thighs. "And that's fine if that's all you choose to do tonight. Watching can be unbelievably hot."

"And being the exhibitionists is the other choice of the two?" she asked, leaning back into him, her body heating beneath his fingers and illicit words.

"Absolutely," he agreed. "Great option as well. But there are more than two choices, Tess."

Her gaze shifted from the triad across the way and landed on Colby, who'd taken off his shirt to reveal a body that would've been at home on Mt. Olympus. *Jesus.* "More than two?"

Her eyes were glued to Colby as he unbuttoned his jeans and pushed them down along with his underwear without hesitation or reservation. What he revealed had her face going hot and her tongue pressing to the roof of her mouth. Part of her felt wrong for staring. She was with Kade and in complete lust with him and his gorgeous swimmer's body. But hell if she could look away from the beast of a man slipping naked into the pool. There were some things that required you to stare.

Kade snorted behind her.

"What?" she asked.

"I asked you something and you didn't hear a word. You're giving me new reasons to hate my best friend. You love his music and can't take your eyes off of him getting undressed. A guy could develop a jealous streak."

She set her drink down and turned in his arms with a grimace. Jealousy. It'd been a running theme in her marriage to Doug. Any time she glanced at a guy, whether with appreciation or not, Doug would get annoyed and call her out. "God, I'm sorry. You're right. I shouldn't have looked, I—"

His smile was slow and knowing. "You really didn't hear what I said before that, did you?"

She bit her lip. "No, what did you say?"

He slid his hand around the back of her neck, pinning her with his gaze. "I said you have the option of watching a threesome tonight or *having* one."

Every muscle in her body froze. "What?"

His fingers drew circles along the nape of her neck. "It's up to you, Tess. If you want to just stick a toe in the water tonight, we can relax here, watch Jace, Evan, and Andre. Enjoy the view. Or you and I can give a little show of our own. Or if you want to really push your boundaries, that man you were just ogling can join us. Your call."

She tried to wet her lips but her tongue wouldn't work. Kade *and* Colby? "You want to *share* me? With your best friend? I thought you said you were getting jealous . . ."

The whole idea had her body stirring and her mind scrambling.

"He's too cocky to get jealous," said a deep voice from behind her. She turned around to see Colby peering at them, his forearms braced along the edge of the pool, body concealed by the water, and his hazel eyes sparkling with mischief. "Plus, he wouldn't make the offer unless he trusted that you're solidly with him."

Tessa's heartbeat was pounding too loudly in her ears and she was starting to sweat—and not in a cute way. She looked back to Kade, who was watching her with evaluating eyes. He pushed her hair away from her face. "This is an absolutely no-pressure decision, baby. I want to give you your fantasies, whatever you're ready for." He looked over her shoulder and raised his voice. "And if Colby's too disgusting to contemplate touching, I completely understand."

"Hey!" Colby said, splashing water their way.

She laughed and pressed her forehead to Kade's shoulder, the joke loosening that fist of tension a bit. "I don't know, Kade. A threesome seems so . . ."

"Hot? Sexy? Dirty?" he offered, a smile in his voice.

"Slutty," she said honestly. Isn't that what had first crossed her mind when Sam had told her she'd been in one?

He ran a hand over the back of her head. "I have a feeling you're not using that word in the positive way. Do you think Evan is a slut?"

She lifted her head. "Of course not."

And she meant that. She'd watched the triad interact with each other. There was so much affection and genuine love there. And those guys looked at Evan like she was the most precious thing ever put on the earth. They were sexy together. Not trashy. Not wrong. They were three people embracing their sexuality and relishing it.

"Then why would you assign that label to yourself if you decide to indulge a little tonight?" There was no judgment in his voice, just genuine concern and curiosity.

"I don't know. Maybe I'm just a little scared," she admitted. "Scared that no matter how much the idea excites me right now or how much I enjoy it, I'll look back at this tomorrow and realize I've lost my mind. I'm also scared that if I keep pushing past fences, I'm never going to find my way back into my own yard. You make me want things I shouldn't."

His eyes went soft. "Why shouldn't you, baby?"

"Because when it goes away,"—when *you* go away, her mind filled in—"everything normal is going to seem mundane."

He cupped her cheek in his palm. "It doesn't have to go away. The people around you right now prove that. If you like kinky, it's out there for those who seek it. Your reactions to this aren't responses I'm creating in you, they're things I'm uncovering. Vanilla sex works for most of the world. It doesn't for me. And maybe it doesn't for you either. And I don't think you need to worry about mundane. I don't plan on finishing your lessons anytime soon."

She smirked, his little speech quelling the rising anxiety in her. He made it all seem so easy, feel so very okay, like she deserved to have whatever made her feel good without shame or guilt or worry. Like he would think no differently of her no matter what her decision was. "You know, if your CEO gig doesn't work, you may have potential in the pied piper business."

He laughed. "Maybe, but really, tonight is your call. I just want *you*. I don't care how we go about that. We could go back to your place and forget all these options altogether. This is about what you want."

She moved her hands up his chest, feeling his heart steadily beating beneath her fingers, and sighed. This man was undoing her—lace by lace, button by button, soon there'd be nothing left to protect her from him or from the secret parts of herself she'd locked away in her own brain. She took a long, full breath and let her chest fall, breathing out the anxiety. "I think I'm ready to be a little scared."

"Yeah?" he said, his brows lifting.

She glanced back at Colby before looking to Kade again, her resolve building block by block within her. "Yeah."

"Brave girl." He gave her that smile that could've melted her panties right off her body and ran his hands along her arms. "I promise you're safe with the two of us. I wouldn't let just anyone touch you. I'd trust Colby with my life. And you always can say the word if you want anything to stop. We're going to make this good for you, Tess."

She nodded, a little too breathless to speak. She was going to do this. She was *really* going to do this. Two men. Doug would've burned her at the stake in a public square if she'd ever suggested a threesome.

Kade gave her one last long look, as if to make sure she was one hundred percent sure, and then he untied the belt holding her wrap dress in place. The two sides fell open, revealing the obscene bra—not that it really had any business being called a bra. All it did was lift and frame her naked breasts for display. Kade's eyes went molten blue when he took in the view.

"Fuck, it's even better than I expected," he said, cupping one of her breasts and running a thumb over her already sensitized nipple. "Lose the dress. But keep the lingerie on."

She scraped her teeth along her bottom lip, the command giving her something to focus on besides her nerves. She tucked her knees under her and slipped the dress off her shoulders, leaving her in the bra and crotchless panties. Kade turned her around so she was facing away from him.

A soft moaning sound came from in front of her, and she peered across the pool. Jace and Andre had divested Evan of her dress as well. She was on the lounger between them, the silver chain that hung between her breasts glinted in the light from the pool. And Andre was shirtless and on his knees, his back to Tessa and his dark head between Evan's thighs. Jace was lying alongside her, kissing her all over, worshipping every inch of bared skin like she was some goddess to pay homage to.

Tessa's body went tight all over, the erotic tableau almost too much to take in all at once. She'd never been particularly interested in watching porn. And most people from the outside looking in would probably label what was in front of her as such, but there was something unbearably gorgeous and right about the three of them together. You could feel the reverence among them. They were in love and unashamed and completely entranced with each other. The scene was dirty, but it was beautiful. And for the first time, Tessa realized those things didn't need to be mutually exclusive.

Kade kissed her shoulder. "Let's get in the pool, gorgeous. Your turn to make those pretty noises."

She let him take her hand and guide her to her feet. Colby peered up at them from the edge of the pool, his hazel eyes tracing over her body with open interest. She should've felt self-conscious or awkward considering her outfit and the circumstances, but somehow Kade's warm hand on her back and Colby's inherent relaxed state sent a sense of calm going through her. She was, of course, nervous about what would happen since she'd never done this before. It was like climbing up the roller coaster tracks, feeling unsure of what the rush down would feel like. But she was no longer freaked out by the idea of it all. This didn't have to be some big, life-changing incident. This was just her and two drop-dead gorgeous men having a fun night together.

Kade guided her down the pool steps until she was submerged to her waist, and then he passed her off to Colby so that he could slip out of his clothes. Colby's big hand closed around hers and he tugged her further into the pool. The warm water lapped at her exposed skin, making her body ache with awareness.

"Hey there, darlin'," he said, his voice as gentle as if he were talking to a skittish deer. "You sure about this?"

She appreciated the question and that he kept a bit of distance between them even though she was intensely aware that he was naked beneath the water. She gave a little nod. "Yes. Are you?"

He chuckled and slicked back his wavy, dark hair. "That saying about there are no stupid questions is a lie. If my best friend wants to share his beautiful submissive with me, I am more than happy to oblige you both."

She frowned. "Submissive?"

The conversation with Sam came back to her. Dominance. Submission. Sam and her training.

The water moved behind her as Kade slid into the water and wrapped his arms around her waist. His naked body pressed along her back, making her insides melt. "Just a term, Tess. The person in charge is the dominant, the one following the commands is the submissive."

She turned in his arms, the water rippling around her. "So you're a dominant?"

Something flickered in his blue eyes. Worry? Concern? "I am. So is Colby. Does that bother you?"

She rubbed her lips together, tasting chlorine and margarita salt, and considered the question. "No, I don't think so. I'm just not a hundred percent sure what that means for me."

He pushed her hair away from her face with wet fingers. "All it means for you right now is that we're going to take the lead. There's no pressure for you to decide what to do next. Just enjoy. And if something isn't working for you, you let us know."

She swallowed hard. Part of her thought she should take issue with this submissive role. Wasn't that what Doug had always tried to make her be—the polite, obedient wife who was there as an accessory to the man of the house? But she had a feeling that's not what submissive meant for Kade. Plus, she'd asked him from the beginning to take charge in bed, so she couldn't exactly blame him for continuing to do that. God knows, she didn't want the responsibility of making the moves tonight.

She took a deep breath and nodded. "Okay."

"Close your eyes, baby," he said, sliding a hand into her hair. "Let yourself go and savor this."

She let her lids fall shut and his lips touched hers—warm and unhurried, a kiss that bloomed slowly and sent a sensual elixir through her blood. Her hands curled around his hips as his tongue stroked hers, and her muscles softened one by one, her nerves melting into the warm water surrounding them.

But when calloused palms closed over her breasts from behind and a hot mouth sucked water droplets from her shoulder, she gasped into Kade's kiss. Kade didn't release her though. He kept his fingers wrapped in her hair, holding her in place, as Colby cupped her breasts and drew her nipples between his fingers. The sensation shot straight downward and she involuntarily rocked her hips against Kade. His erection brushed against the wet lace of her panties, making her clench with need, but he seemed in no rush to stop the slow and tortuous approach.

He pulled back from the kiss for a moment, looking down at her with hunger in his gaze. "Take off her bra, Colby. I don't want anything in the way."

Colby made a pleased grunt under his breath and unhooked her bra. She moved her arms out of it and the scrap of lace and wire floated away. Then Kade dipped his head beneath the water. Rough fingers tugged at her panties, pulling them down and off. Before surfacing, he moved his mouth between her legs and blew, sending bubbles tickling her in a maddening tease. She moaned and leaned back, landing against the wall of muscle that was Colby's chest.

Colby hooked his arms around her, tilting her back, and Kade's bumped against the underside of her thighs. He'd spread her legs and draped them over his shoulders. Her body began to lift. When Kade broke the surface of the water again, he looked like some sort of ancient water god rising from the depths—blond hair slick and dripping and eyes filled with blue flame as he stared down at her open thighs. She was almost completely reclined now and her hips were above the water, her sex exposed to the chilled night air.

But her skin didn't cool for long because Kade's palms cupped her ass and lifted her to his mouth. She let out a shameless groan at the contact. His tongue was unbelievably hot against her clit, the sharp contrast in temperature almost enough to send her over into orgasm. "Oh, God."

"That's it, darlin'," Colby said, all darkness and country swagger. "Watch him fuck you with his tongue. Slow and deep. I bet you taste so good. I can't wait to find out for myself." Colby dragged his tongue along the shell of her ear to punctuate his dirty words, and she thought she might spontaneously combust from the combination of the two men's mouths on her.

She looked down her body, and Kade's eyes met hers, an intense and unblinking connection as he traced his tongue along her folds and dipped it inside her. She lost herself for a moment in the eye contact. He didn't have to say a word. She could hear it all. *Don't look away. Watch me undo you, Tess. Watch me shatter everything you thought you knew about me and about yourself. Nothing will ever feel as good as I can make you feel.*

The thoughts terrified her, but she couldn't grab onto the fear when he was making her body throb and heat with every stroke of his tongue. Colby pinched her nipples again, and she had to close her eyes to try to stave off the climax rumbling to the surface. She wanted this to last, wanted to savor every second of it.

"Don't fight it," Colby said against her ear. "I can see it happening. Your pussy's getting so wet and pink beneath his mouth and your nipples are swelling between my fingers. You look so fucking sexy. Our cocks are both hard from watching you. Let yourself go over. Give in to the pleasure. We've got a lot more for you tonight."

At that very moment, Kade sucked her clit between his lips and ran his tongue around it. Light burst behind her eyes, and she cried out as the sensations took her over. The cool water. The hot tongue. The strong arms around her. It all coalesced and threaded in with her orgasm, turning the dial to eleven instantly. So. Much. Her arms splashed restlessly in the water, seeking something to hold on to, but there was nothing. Only the force of her orgasm and water droplets landing on her heated skin like icy rain. Every inch of her turned hyperaware and electric, the slightest touch amplified.

Kade didn't release her, his tongue and mouth fucking her like he wanted to drink her up and never stop. She couldn't push back, or pull away. Colby held her in place and kissed her neck with hot, openmouthed kisses. She tipped her head back, overwhelmed with it all. In her blurred peripheral vision, she could see Jace standing near the edge of the pool, his jeans open. Both Evan and Andre were at his feet, licking his cock. It was too much. Another wave of orgasm hit her like a bolt. She moaned long and loud and squeezed her eyes shut.

Finally, when her eyes had nearly rolled into the back of her head and she truly couldn't take any more, Kade pulled back and lowered her into the water. The change in temperature was a shock and she gasped, ready to hop back out, but her muscles were useless. She couldn't get her footing. Colby held onto her until Kade took her from his arms. Kade lifted her and cradled her against his chest. She closed her eyes and let her head rest against his shoulder, her body quivering with aftershocks and the growing need for something more than Kade's tongue.

In the background, she could hear another groan as Jace apparently was pushed past his own limit. God, she'd just come in front of a group of strangers and watched them do the same. What planet had she landed on?

"We're not done with you, but I think it's time to get you inside, baby," Kade said gently.

Colby moved into action and climbed out of the pool to grab three big towels. Kade carried her out of the pool and wrapped her in the thick terry cloth before knotting a towel around his waist. Soon, the three of them were heading inside and into a large, toasty bedroom. Kade set her down on the bed and stepped back. She let her gaze move over them, no longer worried about being too bold. Her body revved anew at the sight of the two gorgeous men standing there wet and mostly naked, waiting for her. Whatever planet this was, she wanted to stay.

"Warm enough?" Kade asked.

"Yes," she said, her voice small in the large room.

"Good." He leveled a gaze at her, and she saw the dominance flare in that look. "On your knees. Warm us up, too."

She blinked when they both pulled off their towels. The cold had softened their erections some, but the sight of them flaccid gave her this weird, forbidden thrill. Like she was seeing a more personal version of these two men. Plus, she had a feeling it was going to be fun bringing them back to life.

She slid off the bed and knelt in front of the both of them. Colby took himself in his hand and Kade laced his fingers in her hair, guiding her toward Colby. Her gaze skated upward to Kade for a split second and as if sensing what she was seeking, he nodded, giving her assurance that this was okay with him. She parted her lips and took Colby inside her mouth. This was only the third man she'd done this to in her life, and she was fascinated with the differences between each man. The same parts but all so very unique. Colby was thick even when not fully hard and tasted of musk and man, but as soon as she ran her tongue along his length for a few strokes, he swelled large against her palate. He let out a shuddering sigh. "That's right, darlin'. Fuck, your mouth is hot."

Kade kept his hands in her hair, moving her along Colby's growing erection, and she let her focus move to him. Kade was gazing down at her with an intensity that she felt down to her core. "You like doing this for me?" he asked, his voice as still and calm as she'd ever heard it. "Like being a little slut for me and sucking my friend's cock while I watch?"

She stiffened at the ugly word, but when he tightened his grip against her scalp and grabbed his erection to give himself a stroke, she realized he wasn't insulting her at all. He liked her like this. He wanted her dirty. Just like in her silly prince and captive fantasy, he was using her like a pleasure slave. The thought shouldn't have made her unbearably wet, but her body was forging its own path without her permission.

As if unable to wait any longer, Kade tugged her off of Colby and guided his cock into her mouth. She closed her eyes and made an involuntary *mmm* sound at the taste of him on her tongue. He tasted like salt and pool water and Kade. She swirled her tongue around him and reached out to stroke Colby at the same time, relishing the feel of Kade getting hard in her mouth while Colby heated in her palm.

Kade groaned and pulled back. "On the bed, gorgeous. I'm not feeling very patient all of a sudden."

She got to her feet and moved back to the bed, her body aching like she hadn't just had an orgasm a few minutes ago.

"You've got something to cuff her to the headboard?" Kade asked.

Tessa's stomach dipped.

Colby smirked. "Are you honestly asking me that?"

"You're right," Kade said, with a grin. "Get cuffs and condoms."

Tessa's nerves ping-ponged through her body as Colby wrapped leather cuffs around her wrists and secured her arms above her head. She was stretched out on the bed now, completely at their mercy. No escape. Theirs. She could've told them to stop, could've used her safe word. But she quickly realized it wasn't fear she was feeling, it was the pure adrenaline rush of anticipation.

The two men went to opposite sides of the bed and peered down at her like she was a feast spread out for their consumption. Kade brushed the back of his hand along her jaw. "Still with us, gorgeous?"

Her chest squeezed at the tender touch and the honest question in his eyes. If she told him to stop everything now, she knew without a doubt that he would, and that he wouldn't be annoyed or angry about it. He wouldn't try to convince her otherwise. That unlike most of the people she'd met in her life, his word meant something. That knowledge tugged at a place inside her where she didn't want to prod, and unplanned words tumbled out of her mouth. "I'm with *you*, Kade. Whatever's next, I trust you."

Surprise broke over his face, matching the shock she felt at her declaration. Trust? She was giving out *trust*? But the look Kade gave her when he realized what she'd said damn near split her open. She turned away, unable to take it. It was too close to the looks he'd given her long ago, too close to stirring real feelings in her. That's not what this was about. He was about to let his best friend fuck her. This was not some teenage romance. This was a kinky adventure with a guy who'd probably done all this before with countless women. This was sex and fun and experimenting.

This was not real.

And she couldn't let it be.

# EIGHTEEN

Colby caught Kade's gaze from the other side of the bed, a question plain on his face. *You still want me here?*

Colby had obviously sensed the shift in the room, the shift in Kade. Hearing that Tess trusted him had punched him right in the sternum. He'd told Colby tonight was just going to be about fulfilling a fantasy for an old friend because he hadn't wanted to get into all of the history. But his friend knew him well enough to know that tonight was different than the times they'd shared women before. Kade hadn't allowed himself to take real control tonight, to dominate Tessa. He'd treated her softer than any of the women he was typically with and Colby knew it.

And maybe he should want to kick Colby out. Kade would be lying to himself if he didn't admit that he felt something for Tess. That she was more than a girl he was having a good time with. Hearing her say she trusted him, when he knew she had very little of that commodity left to give, had made everything in him feel lighter, hopeful. But the feelings didn't change how he was wired. Sharing her with Colby, watching his friend give her pleasure, fed

Kade's dominance. Giving permission for another man to touch her was the ultimate feeling of ownership. *You are mine. Others can only touch you when and how I say so. Your pleasure is mine to give and control.*

And he was all too aware that Tessa was not his submissive. He didn't own her, hadn't even had the nerve to talk to her about the depth of what he really desired in a relationship. But for a little while, he wanted to experience how it could be with her.

He gave a quick nod to Colby and brushed his fingers along Tessa's collarbone, enjoying how she quivered beneath the simplest of touches. Then, as if connected by the same wavelength, he and Colby lowered down to the bed and each took one of her dusky nipples in their mouths. Tess arched beneath them at the contact, and Kade let his hand slide down between her legs. She moaned softly as his fingers found her center. She was so wet and hot already, so goddamned sexy. His cock throbbed, need pounding through him, but it was Colby who moved onto the bed first and rolled on a condom.

Tessa's eyes went a little wide as Colby bent her knees and spread her legs. Kade knew that Tessa had only been with her husband and him, so taking another lover was a big deal. But he didn't sense any fear, just heightened awareness and curiosity. She kept glancing at Kade, and it pleased him that she was concerned about what he thought, like she was afraid to show real desire toward Colby.

But he wanted her to relish in that desire, roll around and drown in it. He'd picked his friend for a number of reasons. One, Kade trusted the guy like a brother. Two, Colby was one of the best dominants at The Ranch, so the man knew what he was doing. But also, Kade remembered Tessa's high school crushes on those good ol' boy country singers. Back then, he'd been annoyed as hell over it because those dudes had represented everything he wasn't. But he didn't feel that need to compete anymore. He saw how she looked at him, the deep attraction there. But he also knew old fantasies didn't often go away. And he wanted to give her that experience.

"You ready for him, gorgeous?" Kade asked as he continued to stroke her clit. "He's a big bastard, so you're going to need to relax to let him in."

Colby joined in and dipped his fingers inside her, his knuckles nudging Kade's fingers as he stroked her inside. Tessa let out a whimper, her eyes going hazy already. Nice.

"She feels ready. God, the way she's squeezing around my fingers. I can't wait to have you doing that around my cock, darlin'."

Her belly dipped and her pussy twitched beneath Kade's fingers. He smiled. His girl loved the filthy talk even if she'd never admit it.

"And I promise your boy, Kade, can't wait to watch," Colby added in that low voice Kade knew brought women to their knees.

Her gaze drifted to Kade's as if she wasn't quite sure she believed Colby's assertion. "He's right. Open for him, sweetheart, let me watch you take him inside you. Tell me you want this."

"I want this," she whispered, spreading her knees further but not looking away from Kade. Her features were softening as she watched him, her pupils big, and the sight went straight downward, making his balls draw tight. She was on the edge of subspace without him having to spank her or deliver any kind of pain. She was going there because she trusted him, and some natural response was kicking in. It was the sexiest thing he'd ever seen.

"Fuck her, Colby," he said, his voice calm but his heart pounding. "She's ready now."

Kade turned his head in time to see Colby grab the base of his cock and guide it against Tessa's entrance. She was so slick and pink, and watching the crown of Colby's dick open her and then push inside was almost too erotic of a sight to bear. Most guys would probably want to kill another guy for fucking his girl, but Kade couldn't help his body's reaction when Tessa let out a breathy moan. He was giving his woman pleasure through Colby. On the surface it was a kind of physical pleasure he could easily provide her on his own without any help, but that would ignore the mindfuck part of this. Tessa wasn't moaning simply because of the sex. She was losing herself in it because of the role it put her in. This objectified her. She was his possession to be passed around if he so chose. She was not that proper lady to be kept safe in her big house on the hill. She was no longer the preacher's wife.

She needed to be sullied. She craved it.

And Kade wasn't afraid to give her just that. Colby buried to the hilt with a rumbling groan, and Kade continued to stroke her clit, her arousal coating his fingers and her scent drifting up to him. God, she was perfect. He reached down and gave his own aching balls a squeeze, need growing heavy in his gut, as Colby picked up the pace and begin to fuck her harder.

"You look so gorgeous, baby. Open your mouth." She kept her eyes closed but her lips parted, and Kade tucked his arousal-slickened fingers into her mouth. "Taste how sweet you are."

She wrapped her lips around his fingers and her hot tongue laved her juices from his skin. *Christ.* It was like a match being struck against his fuse. Unable to wait any longer to feel her, he moved to the top of the bed and straddled her. Her lids lifted to find his cock fisted in his hand and poised above her.

"Lick me," he commanded.

Since she was bound, all she could access was what he gave her and right now he lowered himself until only his balls were in her reach. Without hesitation, she opened her mouth and wrapped her soft, wet mouth around one, gently laving her tongue against the sensitive skin. He braced one hand on the headboard above her and groaned.

"That's it, baby. That feels amazing." His free hand stroked up his length as she ran her tongue along the seam of his sac and teased further back along his perineum. Dirty girl. He loved that she was so bold when she got turned on. All her inhibitions fell away. And she clearly had a fascination with the forbidden zones. He'd put that on his list of things to explore with her. But right now, he needed all of her around him.

He grabbed a pillow and tucked it under her head, tilting her at the right angle then pushed the tip of his cock against her lips. She accepted him with a hungry suck, her motions in time with Colby's thrusts. Fuck, she felt like heaven around him, and he had to breathe deep to keep from going off right then. No way was he coming before he had a chance to be deep inside her. But that didn't mean he was going to stand by and twiddle his thumbs while he waited. He liked pushing himself to his edge and holding there, his own version of sweet torture. So he braced his hands on the headboard and pumped into her mouth, no longer concerned about being soft or gentle with her. She was way past the point of shame and had no problem handling the roughness.

"That's right, baby. Take it all. You're so fucking beautiful." All the words falling from his mouth stopped making sense but he let them flow without editing. Her answering moans and whimpers vibrated against his cock and her fists curled in her restraints. "You want to come, Tess?"

The desperate noise she made was definitely an affirmative. And Colby apparently heard the same thing because the bed began to squeak with the force of their fucking. Tessa's back arched and the restraints went taut. Kade pulled back and rolled away from her, letting her grab a breath as her orgasm rumbled through her. She was a sight to behold in climax—skin flushed, eyes closed, nipples dark and pebbled. He coasted his hands over her breasts, her belly, feeling her shake with the force of her release.

Colby was past the point of control as well and soon his groan joined Tessa's gasping sounds as he came. Colby eased back before Tessa had quieted, and she made a sound of protest. "Don't worry, darlin'. We're not going to leave you wanting for long."

Kade had a condom on in record time and was lifting her up and over as if she weighed nothing. The restraints moved with her, crossing her wrists above her head as she flopped onto her stomach. He grabbed her hips and raised her up on her knees then plunged inside without giving her warning. She let out a sharp cry, and he knew this position was letting him get deeper than Colby could have.

"Jesus, you feel good," he said, his voice strained. Her pussy was still contracting from her orgasm, and he thought his head might explode from the self-control it took not to let go, but he wanted to bask in this. Plus, he knew she had more than that one orgasm to give him. "Ready to come for me again?"

"Kade," she panted, "I can't. It's too much . . ."

"You can and you will," he commanded as he pumped into her with long, steady strokes. She was nowhere near done. Her muscles were coiled and her body was slick with sweat. Whether she realized it or not, her whole demeanor said she was bracing for an even bigger orgasm. All she needed was a little added inspiration to push her over.

Kade knew what could send her there but he took his time, moving inside her and teasing her clit with his fingers until she started to beg. Oh, how he loved the begging. Her desperate pleas filled his ears like sweet music and he smiled. Now it was time. Colby had taken care of his condom and come back into the room. Kade mouthed a word to him and Colby dug what Kade needed out of a drawer.

Kade gave the go ahead and Colby flipped the bottle open and drizzled the lube along the seam of Tessa's ass. She jolted in Kade's hold, the cold liquid delivering a shock, but he didn't give her time to contemplate what was about to happen. He ran his finger along her back opening, slicking the tight pucker with lubricant.

*"Oh, God,"* she ground out, but it sounded more like *please yes* than *please don't.*

He pushed his finger against her opening and slid inside. She let out a cry, and her pussy clamped down on him with a grip that he felt down to the soles of his feet.

"That's it, Tess. Feel me everywhere inside you. All of it's mine right now. Nothing is off limits from me."

She made unintelligible sounds in response, the added stimulation pushing her higher and higher. She was all his in this moment. The power of that washed through him and shoved him to his own edge.

"Come for me," he said through gritted teeth as he fucked her ass with his finger in time with the rocking of his hips.

She fell apart beneath him, a crazed, animalistic sound escaping her as her orgasm crashed down on her. With that, he lost all semblance of his own control. Everything in him went tight and hot, his balls drawing up and his cock swelling with release. He thrust into her like an inhuman thing, every ounce of his energy pouring into those last few thrusts as he spilled inside her.

Bliss. Perfection. He rode the high with her. Soaring.

When he'd sapped every bit he had to give and she'd sunk into the bed beneath him, he reluctantly slid out of her and rolled onto his back, fighting to draw breath. Colby tugged on a pair of shorts then quietly undid her restraints and set towels on the side of the bed. He leaned down and kissed Tessa's cheek. "That was amazing, Tessa. Thanks for letting me join y'all tonight. Kade's a lucky guy."

The sentiment hit Kade right in the gut. *She's not mine.* The words were like rusty nails puncturing the bubble of bliss from a few moments before.

Tessa turned onto her back with a sleepy, satisfied smile. "Thanks, Colby, that was fun."

*Fun.*

That's what this was to her. She wanted sexual adventure, and Kade was giving it to her. He needed to get that through his head.

But when Colby left the room and she curled into Kade's arms to fall asleep, he knew he was never going to be satisfied with just that.

Tessa McAllen was meant to be his.

He knew it back when he was seventeen and he knew it now.

But how he felt didn't matter when she was too scared to even be seen with him in public.

He sagged against the pillows, holding her close, and wished, not for the first time, that her prince and captive fantasy could be true. Because right now, all he wanted to do was tie her up, throw her over his shoulder, and keep her.

# NINETEEN

"How's she doing?" Kade asked, setting down the report he'd been looking at when his brother had strolled in and parked in the chair across from his desk. He'd called him in here earlier to get the report on how Tessa's job training was going, but Gib had been tied up with another meeting.

Gibson hooked his ankle over his knee and leaned back, looking like a Kennedy descendant instead of a guy who'd grown up being called trailer trash. "Quick study. Motivated. Still a little insecure soliciting the donations but getting better. When James Alario went all cross-examination on her early on, asking her the financial stats of her organization and business plans and shit, she knew a lot but not enough for Alario, apparently. He didn't donate. Busted her confidence and I thought she was going to throw in the towel, but later that day I saw her with the P&Ls for the charity. I asked if she wanted me to send Marcy in from accounting to help her decipher them, but she said she wanted to try to figure it out herself first."

Kade nodded. "She's taking business classes two nights a week.

And numbers always came easier to her from what I remember, so I'm not surprised. How is the fundraiser looking?"

"She secured Third Sky for the musical headliner, so that's been a huge help because they're a hot ticket right now. Apparently, Billy, the guitarist, grew up in foster care here, too, and Tessa knew him from back then. She called in a personal favor."

"Impressive."

"Yeah, like I said, she's motivated. And she hasn't lost that Ms. Popularity thing she had in high school. She's easy for people to like. So with that and the band's name to throw around, she's landed a few good donations over the last few weeks and has sold some booth spots. It's a solid start. Though, I'm not sure it really matters."

Kade lifted a brow. "What do you mean?"

"Come on. You may be fooling her, but you're not fooling me. I know you'll give her whatever money she needs if she comes up short. You can fix her charity with one quick check."

"She doesn't know I'm willing to do that, though. And doesn't *need* to know. I want her to see that she's capable of doing it on her own."

"She's working her ass off and pulling in any connections she can manage, so I can't fault her on effort." Gib did that little shrug like it hurt him to give her credit.

Kade rested his forearms on the desk, not liking Gib's tone. "You faulting her for something else then, little brother?"

"Only for what's going on between you two," he said bluntly.

"That shouldn't concern you."

"Come on, you're seeing her every night, man."

"And that matters, why?"

He made a face like the answer should be obvious. "Because you're sneaking around like teenagers and letting her do the same damn thing she did to you back then. Taking what she needs from a relationship with you without anyone else having to know. She's dragging you into the pit again."

Kade gave Gib a bemused smile, imagining some she-devil cartoon version of Tessa, digging talons into him and forcing him to have sex with her in her secret lair. "Come on, Gib. Dragging me into the pit? It's not like I'm not getting something out of this deal. Last I checked, *she's* submitting to *me*."

"And *you're* getting attached to *her*," he countered.

Kade's jaw tightened. "Weren't you the one who wanted me to *woo* her?"

Gib leaned back in his chair with a groan. "Into a public relationship that could help you with the case. Not some clandestine affair that's only going to get you burned when she goes AWOL again. Can't you see this is just fun and fantasy for her? A way to soothe her tattered ego after getting cheated on by her ex. If this were something real for her, she wouldn't care who knew."

Kade frowned, Gibson only underlining the things Kade was already worried about. "I'm working on trying to get her to go public, but can't rush her or it will blow up. I have to work her up to it. She was raked over the fire by the press back in Atlanta, so her concerns are valid. No one would want to be portrayed as a gold digger. And you know that angle would pop up. I'm sure Doug Barrett would be more than happy to provide some choice sound bites as well. Plus, with my past, rumors about is she/isn't she into kink would surface. It's a lot of scrutiny to invite for something she sees as a casual hookup."

"But none of that's going to kill her," Gib said, frustration edging his words. "She'll survive the gossip, and I can do spin control with my contacts, have them write stories focusing on her charity work and how you two knew each other from high school. You need to stop worrying about her feelings and focus on the custody case. Reid told you straight up that a stable relationship would improve your image with the court tenfold, especially one with a woman who has never been tied to the scene."

"I'm aware of that," Kade replied tersely. "But it's not your place to decide how I handle it."

"Yeah, well, I'm the one who lost my brother when she fucked you over last time. And I'm also the one who dealt with you after the divorce and when you lost custody originally. I'm not in the mood to watch your self-destruct mode again. The company can't afford that and neither can I."

Kade pushed back from his desk and rose to walk toward the window. He put his back to his brother as he stared out at the buildings and afternoon sky. When he'd first lost custody of Rosalie, he'd been more angry and depressed than he'd ever been in his adult life. He'd reverted back to Kaden Fowler mode, becoming a version of that beat-down teenager filled with angst and rage at the world. All that grief had piled in with old trauma, forming one big, black mess inside his head. He'd drunk too much, plowed through women, and had shirked his responsibilities at work. And he wouldn't let anyone near him to help pull him out of it. He'd almost alienated the very family he'd been so happy to find only a few years earlier and damaged the company he'd worked so hard to start.

Only Gibson had been able to get past all the daggers Kade had been throwing at everyone. He and Colby had come to Kade's house and had taken him by threat of force for a weeklong brocation on the coast. No alcohol or women allowed. They'd cleaned him up, gotten his head clear, and had basically vowed to kick his ass if he didn't get his shit together. But the thing that had put it over the top was Gibson telling Kade that he was on the way to becoming a worthless alcoholic like his stepdad. That had put the fear of God in him. He'd known he hadn't gotten to that point yet. He could still put down the bottle, but he'd sensed the black hole wasn't far in the distance.

Since that trip, he'd done a one-eighty and had put his energy into the business and into getting another custody hearing. He had Gib to thank for it, so he didn't want to jump on his brother's case. But Kade didn't relish the idea of putting Tessa in a position that would cause her drama. It wasn't her problem to fix.

But he also couldn't deny that the desire to do anything and everything to get Rosalie back kept him awake at night.

He sighed and leaned his head against the glass. "It's going to take more than a little cajoling to get Tessa confident enough to step into the spotlight with me. Especially when there's no real benefit to her doing so."

"Tell her about Rosalie then. Maybe she'll understand why it's so important."

"No way. I'm not guilting her into it with some sob story about my kid. Plus, that's asking for months of commitment, which will freak her the fuck out. I still have to work to get her to agree to another night each time I see her. I need her to decide to be with me because she wants to try a relationship and doesn't want to hide."

"You need her to trust you."

Kade frowned and turned to face his brother again. "I need more than that. Trust isn't enough."

Gib leaned back in his chair and ran a hand over his jaw. "Well, you're a pro at getting girls to fall for you. They don't call you the Time Share Bachelor for nothing. You've even got the psycho ex-girlfriends to prove it. I'm assuming you heard the latest on the fire?"

"Yes," he said with a groan. The cops had informed him that Rebecca, the same ex-girlfriend who'd given a statement to his ex-wife's lawyer about his kinky side, was now being investigated for the fire at Barcelona. Brilliant.

"So clearly you can stir up passion in a woman. Dial up your game with Tessa, bro. Jet her off to Rome for the weekend or something. Make her feel like a princess."

He scowled. "You make it sound like I have some playbook of how to make a girl love me. This isn't a game. I feel like this could become something real, Gib. But I don't want to fuck it up by rushing things and scaring her off. She needs reassurance that this is just a fun fling, that I'm just happy to show her some fantasies."

"And you're lying about it being only that," Gibson said quietly.

He turned and faced his brother, the truth like bags of gravel weighing down his shoulders. "Through my teeth. Fulfilling some dirty fantasies with Tessa is no hardship, believe me. But I want the real thing, have for a long time, and everything in me thinks she could be it. There's always been something intense between us, even if we didn't know how to label it."

Gibson eyed him, unconvinced. "But is she really submissive or is she just experimenting with roles? What you want isn't simply a little kink. It's full surrender. The pool of people open to that kind of thing is small already."

Kade tucked his hands in his pockets and leaned against the window. "My gut says she could be capable of it. But she's working so hard to be one hundred percent independent, trying to prove to herself that she can do it all on her own, that I think she'd flip if she knew the depth of what I want in a relationship. She doesn't even like me paying for dinner. I understand it, but it's driving me crazy."

"She realizes that she was bought by Doug. Can't blame her for not wanting to fall into that again."

He rubbed the back of his head. "I know. I get it. But I don't know how much longer I'm going to be able to keep myself in check. The more we're together, the more my instinct to take over completely gnaws at me."

"So take over," Gib said, as if it were the simplest decision in the world. "You're a dom and a sadist. That's not going to change. Colby said y'all got together the other night and that you were so gentle with Tessa, he didn't even recognize you."

"Colby should keep his mouth shut."

"Come on, he didn't give me details or anything. He's just

concerned like I am. He can tell things are getting heavy with this girl, and it's going to lead nowhere good if you don't show her who she's really dealing with. If she's truly submissive and open to your brand of dominance, she'll respond if you dial things up. If she's not, then at least you know before you get in too deep and get your guts handed to you."

In too deep. As if he weren't in it up to his eyeballs already.

"It's not that easy." The fact that he'd been playing the dominance aspect low key with Tessa had been a source of frustration for a while now. She'd been distant the next morning after the threesome, as if she couldn't quite process what had happened, and had needed a few days before she was ready to see him again. So since then, every time he considered amping up the intensity, he'd backed off at the last minute, fearing that he'd scare her off. But he'd promised himself after his divorce that he would always be up front about the extent of his kinks with anyone he considered getting serious with—take it or leave it. And here he was breaking his number one rule by constantly diluting it for Tessa.

"Look, man, I get that she's special to you, and you don't want to mess it up again. But holding back and playing some half-assed version of yourself *will* screw it up, guaranteed. In high school you held back with her, played the game how she wanted you to play it. Don't be that kid again. That kid got his ass kicked and lost the girl anyway."

Kade looked over at his brother, the truth in the words slicing right through him. Gib was right. The moment Tess had stepped back into his life, his normal confidence had been shaken. Something about her always channeled that stuttering kid who wanted to jump through every hoop to be near her. And here he was doing it again. Plus, he *was* getting attached and developing that wicked bastard of an emotion called hope. The deeper he got, the more it'd suck when it blew up in his face.

"You're right."

"Of course I am."

Kade raked his hand through his hair. "Maybe it's time for a trip to The Ranch."

Gibson nodded. "That will at least give your girl a real glimpse of what it could be like with you. And if you see she's not into it, you can save yourself the trouble and end it now. Then I'll set you up with a nice faux girlfriend for the press. I already have someone in mind."

Kade's lip curled. "Does she charge by the hour or day?"

Gibson gave him an offended look. "Hey, I wouldn't do that to you. The high-end ones have weekly rates."

Kade resisted rolling his eyes and sat in his chair again, his mind already drifting to The Ranch. Imagining Tessa in that environment, under his command, wearing his collar in front of his friends, being his—all of it had his blood heating. It'd be a risk to put her in that kind of environment this soon. But she'd enjoyed the boundaries he'd pushed so far, and even if it had shaken her foundation, she had still come back to him. And he was beginning to wonder if there really was any true way to ease someone into the kind of relationship dynamic he needed.

"I guess it's time to lay it all out there," he said, looking up at his brother.

Gibson smiled. "So it is."

Kade drummed his fingers on the desktop. "You're thinking she's going to run scared."

Gibson stood. "Doesn't matter what I think. But I will say that, for your sake, I hope she proves me wrong."

Kade started to reply, but Gibson was already slipping out the door. He waited until the lock clicked shut and pulled out his cell phone to find a number. He hit the name he was looking for.

The call was answered on the second ring. "Hey there, Vandergriff. Another call? Tell the truth. Are you hitting on me? Because I know you have a thing for the Austins."

He smirked. "You're never going to let me live that down, are you, Jace? For the last time, I didn't know she was married or that she was your sister."

And boy had he felt like an ass when he'd made a pass at Jace's married sister.

Jace laughed. "Sure, whatever, home wrecker. What can I do for ya?"

"I'm going to need another order. And maybe a little help setting up something at The Ranch."

"Is this for your lovely girl from the other night? Thanks for inviting us along by the way. The three of us don't bring things out in the open very much except for an occasional weekend at The Ranch, so it was fun to push our own limits some."

"No problem. I'm glad you had a good time." Kade tilted back in his chair, rubbing the back of his head. "And yes, this is for her."

"Yeah, dude, sure, whatever you need. And I know Wyatt and Kelsey are going to be out there this weekend, if you need any extra help putting something together. Kelsey's good at organizing stuff."

He smiled. "Always good to have a load of kinky friends one can call upon."

"You know it," Jace said with a chuckle.

He and Jace made quick plans and exchanged good-byes. After hanging up the phone, Kade ran his palms along the arms of his chair, the gears in his mind starting to turn. It was time to put it all out there, show Tess who he really was.

He just had to hope that by the end of all this, she wasn't running for the nearest exit. Because the last time he'd taken a chance and revealed what he really wanted to Tessa, it had demolished everything.

# TWENTY

*1996*

"I'm starting to think this magazine just rewords everything each month and prints the same stories," Tessa said with a huff. She was flopped across her bed in gym shorts and a tank top, flipping through some chick magazine and chewing her thumbnail.

Meanwhile, Kaden was sitting on Tess's pink beanbag chair on the floor, contemplating if he'd lost his mind. He wondered would someone who had actually lost his mind even be able to contemplate that? But surely something had to be wrong in the universe because he was in Tessa McAllen's bedroom alone at ten at night and there was no tutoring going on. "You should read *Rolling Stone* instead."

"Maybe." She glanced over at the darkened window then over to him. "I'm sorry about this, by the way. Now I feel like a dork for calling you. But I really did think I heard something outside."

"It's not a b-b-big deal," he said, trying to sound casual but the stutter giving him away as usual. "I was heading out when you called anyway."

"Yeah?" she said, her tone hopeful. "Where to?"

He shrugged. "Just out. My mom's working overnight shifts all weekend, and my stepdad really goes full throttle when she's away. I'm sure he's halfway through the vodka supply by now, and I'd rather not be in his path. Even Gib is staying at a friend's house."

She frowned. "That sucks. Doesn't your mom realize how he is?"

He sighed and looked up at her ceiling, which had posters of country singers and bands he'd never be caught dead listening to taped to it. "I don't think she knows how bad it gets. He puts on a decent show for her, but she's got her own issues. When she's not working, she's mostly in bed, zoned out on her pills for her back. I think she's too depressed to bother doing anything about him."

"My real mom was into pills, too," she said quietly, drawing his attention from the ceiling back to her. She never talked about her birthparents, at least not to him. "She had mental problems or whatever and was supposed to take medication. But it made her feel crappy. Or, at least that's what she said. She started doing the nonprescription stuff instead and kind of forgot she had a kid to take care of."

He frowned, not knowing what to say to that. *That sucks* didn't seem like the right response. "What happened after that?"

She looked down at the magazine and started flipping pages again, but he could tell she wasn't seeing them. "One day she just didn't come home. I slept in the closet with my Glo Worm toy because I was scared when it got dark. The neighborhood wasn't great so there were lots of noises at night. I lasted two weeks at home alone until I had to go to a neighbor and ask if they had anything to eat. I'd run out of Captain Crunch and stuff to make cheese sandwiches. They called child services."

"Jesus." Kaden sat up, his heart dropping to his stomach. "How old were you?"

"Six." She closed the magazine and tossed it onto the floor. "That was the last time I ever stayed home alone."

God, no wonder she'd called him in a panic earlier tonight, begging him to come over and check the house when she'd heard something outside. Being alone like this probably terrified her. "When are you foster p-p-parents getting back into town?"

She was chewing her nails again and had to lower her hand to respond. "Not 'til Monday. Apparently, they decided I was trustworthy enough to stay on my own while they went to some work conference."

"And now you have a guy in your room," he said, trying to lighten the mood. "Breaking rules already."

She gave him a little smile. "Not *technically*. They said it was okay for you to come over if we needed to study. I doubt they meant at night, but whatever."

"What about Doug?"

She sniffed and the drawn look she'd been wearing lifted a bit. "Of course *he* can't come over. I mean, they think he's a nice guy and all, but they know we're dating. So you know, high risk of shenanigans or whatever. Can you believe they actually use words like *shenanigans*?"

Doug was high risk. Kaden was no risk. Even her parents saw him that way. How frigging comforting. "Words like that were created to fuck with p-p-people who stutter."

She grinned. "Right? I can barely say it. Stupid word."

Her retort settled some of the tension strumming through the room. Over the last few months, they'd gotten to the point where they could joke about sensitive things without it being a big deal. It was nice to have that ease between them. "So are you going to break that rule—about Doug?"

She sat her chin on her hand. "No. I've learned not to break rules. It's not worth it."

The concept was so foreign to Kaden, he could barely put together a response. "Seriously?"

She laughed at what must have been his stricken expression.

"If you break the rules, your parents get pissed off. I break the rules, the parents can give me back. What I have here is way better than what I've had in the past, so I'm not going to screw it up."

"Damn, that kind of sucks."

She gave a little shoulder scrunch as if it was no big thing. "It's not that bad. I kind of like knowing what's expected of me. If I obey curfew, go to church on Sundays, and help around the house, they're happy. That's way better than trying to figure out what the hell someone wants from you. The last place I was at, the rules were on like some sliding scale with each kid getting different versions. Half the time I got in trouble, I didn't know what the heck I'd done wrong."

"Yeah, that's kind of how my house is. My stepdad changes rules all the time, and it's always the opposite of whatever I'm doing. I've given up trying and just stay out of his way as much as possible."

"Thank God you have only a few months before you go to college."

He wanted to say the same back to her, but he refused to acknowledge that her following Doug to Georgia after they graduated was a good plan.

She sat up and he tried—not very successfully—to ignore how thin her tank top was. "So, now that we've established that parents suck, and I've completely embarrassed myself by dragging you out here for no reason, I should probably let you get back to whatever it was you were going to do tonight."

Her tone was bright but he didn't buy her bullshit. The fact that she kept glancing out the window told him everything he needed to know. "Well, I did have b-b-big plans to skateboard in the parking lot of the Ace Hardware tonight, but I could be persuaded to hang around a while if you agree to give me control over the r-r-remote."

A smile crept onto her face. "Really?"

"And I expect popcorn."

She laughed. "Done."

"Then we have a deal." He pushed up from the floor and she scooted off the bed.

Before he could take a step forward, she wrapped her arms around him and hugged him. The feel of her body against his was like an electric current plugging into his grid, lighting up all parts of him. He returned the embrace, wishing he could freeze the moment, bottle the scent of her.

"Thanks, Kaden," she said against his chest. "I know this is probably the last way you wanted to spend a Friday night."

He pulled back from the hug and looked down at her. God, how many times had he ached to be this close to her? Before he could let the nerves interfere, he pushed her hair behind her ears and let his hands linger on her shoulders. "Then you don't know me very well because there's no place I'd rather b-b-be."

She stiffened briefly, like she always did when he crossed that invisible line. After their initial kiss that day in the cabin, he'd managed to keep things distant for a while. But as the months went on and they opened up about their lives to each other, the barriers had fallen down and more and more they were slipping up and touching each other with a familiarity that should be reserved for a couple. But he'd never taken it quite this far or admitted anything out loud.

"Kaden . . ." Her voice was barely audible in the quiet room.

"Why did you call me tonight instead of Doug? I know it's not just because of the rule thing."

Her gaze slid away. "You live closer, and he's at a guys-only thing tonight."

"Bullshit. That's not why."

She rolled her lips inward but still wouldn't look at him. "Don't make me say it."

He sensed in that moment that it was now or never. He'd never get a better opportunity to make a stand and tell her exactly how he felt. "You called me because you knew you could trust me to t-t-take care of you. You called me because you'd rather spend time with m-me than him."

She shook her head, but he could see she was blinking fast, fighting tears. "That's not true."

"Then look at me and tell me that. Look at me and tell me you don't feel anything but friendship toward me. Tell me you l-l-love Doug, that it's not about the money or his fancy family. That even if I had what he had, you'd choose him anyway."

She lifted her gaze to him, a forlorn look in her eyes. "I love Doug and I'd choose him anyway."

But he saw the truth there on her face as plain as it'd ever been. She was lying and it was killing her. He slid his hands up from her shoulders and cupped her face in the way he'd imagined so many times since that first kiss. "Then if that's the case, t-t-tell me to stop."

He gave her a beat of a moment then lowered his mouth to hers. She didn't turn away, she didn't stiffen, and she didn't say stop. Instead, she whimpered into the connection and stepped closer to him, grabbing his waist. When he tried to deepen the kiss, her lips parted as if they'd been waiting for this moment as long as he had. His tongue touched hers and everything inside him went white hot and urgent. His fingers slid into her hair, and he kissed her like this would be the last girl he'd ever kiss in his life.

A soft moan slipped from her and it went straight to his groin. But he wasn't going to worry about his body's obvious reaction to her or be embarrassed. He wanted her to know what she did to him, how badly he wanted to touch her. He breathed her name into the kiss, and her hands slipped beneath the edge of his T-shirt, the soft touch of her fingers against his bare skin making his stomach clench in anticipation.

Without realizing it, they drifted the few steps toward the bed, hands and lips exploring each other with a kind of stunned wonder. Her touch grew more bold, her fingers tracking along his back beneath his shirt. She moved the fabric upward, as if trying to push it over his head. A brief moment of panic went through him. He didn't go without his shirt even to swim. His pudgy years had scared him off of that. But when she made another breathy sound, he shoved the anxiety aside and pulled back from the kiss to tug his T-shirt up and off. If she wanted to touch him skin to skin, he'd be a fucking idiot not to let her.

She sat down on the bed and looked at him, really looked at him. And what he saw there soothed any remaining self-consciousness. If she cared that he didn't have a six-pack, she sure didn't show it. And, God, what a sight she was—wet lips and flushed cheeks. He was going to die if she told him to stop now. But even though he was afraid talking would break the moment, he also needed to be sure. "Tell me you want me to keep kissing you, Tess."

He braced for her to run like last time, but she held out her hand to him, inviting him onto the bed. "I want you to keep kissing me."

*Thank you, God*. He'd take that earlier threat of atheism back.

He climbed onto the bed and laid her against the pillows, then lowered in for another kiss. This time she wrapped her arms around his neck and they rolled to their sides. Everything inside Kade was flying. Nothing could be or ever would be better than this. Somehow he knew that. This was it for him. The way she smelled, the softness of her. And Lord, her taste—toothpaste and girl and lip gloss that had faded. He'd never forget it.

To his relief, she seemed just as eager for him. Each stroke of their tongues built his confidence and made him bolder. Following her lead from earlier, he let his fingers move beneath the bottom edge of her tank top, the smooth skin of her hip and belly like hallowed ground beneath his fingertips. He kept his touch easy, unsure of how far she wanted this to go. He wasn't exactly experienced in determining the signs. He'd barely made it to second base with anyone before and none of his meager experience had been like this.

Tessa broke from the kiss with a gasp, her eyes searching his. "What are we doing?"

"Whatever we want," he said, pushing her hair back from her face and praying she wasn't going to shut down on him. "What d-d-do you want, Tess?"

She stared at him for a long moment, then shifted position. He thought she was going to climb off the bed, but instead she reached for the hem of her tank top and pulled it over her head, revealing a purple cotton bra and an eyeful of flesh. Kaden's brain nearly melted right out of his ears, and all his blood rushed straight south. "You don't h-h-have t-t-to, there's no p-p-pressure . . ."

Fuck, he couldn't speak on a normal day, but this might short out his system for good.

She met his gaze and reached to the spot holding the two bra cups together. With a flick of her fingers, she unhooked it and let it fall open. "I'm not doing this because I feel pressured."

Yeah, he had no shot at speaking now, so he wasn't going to even try. Plus, he had to put all his energy into *not coming right this very second*.

"I don't know what I'm doing, and I'm not ready to become horror movie bait yet. But I also know I don't want to stop yet."

The words nearly caused wings to sprout from his back he was so damn happy. "C-c-come here. I d-d-don't know what I'm d-d-doing either."

But he was damn sure going to figure out how to make her feel good.

She moved back into his arms and the press of her bare breasts against his chest nearly undid any hope at controlling his body.

But he breathed through it and focused on her eyes. There was so much there—want, curiosity, fear, and a little sadness. He knew why that last one was there. He wasn't under the impression this would change anything long-term. He still didn't have what Doug had to offer her. But maybe, just maybe, he could show her that he had more and better.

He slipped his hand behind her thigh and drew her leg over his, letting her feel how much he wanted her. Her eyes went a little wide, but he kissed her before she could think too much. As soon as their mouths melded again, the tension drained from her body and she sank into his touch. Seconds turned into minutes as they kissed and explored with hands and mouths. When he put his lips over one of her nipples and sucked, the sound she made reverberated through him like a siren call. God, yes. That. Whatever that was, he wanted to give her more of it. Encouraged by her reaction, he let his hand drift to the band of her shorts.

He stayed there a moment, stroking her belly and kissing her breasts, but when she whimpered beneath him, he gathered the guts to move his hand lower. When his fingertips grazed hair, he looked up at her. "Is this okay?"

She bit her lip and nodded.

After a deep breath to calm himself, he let his hand slide downward, feeling her most private of parts. Heat touched his fingers, then wetness. He groaned, the silky feel of her almost too much to process. He stroked along the outside of her folds, listening to the noises she made to guide him. She was so soft and delicate there. He wanted to taste her. But he knew that'd probably be too big of a step for them both.

Instead, he moved his hand lower, finding her opening, and carefully inserted the tip of his finger. He wasn't sure if he could hurt her by doing this, but she made a soft sound—pure pleasure. He groaned and his dick pushed against his zipper. God, he'd never imagined that a girl would feel this hot. He could only imagine what that wet heat would feel like around him. With gentle movements, he moved his fingers back along the folds of her skin, stroking her in a way that he hoped to hell felt good.

She tilted her hips upward. "Oh, right there . . ."

The hard little nub beneath his fingertips swelled against his touch. He'd read enough dirty books and seen enough internet porn to know this was a good spot, the clitoris. He circled it again, and Tessa grabbed his hair. Man, he could do this all day to see her react like this. He lowered his mouth back to her breast and kept his fingers moving.

Her grip tightened against his scalp and she lifted her hips in a little rhythm until she was doing most of the work, rubbing against him like she needed. He figured out quickly that he better not change anything up. He sensed she was building to something and didn't want to ruin it.

"Oh, God, I think I'm going to—" But she didn't finish the thought. Instead, she made the sexiest damn sound he'd ever heard in his life. It was nothing like what was in the movies. No screeching sounds—just these soft, gasping breaths and a moan that made her body shake.

It was more than he could take. With his free hand, he reached for his dick, hoping to do something to hold back the inevitable. But as soon as he wrapped his hand around it, he exploded.

"Fuck," he ground out, rolling back on the bed and letting what he couldn't stop overtake him. He let out a strained groan, and the orgasm happened before he could even unbutton his fly—ruining his cargo shorts and his pride.

Fuck. Me. *Way to go, Fowler.*

Half an hour later, he walked back into Tessa's room with wet hair and pajama pants that were too short for him. He hadn't quite found his pride yet. It was probably still in shreds somewhere on the side of the bed. She peered up from the same magazine she'd been flipping through earlier that night. She gave him a shy smile. "So, hey."

"Your foster dad is too short."

She glanced at the pants. "Maybe you're just too tall."

He sighed and sat on the edge of the bed, embarrassment burning a path to his face. "Sorry about . . . well, y-y-you know."

"Hey," she said, reaching for his hand and giving it a squeeze, "don't be. You made me feel so, I can't even really describe it. If anyone should be blushing, it's me. I can't believe we just did what we did."

"That makes t-t-two of us," he said, rubbing his thumb over the top of her knuckles.

She chewed her lip as if considering what she was going to say next, but the shrill ring of the phone interrupted the moment, making them both jump.

She pulled her hand from his and leaned toward her bedside table. "Dammit."

"What's wrong?"

She picked up the phone and turned away from him. "Hello? Yeah . . . no, I'm just about to go to sleep . . . Did you have fun?"

Kaden's teeth clenched when he heard the male voice on the other end.

"Um, right, sure, we can still do that. You can pick me up here. Can we figure out the rest in the morning? I'm really wiped out."

Tessa exchanged her good-byes with Doug, which involved a "you, too" that meant that prick had said *love you* or *miss you* or some bullshit to her. All when he'd probably spent the night fooling around on her. Guy's night out, his ass. He'd overheard enough of Doug's and his friend's locker room chats to know what happened on guy's night.

When Tess hung up the phone and turned back to him, all the light had gone from her eyes. Fat, ugly guilt sat there instead. And the bitch of it was that he didn't know what the guilt was over. He hoped it stemmed from what she was going to have to tell Doug when she broke it off with him. But Kaden had a feeling it was directed toward him. He could feel the hammer about to fall.

When she didn't say anything, his hope plummeted further. "Are you going to t-tell him what happened? End things?"

She looked down at her hands, her shoulders slumped. "Kaden, I, I don't know what to say. It's just confusing and there's so much . . . you know I can't . . ."

Icy cold moved through him. "No, you're wrong. It's not confusing. It's about as c-c-clear as it gets."

She shook her head, a tear moving across her formerly flushed cheeks. "Maybe if things were different . . ."

*Maybe if things were different, maybe if things were different . . .* The thought circled his head like an ugly buzzard. Crazy ideas brewed. "You really mean that, Tess?"

She peeked up at him, blue eyes shiny with tears. "Yes."

He gave a terse nod and stood. "I'm going to sleep on the couch downstairs so you won't be alone. I'll make sure and be out before Doug gets here to p-p-pick you up for whatever."

She looked stricken. "Kaden—"

"Get some rest. And don't make any plans for tomorrow night. We're going to t-t-talk."

And hopefully by tomorrow night, he could show her how things *could* be different.

When he told her good night, he didn't stutter at all.

# TWENTY-ONE

"But you can't cancel," Tessa said. She wiped her sweaty palms on her pants and tried to keep her voice from sounding as desperate as she felt. "Most of the people coming to the event signed up to see Third Sky perform."

"Look, dollface, I hear ya and I'm sorry," said Third Sky's manager, not sounding very sorry at all. "But the guys landed a gig on Jimmy Kimmel that night. Can't miss that opportunity. I'm sure you understand."

No, she didn't. A commitment was supposed to be a commitment. And Billy, her friend and Third Sky's guitarist, had given her his word. But she'd forgotten to send the contract last week and now she didn't have a legal leg to stand on. Verbal agreements meant nothing. Neither did integrity, apparently. "There's nothing I can do to change your mind. Did Billy agree to this?"

"I'm sure Billy's real sorry, but it's a band decision. Hit us up next year and we'll give you a discount off the booking fee."

*You're all fucking heart.* That's what she wanted to say, but she managed a polite response and good-bye. When she set the phone in its cradle, she lowered her head to the desk and attempted to talk herself out of crying and/or throwing things.

"Hey, what's wrong?"

She took a deep breath and raised her head to find Kade standing in her doorway, wearing a three-piece suit and a sympathetic smile. Her shoulders sagged. "Have you looked outside lately? Is there a dark swirling cloud of doom hovering over the city? I'm waiting for the Stay Puft Marshmallow Man to trundle through at any moment."

"That bad?" he asked, stepping inside.

*Hello, failure, my old friend.* God, she didn't want to tell Kade this. "The band just cancelled."

"They can't. We have a contract."

She glanced away. "I sent it late. It wasn't signed yet. I took my friend at his word. I screwed up. God, I can't believe I was so stupid."

"Hey," he said, his tone sharp. "Never say that about yourself. It was an honest mistake. You trusted your friend."

"Trust. Ha! It bites me in the ass again," she said bitterly.

"It'll be fine. We'll get another act."

"It's not quite that easy, K— Mr. Vandergriff," she said, realizing they should keep it formal in case anyone was still in the hallway, listening. "That band was a big reason I've sold so many tickets to the event. This is going to be a disaster when I tell people they cancelled. And the event can't afford to lose that money. I'm already behind on the goal."

Panic was seeping in. She could see the doors of Bluebonnet being locked for good, those kids having no place to help them anymore. All because she couldn't remember to send a freaking contract in time.

"Take a deep breath. We'll figure out something on Monday. I promise. I have a friend who knows one of the guys in Darkfall. They'd be a big draw. I'll see if they're available."

"But I don't want you to have to do that. This is my fault. I need to fix it."

"Tess, first lesson in running a business that I learned was knowing how to delegate and accept help. If you try to do everything yourself, you'll fail. No one can do it all on their own. I certainly don't."

"But I feel like I should be able to handle this."

"And you are," he said gently. "You're doing a great job. But be smart and strategic. I have a connection you can exploit. Use that."

She nodded, hearing the wisdom in the advice even if it was hard to accept. "Okay. Thank you. It would be great if you could ask them and—"

He lifted a hand to halt her. "I will, promise. But right now, neither of us can do anything about it, so I need you to put a pin in it and we'll work on it next week. All right?"

She nodded, her panic ebbing. She would handle it. Kade would help. Yes. Okay. She would delegate that task. That didn't sound so bad.

Obviously considering that matter settled, Kade stepped inside, shut the door behind him, and turned the lock. "Plus, I'm not here to talk about work."

"Oh?"

"I have something for you."

He had a small unlabeled shopping bag in his hand. She peeked at it, her stomach giving a flutter. He never stopped by her office for personal reasons. They always kept things completely professional and purposely distant at work, but she had a feeling that was about to change. "Is that right? I thought we agreed to no more gifts. You've been giving me too many things."

"You declared. I never agreed. Quitting time was an hour ago, by the way. You're the only one left on this end of the building."

She glanced at her computer screen. "Oh, I know, but I wanted to finish up a few things. I'm still trying to figure out some financial stuff from Bluebonnet, and then I got that call."

"You're done for the day now," he said—a proclamation, not a question.

"Okay," she said slowly. "I thought we weren't meeting until eight."

"Change of plans." He set the bag on her desk. "Things have been a little hectic this week, so I thought it'd be a good time to sneak out of town for the weekend."

She wet her lips, looking at the bag again, nerves creeping in. "Where to?"

He met her eyes with a seeking gaze. "Ready to give me real control?"

"Meaning?"

"To submit to me fully."

"But haven't I been—"

"Not just allowing me to call the shots in the bedroom but giving over complete control in every way. Surrender." He reached in the bag and pulled out a black leather collar.

Her breath caught, her brain snagging on the word *surrender.* "Oh."

"I'm a member of a private BDSM resort called The Ranch. You already know that I'm a dominant, but this will give you a better idea of what that really means. This will be much more formal. You'd wear a collar. Call me sir. Obey me. Everyone who will be there is in this lifestyle, so discretion is rule number one for all. You wouldn't need to worry about anyone seeing us and talking."

She needed water, something to ease the sudden dryness in her throat. Yes, she'd let him mostly take charge since they'd started seeing each other, but going to this place sounded like it'd be graduating from the kiddie pool they were wading in to being thrown into the ocean. "Sounds . . . intense."

"It can be," he agreed, "but based on how things have gone between us so far, I think you might enjoy what you'll find there."

She straightened papers on her desk, needing to channel the nervous energy somewhere. "Is it safe?"

His gaze turned somber. "You are *always* safe with me, Tess. No matter what."

The promise landed heavy on her, the weight of his unwavering assurance almost too much to bear. Safety. It was something of a fairy-tale concept for her. She'd never truly felt safe in her life except when she was shutting everyone out of it. Anytime she'd trusted someone, taken a breath around them and let her defenses down, she'd gotten blasted. Her mother had left her, foster parents had decided she wasn't adoptable, Doug and her best friend had betrayed her. But for some reason, in that moment there in her office, she believed Kade.

She raised her eyes to meet his and nodded. "Okay. I'm open to trying it."

The pure satisfaction in his smile lit up places inside her she hadn't even known existed. "Good. And if you enjoy tonight and decide you want to stay the weekend, I can introduce you to the rest of my friends so you can get to know them. A lot of them will be there."

She stared down at the collar, the simple thing sending her heart thumping against her ribs. But his other suggestion is what really had nerves rising. "You want me to meet your friends? Like not for a fantasy thing, like hang out with them?"

He frowned. "You say that like it's a horrible notion."

She rubbed her palms on her pant legs. "It's not that, it's just, you know, what you'd do with a girlfriend."

"Right." He stared down at her, hands in his pockets, a tired look crossing his face. She hated that shift in his expression, like she was wounding him. But they'd made an agreement, and she planned to stick to it. She wasn't up to being hurt again, and she knew if she crossed that line with him, that's all that would end up happening. She'd already struggled with her feelings after the night at Colby's place. If she let it get serious, Kade would eventually leave or get bored with her. It was a pattern she'd seen too often in her life—no matter how pretty the promises, no one stuck around. Love sounded nice, but it was conditional. And she'd never been able to meet the conditions for anyone she'd loved back for long—not her mother, or any foster family, or even her husband. Everyone had an expiration date.

And if she hadn't been convinced that a true relationship with Kade would be a bad idea already, she'd heard two of the receptionists gossiping in the bathroom the other day about Kade's string of past conquests. Apparently, he'd even garnered a nickname for cycling through women on such a steady schedule. She hadn't caught what that nickname was, but she got the gist. He conquered and moved on to the next, leaving broken hearts in his wake. So even if Kade didn't see it for himself, she was just the next battle to achieve.

When she didn't say anything further, Kade blew out a breath and sat in the chair on the other side of her desk. "I'm not asking you to meet my parents to ask for my hand in marriage or anything, they're just my friends. But if it makes you uncomfortable, then we'll stick to the fantasy. You'll go as my slave and property. You'll be there for my benefit only and not to socialize."

She swallowed hard, the prospect overwhelming. That prince and slave fantasy had fueled her libido more often than she cared to admit in these last few weeks. But it also scared her on an elemental level. There was a big difference between playing games a few nights a week and giving total control to Kade in a place where no one would bat an eye at a slave girl. But at least Kade was giving her a way to keep this in the realm that felt safer—fantasy. Not emotions. Not the girlfriend hanging out with people who were important to him. Just a hot weekend on the edge.

She pressed her lips together and nodded. "Would my safe-word still apply?"

His eyes met hers. "It always applies, Tess. All I ask is that you give this a chance before pulling the escape hatch too soon. I've shown you some things, but going to a place like The Ranch can be overwhelming. I'd need complete control. Just know that you'll be under my care and that no one can touch you unless I give them permission."

She coughed, the last part causing her to swallow wrong. But she nodded anyway. "Okay."

"Good." He took the collar off her desk and put it in his suit's inner pocket. "Put what's in the bag on then put your trench coat over it. When you're done, head out and walk down to the corner by the sushi place. I'll have the car waiting for you over there so no one sees us get in together."

"All right."

He leveled a gaze at her. "From this point on tonight, it's Sir or Master Van. Forget that and there will be a consequence."

The authoritative tone zipped through her like heat lightning. "I'm sorry, sir."

"Better." He stood. "Now get dressed. You have twenty minutes. I'll see you in the car."

Tessa waited until he'd left the office and she'd locked her door before peeking in the bag. She expected to find some skimpy vinyl something or other. Isn't that what one wore to these things? At least that's what she remembered from those old HBO specials. But instead she found a gorgeous chocolate brown leather corset with intricate gold design work and gold ribbons lacing the back. The accompanying skirt was sheer brown fabric and long, but had slits all the way up each side to the hip. It was a gorgeous outfit but the colors gave it the feel appropriate for the slave of royalty. Like she was being dressed for someone's amusement.

It was a costume she would've coveted in the high-end lingerie boutiques she'd gone to when she'd first married Doug and had thought enticing him with sexy outfits would work. She'd usually chosen white, flowing things for Doug, hoping it'd be elegant and ladylike enough for him. But in truth, she'd always been drawn to the more risqué stuff in the shops, even if she'd been too chicken to try any of it on.

Now she'd be wearing one of those outfits . . . in front of other people. Her stomach flip-flopped at the notion, but she couldn't tell if that was fear or anticipation. She pulled out both pieces and laid them on her desk then peered into the bag, looking for panties, but of course Kade had conveniently left those out. Lord, she was actually going to have to walk down the street with only this under her coat.

*Well, here goes nothing.* Fantasy was about to become reality. Hopefully it didn't lose its sparkle.

---

When Tessa saw the black town car idling at the curb, she almost chickened out right there. Kade always drove his own car. He'd told her he didn't like giving up the wheel to anyone. But tonight he was taking her out in high style—like he really was some aristocrat claiming her for a night of debauchery.

She knew in theory this whole dominance/submission thing could be sexy, but now that she was faced with doing it for real, with other people around, she'd broken out into a sweat beneath her coat. Somehow her legs kept moving forward despite her mind's retreat. The corset jostled with each step, threatening to fall down. The thing laced up the back and she hadn't been able to cinch it up tight enough on her own. She'd also tucked the length of the skirt up under her waistband so no one could see the fabric coming out the bottom of her coat. But even though no one could possibly know, it felt like every person who passed her on the street had x-ray vision and could see how little she was wearing beneath.

When she reached the edge of the curb, the driver didn't get out, but the back door opened from the inside. She braced her hand on the door and peered inside. Kade gave her a look that pierced right through her. "Need a ride?"

He hadn't changed out of his suit, but had ditched the jacket and rolled his sleeves up his forearms. His tie was still knotted and his vest was still buttoned, though, giving him an air of power and authority—a ruthless businessman looking for a little entertainment. Or an evil prince looking for a captive. "Yes, sir."

"It won't be a free one," he warned her, and even though she knew these were simply roles they were trying on, the words sent goose bumps along her arms. "You get inside, and you're mine for the night."

She glanced at the partition between the backseat and the driver, happy to see the privacy screen was up.

"I'm sure we can work something out," she said, surprised at the breathlessness in her voice.

Kade nodded as if he could take it or leave it. "Get in."

She ducked inside the car, careful to keep her coat around her, and shut the door behind her. "Thank you."

He eyed her. "Lose the coat. I want to see you."

She smoothed the lapels of her trench, nervous to be getting undressed before they got to the safety of the party, but she had a feeling Kade wasn't in the mood to negotiate. She unbuttoned the coat and shrugged out of it, then tugged the skirt to its full length. The corset tried to slide down and she put her hands to it. "I couldn't get the laces tight enough by myself."

"Turn around." She followed his instruction and warm fingers grazed her back as he cinched her tight enough to make her aware of the corset's presence and to send her breasts rounding over the top. He ran a knuckle along her spine then turned her back around and had the collar in his hand. He touched the hollow of her throat with it. "Lift your chin."

She did as she was told and the leather glided along her skin, making her catch her breath. He fastened it around her neck just tight enough to give the slightest pressure against her throat. The snap of the little lock sent a strange thrill through her. *Captured.* He let his hand slide down her throat and he traced the edge of her corset. "This all looks perfect on you."

"Thank you, sir. It's beautiful. Probably too fancy for a slave."

He cupped her shoulders, his blue eyes meeting hers. "Not for my woman. As much as I'd expect from my slave is how much I'd pamper and cherish her in return. She'd want for nothing."

Tessa's gaze dropped to her hands, the words sparking old sadness. "Having lavish gifts gets old quick, though. I've been that kind of slave."

His fingers touched her chin, cajoling her attention back upward. "I'm not talking about things that can be bought, Tess. She'd have everything I could give that meant something."

She looked away, unable to bear the way he seemed to be looking right to the heart of her. "Come on, Kade, you make it sound like a slave is a real thing. Like you'd really want one."

He moved his hand away from her with a weary sigh, his mood shifting in an instant. His odd reaction made her frown and she wanted to ask more questions, but he started talking before she could.

"I need to get you prepared." He pulled something from his pocket, a strip of black satin, and gathered both her wrists in his hand to wrap the strip of material around them.

"Is The Ranch a big place? Like, are there lots of people there?" She had been naked in front of a few of Kade's friends already, but she still couldn't picture herself walking around in a crowd dressed like this with a collar around her neck.

"It's a large piece of property with a good-sized membership, but it's very private and exclusive so the members know how to be discreet and respectful. And my friend, Grant, the guy who owns it, doesn't tolerate any crap. Anyone who doesn't follow the house rules will be kicked out or disciplined at his discretion—which, if you knew Grant, is not something you'd want to be subject to."

She watched the silk go round and round her wrists. "So are there women there who you've done this with—the dominance thing?"

He frowned. "Come on, Tessa."

His tone held warning and, of course, she knew she should shut up, but knowing and doing were two different things. "Have you like . . . dated any of them?"

"No, not dated."

"So slept with."

He gave her a do-you-really-want-to-go-there look. "Maybe I should've gagged you instead of binding you."

"Well, there's my answer," she said, not sure why she was feeling so petulant and annoyed all of a sudden.

He sighed and leaned back in the seat. "Look, I won't hide anything from you. My lifestyle can be pretty free for a single guy. I haven't had serious relationships with any of the women you may run across at The Ranch. But I have played third on occasion with a couple. And I've helped out with scenes. I've played with a few others."

"You've played *third* with couples? Guys let you touch their wife?"

"Or girlfriend. It's not that uncommon in this world. Sometimes it's because the woman has a threesome fantasy. Sometimes it's simply a part of the dominance and submission, which is why I brought Colby in that night with us. It was another way for me to be in charge of you and your pleasure. If you're my property, it can be exciting to share you in a way that I control. Plus, it can be hot for a dominant to watch, knowing he or she is directing the action."

The images he was painting were almost too much for her to process. She'd had no idea that what they'd done with Colby had been an exercise in Kade dominating her. But even though that night had been beyond hot, she couldn't ignore the bitter taste that crossed her tongue at the thought of Kade doing that with someone's wife. It was way too reminiscent of what she'd walked in on in Atlanta. "So it's okay to cheat?"

"*No.* That's never okay. Anything that happens is with consent and knowledge of all parties. People may set up a cheating role play. Some get off on that humiliation of being cheated on—cuckoldry is the name for it."

"Well, those people are freaking crazy," she said, shaking her head. "There was nothing hot about walking in and seeing Doug screwing someone I thought was a friend."

Sympathy crossed his face. "I'm sure. But like I said, the people that do it as a kink have all agreed to it. And if I've learned anything over the years, it's to not judge what flips someone's switch. If it's not hurting anyone and it's consensual, that's their business. There are people who'd label me as crazy or sick."

Like his ex. Like the courts.

She frowned. "I'm sorry, I didn't mean to imply—"

He smiled and touched her nose. "Shut up, slave. I know you're not judging me. Because right now that would definitely be the pot calling the kettle black."

He gave her collar, corset, and bound hands a sweeping look, and she laughed. "Point taken."

"Now," he said, his tone changing from light to serious in a blink. "I have one more adornment for you. But I can't put it on until we're at The Ranch where I'll need to prepare my slave properly."

She wet her lips. "Okay."

"Until then"—he gripped her shoulders and guided her down to lay her head in his lap—"relax and enjoy the drive. I have a few work calls that can't wait. You think you can stay quiet?"

"Yes, sir." She settled against his lap, not really having any choice but to let him move her how he wanted since her hands were bound. She nestled her cheek against his thigh and he idly ran his fingers through her hair as he put in an earpiece with his other hand. She sighed and let herself relax into his touch. It'd been a long day, and there was something wildly soothing about the position and his slow stroking fingers against her scalp.

She startled when he began talking to whoever was on the other end of his call, but he dragged fingertips along her arm, settling her again. Soon, her eyes were closing and her muscles were going lax. She liked listening to Kade conduct his business. Unlike Doug who'd barked orders at everyone, Kade's voice had an ease to it despite the authoritative edge—like he was talking to a friend even when he was giving a directive. She could imagine that most people wanted to do what Kade Vandergriff told them to, even if they couldn't quite pinpoint why. He was easy to say yes to.

He ended one call and started another, but meanwhile, his hand drifted lower, tracking down her side and eventually ending up under the slit of her skirt. He coasted a palm over her bare hip and the curve of her ass—an easy touch but one that jacked up her internal temperature. Memories of him bending her over his lap and reddening her skin with that very hand were still vivid in her mind. She pressed her thighs together at the answering twinge of awareness between her legs.

As if sensing the growing tension in her body, Kade eased the thigh that was on top toward her chest, opening her to him. She tried to pull the other knee along the seat in some modified fetal position, but he was having none of that. He stopped her other leg in its tracks and gave her hip a quick pinch.

She clamped her lips together, fighting not to make a sound.

He responded to some question the caller had asked and ran a fingertip along her exposed flesh. It was a barely there touch, but even so, she had to swallow down a moan. How this man could barely breathe on her and make her so desperate was a wonder. She had no hope of quelling her body's response to him.

The road continued to rumble beneath them, his phone call went on, and he kept up the stroking and teasing, creating a slow, rolling boil in her system. Her scent filtered into the air as she grew slick from his touch. Kade grew hard beneath her, but if he was in any hurry to alleviate that, he didn't give any signs. Instead, he seemed to be enjoying the languid teasing. He dipped a finger inside her and slowly drew it in and out, then went back to touching everything but her throbbing clit.

Evil, evil man.

When she thought she was going to go out of her mind from need, the car took a turn and slowed. Kade moved his hand away from her as he ended his call, and he flipped her skirt down, making her mourn the loss of his hands on her.

"Come on, baby. We're here."

"No, sir, I don't think I'm quite there."

He smirked and helped her to a sitting position. "Patience is a virtue I expect in my slave."

She sighed in frustration and peered out the window to see a large gate swinging open. The sun was almost gone, so she couldn't make out everything, but when they pulled past the gate, a massive cedar and stone building loomed before them, beautiful gardens lining the front and land rolling out behind it. Trees dotted the property. In the distance, she could see what looked to be smaller buildings, which she assumed were the guest cabins for The Ranch.

The car pulled past the main house and followed a winding road to the back of the impressive compound. Rows and rows of grapevine stretched out to their left. Kade had mentioned the owner also ran a vineyard on the adjoining property. Eventually, they pulled around a bend and stopped in front of a two-story cabin—though to call it a cabin would be an insult. It could easily fit in amongst the high-end homes she'd seen nestled in the mountains on some of her ski vacations.

Before she could really process that they were *here*, that when she stepped outside, she'd be Kade's in whatever way he wanted, the driver came around to open the door. She had a moment of self-consciousness, realizing he was going to see her dressed like this, but then she almost laughed. *Everyone* was going to see her dressed like this. She needed to get used to it quickly.

She took the driver's hand and stepped out of the car, giving him a brief, albeit flushed-cheeked, smile. He simply nodded and to his credit, his gaze didn't drift downward. He was probably used to Kade riding around with half-naked women. The thought rankled.

But before she could let her mind run too far down that road, Kade was by her side again, catching her elbow. "Leave your heels in the car. Slaves go barefoot."

It took her a moment to understand what he was saying since her mind was whirling with so many thoughts, but she quickly slipped off her shoes and set them on the seat.

When she straightened, Kade met her eyes and held out his hand. "You ready to become mine, Tessa?"

The simple question held a thousand warnings beneath it. She shouldn't be here. She shouldn't take this step. But she'd come too far not to see what was on the other side of the neat lines she'd always played inside. She found herself moving toward Kade. Her hand slipped into his.

*His.*

If only that didn't sound so good.

# TWENTY-TWO

Tessa and Kade headed to the porch, and Kade knocked on the door of the cabin.

*Here we go.* Tessa adjusted her corset and tried to smooth her expression so she wouldn't show all the trepidation moving through her. *This is just a game. A fantasy. I can bow out at any time with one simple word.*

But it didn't feel like that. It felt real and intense and heavy all of a sudden. Like this was some test she hadn't studied hard enough to pass. What if she humiliated herself? Or made some mistake and embarrassed Kade? Were there certain rules or customs she was supposed to follow?

The door swung open, and a gorgeous dark-haired man in glasses greeted them with a smile. Tessa blinked, not sure what she had expected, but not really anticipating Clark Kent in a polo and slacks to be at a place like this. He reached out and shook Kade's hand. "Good to see you, Vandergriff."

"Wyatt," Kade said, returning the warmth. "Sorry we're a little late."

"Not a problem, the whole plan's pretty fluid tonight, and you're not the last to arrive by any means. We actually just moved out to the back lawn."

"Everything ready?"

"Yep, Kelsey's taken charge of it all. She loves a party."

*Party?* Tessa swallowed hard. Kade hadn't mentioned anything about a party.

"Glad to hear she's enjoying herself. I'm looking forward to saying hi. I haven't seen her since you guys eloped. Congratulations, by the way, I knew when I saw you two on that island that it would only be a matter of time before that girl had your collar around her neck and a ring on her finger."

Wyatt chuckled, the sound deep and genuine. "I'm a lucky bastard, what can I say?"

"Yeah, you are." Kade's wistful tone caught Tessa's attention, but she didn't have time to ponder it because Kade was placing a hand on her back, drawing her into the conversation. "And hey, we're looking forward to joining y'all outside but I need to prepare my girl before we do. I had sent a few special requests to Jace."

Wyatt smiled and spared Tessa a kind glance. "Yep, he has everything you need set up in the downstairs bathroom. We're using that as the prep room tonight. Take a right when you go inside, second door on the left. I need to go change, but I'll see you two in the backyard in a while."

They exchanged good-byes and it wasn't lost on Tessa that no introductions were exchanged. She'd asked not to be brought into his circle of friends as Tessa, the girl he was kind of dating. And he was sticking to his word.

Kade took her elbow again and guided her forward. "Come on, this shouldn't take long."

The house was rustic-chic and tastefully decorated, but Tessa couldn't take in much because her mind was scrolling through endless possibilities of what exactly Kade meant by preparation.

When they reached the large, slate-tiled bathroom, she began to put the pieces together. A wide bench had been placed alongside the oval bathtub and shaving cream and fresh razors where lined up along the edge. Kade shut the door behind him and locked it.

She turned to him, feeling heat of a different sort flare in her cheeks. "You want me to shave?"

She'd only ever shaved her bikini line. Doug had preferred the natural look. Now she wondered if it was some faux pas now to not be waxed or whatever.

Kade gave a hint of a smile. "No, not exactly. Lie down on the bench on your back. *I'm* going to shave you."

*Oh, shit.* "You're kidding, right?"

His brow arched. "What part of being a slave do you not understand? I'll prepare you however I wish. Lie down and don't make me tell you again."

The firm words probably should've made her run instead of shiver in anticipation, but she'd asked for this fantasy for a reason. She could stand here wasting time trying to decipher her motivations for being turned on by this, but what did it matter at this point? Kade had told her he'd never judge her about her desires, so she needed to afford herself the same luxury.

"Yes, sir. My mistake." Her hands were still bound, but she managed to get herself in position and lie down. It wasn't long enough for her whole body so her feet stayed on the floor, her butt at the edge of the bench. Kade turned on the faucet in the bathtub, and the roaring sound of the water filled her ears.

He touched the top of her foot and she jumped. He gave her shin a little flick with his finger, silently telling her to stay still. Once she complied, something smooth wrapped around her ankle and tightened. "This is a spreader bar. It will keep your legs open for me and will stop you from squirming so I don't hurt you."

He locked her other ankle into the device, and she tried to move but couldn't draw her legs together. "Kade, sir . . ."

"Hush. I want you smooth and sensitive tonight so you can enjoy what I bought for you. Give me the pleasure of preparing you."

She closed her eyes, her heartbeat jumping in her chest. Despite her anxiety about a blade being put to her most delicate parts by someone other than her, she could feel arousal blooming through her.

Kade lifted her skirt all the way up and ran a finger along her folds—no, along her pussy. She needed to own those dirty words and stop being scared of them.

"So damn gorgeous. You should see how wet and swollen you are already." His fingertip traced each tender spot. "And I love these curls of yours. I plan to leave some on the top. But I think you'll thank me once you feel how much more sensitive you'll be after this."

She whimpered softly as he slid a finger inside her, teasing her with easy strokes. She lifted her hips toward his touch, but as soon as she did, he moved his hand away.

"That's not going to do," he said as she opened her eyes. He stepped over to a nearby cabinet and pulled something from it. "I need you completely immobile."

He carried over the new items and wrapped another wider strap around her body, right at her waist, and secured it beneath the bench. She gave a test wiggle and couldn't move. Then he took another strip and covered her eyes. Blocking her vision gave her a little flutter of panic. "I promise I won't move or look."

"That's a promise you may not be able to keep even if you have good intentions. Just relax and let me handle things."

He laid a hot, wet towel between her legs. She sighed as the heat melted into her skin and radiated outward, making everything feel languid. Combined with the steady sound of the running water and her blocked vision, she started to sink into the moment. She could picture Kade standing near her, still in his work clothes, steam filling up the room and his focus on her bound form.

The sound of something electronic broke her meditative state, a quiet humming. Her eyes blinked behind the blindfold. She was desperate to see even though she already suspected it was an electric razor. He moved the towel, but where she expected the feel of cold metal, something smooth touched her clit.

She gasped, her body wanting to arch but having nowhere to go with the restraints.

"There, that's better. No moving," Kade said, his voice sounding soft through the rush of the water. He ran the small vibrator over her, sending delicious, undulating warmth up her nerve endings and making her belly clench tight. She'd already been keyed up in the car, so it didn't take much before she was ready to go off. "Do well and you'll get more of this feeling. Understand?"

She released her bottom lip from between her teeth. "Yes, sir."

He gave her a few more passes with the vibrator then moved it away and spread warm shaving cream over her. She groaned again. Who knew heated foam could feel so good? But she didn't have time to relish the sensation for long. A louder buzzing sound filled the room, louder and more ominous than the vibrator, and she willed herself not to flinch.

"Just breathe, baby. I won't hurt you."

She tried to follow his directive, taking a long inhale through her nose and holding it until she felt his touch. But she shouldn't have worried. The electric razor was gentle against her, the slight vibration actually stimulating her even more. The tension started to slowly drain out of her. But when the buzzing stopped and more cream was spread over her, her ribs pulled tight again.

"Easy, Tessa," Kade said, his voice soothing. "I need you to remain as still as possible for this part. I can't do it all with the electric. And this is what I'm going to enjoy the most, so I plan to take my time."

She held her breath again, and the cool metal blade touched her most delicate of skin. Kade drew the razor over her skin with a steady hand. Cool air coasted over her newly bared skin in his wake. The treatment, which she thought would feel clinical, turned out to be one of the most sensual sensations she'd ever experienced—the warm cream, his confident but easy touch, the care he was taking. In her mind's eye, she could see Kade there between her spread thighs and bound body, studying every private part of her, delicately grooming her for his enjoyment. Her arousal increased tenfold. She had no doubt he could see exactly what this was doing to her.

He spread her with his thumb to get to her most hidden parts and ran the razor across sensitized skin. She sighed softly, sinking into some meditative stillness she didn't quite understand.

"You're beautiful, slave," Kade said, his voice reverent as he continued his work. "Every part of you. Your sounds. Your scent. This pretty pink cunt that's swelling beneath my touch. But most of all"—he ran the blade near her clit—"your trust. I plan to reward you for that."

*God.* She could melt into the bench. Somehow Kade could morph words that she'd normally find offensive or degrading into the hottest things ever. "Thank you."

After a few more draws of the blade, Kade was done. He cleaned her off with another warm towel and left her there while he rinsed everything. Every bit of skin he'd exposed tingled and tightened, begging for his touch. She was dying to see how she looked. She'd never shaved so completely. But she had no choice except to lie there patiently.

The faucet finally went quiet, and all she could hear was her own choppy breathing. She strained her ears, trying to get a sense of where Kade was, but without warning, burning hot heaven touched her between her legs. She groaned loudly as Kade's tongue tracked a path over where he'd just shaved her.

Her hips tried to lift, the sensation almost too much to bear, but the restraints didn't give. *Holy mother of everything good in this world*. She'd never felt so very much down there. It was as if every centimeter of skin were electrified. "Oh, shit."

"Come for me, slave. You've done well."

Fingers slid inside her, and Kade sucked her clit between his lips, teasing it with his tongue. She was so wet and so on edge already after everything that she had no hope of prolonging it. Color streaked behind her eyelids and she cried out, the bench jolting with the sharp force of the orgasm that rocked through her.

Kade took advantage of her bound state, not letting up despite her protests that it was too much, and licked her until she was panting and begging for a reprieve. Finally, he moved his mouth away from her, and she dragged in a deep breath. Fingers touched her lips. "Open."

She did as she was told, too blissed out to think it through, and his fingers dipped into her mouth, the distinctive tartness shocking her for a moment. She made a little sound of surprise, but he didn't pull away.

"Clean me off. Taste how sweet you are."

She sucked his fingers, her body still contracting with the aftershocks of her orgasms. She'd probably look back at these moments and blush over it, but right now, she just wanted to do whatever he told her to.

He pulled his fingers from her mouth and untied the blindfold. When she blinked her eyes open, his gaze could've burned right through her. Her focus tracked down to the prominent bulge in his slacks.

She wet her lips, aching to return the favor. "You probably shouldn't go outside like that."

He stepped down to the end of the bench, trailing his finger along her thigh. "You're forgetting what kind of place we're at. But don't worry, you'll get your chance to serve me tonight if you're lucky. It just might not be in the comfort of a private room."

That sent fresh nerves coiling through her.

He pulled something from his pocket and it caught the light. "Now for your last gift for the evening. A little jewelry."

She lifted her head to try to see what he was doing. The small silver bauble had beads attached. "What is it?"

"A ring." He touched her with gentle fingers, but she flinched anyway, her body still in hypersensitive mode. He moved the smooth metal along her wetness, then slipped it around her clitoris.

She let out a soft gasp. The little pinch the ring provided drew her already swollen clit into full throbbing awareness and set her senses on edge.

"Gorgeous," Kade said, staring down at his handiwork and giving the beads a little jostle. "Does it hurt?"

She breathed through her nose, trying to gauge exactly what she was feeling, deciding pain was far from it. "No, not exactly."

"Good," Kade said as he unstrapped her from the bench. "It's meant to provide a little torture but not the painful kind."

"Torture?" she asked, pushing up on her elbows when he untied her hands. The little ring definitely was making her hyper-aware, but it seemed far from torturous.

His mouth lifted at the corner. "Talk to me in an hour."

After unhooking her from the spreader bar, he helped her to a stand and she soon understood what he was talking about. The little beads swung with the movement, brushing against her like light, teasing fingers. Her sex clenched and her nails dug into Kade's arm. "Oh."

He chuckled and slid his hand along her lower back. "Come on, slave. Time for your debut."

The words made her muscles freeze, and she hesitated when he tried to move her forward.

He looked back to her, a wrinkle appearing in his brow. "What's wrong?"

She glanced at the door then back to him. "Is it okay that I'm kind of terrified all of a sudden?"

He turned to face her, his eyes soft, and put his hands on her shoulders. "All you need to do is focus on me and what I tell you to do. I'll take care of you. That's my most important job as your dominant, and I'll never shirk that responsibility. Trust that you can give yourself over fully to my care without worry."

The words warmed her even though the idea of blind trust always sent a shudder of foreboding through her. She managed a half-smile. "Are you saying I need to let you be my prince?"

A strange expression flickered over his features, but he quickly covered it with a confident smirk and brushed his knuckles along her jaw. "Exactly." He leaned over and gave her a quick kiss. "Not that you have a choice, slave."

She grinned. "I think you might be the nicest evil prince ever."

He slid his hand around the back of her neck and guided her toward the door. "I wouldn't make that call so soon, Tess. The night has just begun."

# TWENTY-THREE

Kade led Tess through the main cabin toward the backyard, feeling like a hypocrite for telling her she shouldn't be nervous when he was barely reining in his own butterflies. Despite how many times he'd been to parties at The Ranch, he'd never brought a submissive whose opinion mattered to him so much. Tonight he was going to show Tessa what this world looked like. Not the easily palatable version, but the real one. She was going to get her first view of the kind of relationship he desired, and he had no idea how she was going to react.

Exploring fantasies was one thing. Most people would be willing to try a little kink as a one off every now and then. But much fewer wanted that dynamic every day of their lives.

Before they reached the sliding glass doors that led to the back, Colby pulled them open from the other side. Tessa halted her step, no doubt confused by his appearance, and intimidated. Colby was a big, scary bastard in normal clothes, but in his leathers he probably looked downright terrifying to Tessa. Kade cupped the back of Tessa's neck, the collar pressing into his palm. "Ready for her?"

Tessa's head swung toward Kade, question marks in her eyes, but he gave her no reassurance. If he was going to give her this night, he wasn't going to dilute it for her.

Colby gave a brief nod. "Yep. She'll fetch a good price in that outfit."

"A what?" Tessa asked, panic underlining her voice.

"Hush, slave. I didn't give you permission to speak." He reached for the buckle on her collar and undid it. "I was only transporting you and preparing you for the auction. Highest bidder gets to take you home."

She reached up and grabbed at her neck when the collar slipped away. He liked the glimmer of loss in her eyes, the sudden awareness of what the collar represented and what he was stripping from her. It'd make it all the sweeter when he got to put it on her again.

He took her elbow and handed her off to Colby, who was doing an impressive job of keeping his stern expression.

"Kade," Tessa protested when he stepped away from her.

"It's Master Van or Sir," he reminded her. "And you'd best remember how to be respectful or I may not be inspired to bid on your services tonight."

She wet her lips, the words probably sinking in, understanding dawning. "Yes, sir."

"Master Colby will take you where you need to go."

Another pleading look passed her face, but he wasn't going to give her more information than that. He gave Colby a quick nod, and Colby led her out. Kade turned around, knowing she was safe with Colby, and went back down the hallway to get the last of what he needed for the plan.

*Tessa McAllen, welcome to my world. Hope you enjoy your stay.*

Tessa's knees were weak with nerves as Colby led her toward the open field behind the cabin. She could hear voices before they turned around the back corner of the house, but when the party came into view, she couldn't believe what sprawled out in front of her. Women were milling around in . . . gowns? She blinked a few times, unsure she was really seeing it. But it was like she'd walked into some evening soiree in Regency England. The men were dressed in long tailcoats, vests, and breeches—at least she thought that's what the pants were called. The whole scene was enough to root her to the ground.

Colby looked down at her. "What's wrong, slave?"

For some ridiculous reason, her eyes went wet. She'd told Kade her fantasy about a prince as an aside. It had been an offhanded comment, silly. And though he'd said he planned to give her the role play tonight, she only thought he meant in a general way—just between the two of them. But what spread out before her was a scene from one of her historical novels come to life. She shook her head. "Kade did all this?"

"It's Master Van," Colby reminded her, but his voice was gentle. "And yes, he did. We didn't expect this many people to show up on short notice, but give kinky people a chance to wear costumes and they're all in."

She laughed, swiping at the ridiculous tears that had escaped. "I can't believe he went through this much trouble."

"Can't you?" Colby's tone and frown fastened her to the spot. "My guess is that there's not much he wouldn't do for you."

She glanced away, the comment hitting her right in the chest. "It's not like that. We're just having a good time together."

Colby sniffed. "Uh-huh. Now come on, we can't get started without you."

She swallowed back the anxiety Colby's comment had stirred up again and let him lead her toward the crowd. Heads turned, people openly giving her head-to-toe evaluations. The vibe amongst the group was anticipatory, like she was the roast pig about to be served for dinner. It was damn unnerving, and Tessa couldn't help but feel wildly self-conscious about her state of dress. The other women were wearing full gowns. Though, admittedly, some of the low-cut bodices left little to the imagination. But here she was with a corset and a skirt that was so thin, she knew it was nearly useless at covering anything. The little jewel dangling against her sensitive parts mocked her, making her all too aware of her bareness beneath the skirt.

But despite the predatory mood of the crowd, no one touched her as Colby moved her through the knot of people. If anything, they backed up so as not to brush against her. Kade's words came back to her—*no one will touch you without my permission*. But she didn't know if that applied when she wasn't wearing his collar. She moved a little closer to Colby, seeking protection from the only other person she knew would watch out for her.

He moved his arm around her in a friendly but reassuring gesture. "It's okay, darlin'. No one can touch you until they buy you."

That was supposed to make her feel better? Who exactly had the option to buy her?

Comments whispered on the breeze around her as they walked, lewd ones, suggestive ones, curious ones. But she got the sense this was all part of the production Kade was putting on. Everything about this was making her feel like she was less than the people around her—the commoner, the slave. It should have upset her, but instead it made something settle inside her. There was some comfort in knowing what her role was, what the expectations were.

Once they made it to the other side of the yard, a wooden deck came into view. Men and women who were not dressed in the fine clothes of the crowd but rather like her were lined up along it, kneeling. Around each of their necks was a crude leash made of rope, which was tethered to bolts in the deck. The two men of the group were shirtless and wearing nothing but strips of rough brown cloth around their waists. When one lifted his head, she was stunned to see it was Andre. His eyes met hers and he gave her a little smile.

The simple gesture made her feel better, but then a startling *thwack* ripped through the air and Andre flinched. The man standing in the shadows behind the line of slaves had swung a small multi-tailed whip across Andre's back. "Eyes down, slave."

Tessa winced, but when the man in charge stepped into the light, she realized Andre's tormentor was also his lover. Jace put a booted foot between Andre's shoulder blades and pushed, bringing Andre all the way down to his elbows.

It seemed cruel and degrading, but it was hard to miss the obvious erection hiding beneath Andre's cloth. This was turning him on. And the logical part of her said that should be wrong. That it wasn't normal. But her body was responding differently. Just watching the exchange had her mind drifting to Kade and her body warming. What would it be like to surrender like that? This was the opposite of everything she'd ever known. It was everything she'd been taught was wrong and deviant, not to mention completely incongruent with any feminist ideals she held dear. But she couldn't bank the curiosity. It was overflowing inside her, bursting through the seams. She needed to feel what this was like with Kade. She needed to see what he really meant when he said he was dominant.

So as Colby led her over to the platform, she didn't use her safe word, she didn't say no, and she didn't fight when he guided her to her knees between Andre and a woman she didn't recognize.

Jace looped rope around her neck. "You are to remain here, head down, until your turn on the block. Do you understand?"

"I understand," she said, unable to bring herself to call him sir. That felt wrong for some reason.

He didn't correct her on it and left her there on her knees. The party went on for a while around them, and she had to fight hard not to look up or rock back into a sit. Occasionally, someone would walk over to observe them. Boots or heels would cross her view as the newest visitor circled the group, evaluating the goods for purchase. No one touched her or talked to her.

But the longer she kneeled there, staring down at her hands, the more wired she felt. The not knowing what would happen next was both exciting and completely terrifying. Could any of these people "buy" her and touch her? Would Jace hit her with that scary-looking whip? She didn't know the answers and no one was going to give them to her. All she could do was trust in Kade. He said he would keep her safe, and she had to believe that.

After about half an hour, the crowd noise started to take on a more energetic sound. Jace came back up to the deck and gave a sharp whistle. The sound startled her, and she almost lifted her head, but quickly corrected the involuntary reaction.

"Ladies and gents, can I have your attention?" Jace called out, quieting the crowd. "I'm very happy you decided to come to our late night garden party. But let's not pretend you're here for the canapés. I know you've all come here tonight to feed your desires with an illicit night. Luckily, you won't be left wanting. Our very generous host has kindly provided a number of very lovely pleasure slaves for your consideration. They won't be cheap, but I assure you they will be willing and obedient. And if they're not, I know you all have your wicked ways of gaining compliance."

The audience laughed, but Tessa could barely hear them over the pounding of her heart. Even though it was cool outside, her skin was growing damp with sweat. She was tied to a deck in front of a group of people, half-naked, and up for auction as a pleasure slave. A few months ago, her most daring night had involved staying up until two in the morning on a work night to watch a marathon of Nora Ephron movies. How had she gotten here?

But she didn't have time to contemplate further because Jace was untying Andre from the spot next to her and pulling him to his feet. She dared a peek upward and Andre sent her wink before Jace dragged him toward the makeshift staging area.

Jace kept Andre's rope wrapped around his fist. "Our first slave up for auction is over six feet tall, is strong enough to take a good, solid beating—which he enjoys by the way—and can make a woman scream with his talented tongue. He also sucks cock like a champion. In fact, I'm putting in a bid myself just for the chance at that fine experience. Two thousand pounds."

Tessa had to smile at the fact that they were pretending to use pounds. Kade really had thought of everything.

Another bid came from the audience, this time from a woman. Tessa dared to lift her gaze a hair since Jace was obviously busy, and saw a gorgeous blue-eyed woman in a green gown raising her finger in the air to note her bid. *Evan.*

The sight was more than a small relief. Andre's lovers were bidding on him. They weren't really auctioning him out to strangers. A few other people threw out bids but it was clear that the bidding war was going to happen between Jace and Evan. Andre looked more than happy to be caught between them. In the end, Evan won Andre with a bid of five thousand pounds. Jace handed the leash to her, but Andre swept Evan up and over his shoulder before she could use it and clamped his arm over her thighs to keep her in place. She smacked his back, but he simply grinned and carried her off. So much for an obedient slave.

The rest of the slaves went up on the auction block one by one. Some Tessa could tell were auctioned to their lovers, but for others it was clear that it really was an open bid. One woman was bought by a couple. The other guy was purchased by a petite woman wielding a riding crop. She even gave an onstage demonstration of how well she could use that crop when she lifted up her skirts and demanded he give her a sample of what she'd bought. He'd gone down on her in front of everyone while she hit his backside with the riding crop. The show had gotten the audience more than a little stirred up. The chatter among them was at a mild roar, and watchers became participants. Bodices were being unlaced and hands were roaming. Some in the crowd were on their knees.

Tessa was enthralled with all the sights. She'd thought she couldn't be shocked seeing people be publicly sexual after the night at Colby's, but it was impossible not to be. It was compelling. And sexy. And overwhelming. She was so caught up in all the watching that before she knew it, she was the only one left up there.

She still hadn't seen Kade. She'd stolen glances at the crowd with each new auction but she hadn't spotted him. Her limbs began to tingle with nerves and from being so still. Jace gripped her upper arm with gentle pressure. "On your feet, slave. Time's up."

Her head spun as she climbed to a stand, and the little bead between her thighs teased her with its swaying. How she could be so simultaneously freaked out and turned on was a wonder. But as Jace led her to the edge of the staging area, freaked out was starting to take the lead over the other. "Last but not least, we have a brand new capture. She's never been purchased before and is new to the ways of a pleasure slave. She would be good for a patient master who isn't afraid to teach and discipline her."

Hands went up in the air faster than Tessa could count them. Bids flew. Men. Women. Two couples. Her gaze darted around the crowd, seeking, looking for the one man she wanted to hear a bid from. Where the hell was he?

"I hear six thousand pounds. Anyone else?" Jace asked. "Going once."

True panic began to set in for Tessa. Maybe Kade had gotten

held up somewhere. Maybe he didn't know it was time yet. What was she going to do if the man who'd bid the highest won?

"Going twice."

Her safeword was poised on her tongue, when a voice from the back of the crowd silenced Jace. "Ten thousand pounds."

A murmur went through the crowd, and everyone turned. Tessa squinted, knowing who the voice belonged to but not allowing herself to believe it until she saw him. When the group parted and Kade strolled up the center, Tessa lost all of her starch. In that moment, it really did feel like her prince had come. Kade had changed out of his suit and replaced it with a luxurious dark blue tailcoat with gold buttons, a matching vest, tan breeches that hugged him in just the right way, and riding boots. He looked regal and proud and absolutely lose-her-mind gorgeous.

Her fantasy hadn't been even close to seeing it live and in the flesh. This was the sexiest man she'd ever seen in her life. With his dark blond hair and that aristocratic tilt to his chin, he really could've stepped out of another time. No other person in that garden looked half as distinguished as he did standing there. Royalty among the commoners.

"Seems we have a big spender," Jace observed. "Anyone want to top this gentleman?"

The crowd was silent and Jace declared her sold. Kade made his way to her with intent on his face. He stopped in front of her, towering over her in both stature and attitude. She was shaking.

"You're all mine now," he said, his voice silky and dark. "Kneel down."

Her gaze never left his as she knelt slowly at his feet. Jace handed Kade a pocket knife, and she held her breath as Kade ran the blade beneath the loop and released the rope. He handed the knife back to Jace and then pulled her collar from inside his jacket. She closed her eyes as the leather touched her throat, the feel of it around her strangely comforting.

When she lifted her lids again, Kade cupped her chin with one hand. "Your training starts now. Let me see what I've purchased."

With his free hand, he undid the old-fashioned pants, the flap falling open. He had no underwear beneath so she first got an eyeful of hard, flat stomach, then the impressive state of his cock came into view. He took himself in hand and stroked upward. In front of God and all the people in the crowd, he rubbed the tip of it over her lips.

She glanced at the crowd and he tapped her cheek with the back of his hand. "Eyes on me. No one else here matters. I'm your master. Open for me."

She licked her lips, blood rushing loudly in her ears, and opened her mouth. The minute he slid along her tongue, she centered all her focus on him. She knew people were watching. She knew how she must look. But instead of being embarrassed, this surge of determination filled her. She would give Kade the blow job of his life. She would show him and all these people that she knew how to please him—this beautiful man who'd gone through so much trouble to give her this fantasy. He hadn't declared her desires silly or unworthy or dumb. He'd honored them by going above and beyond to create it for her, down to the most minute detail. She would show her gratitude in the most obvious way possible. She would please him as if he really were her master. She would put her all into the fantasy, too.

She closed her eyes as he laced his fingers in her hair and guided her down his length. "That's right, girl. Take all of me. I want all these people to see that I got the best slave of the bunch. My own little harlot."

She ran her tongue along the thick vein on the bottom of his cock then drew back to lave the crown. She didn't know if there were fancy techniques for giving head, but what she lacked in skill, she would make up for in enthusiasm. Kade groaned loud enough for anyone nearby to hear and his fingers tightened against her scalp.

"You look so beautiful sucking my cock, Tess," he said, his voice filled with grit. "You've got every man who's watching jealous because no one has a sexier slave than I do."

The words drifted over her like soft, stroking hands, the sincerity in his voice and use of her first name making something inside her lift and lighten. She pulled back slowly, letting her tongue circle him, then looked up. "Thank you, sir."

The look in his eyes almost undid her. But she reminded herself that every man probably looked at a woman like that when she had his dick in her mouth. It was nothing more than that. But she couldn't stop stupid emotions from blooming in her chest like big, fat flowers. She closed her eyes and redoubled her efforts on pleasuring him.

Soon, she lost all sense of everything except the feel of his grip on her hair, the way he was moving her over his cock, and the sounds he was making. He was rough, grinding his hips against her mouth and not giving her leeway to pull off. But she relished the sense of being at his mercy, could feel her body relaxing and giving over to it. And when she opened her eyes to enjoy watching her well-dressed duke lauding his power over her, that sent him over the edge. He pulled out and spun her away, leading her with his grip on her hair and pushing her down on all fours. She hit the grass on hands and knees and he shoved her skirt up her thighs. The night air hit her damp skin. His fingers dipped inside her. "Look how fucking wet you are, girl. So damn sexy. Everybody can see how badly you need me to fuck you."

Her fingers dug into the earth as he pumped fingers inside her, jostling the clit ring and sending pleasure straight up her spine. She couldn't think about anyone watching. In that moment, there was no one there but the two of them and what he was doing to her.

"Tell me you need to be fucked. Beg me for it." He curled his fingers along her G-spot.

"Please, sir," she gasped.

"Please, what?"

"Please, fuck me. I need you to."

She heard him opening up the condom packet and then he was at her entrance. He shoved forward without finesse, but her body was so ready for him that he met no resistance. His hand reached around and gently tugged her clit ring, the simple move nearly sending her over into orgasm. Her teeth clamped together, the combination of the stimulation and her sensitive, freshly shaven skin almost too much. But she didn't want this to end too fast. He thrust into her with long strokes and her head lolled between her shoulders as he buried deep over and over again, his fingers constantly teasing her hot button.

She lowered to her elbows, her body going into surrender mode, and put every ounce of energy into not coming. But Kade seemed intent on keeping her on the edge and holding her there. He knew when to move his fingers more gently and when to tug and pinch. She was outright begging after a while.

"That's it," he said, his voice strained. "Beg me for it. You want to come?"

"Yes, sir."

"Tell me," he demanded.

"I want to come."

"Then come, slave." He sunk all the way into her and slid the ring off.

Every ounce of energy burst out of her in one shrieking cry as the orgasm crashed down on her. Her nails sunk into the grass and she let it all go. She didn't care where she was or who was watching. All she cared about was Kade inside her and the overwhelming sensations overtaking her.

Soon Kade's groans joined hers and he came hard, dragging

her hips against him with a bruising grip and pumping into her with unchecked force. Tomorrow she would be marked. She would be sore. She would probably be shocked that she'd done this in front of others.

But at that moment, she didn't fucking care. She was sailing.

When the last of his release was emptied inside her and their breathing had slowed, he eased his grip on her and backed off. He slipped her skirt down to cover her and helped her off her knees. She sat down in the grass, watching him tuck himself back into his pants.

When he was done, he crouched down in front of her and tapped her nose with the tip of his finger, a twinkle in his eyes. "I guess you'll do, slave."

She snort laughed, an indelicate sound that she tried to cover, to no avail, especially when he gave her a broad grin.

"Perhaps I'm worth more than ten thousand pounds, sir," she teased.

"Oh, I assure you, I'd empty my coffers for you." He leaned forward and gave her a long, openmouthed kiss that garnered a whistle from another partygoer.

Only then did she remember that others were still watching them. Kade helped her to her feet and they turned to face the party. Some people had moved on to do their own thing, but there were a significant number of people with their gazes still on them. Most were smiling their way and one clapped. Not knowing what else to do in such a bizarre situation, Tessa grabbed her skirt and gave a little curtsey.

Kade laughed and wrapped his arm around her. "Already practicing to be a princess."

She smirked and leaned into him. "Don't tease me, sir. I know how the aristocracy works. I've got no shot."

He turned her away from the group and pulled her against him, his hands cradling her face. His eyes were clear and determined when he looked down at her. "You've always got a shot with me, Tess. Always have."

*You could be my princess.* He didn't say it, but the meaning was there. The sentiment made everything inside her ache. She'd had the princess life. It was a farce. "Don't, Kade. Please don't say things like that."

He pressed his forehead against hers with a sigh, but didn't push the issue. "Come on, I'm not done with you. There's a table I need to spread you across. I plan on having you as a side with my meal."

She took his hand and let him lead her into the party. And the night turned out to be sexy and amazing. Magical. A fairy tale coming to life and dancing around her. But she knew when he tucked her back into the car that night, exhausted and sated, that there was no way she could stay at The Ranch for the rest of the weekend. No way she could play his submissive for that long, seeing him look at her with more than lust in his eyes, feeling more than she wanted to feel.

Her body may crave it.

But her heart wouldn't survive it.

She couldn't be what he wanted.

# TWENTY-FOUR

"Calm your ass down. Falling for someone is a *good* thing, chickadee." Sam scanned the bottom shelf of the romance section in their favorite used bookstore.

"No, it's not. Not for me. Not right now. I'm doing that thing all over again—looking for love in all the wrong places."

She snorted. "Should I slap a cowboy hat on you and call you Sissy?"

"This isn't funny."

Sam ignored her, happily humming the soundtrack of *Urban Cowboy*.

Tessa adjusted her stack of books before they slid from her arms. She'd gone for all horror and thrillers today. Enough with the romance. No more princes or dukes or anything in between. She needed to break this fairy-tale addiction. "And I don't know why you're all for this now. Weren't you the one who sent him packing when he tracked me down to your place?"

She shrugged. "I sent him away then because I wanted to see how bad he really wanted to find you. If he'd just wanted booty call number two, he would've let it go at that point. The fact that he went as far as he did to find you is kind of romantic. Frankly, I'm kind of pulling for Team Kade now."

Tessa tilted her head back, staring at the water-stained ceiling tiles and trying to talk herself out of shaking her way too optimistic best friend. "You don't get it. I *know* the type of guy Kade is, how relationships are for him. It's the whole reason I let this go beyond that first night. I knew the freaking score, and I'm getting all attached anyway."

"You know what kind of—" Sam sat back on her heels, peering up at her with a frown. "Oh, honey, you Googled him, didn't you?"

"Maybe a little. Aren't those necessary dating steps these days?"

"Not if you want to actually *enjoy* dating." She sighed and pushed herself up from the floor, a highlander romance tucked under her arm.

"I needed to know what his life has been like since I knew him. He's done some amazing things with his company. But his personal life . . . well, the gossip columns call him the Time Share Bachelor. A month or two with him and a girl falls head over heels and is picking out china patterns. Then he dumps her."

"That's probably because—"

"It's because he likes the chase. The challenge is in getting a girl to fall for him. So he lays it on thick, is the perfect guy, irresistible. Remember how Doug could dial up the charm?"

She shook her head. "Doug was never charming. You saw what you wanted there. This isn't that. From everything you've told me about him, Kade wouldn't be that ruthless."

"I'm not saying Kade's doing it with bad intentions. Maybe each time he really does think the girl could be the one. But I told you how things were for him in high school. Girls ignored him at best and teased him at worse. Think how satisfying it must be to get the most beautiful women in the city crawling after him. He can bed them, get them desperate for something real, then leave them in his wake when he gets bored. And I"—she pointed to her chest—"represent the ultimate prize in that game. The girl he wanted in high school who basically told him he wasn't good enough."

Sam laid her book on top of Tessa's stack. "I think you're taking your Intro to Psych classes too seriously."

Tessa followed her to the next aisle. "All I'm saying is that his exes don't go away gracefully. The main suspect in that restaurant fire is one of his former girlfriends. Batshit crazy stuff. Women fall in love with him. And God, believe me, I can see why. But then he's on to the next. I was okay with that. I figured since I knew what I was getting into, it was fine. I didn't want anything serious anyway. Then fast-forward a few weeks and here I am, cruising down the same goddamned path. And your head would explode if you knew some of the things we've done together. I should be running fast and far. He wants a *real* submissive, Sam. He hasn't said that, but I know it's more than fun for him. We went to this resort this weekend, and I saw how natural he is in that world. I'm not cut out for that. I just left a marriage where I was treated like property. Why the hell would I even want to mess with that role? How could I find that sexy? What is wrong with me?"

Sam tilted her head in sympathy. "*Nothing* is wrong with you, hon. Maybe you're just as kinky as he is. Have you considered that? And you've been dealt a shitty hand with people in the past. That doesn't mean that this guy is going to screw you over, too. You said it yourself, he had feelings for you back then. Maybe that never totally went away. Maybe you *are* different for him."

"Or maybe as soon as he knows he's got me, he'll walk away. It would be kind of poetic justice considering what I did to him." She bent down and set the teetering stack of books on the floor, then sat down next to them.

Sam sighed and sank down next to Tessa. Hopefully, no one

was looking for romances by authors with Q last names because they were now blocking the whole section. "So just break it off with him then."

"What?" She looked at Sam, wondering where her hopeless romantic of a friend had wandered off to.

"You don't want to get hurt. I get that. But that's the only surefire way to ensure that you don't. Tell him you need some space right now, that you need to focus on your job and school."

She blinked. It was the exact thing she'd been thinking she needed to do, but hearing it out loud made her chest pull tight. "I'm not even sure we have anything to really break off. We've never put a label on any of it. It's just been sort of this super intense adventure."

Sam patted Tessa's knee then grabbed half the stack of books before standing up again. "Well, there you go. Problem solved. You can go back to focusing on your list. There's a Mexican cooking class at Central Market next week. We should go. And I think this store has a book club we can join. You can meet some new girlfriends."

The words turned into droning noise in her head. She managed a wan smile. "Right. Sounds great."

"Perfect," Sam said brightly. "Now grab the rest of those books. We've got to get back to work."

---

Tessa hung up the phone and raised her arms above her head in victory, sending a broad smile to the man leaning in her doorway. Finally, after her shitty morning and her stress about what to do about Kade, she had some good news.

Gibson grinned back. "Got 'em?"

"Doubled his donation from last year and is going to sponsor the swag bags."

"And the crowd goes wild," he announced, complete with

sound effects of a cheering arena. "I told you you'd get him. The guy is a hard-ass in business but he's a softie when it comes to kids. Plus, I heard you talking to him. You could've charmed the watch off his wrist if you'd wanted it."

Tessa leaned back in her chair, grinning like a cartoon character. She knew she had a long way to go. But after the drama with losing the band booking, this was definitely the biggest victory she'd had in a while. "I researched the crap out of his company, his life, and the causes he's championed in the past. Your tip on jotting down talking points before calling was brilliant. It helped me not to stall out and have those awkward silences like I did with that guy James Alario. God, that one was awful. But with this guy, as soon as I asked him about his dogs, I was in and it became a relaxed, normal conversation."

Gibson crossed his arms, looking pleased. Something about the expression reminded her so much of Kade that she had to rub chill bumps from her arms. There was no blood relation between the two, and they certainly didn't look alike with their opposite coloring. But it was obvious that the brothers had been cut from similar cloth—and mighty fine cloth it was. She was still a bit in shock that the gorgeous, confident man standing before her now used to be that angry, gangly boy who'd called her a bitch to her face when she hadn't stood up for Kade in high school when his name had been trashed.

At the time, she'd deserved Gibson's anger, had almost welcomed it as penance for all that had happened. But when she'd found out that Gibson was going to be her new boss, she'd been convinced that all that hate would still be there. She'd braced herself for getting fired on the first day. But instead, Gibson had been nothing but professional and helpful during her time here. If he still held any ire toward her, he'd been successful in hiding it.

"You're good at talking to people," Gibson said, nodding at the phone. "These bigwigs are used to people blowing smoke up their asses with all that fake flattery and fawning to get what they want. But you can tell you're not doing that. You're a straight-shooter and once you start talking about your charity, you'd have to have a heart of ice not to be at least a little affected by that. Hell, when I heard you talking to Mary Fielder the other day, you had *me* wanting to take in foster kids."

"Hey, don't rule it out," she said, pointing at him. "They're always looking for good people to help."

He laughed. "No way, not right now anyway at least. I can barely keep a plant alive. Kade got the daddy gene. That one might've been left out for me. You've met my train wreck of a father."

She shuddered, remembering the few brief times she'd come across Kade's stepdad. Even in just the short glimpses, she'd sensed the poison in that man. She'd stayed with enough families over the years to pick out the evil that glimmered beneath the surface in people. Kade's stepfather had been ripe with the stench of it. But before her mind could run away with memories, her attention snagged on something else Gibson had said. *Kade got the daddy gene.*

"Kade wants kids?" she asked, the idea not quite gelling with the image she had of him.

Gibson frowned, opened his mouth, then thought better of it and shut it. He pushed off the wall. "Never mind, not my place to say anything."

That had her sitting up straighter in her seat. Gibson was the only one besides Sam who knew she was seeing Kade. "What is there to say, Gib?"

Gibson looked toward the open door, obviously debating, then gave in. He turned back to her. "Kade already has a kid, Tessa. A daughter from his first marriage."

All air evaporated from her lungs. "What?"

Kade had mentioned a previous marriage in passing, but it hadn't even crossed her mind to ask if there were children. And in all the time they'd had together so far, he'd never said anything about having a child.

"Don't take offense if he hasn't brought it up. It's not the easiest topic for him. He's even managed to keep it out of the press because he doesn't want any of that attention directed at his daughter. The custody situation is messy, and he doesn't get to see Rosalie very often. His ex has gone through a lot of trouble to limit it to only a few hours a month."

"Why? Does she live far away?" she asked, not understanding why a mother would keep a child away from her dad if he was a good guy and wanted to participate.

Gibson shut her office door and stepped forward, bracing his hands on the chair across from her small desk. "His ex-wife had the judge in her pocket and painted Kade's lifestyle as deviant and endangering to a child even though he, of course, would never expose Rosalie to any of that. He keeps his sex life private just like any other responsible parent. But his ex paid one of the maids from the service Kade used at the time to take pictures of a room he had upstairs at his house. It held all his kink equipment, which, of course, would look terrifying to an outsider. And she also got one of his former girlfriends to give a statement about his proclivities. You know how things can be twisted out of context. Throw out to your average person that he ties up women and beats them for enjoyment, and you've got people ready to burn him at the stake. The accusations and evidence did enough damage to get him only limited, supervised time with his daughter. Rosalie's not even allowed over to his house."

"Jesus," Tessa said, her shoulders sagging with the knowledge.

"Yeah, he has another court date coming up, so he's hoping for a better outcome. He's locked down his private life. Up until you, for the last two years he's kept things at The Ranch where everyone knows how to keep things quiet. Publicly, he's said that he isn't in that lifestyle. But I don't know how far those things are going to go. People are still suspicious since he only goes out to public events with friends or his assistant."

"They know he's not living like a monk," she said flatly.

"Exactly," he said with a tired huff.

It warmed her to see how much Gibson seemed to care about his stepbrother, like he would do anything to fix it for him. Hell, she wished *she* could fix it. The thought of Kade being cut off from his daughter, and some little girl out there missing out on time with her dad. God, what she wouldn't have given to have had more time with her father. Her mother had gone off the deep end with her bipolar disorder, trading her meds for drugs of another sort, right around the time her dad had gotten sick. She'd dragged Tessa to a new town and kept her from him. By the time child services had stepped in to remove her from her mother, her father had been too ill to care for her. He'd died of brain cancer three months after she'd been placed in foster care.

"There's nothing else to do but hope?" she asked.

Gibson shrugged. "He's got a top-notch lawyer who told him he needs to create an image of stability. Kade's cut down on a lot of his travel and regulated his work hours. That playboy, being seen at all the hot spots version of himself is in the past. He has a room set up for Rosalie. But that judge is all 1950s values and conservatism . . ."

"Kade needs a wife and a picket fence," she said, the words landing like rocks in her belly.

Gibson looked up with a smirk. "His house has an iron fence around it. That'd probably do. But yeah. Maybe even throw in a golden retriever because that image of the scary whip-wielding, leather-clad freak is going to be hard to overcome in court."

She pressed her fingers to the spot between her brows, a headache forming. "And instead he's wasting time with me."

Gibson sat in the chair like the conversation was exhausting him. "Whatever y'all have going on is none of my business. But know that I told him he should take your relationship public, even if y'all were just doing the casual thing, and make it look more serious—even to you. But Kade's a better guy than I am. After what you did to him, I wouldn't have had qualms about breaking your heart back."

Her ribs cinched and her attention snapped upward.

Gibson shook his head. "Maybe that makes me a dick, but you crushed him, Tessa, and sent him into a lion's den with no weapon. The shit Doug did to him that night . . . he wouldn't even talk to me about it. But I know it was more than just your average beating. Something in my brother died that night. He was in therapy for a year after he moved in with his father because everyone was so worried about him. He'd never tell you that because he thinks it makes him look weak. But you have no idea what he went through. None of us really do."

Tears pricked her eyes between blinks, guilt raking through her with jagged force.

"I don't have a problem with you now. I can see you're trying to change. But whether you realize it or not, keeping your relationship secret is a selfish move, especially if you know there's no future. You get to date Kade for whatever purpose you want, you get to have a new job, you get to help your charity. It's the same as it was in high school. Kade helping, you taking. Kade tutored you when you needed help, he gave you friendship when you hadn't done anything to earn it, and he protected your secrets at great cost to him. And he never asked for anything back from you."

Tessa swiped at the moisture that tracked down her cheek. With each jab she felt smaller and smaller, but he was only speaking the truth. "I know. I didn't mean for it to be that way . . ."

"Doesn't matter what you meant, only what is. So, if you really feel bad about it and want to make it up to him, now's the time. Either suck up whatever consequences you might suffer and be seen on his arm or cut him loose so he can find someone who isn't scared to be out in public with him and who isn't opposed to the kind of relationship he wants. You two have been seeing each other a lot, so I know you're not blind. Kade cares about you. You knew it back then and you know it now. So it's your turn to take a hard look at your motivations. From the outside looking in, I see a girl who's enjoying a wild adventure and is soothing her wounded pride from getting cheated on with a guy who openly adores her. I don't see a woman willing to give herself to something real. My brother deserves better than that."

She stared at him, words leaving her.

He pushed up from the chair and tapped the top of her desk with his palm, returning to cool business mode. "I have to get to a meeting. Give it some thought. And call me if you need any help with the rest of that potential donors list."

He walked out without waiting for her reply, leaving her reeling. So much for speculating on whether or not Gibson still held any bad feelings toward her. He'd been better at hiding his low opinion of her than she'd thought.

But harder than fielding the barbs he'd thrown her way was wondering if he was dead-on right. Maybe she hadn't changed at all.

Maybe she'd never be able to be the kind of person Kade deserved.

Because even knowing how much hurt she'd caused him back then and how he needed her help now, she still felt like running.

# TWENTY-FIVE

Kade sat on a bench under the massive oak tree that served as their meeting place and turned his phone on silent. Work wasn't allowed to invade this little sliver of sacred space. The park was pretty empty this afternoon, the chilly overcast day chasing cold-sensitive Texans indoors, but Kade didn't mind the quiet. Sometimes there were so many people out here that it was like trying to spend quality time in a fish tank.

A car door slammed a few yards away and he turned toward the parking lot. A small tornado of blonde curls was already hurtling his way. He stood, holding out his arms to prepare for impact. Rosalie was wearing white tights, a pink skirt, and a flower-patterned sweater—perfect princess wear, but he knew that pristine outfit wouldn't last long. And sure enough, as soon as the thought crossed his mind, her foot smacked into a mud puddle, creating a Jackson Pollock version of her former self. Her mother shrieked her name from behind her, but Kade just laughed. Rosalie was rough and tumble wrapped in glitter. If Angie kept putting her in white, she was just asking for it.

Rosalie didn't even break stride and before he knew it, she was barreling into him like a mini-linebacker. "Daddy!"

"Spark!" He lifted her into his arms, spinning her, and she wrapped herself around him like an octopus. He closed his eyes as he hugged her back, inhaling the smell of banana Laffy Taffy and Burt's Bees baby shampoo. Angie had never changed the shampoo, and the scent reminded him of those early days when he'd rock Rosalie to sleep after Angie had nursed her. Back then, even when he knew his marriage was struggling, he never once considered the possibility that he'd be relegated to cameo appearances in his daughter's life.

Rosalie leaned back, her arms looped around his neck, and grinned a semi-toothless grin. "Look, I lost a front one. The tooth fairy brought me *ten dollars* for it. 'Cause those are more special."

Everything was a little lispy with the missing tooth, and he couldn't help but chuckle. No matter how hard it was knowing that he'd only get a couple of hours with her, there was no way he could maintain a grim mood under the power of a seven-year-old ball of sunshine. "Wow, you're rich, Spark."

"Yep. I bought *five* packs of glitter stickers," she said, a touch of awe in her voice.

He set her down, shaking his head. At least she was doing justice to the nickname he'd given her. Since age two, she'd never been able to resist something sparkly. Rosalie started to chatter again, but Angie stepped up behind her and put a hand on her shoulder. "Baby, can you go play on the swings for a minute? I need to talk to your dad."

Rosalie stuck her bottom lip out for a second and looked to Kade as if to get a veto, but he nodded toward the swings. "Go on, Spark. I'll be there in a second to give you a push."

When she was out of earshot, Angie crossed her arms and glanced toward the car. No doubt her husband, Chris, was there waiting for her. They would sit and wait for Kade's two hours to be up, watching him like he was some sort of prisoner on leave for the day. "I heard Barcelona burned down."

"Yeah," he said, not in the mood to talk with her when the clock was already ticking for his visit.

"I'm sorry. That's terrible."

He sighed. "Why are we having small talk, Angie? This is my time with Rosalie. Get to the point."

"You need to drop the custody case."

He scoffed. "Good-bye, Angie."

She reached out and grabbed his sleeve. "Wait, listen to me. I'm serious. It's just going to go like it did last time and will waste my money and yours. And even if they do make some adjustment to the arrangement, you're going to be doing Rosalie more harm than good by disrupting everything. Things are stable for her now. Every time she comes home from these visits, it takes me days to get her back on track. It confuses her and fills her with all these questions she doesn't need to be worrying about."

Kade's jaw clenched so hard, his teeth hurt. "What? Like why don't I get to see my daddy more? Why can't I go to his house?"

Angie's gaze flicked over to where Rosalie was playing, her pixie-like features going hard.

"Those are valid questions, Angie. I'm her father. Just because you don't want her to love me, doesn't mean you get to make it so. You can't just insert a replacement dad and expect me to disappear from her mind."

She made a disgusted sound in the back of her throat. "God, it's always about you, isn't it? This is about winning to prove a point and punishing me for moving on. You wouldn't even know what to do for Rosalie. You haven't had to parent her since she was two. You get to just walk in for two hours every now and then and be fun times guy. Skip all the hard stuff. You don't have to comfort her when she's sick or clean up the vomit. You don't have to make sure she gets to bed on time or deal with her crankiness when she doesn't. Chris and I handle that."

The trees around them seemed to turn from brown to red as fury leaked into Kade's system. "Are you seriously throwing that in my face? I don't handle it because *you won't let me.*"

Her attention zeroed back on him, eyes narrowed. "When exactly would you fit in her bath and bedtime story? Before the threesome you have on the docket that night? Or maybe right after you chain some woman up in your bedroom?"

He gritted his teeth and tried to keep from shouting. He didn't want Rosalie to know they were fighting. "That's not my life anymore."

Her lip curled. "Sure it isn't."

"Daddy! Push me!" Rosalie called. Her little legs were pumping but she wasn't getting the swing going like she wanted.

"Be right there, Spark." He spared Angie one last look. "I expect an extra ten minutes today since you've wasted my time."

He didn't wait for her response. There was no reason to. No matter what he said, Angie wasn't going to listen. If he'd hoped for her to one day grant mercy or become reasonable on this topic, he was a fool. She knew that he'd lay his life down before he'd hurt Rosalie or expose her to anything she shouldn't see. But ever since Angie had gotten remarried, Kade's presence in Rosalie's life had become a blemish on the picture perfect family image Angie wanted to create.

She'd come from divorced parents who'd remarried so many times and had so many combinations of step and half-siblings that Christmas had become a weeklong marathon just to visit all the different families. He knew how much she'd hated it both as a child and adult, so on some level, he understood why she was being so ruthless about this. But he no longer had patience for her fucked up view on things even if she'd come by it honestly. See a shrink and get over it. Don't cut your child's father out of her life just to make yourself feel better.

"Are you and mom fighting?" Rosalie asked when he made it over to the swing set.

He sighed and squatted down in front of her. "Nah, we were just talking." *Heatedly.*

She tilted her head, considering him in that evaluating way only a seven-year-old could. "Did you ask her if I could come to your house? I want to see the room you told me about, and you could help me make those cupcakes like we did at your restaurant that time."

His chest felt like a bale of hay had been dropped on it. "No, baby, we can't go to my house."

"Why not?"

Her big blue eyes flickered with sadness and a hint of betrayal—like he was the one who didn't really want her there—and he had the sudden urge to swoop her up and just take her home, rules be damned. Show her the room he had designed for her. Tell her that he wanted her there more than anything in life. But through all of this, he'd worked hard not to show the strain. She didn't need her parents' drama set on her little shoulders. "I'm hoping that will happen one day soon, Spark. But today we get the whole park to ourselves. And I brought you a special present for later."

Her grin returned with extra wattage with the mention of a present. And she jumped off the swing and challenged him to an epic game of hopscotch. When he lost that, twice, and not on purpose, he brought out her gift—a sparkly purple pair of roller-blades and helmet. Kade spent the rest of his time with her trying to teach her how not to be a crash test dummy. He was only partly successful. And before he knew it, Angie was heading back over, calling to them that it was time to go.

Rosalie whined, but he knew she wouldn't get too out of hand.

She, unfortunately, knew the drill. She pulled off her rollerblades and helmet and walked them over to Kade. "Thanks for the skates, daddy. I love them *so* much."

He squatted down to her level and ruffled her hair. "You don't have to give them back, peanut. You can take them home."

"Yeah, sweetie, Chris can help you practice. He has rollerblades in the garage," Angie added, her tone a little too bright.

Rosalie shook her head. "*No.* I want daddy to teach me. He's good at it."

Kade coughed over the snort that tried to escape. His kid was awesome. "You sure?"

"Yes," she said, determination in her little voice as she thrust the rollerblades toward him.

He could tell it was costing her something to part with the glitter-coated gift, but he took the skates and set them down on the ground, his heart swelling and breaking at the same time. Whether Rosalie knew it or not, this was her way of showing him that he still meant something important to her, that she was holding a spot for him in her life even if no one else wanted him there.

He pulled her into a hug and gave her a squeeze, smiling even though everything inside him felt off-center and broken at the thought of not seeing her again for another two weeks. "You be good for your mama, okay?"

"I will," she said, giving him an extra tight squeeze before letting him go and taking Angie's hand. "I love you, daddy."

He swallowed hard. "Love you, too, Spark."

Watching her walk away and then peek over her shoulder for one last wave before climbing into the car was about all he could take. He waited until the car pulled away then he sat down on the sidewalk, laced his fingers behind his head, and let the anguish overtake him.

It was a full fifteen minutes before he had the energy to get up, grab the rollerblades, and head to the car.

But when he rounded the grove of trees by the parking lot, he stopped midstride. Tessa was sitting on his back bumper with her chin in her hands. When she saw him, she lifted her head and her gaze flicked to his face, then to the skates, then back. Sympathy shrouded her features.

She knew.

"What are you doing here?" he asked, his voice croaky from the tears he'd shed.

She stood, clasping her hands in front of her like she was afraid he was going to tell her to fuck off. "Gibson told me where I could find you. I thought maybe we could go to dinner . . ."

"Dinner? Like pick up take out." That'd been their MO for the last few weeks.

She shook her head and stepped forward, holding her hand out. "No. Dinner. Like a date. In public."

"Tess, you don't have to . . ."

She closed the distance between them and took the skates from his hand. "Hush, I still plan on using you for your body later. Don't worry. I'll even pay for dinner so you feel really cheap and tawdry."

He laughed and drew her into his arms, setting his chin atop her head. Somehow she knew exactly what to say to make the load on his shoulders not feel so damn crushing. "Thank you."

She tilted her face up and pecked him on the lips. "Thank me later. Come on, the line at Dairy Queen's going to be killer if we don't get there soon."

"Ooh, big spender."

"You know it. I may even spring for a peanut butter sundae."

He released her from his hold and let her lead him to his car. "Well, now I'm just feeling pressure to put out."

She peeked back over her shoulder with a saucy smile, but he saw the tenderness lingering there in her eyes and felt it reach down into his bones, setting up shop like it'd never left. He knew then that he hadn't learned a thing since he was seventeen. This girl was going to break his heart all over again.

And if he didn't do something soon, all he was going to be able to do was stand by and let her.

# TWENTY-SIX

Kade swirled his spoon in his chocolate chip cookie dough shake, contemplating it like it was some exotic foreign food he'd never tasted.

Tessa rolled her eyes. "I told you I was just kidding about coming here. We could've gone somewhere else. I know you're used to haute cuisine, Mr. Vandergriff."

He lifted his gaze from his dessert with a smirk. "It's not that, smartass. I'm just not used to indulging like this. I gave up fast food sophomore year after getting oinked at one too many times. It still feels like the enemy, I guess."

She tilted her head. "I never understood why they called you those names. You weren't overweight when I met you."

"The universe granted me mercy and I had a growth spurt at sixteen that, along with my diet, thinned me out some. But it didn't matter to the other kids. You know how things stick. Though, to their credit, they did shift over to teasing me more about the stutter instead since that was still fair game."

She took a bite of her sundae, remembering how he'd stumble

over his words the more nervous he got. Part of it had been kind of cute and endearing because she could tell when she was knocking him off balance, but she'd seen how brutal the other boys were when the stutter would appear at school. She remembered wishing with everything she had that Kade's mouth would just cooperate with him. "How'd you get past that? You can't even tell that you used to struggle with it."

He held out his spoon so she could taste his dessert. "When I moved in with my dad, he got me a top-notch speech therapist and had me see a psychologist. They think a lot of my problem was tied to all the stress at home and the social anxiety of being bullied or whatever. Either way, by my third year in college, it was almost completely gone."

"And smooth and charming Kade Vandergriff emerged," she said, trying to sound upbeat even though she knew he was glossing over the story about why he'd been in therapy. Gibson had made it clear Kade had been going through more than dealing with a stutter.

He shrugged. "I don't know about all that, but I owe my father a lot. He didn't have to accept me into his life like he did. He didn't even know me. But he took me on like a project. Taught me about life, confidence, and business."

"Are you still close?"

"Yeah. He retired a few years ago and spends a lot of time on the coast now, but we get together pretty often. I also have two half-sisters who live in town. One took over my dad's restaurant supply business, the other is a teacher."

"Wow, that had to be crazy walking into an entirely new family with relatives you had no idea existed."

"Yeah, it was overwhelming. But after the initial shock, they took me in like I'd been part of the family my whole life. Maybe because I look just like my dad—that made it more believable. I eventually did the DNA test thing, but really, that was more for my reassurance than theirs. I'd never experienced that kind of open acceptance before. I mean, my mom loved me, but she had her problems. And I knew that when it came down to it, she'd always choose my stepdad over me. So for a while, I didn't trust the Vandergriffs."

She smirked. "I know how that is. When new foster parents were nice to me, I was more likely to be suspicious than thankful. Normal families still freak me out a little."

"As if there's such a thing as normal." He went back to staring at his cup for a while, lost in thought, and she knew his mind had drifted back to his own fractured family. He let out a long, tired breath. "So why are we here, Tess? You haven't wanted to go out in public since day one. Why now?"

She watched him, trying to choose her words carefully. "Gibson kind of told me about your situation with your daughter and ex-wife."

His expression turned wry, but he didn't look up. "Gibson has a big mouth."

"He cares about you."

He leaned back in his chair, meeting her gaze head-on. "One doesn't negate the other."

"He told me I should break things off with you."

He shifted forward so swiftly the table rattled. "He *what*?"

She wet her lips, that glare of his scrambling her thoughts for a minute. "He told me to set you free so that you could find someone to date for real or to step up and be on your arm in public."

Kade's expression darkened like spring storms rolling in over a formerly sunny day. "It wasn't his place to give you that ultimatum. My problem isn't yours. And even if it was, I think Gib's plan is shaky at best. Having a girlfriend on my arm isn't going to really prove anything. I don't exactly have the best track record with long-term relationships. The court date is in less than three months. Who's going to care that I've been seeing some chick for a few months? They'll just think it's another fling."

She swirled her ice cream with her spoon, watching the vanilla melt and become one with the peanut butter syrup. Nerves were flailing around in her stomach like epileptic sparrows, but she kept her expression smooth. "Agreed. That probably wouldn't matter."

"So why are we even worrying about it?" He shoved a spoonful of ice cream into his mouth, almost as if he was in combat with his dessert.

She took a deep breath. "Because having a new girl on your arm won't make a difference, but having your former high school crush and brand new fiancée who you've been dating in secret for six months on your arm is an entirely different matter."

Kade went still and silent, spoon abandoned in his cup.

"Think about it," she hurried on, worried that if she didn't barrel forward, she'd chicken out and run away screaming for the hills. This was so completely off her fucking list and life plan that she may as well have transported herself to a new dimension. She knew the smart thing to do would be to break it off now, let him be with someone else. But after seeing him with his daughter today, she couldn't bring herself to go through with it. Her heart had broken, watching him fall apart after his little girl had left. He needed someone to be there for him. He needed her. "I haven't dated anyone in a year and you haven't been seen with anyone publicly in a while, so the timing is totally believable, especially since we knew each other before."

"You're being serious right now?" Kade asked, something akin to awe in his voice.

"I know it sounds insane, but we'd only have to keep up appearances until your court date. And you know the local press would eat it up. My ex will freak the hell out, but the more I think about it, the more I might kind of enjoy that."

"Tess, do you even know what you're saying? What that would involve? It's everything you hate . . ."

She glanced past him toward the window, staring out at the orange and red shafts of setting sun and absorbing his very valid warning. Yes, it was everything she dreaded. Playing a fake role for everyone else. The media turning their evaluating eyes on her and dredging up her past. All of it had her near the breathing in a paper bag stage. But once upon a time there was a boy who'd needed her to stand up for him and she hadn't. "Kade . . . I saw you, when your daughter left. I saw how much this is killing you. And how much she didn't want to go."

He made a sound in the back of his throat, and she could almost feel him bracing to keep the grief from surfacing again, to stay the cool, calm Kade.

She turned back to him and reached across to thread her fingers with his. They were chilled, whether from being wrapped around his shake or from the bomb she was dropping on him, she wasn't sure. "I want to help. So what do you say? Will you accept my proposal or do I need to get down on one knee?"

The emotion that broke over his face nearly unraveled her. She was so used to the strong, nothing-bothers-me version of Kade that the flash of raw vulnerability left her breathless. He stood, tugging her up with him, and gathered her against his chest. "Tessa, I can't even, this is . . . I don't know what to say."

"Just say yes. Let me do this for you." She pushed up on the balls of her feet to give him a peck. But Kade wasn't satisfied with that. He grabbed her legs, lifted her off her feet, and wrapped her legs around his waist, going in for a real kiss. She let out a little gasp of surprise but quickly melted into his hold. He tasted like cookies and vanilla and pure temptation.

A few teenage boys who'd been eating burgers in a corner booth sent catcalls their way, reminding her where they were. She broke off the kiss with a laugh.

Kade grinned and set her down. "Maybe we should get out of here. Don't want to traumatize anyone."

"Good idea." They gathered their trash in a rush, tossed it, and were out the door before the manager who'd been giving them the stink eye could give them a stern talking to. When they climbed into the car, she looked over at him. "My place or yours?"

He stuck the key in the ignition. "Yours is closer. I'll drive you back to the park to pick up your car first, though. It's not safe to leave it there too late at night."

They did the car exchange in record time, and he followed her to her house. Her body was still buzzing from the kiss and all the adrenaline over the decision she'd made, so by the time she turned the corner onto her street, she was ready to ravage and be ravaged. But the unfamiliar car parked in her driveway had her slowing down.

Her phone rang. Kade. She hit the speaker button on her steering wheel. "Looks like you have company, Tess. Expecting any?"

"No, I don't recognize the car."

"Want me to lay low until you know who it is?"

She frowned as she pulled in front of her house, squinting to see if she could see who was in the car. "No, if we're going public, we don't need to hide. Maybe someone has the wrong house."

She parked her car in the driveway, and Kade pulled his along the curb. When she climbed out, she could see that her visitor had helped himself to her porch swing. Even in the dark, the shadowed figure was all too familiar. Doug had a certain way of holding himself, like he had a steel rod up his shirt. "Fuck."

A warm hand touched the small of her back as Kade stepped up behind her. "What's wrong?"

"I guess this is the answer to the question: What happens if Tessa changes her number and doesn't answer his calls?"

Tessa could feel Kade shift gears almost instantly, like a tuning fork being struck. And the energy vibrating off of him wasn't at all friendly.

"Well, isn't that sweet?" Doug said, strolling down the porch, his ever-present suit swishing in the silence. "Did I interrupt date night again?"

The words were spoken with a light tone but there was no misinterpreting the cold maliciousness in his gaze. Kade stiffened next to her.

"What are you doing here, Doug?" Tess said, stepping forward in front of Kade, almost in a protective motion—like they'd slid backward on their timeline and Kade was still the kid who could be protected by the power of the popular girl.

Doug ignored her, something he was well-practiced at, and gave Kade and his casual jeans and T-shirt attire a dismissive once-over. He stuck his hand out toward Kade like he was the president of the fucking United States greeting a mere mortal. "Douglas Barrett."

Kade ignored the outstretched hand and moved next to Tessa. "I know who you are."

Doug's eyes narrowed, and he lowered his hand. His attention shifted to Tessa. "Is this the same jerkoff I talked to a few weeks ago or are you on a leg-spreading rotation? Hard to keep up."

Kade lurched forward, biblical-level wrath in his eyes, but Tessa scrambled in front of him, putting her hands to his chest and a plea in her voice. "Don't. Please. Not worth it."

Plus, she was afraid if let loose, Kade could possibly kill Doug. She didn't know exactly what had happened that night between them all those years ago, but she sensed murder might not be an unjustified response.

Doug chuckled behind her. "Ready to attack already? Who is this guy?"

She turned around, Kade at her back. "You need to leave. I didn't invite you and you're not welcome."

The amused expression faded. "You haven't answered my calls, and I still haven't found my grandfather's watch. And now my dad's coin collection is missing, too. You need to let me in that house, so I can get what you obviously took."

She scoffed. "You're so full of shit. You know I don't have those things. You're here because you can't stand that I'm ignoring you."

"Maybe you took them to pay off the bills at your pathetic little pet project. I've heard it's quite the cash sieve."

Calling the charity pathetic sent all her bitch buttons blinking, but if she let herself get out of control, it'd only be minutes before the guys were scrapping on her lawn like junkyard dogs. "I don't need your help with my charity anymore. I'm handling it."

"Sure you are." He nodded at Kade. "Hope your pockets are deep, my friend, and that the pussy's worth it."

A bomb went off behind her. It happened too fast for her to intervene, her hands grasping air as Kade flew past her. Kade grabbed Doug by his lapels and hauled him up the porch and against the wall with a crushing bang. Tess ran after them.

Kade's voice was murderously calm. "If I were you, Douggie, I'd be real careful what you say next. You want to know who this guy is? Maybe I should stutter and jog your memory. I'm the guy who despises you enough that jail might be worth the chance to beat you until you cry and beg and break. Maybe I should do to you exactly what you did to me."

Doug's eyes went wide at that, and it was the first time Tessa could recall seeing real fear flicker there. Doug's gaze darted to her then back to Kade. "Fowler?"

"Apologize to Tess for being a crude and obnoxious prick tonight," Kade said, his grip on Doug not relenting.

Doug's jaw clenched and she could tell, though he was wary of Kade, he wasn't quite ready to concede. "I apologize, Tessa."

The lack of sincerity was clear to them all, and Kade looked ready to kill him with his bare hands. She'd never seen anyone look so deadly. The hate was like a palpable flavor in the air around him. But when she called Kade's name, truly scared he might do something, Kade released Doug with a shove, and stepped back. Tessa let go of the breath she'd been holding and went to stand next to Kade, taking his hand. His was shaking.

Doug glanced down at their linked hands and snorted. "You've got to be kidding me. *Him*, Tessa? Seriously?"

"You need to go," she said.

"Guess it's true what they say about the law of attraction. Trash attracts trash. Have fun playing in the gutter."

Kade made some growly noise under his breath but she put her other hand on his upper arm, keeping him from launching at Doug and doing real damage this time.

Doug shook his head like he couldn't believe he had to suffer the presence of such pathetic creatures. "You'll be hearing from my lawyer about the watch and coins."

She chose not to take any more of his bait and watched him smooth his jacket then head toward the rental car. She squinted, catching what looked to be movement next to the car, but it was too dark to tell. Probably a neighbor peeking over the hedges for the show. Great. She gave another investigating look as Doug pulled out but didn't see anything else. And not until his taillights disappeared off the street did she let herself ease her grip on Kade's hand. She leaned into him. "You okay?"

"No, not really," he said, his voice so quiet it almost didn't sound like him.

She looked up at him, concern lacing her. "What's wrong?"

He leaned against the railing of her porch, the lines of his jaw flexing. He'd gone pale and sweat had broken out along his brow. "You saw me. I almost fucking lost it. I *hate* that he can still get to me."

"Don't be so hard on yourself. He would've kept provoking you until you snapped at the bait. That's his way. Provoke and then make the other person feel like they're the ones acting irrationally. He used to do it to me all the time."

He shook his head, tension still swirling around him like a fog. "You don't understand. I hate feeling out of control like that. I'm not that person anymore. He shouldn't be able to affect me at all. But it's taking everything I have right now not to get in my car, hunt him down, and wring the life right out of him." He met her gaze. "I could kill that guy in cold blood and not feel remorse. I don't want to be that person."

"No," she said, her voice firm. "You aren't that person. You had the chance to hurt him tonight and you let him leave."

"Only because you were here," he said, running a hand through his hair and stalking the length of the porch. "God, I hate that he can get to me like that. It makes me feel crazy, out of control."

She rubbed her arms, worried at this shift in him. He looked like he needed to punch a wall or pummel something, like all this energy was built up with nowhere to go. But she didn't have a punching bag to offer. And she sure didn't want him going after Doug and getting himself in trouble.

She wet her lips, another idea hovering. It was a risk, but some instinct inside her told her it may be just what he needed. She walked backward toward her door, slid the key inside by feel, and turned the knob. "So take the control back."

He glanced over at her, brows still low over his eyes. "What are you talking about?"

She pushed the door open behind her. "Forget about him and take some control back. I'm here. I won't fight it."

His expression darkened. "I don't think that's a good idea right now. You haven't seen my mean side, and I'm not sure I trust myself to keep it light and easy right now. Just give me a few minutes to calm down."

"Maybe I don't want you to calm down," she said, the words escaping before she could evaluate their possible consequences.

"You've given me my fantasy. Maybe it's time you show me yours. What would you do if you weren't worried about what I'd think?"

He stared at her for long seconds, and she almost chickened out and took it back, but then he was stalking across the porch in a blink. She backed up into the house, and Kade kicked the door shut behind him. "Tell me your safeword, Tess."

Her voice went hoarse in an instant. "Red."

He moved forward, wrapping his hand around the base of her neck. "Tell me you really want this."

The grip on her neck and his words coalesced in the small space of her entryway, creating a foggy, heady feeling that wasn't altogether unpleasant. This was it. No more safety net. Even though she'd surrendered to him at The Ranch, she knew he was still holding back parts of himself. She'd seen the things the other dominants did to their submissives. Kade had never tried any of that with her. The only pain had been spanking.

She'd realized that night that he'd been going easy on her, introducing her slowly to his darker side, keeping it all playful, fun fantasy. She'd been thankful for it at first, the heavier stuff scaring her. But she couldn't deny that lately, she'd found herself imagining more, amping up the intensity in her mind and wondering what it would be like for Kade to go into full primal mode with her—she'd sensed it there right beneath his surface and now it was glittering on the forefront like moonlight on black water. The idea of exposing herself to that primitive side of Kade both turned her on and scared her. But in her heart of hearts, she did trust him to not physically harm her.

"I want this—whatever *this* is."

"This," he said, guiding her none too gently down to her knees by her neck, "is the ugly part."

# TWENTY-SEVEN

Kade loomed over her, every trace of his normally easy-going expression gone. "On all fours. Crawl to the bedroom."

She got in position but peeked upward before moving. He couldn't be serious. "You want me to crawl like a dog?"

His expression hardened and he wrapped his fingers in her hair. "No, I want you to do what I say without question. Understood?"

"Yes, sir," she managed, though her heart seemed to be pounding so hard it was affecting her vocal cords.

He tugged her forward, not hard enough to do damage, but enough to make her scalp tingle in protest and her body move beneath her. He led her into her bedroom and left her there on the floor while he turned on her bedside lamp. When he swiveled back around, he gave her an appraising look. "Are you wearing anything important to you? Something that can't be replaced?"

She shook her head.

"Good. Stand up."

She scrambled to her feet, her body going on autopilot for the commands. The whole thing should have freaked her out, but for some reason, everything inside her pinged with anticipation—like watching a horror movie and knowing something was about to jump from behind the curtain but unable to look away. This was Kade without a filter.

Kade closed the distance, his gaze like lead weights anywhere it landed on her. He reached out and grabbed the collar of her blouse with both hands and yanked, sending the buttons flying.

"Kade! What are you doing?"

The buttons skittered along the wood floor, and he tossed the shredded blouse to the side. His hand went to her neck, collaring it. "I'm doing what I want. Take the jeans off."

*Oh, shit.* Hello, deep end of the pool, nice to meet you. She fumbled with her snap and zipper, the presence of his hand on her throat making her thoughts branch and divert in directions she couldn't quite follow, but eventually she managed to work the jeans down and off.

"Good girl." He ran his fingers along her jawline. "Scared?"

She rolled her lips inward, considering the question, but then shook her head. "No, not exactly. Confused maybe."

He watched her as she spoke, as if recording every verbal and physiological response she had. "By me or your reactions?"

"Both."

That answer seemed to give him what he was looking for. He turned her in his hold, putting her back to his front. His erection was hot against her backside, and everything went liquid inside her. She almost didn't want to admit to herself how turned on she was already. His lips brushed her ear. "We all have sides that we don't show the world, Tess. The back of the coin. This is mine. I like some violence, some edges. A little darkness. Let's see what your flipside looks like."

He grasped her upper arms and walked her to the bed, then pressed a palm to the center of her back bending her over. He nudged her ankles apart.

"Eyes closed. Stay there."

"Okay," she whispered, her heart beating so hard she wondered if it could leave an imprint in the mattress.

The sound of his footsteps receded. He'd left the room, but she didn't have the guts to look back to see where he was going. A rummaging noise came from somewhere in the house, and then Kade was back, his presence seeming to charge the room with static. Something cool touched her shoulder. She sucked a breath.

"Don't. Move."

A metallic edge ran over her skin and under the strap of her bra, sending fear pulsing through her. *Oh, God.*

---

Kade knew he was pushing it as he ran the dull edge of a knife along Tessa's skin. Fire was still running through his veins from earlier. And he needed this more than Tessa could even understand. But he also was acutely aware of how wrong this could go if he wasn't one hundred percent on his game.

He'd learned early on that when a submissive dropped an unintentional hint or said something then wanted to take it back, more times than not, it was a desire that scared her. Which meant it was what he most needed to give her. And Tessa had slipped when she'd said she didn't want him calm. His anger had affected her in a way she may have not understood, but he'd seen the reaction.

The little whisper of roughness, of violence, had made her challenge him instead of shrinking away. And it'd flipped every single one of his dominance switches. He'd been keeping his sadistic side mostly in check around her because he didn't want to scare her. But she'd shown the most important component of all tonight. She *trusted* him. At the most basic level, she knew that she was safe with him.

And then she'd asked for it. Asked for what he so needed in

that moment after Doug had left. *Maybe I don't want you to be calm.* It had broken open something inside him and the part of him he usually kept locked away, even at The Ranch, had trampled through the door.

So now when he ran the knife under her bra strap, he prayed that he hadn't misjudged her signals. Because he was pushing her far beyond where they'd ever treaded before. But when he turned the blade, careful to hold the sharper edge away from her skin, and sliced through the bra strap, the quiet whimper she made was the perfect kind of fear.

"Brave girl," he said softly.

"Or a stupid one," she murmured, her body as still as a stone but her tone sardonic.

He smirked and smacked her across the fleshy part of her thigh. "Not nice to talk back."

But in truth he loved that her defenses were rushing up. The more sarcastic she got, the more he was getting to her and the more what had happened outside was becoming a distant memory for him. He hooked the band of her underwear with his finger, pulling them away from her waist, and ran the knife through them. Yes, he could've just taken them off of her. But he knew well how powerful a mental image could be. Cutting her clothes off sent a clear message—*your things and normal protections are worthless right now, you own nothing, only I can give and take away.* He set the blade on the dresser and then tugged the scrap of panties away. The satin was soaked against his palm.

He had to swallow back the groan at the victory. His instincts had been right. "Do you know what it does to me to see how wet you are right now?"

"You're a bad, bad man, Mr. Vandergriff."

He pressed his lips together, trying not to smile, and unhooked his belt buckle. "Keep up the sarcasm and see how that works out for you."

At the sound of the leather belt pulling out of the loops, she lifted her head and peered back over her shoulder. He looped the belt and tucked the buckle into his hand. All shreds of attitude fell away from her, self-preservation kicking in. "Kade . . ."

"Do you have a vibrator, Tess?"

She blinked. "What?"

"Simple question."

She pressed her face back into the comforter as if she were too embarrassed to say it to his face. "Bedside table, top drawer."

He headed over and pulled the little pink bullet out of its clear box. Simple and utilitarian. Perfect. What he was about to do to Tessa was not meant to be a punishment. Even if she didn't realize that yet. But it certainly would be better with a little extra motivation.

He walked behind her again and gave her a little pop on her left ass cheek. "Lift your hips."

She pushed up on her toes and did as she was told. He rubbed the rounded tip of the vibe against her slick folds and her fingers curled into her comforter. He hadn't even turned it on yet, and already she was desperate for it.

"Put your hands beneath you and hold this against you. Don't move it away unless I tell you. Understand?"

"Yes." She nodded against the sheets and slipped her hands downward, pinning her arms beneath her body and taking the vibrator with her. She adjusted into a position that allowed her to hold it where she needed, and he turned it on. She jolted and her knees buckled slightly before she regained her balance. "God."

"So keyed up already. But no coming until I tell you." He coasted his hand over the curve of her ass, while the belt buckle warmed in his other palm. "Now, ask me to hit you."

"What?" Her voice held disbelief. "Why would I ask for it?"

He ran the loop of leather along her spine, barely brushing her skin, and smiled when she visibly quivered. "Because it's what you want. You didn't goad me outside and tempt me while I was angry, so I'd come in here and be sweet and cuddly. Correct?"

Her back rose and fell with quick but deep breaths. "No."

"Then ask for what you want, and you may be lucky enough to get it."

She was quiet a few long seconds, only the soft hum of the vibrator filling the room, but then she rallied her nerve. "Please hit me. I want you to."

His blood surged at the admission, his cock throbbing against his zipper and his heart knocking against his ribs, but he didn't make a move yet. "Why?"

"Goddammit, can't you just do it?" she asked, defensiveness edging her voice. "I don't want to think about why."

But he wasn't in the mood to let her get away with that. What he wanted to do with her was not for the faint of heart. He needed to hear that this was more than just curiosity or some show of bravado. "Nope. Try again."

He could almost hear her gritting her teeth. So stubborn, his Tess. He backed up a few steps, making sure she could hear his retreat, and that got her. She shifted restlessly against the bed but started talking. "All my life, everyone's treated me with white gloves, like I'm some porcelain doll to be left in the box or I'll shatter. With foster parents, they were scared I'd snap and become crazy like my mother. With Doug, he wanted the untarnished trophy."

His heart squeezed in his chest at the honest words, and it took everything he had not to reach out and caress her, but he could tell she wasn't done.

She turned her head and looked back at him, her gaze stripped clean. "I want you to hit me because being with you like this makes me feel less fragile. You aren't afraid to push me, to break me. And sometimes . . . I wonder how it'd feel to be broken."

The admission reached inside him and twisted things around into something new, opening up an ache that echoed through his deepest chambers. He walked forward again and pushed her hair away from her face. It'd be the last bit of tenderness he'd show her for a while, but he needed her to know that he'd heard her. *Really* heard her.

She'd gone through life and no one had bothered to leave a mark.

Well, that was about to change.

He let his hand slip away from her face, raised his other arm, and let the belt stripe across her ass. The sharp curse she made was one of the sweetest sounds he could ever remember hearing.

He gave her a breath to call a safeword if she needed it, but when none came, he landed another lash on her backside, creating angry parallel marks on her skin. So fucking pretty.

"You still with me, girl?" he asked, purposely using a term that had a humiliating tone to it. He knew she'd never admit it, but verbally taking her down a notch did something for her. He'd seen it when he teased about the word *slut* being an endearment in his world. And he'd seen it when he called her slave that night at The Ranch.

"Yes, sir."

"Good, because I'm not even near done with you." He let the belt come down again, this time across the backs of her thighs. "I want you to be thinking of me every time you sit down for the next few days at the office, remembering how badly you wanted to be my pretty little slut tonight."

She groaned with such gritty desire that he had to pause for a second to reel in his own stampeding desire. He unfastened his jeans to get some space before he had a permanent zipper imprint on his cock and tugged off his shirt.

"I can just picture you there in your office, my dear brother droning on about some PR initiative, and you'll be squirming and wet in your seat while you remember what it felt like to be under my belt." He hit her again. "And Gibson will know. Anytime you wince, he'll know."

A soft gasp escaped her.

"Does that bother you?" he asked, his tone teasing as he landed another lash across her back.

She bowed up at that, and he could see her arms shift to get the vibrator back in place. Her skin was fully flushed now, a gloss of sweat coating her, and her breath had gone choppy. She was fighting that orgasm hard. Good.

"Answer me, girl." He punctuated it with a quick pop on the ass with his free hand, catching her off guard.

"I—I don't know if it bothers me."

He set the belt aside for a second and pressed one palm to her lower back, reaching between her legs with his other hand. Hot, wet arousal coated his fingers as he tucked two inside her, the device vibrating against his knuckles through her inner wall. She clenched around him and whimpered.

"Does it bother you or does it turn you on? Knowing that others know how down and dirty you can be? That you like to be used?"

She was rocking against his hand as he pumped his fingers slowly into her. He'd wondered if he'd get a reaction to calling her dirty, but any shame had apparently been left two near-orgasms ago. "It makes me feel embarrassed . . ."

He could tell that wasn't the whole answer, but she seemed reluctant to say the rest, so he helped her out. "And the embarrassment makes you hot."

She made a desperate sound as he moved a third finger inside her. "Yes. God, none of this makes sense."

He smiled. His girl had quite the exhibitionist streak. The things he'd put her through already would've made most girls die of panic. He loved that she could lose that fear and be free in front of his friends. "Don't be too embarrassed. Gib's no stranger to this world. Your secret is safe with him."

Without giving her warning, he slipped his fingers from her and picked up the belt again.

Earlier tonight she'd given him a gift so amazing, he could never repay it. But that wasn't going to stop him from trying.

She may be his slave right now, but he would forever be in her service.

And tonight, he'd start with her first request.

It was time to break the porcelain.

# TWENTY-EIGHT

The belt came down on Tessa in a ruthless pattern of blows, never quite hitting the same spot, but sending a continuous wave of burning, humming energy over her body. She wouldn't be surprised if she glowed in the dark. Pain had become something unrecognizable by the fourth or fifth swat, and now the throbbing kept time with the pulsing ache in her clit. Everything was sensitive and on high alert, even the parts of her that hadn't been touched.

She wanted to claw at the sheets, but her hands remained trapped beneath her, desperately shifting the vibrator from spot to spot so as not to explode in orgasm. She'd never felt such a grinding need to come. But Kade seemed to be in no hurry to give her the go ahead.

She peeked back at him, hoping to distract her from all the sensations, but seeing him looming above her in nothing but an unzipped pair of jeans had another flood of arousal slicking her thighs. Her gaze drifted down the planes of muscle in his chest and abdomen to the thick outline in his boxer briefs and back up to his face. God, every part of him was beautiful. It was as if the universe had forced him to bloom late because high school girls wouldn't have known what to do with this version. But she'd sensed it in him back then, beneath the stringy hair, hunched shoulders, and stutter. That quiet intensity and unshakeable strength had always been there. She'd been drawn to it even when she hadn't quite been able to pinpoint what was drawing her.

His focus flicked over to her face, his eyebrow lifting. "Enjoying the view?"

"You have no idea," she said, her voice strained from the still coiling tension inside her.

He dipped his hand inside his underwear, freeing his erection. He gave it a long, slow stroke that nearly sent her over the edge just from watching. "This is what you do to me, Tess. Seeing you like this, knowing it's turning you on, too."

He set the belt aside and glided his hand along her fevered skin. She could picture the welts rising on her back beneath his fingers, but somehow the image didn't appall her. Instead, every sensation racing through her amplified, her entire being ready to burst open. "Please, Kade."

His hand grasped the back of her neck. "All the way on the bed. Grab the headboard and get your ass in the air for me. Legs spread."

His movements were rough, his commands coarse, as he guided her along the mattress, but the manhandling was kicking up some unknown hunger inside her. Her mind was tumbling down a path she didn't understand, one where she pictured taking it even further, imagined him grabbing her hair, tossing her down, holding her against the bed and making demands.

But before she could get freaked out by where her mind was scampering off to, Kade gave her a pop on the thigh right over the angry belt marks. "I said, legs spread."

She gritted her teeth at the sting, wishing the vibrator was still against her, but managed to get in the right position.

"Good girl," he said, as he pulled his pants and boxers off. He donned a condom and climbed on the bed with her.

She expected him to immediately enter her, wished for it—because Lord, she needed to come—but instead the soft, wet heat of his tongue ran over her. She jolted and almost lost her grip on her headboard.

"Mmm," he said, his breath tickling her labia. "You have the sexiest cunt—so sexy and pink. I could spend all night torturing you with my mouth."

At that, he parted her with his thumbs and his tongue slid inside her. Everything broke apart. She couldn't stop it. Orgasm, bright and powerful, overtook her and she cried out with the force of it. Kade didn't let her squirm away. He worked her harder, holding her against his mouth as he fucked her with his tongue, the scent of her arousal filling the room.

She gripped wood slats of the headboard with all her might as she let the orgasm envelop her and take her down.

Kade pulled back after her gasping breaths ended. "I don't remember giving you permission for that."

"I'm sorry," she said, her voice cracking. "I tried. I really did."

"You'll find another one for me. He leaned over to her bedside table and grabbed something else from her drawer. He gripped her thighs and positioned her again since she'd sagged to the mattress.

"I'm not sure I can—"

He gave her thigh a smack, and the sensation went straight to all her throbbing parts. "I wasn't asking you. I've been waiting to claim this ass since the first night. You're about to be very, very happy that you keep that little bottle of K-Y in your drawer."

*Oh, God.*

Without preamble or finesse, he dripped the cold lubricant along her back entrance. She clenched automatically but when he pushed a finger in, everything went quivery inside her. *Good God.*

"Reach down and grab the vibrator to hold against yourself.

That will help things." He held her steady while she got into a workable position. She pressed the vibrator lightly against her clit, still too keyed up to take the full stimulation, and Kade positioned himself behind her. He felt huge and like there was no way he'd ever get inside her.

"Kade—"

But the pressure increased as he moved forward. "I need you to relax and push back against me, baby. Let me in."

She closed her eyes and focused on doing what he said. The vibrator hummed softly against her, making the discomfort bearable as he pushed past the ring of muscle. If she hadn't been so keyed up with arousal and near orgasm again, it probably would've hurt. But as soon as he got past the initial resistance and slid deeper, she knew he'd been right when he'd said she could come again. Every nerve in her system roared at the edgy invasion. Sensations she didn't know existed crackled through her with every inch he added until he was seated all the way inside her. She had to breathe through the fullness of it all, the sexy forbiddenness of the act.

He didn't ask if she was okay. This was not about her. But she wouldn't have told him to stop if he'd asked anyway. She felt overtaken in the best way possible.

Instead of thrusting into her, he gripped her hips with harsh fingers and dragged her back and forth along his cock in a slow glide, handling her like she was simply some inanimate object to use as he pleased. Her one-handed grip slipped from the headboard and her muscles turned rag doll as he handled her. Her chest lowered to the bed, her nipples dragging back and forth along the comforter with his motions. Every part of her felt both alive and separate, a thousand entities trying to cooperate at once. Her mind began to fuzz, launching her into some dreamy, sensation-filled state.

"I can feel your fucking surrender, baby," Kade said, his voice roughened with his own restraint. "You're all mine now, aren't you? All you're here for is to give me what I need."

"Yes, sir," she said in her haze, the words sending desire coiling tight inside her.

He pulled her thighs from under her and put her flat onto her stomach, then worked the vibrator between her and the bed. He braced a hand next to her and pressed the other to her face, his palm spanning the side of her head. The move made her feel pinned and insignificant, like he couldn't even bother to look at who he was fucking. And the idea should've pissed her off, somewhere in her foggy brain she knew that, but instead the hold, the vibrator, and the feel of him filling her had her barreling into hyperspace.

He increased his speed and rocked into her ass without reprieve as she clung to unraveling threads of her self-control, trying to keep from coming again without permission. For all the foreplay, she'd expected this part to be short, but Kade seemed to be in complete control of his own release.

"Come, Tessa," he demanded.

The words sliced right through those last threads and she moaned, low and long, as a second, sharper orgasm hit her. He didn't slow his pace and if anything, he plunged even deeper and harder. The pressure of his hand on her head increased.

Soon, she was gasping and writhing beneath him, the stimulation almost too much, but he wasn't letting her go.

"Now you fucking do it again," he said, his voice hard. "You aren't done."

The vibrator was trapped against her clit, Kade's body weight holding her against the bed, and she whimpered. Her muscles were quivering and her skin felt electrified. It was all so much. *So* much. There was no way . . .

Kade moved his hand away from her face and dropped to his forearms above her. His lips touched the curve of her shoulder, and she thought he was going to kiss her, but instead his teeth sank into her skin, holding her like an animal as he tunneled again and again into the most private part of her.

She shattered, a silent scream searing her throat, as she launched into some other dimension where she no longer had conscious control of her body. Kade let go then, too, sinking deep and pouring his release into her with unintelligible words and coarse, groaning pleasure. But even when he was through, he held her in place beneath him. Her orgasm went on and on, like light trails from fireworks, leaving afterimages and scorch marks on her psyche.

She couldn't stop. She could barely breathe. She bit the sheets to try to hold back the screams.

But when she started to cry from the overwhelming bigness of all that *feeling*, Kade gently rolled off of her, taking her with him and getting her off the vibrator. Sobs overtook her as he tucked her against his side, flipped the comforter over their bodies, and kissed her hair. "Shh, just let it happen, baby."

She had no idea why she was sobbing, but she couldn't seem to quit. She tucked her face in the crook of his shoulder and cried without reason or understanding. Through it all, Kade simply held her, stroking her and giving her silent support. Unlike many men, he seemed completely at ease with her tears. He didn't try to talk her out of them or fix them or ask her why. That alone made her want to never get up out of this bed.

When she finally got her breathing and emotions mostly under control, leaving her a sniveling, swollen-eyed disaster, Kade looked down at her with a soft smile and wiped the streaks from her cheeks. "Still with me?"

She made some sound that could've been a laugh if she wasn't so hoarse. "I feel like someone else has taken over my body and brain."

He touched the tip of her reddened nose, amusement glittering in his eyes. "Someone did. Me."

"I—" With what little strength she had left, she pushed herself into a sitting position, but her sensitized backside protested the movement. She quickly changed to lying on her side. He followed, mirroring her. She attempted to put into words what she was feeling, to ask the questions hovering at the edges of her mind, but nothing would come together. She let out a frustrated breath. Everything felt fragmented.

*Broken.*

She looked to Kade, but before she could speak, he cupped her cheek. "Hey, why don't I get you something to drink and run a bath. Give us both some time to come down. We have all night to talk if we need it."

She sagged against the pillows and nodded. "Sounds like a good idea."

Over the next hour, Kade did exactly as promised. He brought her juice and put her in a bathtub, washing her body and her hair with gentle hands, then letting her soak while he took a quick rinse in the shower. She didn't have to say or do anything. He took care of it all. The intense dominance from earlier had sunk back into the soil, and now he was all kindness and care. Even though the two sides of him appeared to be so very different from the outside, the combination worked.

After drying her off, he forbade her clothes and led her back to the bed. He left for a few moments and returned with a glass of water and some ibuprofen. "You'll thank me for those in a few hours."

She took the pills and swallowed them back. "This definitely goes on record as the first sex I've had that required medication afterward."

"Gold star for me."

The completely shameless grin he gave her made her laugh. "Hey, I'm the one who's not going to be able to sit down tomorrow. Don't I get some stars?"

He climbed in the bed next to her. "Tess, I'd give you all the stars in the sky right now if I could."

She turned to him, expecting to see that cocky smile, but his expression was intent. He wasn't feeding her a pretty line. She sighed and tucked her arm beneath her head. "I'm not going to pretend I understand this. If I look back at tonight or any of our nights together with my logical brain, I should be kicking your ass out of the house."

"A lot of women would," he said, facing her. "My ex did. I didn't even have to show her this part of me. I just talked about some desires and that was enough to send her running. It's scary shit to most."

She met his gaze. "It *is* scary."

"I know," he said, reaching out and brushing a lock of hair from her face. "But you're still here. Want to tell me why?"

She closed her eyes and rolled onto her back. The sting was almost welcome. "Isn't that the question of the month? I thought I understood this whole thing. It's role-playing, fun and games, a kinky thing to check off a list. But tonight . . ."

"Tonight?" he prodded gently.

She stared at the ceiling, trying to process everything that had happened. "Tonight felt real, Kade. This wasn't like that night at The Ranch with the roles to play and the costumes. That was an exciting fantasy. But whatever you did to me tonight, put me in this place . . . like I really was a slave to you, an object. It morphed something in my mind."

He shifted next to her, but didn't say anything, giving her time to put her thoughts in order.

She turned to meet his patient gaze. "You make things I should be repulsed by seem appealing."

He considered her. "And that scares you."

A statement, not a question.

"Yes." She sat up on her elbow. "Of course it does. If you had hauled me off the bed and slapped me for coming too soon, I probably would've let you and gotten more turned on because of it. You covered my head with your hand like I was some whore you didn't care to look at, and I nearly came from it. You made me *want* the ugly parts. Why would I want that?"

His eyes went soft. "Baby . . ."

"I mean," she continued, unable to stop talking now that the anxiety was bubbling up. "I spent a marriage with a man who treated me like I was less than, who had the ability to make me feel worthless with one well-placed insult. I don't understand why I'd want to be bullied in bed. Shouldn't I want a guy to worship me or something?"

The corner of his mouth lifted. "Maybe you do, but that worship looks different than what you thought. In my world, nothing is more precious to a dominant than his submissive. I would break someone's fingers if they tried to lay a hand on you without permission. I did what I did with you because I enjoy it, yes, but I also did it because it's what you needed and craved tonight."

She lifted a brow. "I needed and craved to be beaten with a belt and sodomized?"

"You asked to be broken. Kissing you from head to foot and telling you how pretty you are wouldn't have done that. You don't trust people who are satisfied with the surface. You've catered to them but you don't trust them. It's one reason you've been so scared to put full trust in me. I needed to get to the woman beneath all those coats of gloss you've put on. And you needed to see what I'm like underneath it all, too.

"So take a good look and see, Tess. I'm a nice guy, but I'm also a sadist who gets off on seeing those welts on your back. I'm a guy who likes grabbing you by the hair and treating you more like property than a person in bed."

She looked away and he grasped her chin, turning her gently to meet his eyes. "And you're a nice girl who didn't deserve to be treated like you were in your marriage. But you're also the woman who gets turned on by being manhandled and likes a little dose of humiliation in bed. A woman who just came three times because I forced her down on the bed, fucked her in the ass, and demanded she obey. And there's nothing to be ashamed of about it because it's real. And maybe this friend or that neighbor would think it's deviant or demented, but who the fuck cares? *I* love this side of us. Because where else in life do we get to indulge in the darkest parts of ourselves without fear of judgment or censure? You couldn't tell me one thing you want that would weird me out. Truly. Even if I'm not into that particular thing. This is a safe place to be exactly who you are—even the portions others would label wrong. You won't scare me away. And I'm not going to try to fit you in some box to suit my needs. It's why I waited for you to open the door to more before I just ran roughshod over you, demanding you handle whatever I wanted to mete out."

She stared at him, his speech seeping into her skin and settling into her bones. Acceptance without judgment. No predetermined expectations. It was a completely foreign concept to her. She'd jumped from box to box all her life, trying to morph herself into whatever other people expected her to be.

And this man had just burned down the box.

"I don't even know what to do with all that," she said honestly.

He leaned over and kissed her, then tugged her closer to settle her against his chest again. "You don't have to do anything, Tess. Just close your eyes and rest. You can worry about the rest tomorrow. Right now we simply bask in the afterglow."

She smiled at that, but when she snuggled closer and let her eyes drift shut, she knew she had far more to worry about than her newfound sexual desires.

She was about to get faux engaged.

To a man who was inspiring anything but faux feelings.

She was falling for him all over again.

And she wasn't sure she had the strength to fight it anymore.

# TWENTY-NINE

Tessa jolted awake, the morning light burning her eyes as she tried to figure out what was going on and what all the god-awful noise was.

*Boom! Boom! Boom!*

Kade groaned and rolled over, his arm thrown over his eyes. "What the fuck is that?"

She peeked at the clock. Right past six in the morning. "I don't know. I think someone's at the door. I'll go see."

She hauled herself out of bed with a grunt, everything achy and sensitive from the night before, and started to head to the front of the house but quickly realized she was still naked. The loud knocking came again, and she shuffled to her closet to grab her robe. Kade was climbing out of bed behind her when she made her way toward the living room.

"Who is it?" she asked, wishing she had a peephole.

"Police," a voice called. "We need you to open up."

*Police?* What the hell?

Maybe something had happened in the neighborhood. There'd

been a few break-ins two streets away a month ago. She knotted her robe around her and opened the door. "What's going on?"

Two officers, a man and a woman, stood on the other side, wearing matching stern expressions. The man spoke first. "Ma'am, we need to know if Kade Vandergriff is here."

She blinked. "What? Why?"

The female cop stepped forward. "We have an arrest warrant, ma'am."

Tessa's heart climbed into her throat.

Kade walked up behind her, wearing his jeans and wrinkled T-shirt from last night. "A warrant? What the hell for?"

"Mr. Vandergriff," the male cop said, and Kade nodded. The cop walked toward Kade, his hand on his gun belt. "We need you to step outside and come with us. You're under arrest for assault and battery of a Mr. Douglas Barrett."

Tessa's mouth fell open. "*Doug*? No, wait, there's been a mistake. Kade didn't hurt anyone."

The male cop moved past her, unhooking his handcuffs from his belt. "Well, Douglas Barrett disagrees and spent the evening in the hospital getting patched up from a beating he claims Mr. Vandergriff is responsible for. He also claimed you threatened his life."

"A *beating*?" Kade said as the cop snapped handcuffs around his wrists. "I didn't hit him."

The cop began the Miranda warning and ignored Kade's protest.

Panic welled in Tessa. She looked to Kade who appeared to be either intensely calm or intensely pissed, then tried to implore the female officer. "Nothing happened. Doug's my ex-husband and is making this up."

"Not my call, ma'am," she said, all business.

"Tess," Kade said, dragging her attention his way. "Call Reid

Jamison, he's my lawyer. Tell him what happened and to meet me wherever they're taking me."

She grabbed a scrap of paper and pen from a drawer in the entryway table and scribbled the information down as he rattled off a number. "Okay. Reid Jamison. God, this is ridiculous. I'm so sorry. Doug must've—"

"Doug's doing what he always does. Lying. Don't worry. We'll get it sorted out."

He seemed confident that it'd be resolved easily, but worry rolled around in her gut like a heavy boulder. Nothing was ever simple with Doug. He wouldn't do this if it was a quick fix. There was more to it. She knew him too well.

Tess watched with dread as they tucked Kade into the back of the squad car. The cops pulled away, and she put in a call to Reid. He asked for details of the night before, and she told him the quick version of what had happened.

"Okay, Tessa," he said, as calm as a judge. "I'll head out that way. You should probably go there, too, to give a statement. You're a witness to what really happened last night."

"Right. Of course. I've got to get dressed then I'll drive up there."

She said her good-byes and hit the End button on her phone. She hustled to her room and grabbed jeans and a sweater. She tugged her clothes on and ran a brush through her hair. But when she pulled the door open to go to her car, Doug was standing on the other side. And he looked like absolute shit—eye swollen and bruised, lip split, surgical tape over one of his eyebrows.

She recoiled. "What the hell are you doing here?"

He smirked, which looked macabre with his cut lip, and walked past her into the house without invitation. "We need to talk."

"You need to get out," she said, staying by the open door as he took a spot on her sofa. "I don't know what happened to you or who did it, but you need to go tell the police that it wasn't Kade."

"Oh, but it was. Didn't you see? He laid me out on your front lawn last night. I even have a witness who saw it happen."

She stared at him, her heart sinking as she remembered the shadowed figure near Doug's car last night. "You've lost your goddamned mind."

"And I've heard Vandergriff has a nasty little custody fight on his hands. You'd think he'd be more careful with his anger. I mean, who would trust him with a little girl when he can't control his temper or his fists?"

Her whole body went cold.

"Shut the door, Tessa," he said evenly. "Like I said, we have a few things to discuss."

Her bones felt like they would splinter she'd gone so stiff, but she managed to reach out and slowly shut the door. When she heard the click, it felt like she'd just locked herself in a cage with a venomous snake. On wooden legs, she made her way into the living room and sat down in a chair. "Why are you doing this? Haven't you done enough to Kade?"

"Ah, poor Kaden Fowler, always getting in my way when it comes to you. He should know that's not going to work for me." He pointed to his battered face. "I'm willing to go to any lengths to handle my business."

Her jaw clenched. He'd probably paid some bum to beat the shit out of him. "I'm not with you anymore. He's not in the way of anything."

"No, maybe not, but you are. Do you know how much of my congregation I've lost over the last year because of the scandal you created? Not just because of the rumors that I cheated but because I got a divorce? You know how long I preached about the sanctity of marriage and how it was a sin to give up on that sacred bond. You made me look like a hypocrite and a fool. The church has lost a lot of money, Tessa. *I've* lost a lot of money and respect. And that's on you."

"You *are* a hypocrite. I told the truth. If you didn't want scandal, you should've kept your dick out of other women."

His eyes narrowed. "You talking like a whore now, too? I know Fowler has made you his bitch. What kind of sick shit have you gotten into with him?"

Her fingers tightened on the arms of the chair. "What are you talking about?"

He pulled folded pages from inside his coat and flattened them on the coffee table. In them, though the images were hazy from being shot through her sheer curtains, was Kade standing over her, her hair looped around his fist, as she crawled for him.

Her stomach lurched. "You fucking bastard. You *watched* through my windows?"

He shrugged. "No, but you know how Marilyn is, always the reporter. She came with me last night because she really did want to apologize for the bad blood between you two, so she stayed behind when you sent me off. But when she went to knock on your door, she saw what was going on and was worried for you. She snapped a few cell phone pictures for evidence in case you wanted to press rape charges. But of course, she figured out quickly that you weren't saying no to him." He leaned over the coffee table as if examining them closely. "But really, it's hard to tell. If the press got ahold of these, Kaden would have lots of explaining to do."

Everything in the room was spinning, her skin like ice. Assault charges and hard proof that Kade was rough with women. He may never see his daughter again if all this got out. She swallowed past the jagged knot in her throat. "What do you want, Doug?"

He gave her a sharp-toothed grin and slapped his thighs. "Now, we're talking. There's my practical Tessa."

She wanted to vomit on his expensive shoes.

"I will drop the charges and give you these pictures if you agree to come back to Atlanta with me. You'll give Marilyn an exclusive interview and tell everyone that I never cheated. Tell them that you were the one who strayed in the marriage because you're into this demented S&M shit. But you're ready to come back to me, get help, and work on putting our marriage back together. And you will *beg* my forgiveness in front of the congregation on the live Sunday broadcast."

The walls around her seemed to shrink inward, pressing on her. He wanted her to go back to Atlanta with him? She'd rather be dead. But if she didn't do something, Doug would annihilate Kade's chances with his daughter and his reputation. She couldn't do that to Kade. Wouldn't. Last time she'd had to make a choice between herself and Kade, she'd chosen the easiest path for her. But she refused to hurt the man she loved, maybe had always loved, again.

"I can't be your wife again," she whispered, almost more to herself.

"Sure you can," he said, malice underlying his easy tone. "You know how to put on a happy face. You'll get your nice house back, a generous allowance in your account each month. You can drop this ridiculous pauper's lifestyle you've been trying out. I'll even throw some money at your precious charity. All you'll need to do is turn your head and keep your mouth shut if you see something you shouldn't. Isn't that what you're setting yourself up for with Kaden anyway? You get to be his little whore and he takes care of everything for you? You strive to be useless. It's always been your career goal."

She lifted her head, wishing she could kill him with the look she shot at him. "If you think so poorly of me, why do you want me in your life again? Get Marilyn to divorce her husband and marry her."

"Marilyn will never leave him. He has more money than I do.

Plus, she's stated publicly that she's an atheist. I can't have that in my church. And maybe I won't need her around anymore anyway. I'm thinking you may be more fun to be around now. I tried to treat you well before, respect you like a wife. But I see now that you needed something different. If you want to be treated like my whore, I can happily oblige you."

The up and down look made her feel like bugs were running over her skin. She wrapped her arms around herself. "You will never touch me. *Never.* Do you understand? I'll go with you, but you're not ever allowed in my bed."

He smiled. "That's going to get mighty lonely for you. We'll see how long you last. But I can agree to that for now, if you come with me this morning."

"Now? I can't. I need to go to the police station and see Kade. Tell him I'm leaving."

"No," he said, standing and smoothing his slacks. "You don't get to talk this out with him. Pack a suitcase. We have a flight that leaves in two and a half hours. He can figure it out. He's used to you walking away from him to be with me."

The statement was like a slap across her cheek.

"And if you think you actually mean something to him, you're deluding yourself. Men don't marry women they fuck like dogs. They use them. That's all he's doing with you. You're his temporary diversion. Another slut will step up in line behind you."

She ignored the insults he was lobbing her way. "I'm not telling anyone anything until you drop the charges and give me those pictures."

He smiled. "When we land in Atlanta, I'll call the police station and will give you the pictures then. You can also verify that Marilyn deleted them from her phone."

"Fine."

"Now go pack. I don't want to be late."

She pushed up from the chair to stalk toward her bedroom.

"And sweetheart—"

She turned to glare at him.

"I so can't wait to see you on your knees in front of the congregation. I'm starting to see the appeal Kade finds in putting you in that position."

"Fuck you, Doug."

"I'm sure you will. Soon," he said with smarmy confidence.

She was glad she didn't have a gun in the house because, right now, life in prison was sounding worth it.

# THIRTY

"What do you mean she's gone?" Kade asked, once again, standing in Sam's doorway and praying the woman would help him. He'd already been to Tessa's house to find it locked up and her car sitting in the driveway. She wasn't answering her phone. And she'd been a no show at the police station the day before. He'd been climbing the walls with worry waiting to get the bail processed so he could get out. Then this morning, they'd let him out saying the charges had been dropped.

"She's in Atlanta," Sam said, lines of strain around her mouth. "She called me a few hours ago."

"*Atlanta*? Fuck. Why would she go back there?" Then a sickening realization wrapped around him. "What did that asshole do?"

"I don't know the whole story, but I'm guessing there's a reason charges were dropped for you."

"Christ." He scraped a hand through his hair. "She didn't need to go anywhere with him. I would've handled it. He'd have to prove it in court, and I don't care if he claims to have a witness or not."

"She was worried about your custody case. And honestly, I think he's holding more over her than the charges. She wouldn't have gone with him easily."

His fists curled at the thought of Doug laying one finger on Tessa or threatening her in any way. He would kill the sonofabitch. "I'm going to get her."

Sam's hand darted out, grabbing him before he could leave. "Hold up."

"Don't try to talk me out of this, Sam. You don't know what that guy is capable of. He's demented, sick, and cruel." Flashes of the night Doug had jumped him in high school flickered through his mind in painful succession, ripping open old scars he thought long healed. "She can't be near him."

"Look, you don't have to convince me of that. But she gave me specific instructions to tell you not to come. She needs a little time. She has to take care of some things, and you'll only get in the way."

"In the way?" The words stung. "I can't let her stay there with him. He could hurt her. She needs my help."

Sam's expression turned sympathetic. "I know how you feel, believe me. I've been sick about it since she called me. But she said to tell you to trust her, to focus on keeping your image clean for the courts. That she has a plan and can handle herself. And you know, I think she can. She's a lot tougher than she used to be."

He leaned back against the wall. Trust. Letting her handle herself. He could deal with the first. He did trust her. But he also knew she could put herself at more risk than she realized with Doug. He'd never told her or anyone the extent of what had really happened that night. Everyone knew he'd been beaten up. The groundskeeper had found him naked, bloodied, and hog-tied behind the bleachers on the football field the morning after and word had spread fast. But no one else had seen how broken he'd been; no one knew how cruel Doug had gotten.

He'd been too damaged, humiliated, and disgusted afterward to cope. He hadn't been able to bear the thought of Tessa seeing him that way. Of anyone seeing him like that. It felt like the shame of that night was printed on his skin, like everyone would see all his secrets just by looking at him. So when he'd left home, he'd closed that chapter of his life and tried to forget it. But now blind panic filled him, knowing Tessa was with Doug. Doug who was capable of far more than verbal abuse.

"She's not safe with him," he said, rubbing his hand over his forehead. "I have to get to her."

"Kade—" Sam called.

But he was already striding away, the visions of that horrific night coming back. Back then, he'd let Tessa go because he couldn't face her after what happened. Yes, she'd turned away from him, rejected him in front of everyone, but he'd seen in her eyes that it was killing her. He could've stayed in school and given her time, tried to convince her again. But after that night, he didn't want to think about her or anything related to that night. He couldn't even look in the mirror until the visible scars had faded. Everything would cause a flashback, a spiral into darkness. So he'd slammed the door shut.

All this time she thought she'd abandoned him for Doug. But in truth, *he'd* abandoned *her.* He'd been broken and full of rage and couldn't get past it. He'd left her there with him even knowing who Doug was, praying she'd move on when she heard Doug had beaten Kade. But he hadn't done anything to protect her from that sick fuck. He'd run and protected himself instead. He'd given up.

*1996*

Kaden's chest pulled tight as he headed up to the brightly lit house in a cul-de-sac of one of the nicer neighborhoods in town. The music could be heard drifting on the breeze, but not enough to make a neighbor call in a noise complaint. Toby Wallace was a professional party giver. He'd cover all the bases to make sure they didn't get a visit from the cops. At least that's what Kaden had heard. He'd never actually been to one of his parties. But Tessa was here. So this is where he needed to be.

*Maybe if things were different.* Tessa had said those magic words, and the statement hadn't stopped running through his head since he'd left her house the night before. But when he'd tried to set up a time to talk to her tonight, she'd told him that she had to go to a party.

With Doug.

She hadn't said the last part, but he'd known it. She wouldn't have gone to a house party solo. But this couldn't wait. He needed to talk to her tonight.

He loved her. He knew without a doubt and was ready to do anything to show her why she should be with him. He only hoped he could get her alone to talk and that it was enough. He checked to make sure no one was around to see and slipped through the gate into the backyard. He hadn't been invited to this party. Hell, he wasn't invited to any of the parties. But he hoped he could blend in well enough if the crowd was from a few different schools.

Kids were crowded around the pool, most had beer in their hands. There was laughing and guys shoving each other, joking around. Girls stood nearby, giggling at their antics. To Kaden it was like turning on the National Geographic channel and observing a society he wasn't a member of. He stayed in the shadows for a good while, watching the crowd, picking out who he recognized and who was from another school. If he could latch on to a group going inside, he may be able to slip in unnoticed.

But before he had the chance, he saw Tessa step out into the backyard with a few of her girlfriends. Unlike her friends who had wine coolers in their hands, she was carrying a Dr Pepper.

Probably because she knew she'd have to drive Doug's drunk ass home. She smiled at something one of the girls said, but she looked bored, distant.

He waited for her to go off on her own, but the girls were traveling in a pack just like at school. He sighed, knowing he was going to have to suck it up and risk being seen because they weren't going to leave her side. But what did he have to lose? At worst, she'd ignore him or laugh for the sake of her friends. With one last deep breath, he moved out of the shadow of the hedges and headed her way.

One of her friends, Lexi, noticed him before Tess did. She curled her lip. "What is *he* doing here?"

Tessa turned, her eyes going wide, her expression panicked. "I don't know."

He walked over to the lounge chair she was sitting on. "Hey, y'all know where the d-d-drinks are?"

"Oh my God. Are you even invited?" Lexi asked. "No way Toby invited you."

"Here, I'll get you another drink, Tessa. This one looks like it isn't c-c-cold anymore."

She sucked in a breath when he wrapped his hand around the soda she was holding. The note he'd tucked in his hand slid into hers. She immediately closed her fist.

"Get the hell away from her," said a voice from behind him. Doug, of fucking course.

Kaden lifted his hands in a surrender motion and turned toward Doug with a snide smile. "No problem. J-j-just trying to be helpful to the homecoming queen. Don't want her drink getting hot."

"Well, j-j-just get the f-f-fuck out of here," he said, spitting with the stuttered words. "I'll take care of her drinks. You don't belong here, freak."

"Leave him alone, Doug," Tessa cut in. "He was trying to be nice."

"Yeah, sure he was." Doug said, sitting down next to Tessa and draping his arm around her like some gorilla marking his territory. "It has nothing to do with the fact that when he leaned forward to get your drink, he could probably see straight down that top you're wearing. I told you it was too low cut. You're bringing out the perverts, babe."

Kaden's teeth ground against each other. This guy was such a freaking asshole. Kaden tossed the drink on the ground and turned to head out of the yard. "This party's l-l-lame anyway."

The group laughed behind him. But he didn't give a shit. All he cared about was Tess reading that note.

Fifteen minutes later, Tessa met him at the corner of the neighborhood's kiddie park. She wrung her hands and kept looking over her shoulder, the moonlight making her look even more drawn and worried. Finally, she pinned him with a stare and wrapped her arms around herself. "What are you doing here? And we need to get out from under the streetlight."

He took her arm and guided her to a darker spot over by the swing set. She sat on one of the swings and dragged her feet through the mulch.

"Where's Doug?" he asked, even though it hurt to say the shithead's name.

"Distracted with his friends."

"I guess you didn't tell him anything about what happened last n-n-night."

She rolled her lips inward and shook her head. "I can't, Kaden. You know that. I told you."

"You told me if things were d-d-different, your answer to that may be different."

She blew out a tired breath. "But things *aren't* different."

He pulled an envelope out of his jacket pocket. "What if they were?"

She eyed the envelope warily. "What's that?"

"I've been working since freshman year—tutoring, cutting grass, whatever anyone would p-p-pay me for. I've saved every cent for when I go to college. I have over four-thousand dollars in a lockbox in my room, and I know my mom has saved up a little for me on the side that she hasn't told my stepdad about. I've looked into living expenses. I can get an apartment near campus for a few hundred bucks a m-m-month. It's not going to be fancy or anything, but I can get a two-bedroom. Plus, I'll get a work-study position, so I'll be bringing in more money after that. And there's a community college nearby. These are all the printouts with the information about the school." He handed her the envelope. "You'll qualify for financial aid, and it's not that expensive to take classes there. Especially when you w-w-won't have to worry about rent and stuff. You can stay with me for free."

She blinked, peeking down again at the envelope. "Kaden—"

"And I'm not saying you have to d-date me or whatever. I'm not doing this to make you do that. Though, if you want to, you know how I feel."

She stared at him, shaking her head, her expression stunned. "Why are you doing this?"

He ran a hand over the back of his head, more nervous than he could ever remember being in his life. "I l-l-love you, Tess."

She closed her eyes like the words had caused physical pain. "Kaden."

But he could see the tears welling when she lifted her eyes to him again, and he stepped forward into her space and kneeled down in the dirt in front of the swing. He folded the envelope and tucked it in the back pocket of her shorts. She didn't back away or flinch when he moved his hands to her waist so he kept talking. "I don't want you to be with Doug just because he can help you with money. He doesn't deserve you. I can t-t-take care of you."

She was shaking in his hold. "I can't ask you to do that. It's your money. Your life. You worked hard for all of it."

"And none of it means shit without you, T-Tess. I can't picture next year without you there. But if you can stand here and tell me that you don't have f-f-feelings for me, too, I'll leave you be. I will never try to touch you again. My offer for coming to Dallas and sharing my place stands either way."

Her tears fell down her cheeks when she blinked this time, her green eyes big and sad in the moonlight. "I can't just go with you."

"You can, Tess. All you have to do is say y-yes. Come with me. I c-c-can't buy you fancy shit like he can, but I can p-promise I won't let anything bad happen to you."

He kneeled there, bracing for the gauntlet of no. But instead of finishing her no like he expected her to, she leaned forward and kissed him. The feel of her lips against his made his stomach turn over with relief and pure happiness. She wasn't running. He'd changed things. Really changed them. It'd worked. He'd made things different.

He slid his hands into her hair and her lips parted, letting him deepen the kiss. God, she was so sweet and pliable in his hold, so goddamned perfect. She could be his. He'd gotten the girl of his dreams. Something would finally work out.

"What the *fuck*?"

The booming voice cutting through the silence of the night sent Kaden jumping back to his feet and Tessa hopping off the swing. They turned to find Doug standing at the edge of the park with a few of the people from the party.

"Oh, no," Tessa said, her hand going over her mouth and fear filling her eyes. "Doug, it's not—"

"What is he doing with his hands and mouth on you, Tessa?" Doug demanded, his eyes filling with fury.

She lifted her palms to him. "It was nothing, just a misunderstanding."

"That didn't look like a misunderstanding. That looked like he was trying to maul you."

She shook her head.

"Did you tell him no?" he demanded.

Kaden looked to Tessa, his heart pounding hard in his ears. He had no shot in this fight if Doug started one. Kaden was way outnumbered, but he was willing to fight for Tessa if need be. He willed her to tell Doug to fuck off, that she was with Kaden now. But as he watched the panic envelop her like a fog, saw her gaze jump from one person to the next, the old Tessa he used to know took over.

"I didn't have a chance. It was just a mistake," she said softly. "It doesn't have to be a big deal."

"When a guy tries to put his fucking hands on you, it is a big deal," he said, his voice rattling Kaden's ears. He nailed Kaden with a glare. "I always knew you were a freak. Goddamned rapist in training."

Kaden clenched his jaw, and Tessa didn't say anything to defend him.

"Tessa, go back to the house with these guys and find a ride home. Kaden and I need to have a chat."

"No," she said, her voice rising. "Don't hurt him, Doug. He didn't hurt me. It wasn't like that. Just let it go."

Doug grinned, but it had no humor in it. "Don't worry, babe. I'm not going to hurt him. We're just going to have a talk to make sure he's never going to come near you again."

Tessa looked to Kaden, her frightened rabbit expression tugging at him, but he couldn't bear to meet her eyes. She wasn't standing up and telling the truth. She was letting all these people think he'd tried to take advantage of her. She wasn't going to come with him to Dallas. She never had planned to. That kiss was going to be her kiss good-bye.

"Just go, Tess," he said quietly. "I'll be f-f-fine."

"Kaden—"

He lifted his gaze to hers. "Go b-b-back and be with your friends, *homecoming queen*. Your court awaits."

She winced like he'd backhanded her. And he immediately regretted the snark in his voice. But he couldn't stop the emotions from spilling out. He'd pinned everything on tonight, had hoped that if he could really make things different, he could change the path for them both. But it'd been stupid to hope.

Things never changed. People were who they were. He was the freak and she was the future debutante. Their worlds would never fit together.

He would never fit.

And it probably wouldn't matter because based on how Doug was staring at him, he may not make it through the night.

Tessa left with the group, peering back over her shoulder one last time, and Kaden waited for her to be out of sight. Then he did the only thing he could do. He ran. Like a coward. He knew Doug had no interest in talking. This was going to be a conversation of fists. He wasn't stronger than Doug. The dude lifted weights daily for football. But he hoped he might be faster.

However, when he ran into the woods behind the high school, he could hear Doug calling his name from not far behind. Branches cut at Kaden's face as he raced through the trees in the dark. He figured if he could make it home he could lock himself inside and call the cops. His house wouldn't be far once he made it to the main road. But his Vans were no match for the gnarled roots and slippery ground of the forest floor. His foot caught a raised root, turning his ankle, and he went sprawling face-first to the ground. All his air left him as he hit.

He did his best to scramble upward, but before he could, a foot planted against his spine and shoved him back to the ground. He landed with an *oof* and pain shot up his back.

"Where you going, freak? Think you could outrun me. That proves you're not just a freak but stupid."

"Fuck off," he ground out.

"Excuse me?" His booted foot swung into Kaden's ribs with a painful crack. "Someone needs to teach you manners, son."

Kaden's knees pulled up and he rolled into the fetal position, the pain blinding him for a second. He tried to curl tight, protecting his midsection from another blow.

"You trying to take advantage of my girl?" Doug asked, his voice disconcertingly calm. "Think she could ever want a piece of shit like you when she has someone like me?"

"I'm n-n-not t-t-trying to take advantage of her," he said, hoping to placate him, willing to suck up the humiliation if it meant he wouldn't get kicked again. He needed to get up, get away, but his body wouldn't cooperate. Knives of agony were stabbing his lungs.

"You're n-n-not?" Doug mocked and kicked him again. Harder. "Then why is she kissing the guy who's supposed to be her tutor?"

Kaden yelped even though he hated letting Doug know he'd hurt him. But that time he knew a rib had been broken. Tears sprung to his eyes, the sheer pain making it impossible to breathe.

"Yeah, I knew about that. I let it go because her parents are riding her about her grades. And I figured you weren't worth worrying about. But Tessa's weak. I realize that now. She buys into your *poor me* crap. She pities you and is mistaking that for feelings." He shoved him in the side with his heel, flipping him onto his stomach and sending agony through his ribcage. Doug wrenched Kaden's arms behind him and looped his belt around his wrists. Kaden tried to fight back but every movement made him want to weep. The pain made his head spin. "But you have nothing to offer her. You're a fucking pussy, Fowler. You can't even protect yourself, how would you take care of her?"

The toe of Doug's boot made contact with his side and Kaden tasted blood. He tried to crawl away but it was near impossible without the use of his hands. He was going to die out here. Doug loomed over him and pulled him onto his knees.

"At least be man enough to look me in the eye and apologize."

Kaden refused to lift his head and Doug started in with his fists. When knuckles crashed into his jaw, Kaden knew he was close to losing consciousness.

Doug crouched low, getting in his face. "Apologize, you pathetic piece of shit."

Kaden spat blood in his face and Doug roared, backhanding him.

Kaden choked, his chest wheezing with effort. Black edged his vision. He forced words out through gasping breaths. "I'm sorry. Please. Just stop. Can't breathe."

"Oh, what was that? I couldn't hear you," he mocked.

Kaden swayed on his knees, half-hoping that if he passed out Doug would stop and go away, the fun gone, but he didn't put it past the guy to kill him in cold blood. He swallowed down any pride he had left, hoping to survive the night. "I'm s-s-sorry, Doug. Please, just stop. I'll leave her alone. I'll do whatever you want. Just. Stop."

Doug grinned and his teeth seemed to glow and sharpen in the dark. "Is that right? You'll do whatever I want."

Kaden's vision blurred, two versions of Doug dancing before him. He closed his eyes, pleading. "Yes. Please. Stop."

But Doug wasn't going to be appeased that easily. The humiliation wasn't complete. The sound of a zipper brought Kaden back from the edge of consciousness. His eyelids snapped open, though one was already starting to swell, and he watched in abject horror as Doug pulled his dick out of his pants.

Pure panic seized Kaden, and he tried to scramble to his feet, the pain in his ribs like daggers slicing through his organs. But Doug just shoved him back down and laughed. "Where you going, asshole? I'm not done with you. Ready to show me what a pussy you are? Or maybe I should say cocksucker. I know that's why you stutter. All that dick you suck."

Kaden gagged both on blood and fear, choking out his words. "You'll have to kill me first."

"A valid option," Doug said with a sneer. "But you're not worth jail time."

Kaden spit blood at him again, using the last shred of energy he had and Doug hit him in the side of the head, knocking him to the ground. He couldn't move. He'd been beaten until his ribs had cracked and he could barely breathe. He wasn't going to make it out of these woods. And that end would've been welcome because the next thing that happened was worse than death. Doug grabbed Kaden by the hair, took his dick in his hand, and forced it down Kaden's throat. It was sweaty and hard and disgusting. Doug laughed at him, calling him a bitch, and telling him to act like a good one. Kaden tried to bite down but Doug yanked on his hair and told him if he used teeth, he'd put him in the dirt and fuck him with one of the fallen tree branches. Kaden gagged and choked, fighting for breath and the urge to upchuck, but Doug was enjoying it all, getting off on Kaden's ultimate humiliation. When Doug came, Kaden did vomit, then he blacked out.

When he woke up, he was naked, tied up, and bleeding under the bleachers of the school's football field. And he'd had no idea how he'd gotten there, where his clothes had gone, or what Doug had done after he'd passed out. He refused to talk to the groundskeeper who'd found him. Everyone would already know who'd beaten him. Nobody would tell. Including him. There were some things you never wanted to relive, things you never wanted anyone to know, things you didn't even want to acknowledge in your own mind had happened. And that morning as they patched him up in the hospital and asked him a hundred questions, he'd slammed the vault shut on that night. His secret would stay in those woods. Buried. Along with that boy who was bullied. He would never let anyone have that kind of control over him again. He would never be weak or vulnerable. He would become someone else.

Kaden Fowler died that day.

Doug Barrett had killed him.

# THIRTY-ONE

Tessa lay in the bed in the guest room of her former house, trying not to make a sound so that she could hear any little noise in the place. She hadn't heard anything in a solid hour. Her heartbeat had finally slowed when she realized that if Doug planned to make some sort of move on her, it wouldn't be tonight. Not that she would've let him. She loosened her grip on the chef's knife she'd tucked under the pillow. Kade had informed her that first night that an expensive one was sharp enough to cut off fingers. And God knows she'd never used this one when she lived here, so it was as sharp as the day it was honed. But thankfully, it didn't look like she was going to need it to protect herself.

The chilling text message Kade had sent her earlier was still burning in her mind. I'm coming to get you. Don't stay in the house with him. He's a sociopath and a rapist.

*Rapist.* The word made what little she'd eaten in the last twenty-four hours want to come up. At first the accusation hadn't made sense. Kade hadn't seen Doug since high school. How would he know that? But then the answer had come crashing down on her. Because Doug had done something more than beat up Kade that awful night. The thought had almost been too much to take in.

No one had seen Kaden afterward. Rumors had spread that he'd been beaten badly, but she hadn't known what to believe. She'd tried to go to his house, but his stepdad had told her he wasn't there, that he was moving in with his real dad. She'd wanted to tell Kaden she was sorry and make sure he was okay. She'd wanted to tell him she'd go with him to Dallas. But he'd left town before she'd gotten a chance.

Then over time, Doug had convinced her that nothing bad had really happened that night. That it was all just rumors. He'd said that he'd told Kaden not to come back to school or he would beat him down. That's all. He said he didn't want Kaden around her and did it to keep her safe. And she'd wanted to believe him because she didn't feel like she had any other options. Her eggs were in Doug's basket, and she'd wanted to believe the good parts about him. He'd lavished her with attention and made her feel like he was being overprotective because he loved her. She'd been stupid to let herself believe it. Stupid and too scared to do anything on her own.

Doug had been across the room when she'd received the message from Kade, and she'd had the instant urge to take the very knife under her pillow and *damage* him, make him pay for every sick and cruel thing he'd ever done to anyone. But she'd held back, bided her time. She needed a plan. She needed him to think she was cooperating.

And now she was lying here, counting on three things she knew about Doug for sure.

One: He always took a sleeping pill before bed.

Two: He obsessively documented everything down to how many minutes he ran on the treadmill.

Three: He always underestimated her.

He would regret all three of those things tonight. Once she was sure he was asleep, she slipped out of bed and put her tennis shoes on. She quietly made her way downstairs and put in the code to turn off the alarm. She held her breath at the beep signaling the disarmed state, but the walls were heavily insulated and she knew it was hard to hear what was going on downstairs when you were upstairs. After waiting a few minutes to make sure Doug didn't come down the stairs, she went to the sliding glass door at the back and opened it.

The crickets and other night bugs greeted her, but she knew they weren't the only ones out there. She gave a little all-clear signal, and Kade melted out of the darkness at the side of the yard. Stress had morphed his features into a hard mask, but the instant his arms were around her, she saw the relief there. "You're okay?"

"I'm fine."

He kissed the top of her head, whispering thanks to God. "You should've never left with him. You had me out of my mind with worry. Why would you do that?"

"I was trying to protect you. He had charges against you and a witness, he has pictures of us from the other night—ones that would ruin things for your case. I needed to do what he wanted and come with him. But I have a plan. You didn't need to come here and be around him again." She shook her head, tears gathering in her throat. "I can't imagine what it must be like to be anywhere near him."

"Hey," he said, cupping her face and forcing her gaze to his. "Don't do that. Don't pity me."

"Why didn't you tell me?"

"I couldn't tell anyone, Tess. Seventeen-year-old boys aren't supposed to get raped. You know what people would've said? That I wanted it. That I should've been able to fight him off otherwise. I just wanted to forget it ever happened. I needed to bury that person I was that night in order to move on with my life."

Tears fell and she pressed her face into his shoulder. "I'm so sorry. It was my fault. If I'd have stood up for you that night, he wouldn't have gotten you alone. Everything would've been different."

"Don't do that to yourself, baby," he said softly. "It wasn't your fault. We were young and neither of us could've guessed he would've taken it that far. And it's truly in my past. My dad saw the state I was in when I showed up. He didn't know exactly what had happened to me, but he saw enough of the depression to know I needed therapy. I worked through it. The only other time it came up was when I started realizing I had dominant urges. I thought at first it was because of what had happened, my need for control in all things, but then I started looking back and seeing all the signs that were there way before that night. Maybe that night fast-forwarded my desire to be in charge, but it would've shown up eventually anyway. I truly hadn't thought about Doug in years until you showed up in my life again."

"And, of course, I bring all that bad stuff back up."

"Baby." He grabbed her shoulders and leaned back to look at her. "You coming back to me has been the best thing that's happened in my life since Rosalie was born. I feel like all this time I've been cycling through relationships, I was just waiting for what I really wanted. Who I always needed. You."

"Kade—" Her chest squeezed, words leaving her.

"And I don't care what the fuck Doug has on us, I'm not letting you do anything for him. I will figure out the custody situation. Reid just found out that my ex's husband plays tennis with the judge who ruled on our case. So he's petitioning for a different judge based on conflict of interest."

"Maybe we won't have to get faux engaged after all."

"No, we won't. I'm not going to allow it anyway."

She blinked. "What?"

He took her hand and kissed her left ring finger. "When I put a ring on this, it will be for real or not at all. I'm done hiding it. I love you, Tess. I did then. And I do even more now. You're it for me."

She lowered her head, the weight of the words making her want to slide down to the ground. *Love.* It'd been said to her before. But somehow this felt like the first time anyone had truly meant it.

"I'm willing to give you the time you need to figure out what you want because I know this has happened quickly and that I come with a lot of fine print. I'm dominant and that's not going to change, so being with me would mean being my submissive. And I have a little girl who will hopefully be a big part of my life. Plus, I'm in the public eye, so people would scrutinize us. I realize it's a lot. But I need you to know that this hasn't been a fling for me. This hasn't been about fantasy. This has been me falling in love with you all over again. Day by day. Moment by moment." He laced his fingers with hers. "You walked into my restaurant that first night, and before I even realized who you were, it was like the world shifted beneath my feet. Nothing has looked the same since."

She was crying now, full, heavy tears. And not in that pretty Demi Moore kind of way. It was all so overwhelming, so much.

He brushed her tears away as they fell. "You don't have to say anything back right now. I just needed you to hear how I felt. When I got out of that jail and realized you'd left town with him, I hated how much I'd held back and left unsaid. I can't believe you had the nerve to think I'd be okay without you."

She smiled and swiped at her runny nose. "How dare me."

"Exactly. So now you know, and I'm here to help however you need." He bowed his head. "I'm in your service, ma'am. Give me my orders. And please tell me it's to beat that fucker Doug until he weeps."

"All I need you to do is to be a lookout and make sure he

doesn't come downstairs. I grabbed the key to his office off his key ring while he was showering, and I know he just rotates the same passwords and changes the first number. So I'm going to go search through his computer."

"What are you looking for?"

She wet her lips and looked toward the house. "I've been digging through Bluebonnet's older reports, and I noticed some transactions that were strange. The balances also didn't add up the way they should. I couldn't figure out what was wrong and thought I must be reading them wrong, so I asked Gibson if I could take him up on that offer to work with Marcy in accounting for a few days. She helped me understand what I was looking at and what else to search for. Doug had been accessing the accounts under my name, pulling donation money earmarked for services for the kids into his personal account, then charging the charity for services rendered. No one thought to question it since I owned the charity."

"So he's stealing money from foster kids," Kade said with disgust.

"And it's not a huge amount because that would've been questioned. And even if it was, I would've looked like the culprit. But I'm thinking that if he's doing it with Bluebonnet, he's probably doing the same thing with the church. You should see how full the donation box is every Sunday. A lot of church members take the notion of tithes very seriously, donating even when they can't really spare it. People assume he lives this good because he still has his hands in his father's real estate company, but I can tell you his dad doesn't have the kind of money Doug does. His father gambled most of their family fortune away."

"And you think you can find proof?"

"Doug is anal retentive about documentation. He keeps a record of everything. I know something's got to be there if I delve deep enough."

"And when you find it, you won't just have a little blackmail, you'll have a way to take down everything he's ever built." Kade smiled and gave her a quick, firm kiss. "Has anyone ever told you that you're brilliant?"

She laughed. "I can honestly say no."

"Well, you are," he said, giving her another peck. "Brilliant and brave as shit for coming up with this plan."

The compliment wrapped around her like a warm blanket. Brilliant? Maybe not. But for the first time in her life, she felt smart and capable, like even if Kade hadn't insisted on showing up, she could've accomplished this on her own. She hadn't looked for someone else to save her or fix it for her. But she also wasn't going to be too proud to accept his help now.

"Come on," she said, taking his hand. "Let's get what we need and get out of here. I've got a life to get back to in Texas."

# THIRTY-TWO

Kade listened to the clicking of the mouse and the tapping of keys as he held down his post by the stairs, watching for any movement on the second floor. An hour had passed, and he was beginning to worry that Tessa wouldn't be able to find anything. More than once, he wanted to go in there to help. He'd been studying financials for ten years, so he probably could find things quicker. But he knew it was important for Tessa to do this on her own. Plus, he had to learn how to tamp down that urge to take over and handle things for her. It would be a challenge for him, but he didn't want to crush that independent spirit she had. That backbone and determination were a big part of why he'd fallen in love with her.

All these years he thought he'd needed the ultimate control in all things in a relationship. Looking back, he realized he'd probably been a nightmare for his ex-wife to live with even before he discovered his dominant tendencies in the bedroom. He hadn't negotiated, he hadn't compromised, he'd needed things his way all the time. No one could ever get the best of him or have authority over him. And now he could see that part of him had always been that scared teenager in the woods, determined not to give anyone an opening to break him down.

Confidence. Decisiveness. Fearlessness. That's what he'd layered on to protect himself. He could be the nice, fun times guy on the surface. To most who knew him, he appeared laid back and open. But in every situation, including with women, were opportunities to conquer and hold all the control. It'd made him successful in business and desired by the women he thought he wanted. But he'd never let anyone past that armor. It'd left him with empty relationships and a constant sense of restlessness.

Until Tess.

She'd walked into his life and in the matter of a few weeks had turned him back into Kaden Fowler, the boy who wore his heart on his sleeve, the boy who had hope for real love, and the boy who had always loved Tessa McAllen.

And he'd sworn to himself that he'd never let any piece of that loser, Kaden Fowler, back into his psyche, but maybe that boy wasn't such a loser after all. He'd known what he wanted and hadn't been afraid to lay everything on the line. He'd been brave. Even in the woods that night with Doug, he'd managed to survive. And maybe it was time to forgive that kid his insecurities and weaknesses and stuttering words.

Maybe he could stop being so afraid of him.

"Kade." Tessa's urgent whisper broke him from his thoughts.

He glanced up the stairs once before heading over to the office to peek inside. Tessa's face was glowing blue in the reflection of the computer screen but there was no mistaking the awed expression. "Look at this."

Kade stepped around the desk. What greeted him on the other side made him do a double take. Instead of rows of numbers like he expected, pictures were playing on the screen in a slideshow. A pornographic slideshow. With all the photos featuring the house they were in as a backdrop. Naked women, some whose faces were visible, others not, all in compromising, often unflattering positions. And all from the same angle in either the living room or a bedroom with a man's back to the camera. A man who knew how to keep his face concealed from the hidden cameras he'd placed. Doug. Some of the photos had the little Play button superimposed on top, indicating it was a video clip.

"Holy shit," he said under his breath.

"You have no idea," Tessa replied, glancing up at him. "That blonde is the wife of a congressman. And that girl in the pink underwear is the daughter of one of his closest friends. I'm not even sure she's out of college yet. And there're so many of Marilyn in here, I can't even count. He's documented them all. Why would he keep all this?"

"To relive it and jerk off," he said bluntly. "Or to have dirt on them in case he ever needs it."

"They can't know that he's taping them. I know Marilyn would never allow it for sure. She's a reporter and knows how damaging this stuff can be."

The pictures continued to slide by, but Kade could tell they were going backward in time. The locations changed and quality got grainy. Some looked to be scanned instead of digital. Instead of full sex, they also switched to blow job shots, taken from Doug's perspective from above, ones where the participants probably knew they were being photographed. Prostitutes most likely, based on the heavy makeup and come hither eyes. And not all of them were women. Kade's stomach turned with his own memories.

Then there was a photo of a familiar blonde stretched out naked and sleeping. Tessa.

"Oh, God." Tessa's hand flew to her mouth. She hit a button, trying to get the slideshow to stop, but instead it just sped it up. Photo after photo of Tessa scrolled through. Most where it was clear she was completely unaware he was there—shots of her in the shower or getting dressed. But there were also a few sex shots in their bedroom, and Kade had to turn away. The thought of that slime touching Tessa, recording her when she wasn't aware, made him want to break things.

"I feel like I'm going to be sick," she said, gripping the desk.

He reached out and put a hand on her shoulder, trying to calm her but also working to keep himself in check. "Delete the ones of you and let's go. If I don't get out of here soon, I'm going to go upstairs and murder the sonofabitch. Did you get anything else we could use?"

She gave a quick nod as she clicked the mouse in rapid succession, deleting things. "Yes, I emailed a bunch of stuff to myself. There are definite quirks in some of the reports. But I need more time to look at them and maybe show them to someone more experienced."

"Good, then let's move."

She closed out all the programs and shut down the computer, then let him lead her out into the living room. She'd tucked her suitcase and purse into the closet and retrieved those before they both headed out through the back door. But when Kade slid the glass door shut, he heard a yelp and a thud behind him.

He spun around to find Doug with one hand over Tessa's mouth and the other hand pointing a gun at Kade. Her suitcase and bag had dropped by her feet. Doug nodded at Kade. "Either of you make a sound and I pull the trigger. No one would blame me for shooting an intruder, especially one trying to break in to rape my wife."

Kade put his hands out on front of him with calm, slow movements, even though he wanted to charge the bastard. "She's not your wife, Doug."

"All these years and still trying to take my girl," he said, holding Tessa against his chest. "You think you would've learned your lesson last time. Found what you were looking for in my office?"

"We found your photo collection," Kade said, knowing that if he said they found nothing, Doug wouldn't buy it. "Interesting hobby you have."

"Profitable one. It's amazing what people pay for that type of stuff online. The people that leaked my mother's sex tape made millions off of it. You should see how much I got for those photos of you, babe."

Tessa made a horrified noise beneath his hand.

"I would've never released any of yours if you hadn't left me. No one deserved to see my wife, but once you weren't—well, I needed the cash to make up for the money you got in the divorce. Of course, I always blur out the faces. I wouldn't want to embarrass anyone. And don't worry, they're not all out there. I keep my favorite ones for my private collection. Some things are too good to take money for." He looked to Kade. "I wish I would've had a camera that night with you. Seeing you sucking my cock like a bitch, those crying blue eyes begging me for mercy, could get me off every time. Bet you haven't been fucked unconscious since."

The words made bile rise in the back of Kade's throat and that old feeling of shame tried to leak in, especially with Tessa there hearing it all. But he refused to let it claim him.

"Hey, I may have even cured your stutter," Doug added.

Fury rose up in Kade like a tsunami, demanding that he rip this guy apart with his bare hands. But he didn't take the bait and let himself lunge at Doug. He had no doubt Doug would shoot him, and then Tessa would be left with this sociopath. "Glad you're so proud to be a rapist, Douggie. How many of those people in your photo collection were willing? My guess is less than half."

His mouth twitched in a half smile, like he was fucking proud of himself. "You know how it is, don't you? You're into that dominance shit. I saw that picture of Tessa crawling for you. The fear is what gets guys like us off."

Kade's fists curled. "I'm *nothing* like you, you sick fuck."

People like him were the reason he was fighting in court for his kid. Psychos who took everything true dominants held sacred and twisted it into ugly, criminal things.

"Sure, if that's what helps you sleep at night," Doug said with a sneer. "But I bet my dear wife here is soaking wet right now. She has no control. That's what she likes, right? You make her your whore. Maybe I should try it out. I could do whatever I wanted to her right now."

Tessa's eyes darted from left to right, fear there, but also determination. Kade got the sense she was scanning the yard, looking for some escape or weapon. But Kade knew even if there was something available neither of them would be able to get to anything without Doug seeing. Kade was going to have to do this with talking.

"Let her go, Doug. If you hurt either of us, you know it's going to be too suspicious to write off as an accident or self-defense. We can work this out with no bloodshed. You've got photos we want back. And we have ones of you. I'm thinking that's an even trade. Everybody walks away and moves on."

"No," he ground out. "I need her to tell everyone she cheated and that I was a good husband. My congregation doesn't trust me and it's hurting my business. I'm not going to stand by and watch the reputation I built crumble. She needs to fix the shit she caused."

Tessa made a muffled noise.

"Let her talk," Kade said. "She's not going to scream while the gun's on me."

Doug moved his hand from around her mouth to a loose chokehold around her neck. "Talk, but one loud noise and your boyfriend's got a bullet in the head."

"I'll say whatever you need me to say," Tessa said in a rush. "I can't marry you again. But I'll say whatever you want at services tomorrow. I don't care about what anyone thinks of me. They can call me what they want. I just want to go back to Texas and live my life."

"To be his *slut*?"

She lifted her gaze to Kade's, a glimmer of something beautiful there. "Yes. To be his. I love him."

Kade's chest expanded with the words, everything in him soaring. She loved him back.

But they weren't going to be able to celebrate that if they didn't get out of this backyard and away from Doug's gun.

"Listen, Doug. It's a simple business transaction. We can trade photos, and Tessa will go to the church tomorrow to say what you want her to. Then we walk away from each other and never speak again," Kade said, trying to use his reasonable voice.

"You fucking love him?" Doug asked, turning red.

"I always have," Tessa said, venom in her voice. "I married you for your money because I had no choice. But you were always a jerk. And by the way, *you* were the one who was boring in bed. You've got a dick you have no idea how to work. Now I realize just how bad at fucking you were. I used to fake coming just to get it over with."

*Oh, shit.*

"Tess, *stop*." Panic zipped through Kade as she continued her rant. He could see what her words were doing to Doug. The man was about to explode with rage. This was not the way to get him to calm down and cooperate.

"Is that right?" Doug yanked Tessa away from him, holding her by the front of her shirt and pointing the gun her way. He shook her hard and shoved her to the ground. "You think I don't know how to fuck? I tried to be gentle with you. I tried to respect you. You were *my wife*. But, you're about to find out what it feels like when I fuck a whore."

Tessa was on her back and lifted herself onto her elbows. "Come on, then. Take out your dick. I'm ready to laugh."

*Jesus Christ*, what was she doing? But when her gaze flicked Kade's way and then to the gun, which was now lowered at Doug's side while he unbuttoned his pants, he realized what she was doing. Raping someone would be a two-handed event. And in his moment of fury, Doug had lost sight of the man standing nearby.

Kade gave Tessa a quick nod and she rolled out of the way in one swift motion. Before Doug realized what was happening, Kade was barreling forward linebacker style and knocking him sideways. The momentum carried them both to the ground and the gun went off. Tessa screamed and pain lit up Kade's leg, but he wasn't going to let that stop him. He pinned Doug to the ground and grabbed his wrist, banging it on the lawn with all his strength until the gun fell from Doug's grip.

Doug struggled beneath him, but Kade had learned a lot since that night in the woods. He knew how to restrain someone in more creative ways than he could count. He pushed Doug onto his back and wrenched his arms above his head. Doug was still fighting and writhing beneath him.

"Take my belt off, Tessa, and get the gun," Kade said in a rush. Tessa hurried over to help, and Kade tied Doug's wrists tight enough to cause pain. "Put your foot against his wrists to make sure he keeps his hands down."

Tessa did as she was told, and he took the gun back from Tessa. Without hesitation, he put it to Doug's mouth. "Open, motherfucker."

"Please. Don't." Doug's eyes were huge, true fear there, and he shook his head frantically. Kade tapped Doug's teeth with the gun and got a whimper of pain. But he also got compliance.

He shoved the gun into Doug's mouth. "I wonder if this is what I looked like, Doug, when you raped me? Are you giving me the look that you got off on?"

Doug mumbled around the gun, some kind of plea, and drool

leaked out the side of his mouth. But pure fury was filtering through Kade's blood, all the memories of that night fueling him, and he couldn't stop himself, couldn't stop the rage.

"Suck it, Doug," Kade—or rather Kaden—said. Because right now that boy from the woods was rising from the ashes and getting his revenge. "Take it down your throat and make it come. Or maybe I should turn you over. Because that's what you did to me after I passed out wasn't it?"

"Kade," Tessa said, fear in her voice. "We've got him tied up. We need to just call the police."

But Kade wasn't ready to listen to reason right now. He pushed the gun to the back of Doug's throat and Doug sucked.

"You said we weren't very different." He moved the gun in and out. "If that's the case, if you were right, then I guess I should pull this trigger. Because you would. Then you'd probably defile the body afterward. You certainly deserve no better after what you did to me and all those people in the photos."

Doug mumbled something that sounded distinctly like *fuck you*.

Kade yanked the gun from Doug's mouth, put it into the earth next to Doug's head and pulled the trigger. Screams—both Doug's and Tessa's—filled the night and dirt flew.

Kade climbed off of Doug in time to see the dark stain appearing on the front of Doug's pants as he wet himself. Sirens sounded in the background.

Kade crouched down to Doug and patted his cheek, which was wet with tears. "Guess it's a good thing for both of us, Douggie, that I'm nothing like you."

Doug spat at him. "I'm going to tell them you two attacked me. That you were trying to break into the house."

"And I'm going to show them the video of what really happened," said an unfamiliar voice.

A woman stepped out from the shadows by the fence. She was

in a robe, her dark hair twisted on top of her head, and looked vaguely familiar. In her hand was a cell phone.

Tessa stepped away from Doug and looked to the woman. "I hoped you were still an insomniac."

The woman nodded grimly. "I got the photos you texted me. I was coming over to rip his computer out of the wall but when I saw what was going on, I called the police."

Tessa blew out a breath. "I prayed it was you moving in the shadows. Thank you. The video will help."

"You know me, always the reporter," she said without humor.

Kade realized this was Marilyn. The woman in the photos. Doug's mistress and Tessa's former best friend.

Doug rolled over, no doubt one last-ditch attempt to escape, but the police were pouring into the yard a moment later.

And this time, Kade was the one pressing charges.

But he couldn't feel triumphant about it. He felt sick. Because for those few moments when he had the gun to Doug, he knew he'd been far too close to crossing the line. The I'm-past-this bullshit had lost all validity. And it had put doubts in the head of the one person whose trust he'd worked so hard to get.

He'd scared her.

He'd scared himself.

# THIRTY-THREE

Kade was quiet on the plane ride home. They'd spent the previous night in the hospital to get his leg treated—luckily, the bullet had only grazed his thigh. Then they'd spent the morning in the police station giving statements. So they hadn't had any time to talk. And once they'd gotten on his company's private jet, he'd closed his eyes and pretended to sleep. She could tell he was faking because his breathing never turned even.

He was beating himself up over how he'd tortured Doug at the end. He hadn't said so, but she knew that's what lurked behind the dark shadows of his expression. After the police had come into the yard, Kade had stood to the side, stricken. When he'd looked to Tessa, it was as if he was looking through her. Empty. Gone. And when she'd gone to stand with him, he hadn't reached out for her. There'd been this invisible steel shell encasing him.

And part of her had been scared to embrace him in that moment. It had been frightening to see the cold hate in Kade's eyes, the capacity for true violence. Something had overtaken him there in the backyard, morphing the kind and loving man she knew into one with single-minded vengeance. But knowing what he'd been through in the woods, how Doug had violated him so viciously, she couldn't blame him for his instinctive reaction. She'd been most afraid that Kade would do something he'd regret, something that would land him in jail. But through the rage and trauma and all that memory, he'd been able to pull back and walk away anyway.

She couldn't imagine the amount of self-control that had taken. She wasn't sure she would've been able to do the same had she gone through what he had.

But she hated that it'd sent him into shutdown mode. She reached for his hand and threaded her fingers with his. He gave a little squeeze back, proving that he wasn't asleep, but didn't open his eyes.

"Only about an hour before we get there," she said softly.

"Good, I'm ready to be as far from Atlanta as possible."

"You and me both." She glanced out the window at the inky blackness. "Dallas almost doesn't seem far enough."

He gave her hand another squeeze. "I know what you mean."

She rubbed her thumb over his ring finger back and forth, back and forth, thinking. "Maybe we should keep going further then."

He cracked his eyes open and peeked at her, the sadness that had been sitting heavy there earlier still glimmering in the blue depths. "What are you talking about?"

She shrugged. "I heard Vegas is nice this time of year."

That got him fully awake. He sat up straighter and turned toward her. "Have a hankering to gamble?"

She rubbed her lips together, considering him. He looked so much like the boy he used to be at times—sleepy-eyed, mussed hair, vaguely wary look on his face. "Yeah, I think I do. I've never been good at taking risks. Maybe it's a good place to get over that. What do you think?"

He sighed and stared down at their joined hands. The weight of everything left unsaid about the night before, about what really happened in high school, about the darkness that had chased the both of them through the years—all of it infiltrated the cabin, piling in and filling all the spaces with the heavy baggage they'd gathered over the years.

When Kade finally spoke, his voice was unbearably quiet. "I'm so sorry about how I acted last night, Tess. How I . . . lost it. I thought I'd shown you my ugly parts, but even I didn't know that side of me was in there. Being near him again brought all that shit up, and I was there in the woods again, seeing it all again, feeling every kick, every broken bone. All logic went out of my head. I wanted to make him suffer. I wanted to humiliate him and tear away every thread of pride he had. Destroy him. I needed him to feel what he made me feel that night."

"Kade . . ." she said, her heart breaking at the anguish in his voice, the disgust with himself.

"Maybe I'm not as different from him as I thought I was. I could've killed him and not felt bad about it. Part of me wishes I would've. And I don't know what to do with that."

"Hey, look at me," she said, her voice firm. He lifted his gaze to hers, all the pain shining there. "Don't ever say stupid shit like that again. You're as far from someone like him as anyone can be. You may have wanted to kill him, may still want to, but you didn't and you won't. You had the chance twice, and you didn't hurt him. Your reaction was human. The things he did to you left scars that you may have moved past but are always going to be there on some level."

"I just hate that it's still there at all. I thought I'd exorcised it all. I never wanted you to see that side of me. I know I scared you."

She shook her head. "I was scared that I'd lose you if you did something to him. That's where my fear was. And you don't have to pretend that those things never happened to you. That stuff fades but doesn't disappear. We just learn how to deal with it better. It's why any time you mention the word *relationship* I get a fat dose of panic rushing through me. No matter how much I try to convince myself that I'm not that insecure foster kid anymore, part of me will always expect people to let me down and leave."

He reached out and pushed her hair behind her ear. "Then why do you want to go to Vegas?"

"Because I love poker, duh."

He laughed, and the rich sound was so welcome after the last forty-eight hours that she nearly climbed into his seat with him to absorb it fully.

"I want to go because, just like you, I'm tired of all that stuff from the past holding me hostage. The times I've spent with you since that night in the restaurant have been the most exciting and happiest I've ever had. Yes, you're intense and dominant, and I know I still have a lot to understand about that. I will warn you now that if your idea of submission is having some kept woman who sits around the house and waits for you to come home, that isn't going to fly for me. I will never be a housewife. I suck at it. And I don't care how adorable and sexy you are, how convincing you can be when you get that badass dom look on your face, or how madly in love with you I am, that's not going to change."

He gave her a roguish smile filled with that trademark confidence that had been absent in Atlanta, and her belly did a flutter. "Madly in love, huh?"

"Yes. Madly. Deal with it."

"I kind of want to hear you say that over and over again. Possibly while I'm deep inside you."

A pulse of desire heated her from the center outward. But she was not to be distracted from her demands.

"I want to keep going to school. I want a career. I need to stand on my own two feet in the world. I won't be anyone's trophy again."

He lifted an eyebrow, his expression amused. "Is that all Mistress McAllen?"

"Well, I do agree that you can have your wicked way with me when I'm not working or in school. I mean, I do have to concede some things. Plus, you're so very good at that part."

He brought her hand to his mouth and kissed the center of her palm, sending a shiver up her arm. "I would never make you quit school or give up a career. I want you submissive to me. I don't want a Stepford wife."

"Good."

"But I'm going to give you my own warning right back," he said, his gaze meeting hers. "I want to take care of you, Tess. That doesn't mean making you dependent on me. But it does mean that I want to pamper you and surprise you and take you places on a whim. It means that I'll worry about you and make sure you have everything you need. I'm madly in love with you right back, and I'm going to want to show it in every way available." He kissed up her arm. "And I have *lots and lots* of ways available to me."

She closed her eyes, his simple touch soothing something inside her. "I think I can work with that."

He unhooked his seat belt and got to his knee, wincing slightly from his injury, then took her hands in his. His shoulders rose and fell with a deep breath before he met her eyes. "Tessa McAllen, I fell in lust with you the day I first saw you walk across the cafeteria in that purple flowered sundress you used to wear. I lost my heart to you when you hugged me that day in the cabin after your test and looked at me like I mattered to you. And I fell in love with you when I discovered the strong, smart, unfairly sexy woman you've become. I want nothing more in this life than to make you mine and to be yours in return. I know it may take you a while to trust that, but I will give you my love without limit or conditions, without an end. I'm not going anywhere. You're it for me, Tess. Always. No matter what."

Her throat felt filled with cotton, and fat tears rolled off her cheeks, splashing onto their joined hands. It was everything she'd always wanted to hear, the promise of forever. A real forever. And for the first time, she believed it could actually exist. She'd waited all her life for this man. For this kind of love.

"Will you be mine, Tess? Wear my ring and my collar?"

She looped her arms around his neck and slid down to her knees between the seats, almost too filled with joy to breathe. The truth poured out of her, without filter or fear. "It's always been you, Kade. I walked away back then, but I never collected all of my heart back from you. Before this, if someone had told me there was a perfect match for me out there, some person destined to fit just right with me, I would've laughed. Especially if they told me that guy was someone who'd want to put a collar around my neck. But when I landed back in Atlanta and thought that I may have to give you up, give this up, I realized that I can never go back to the before state. I don't want to. I thought I was happy with my new life in Texas. And I was. But not like this. I love you, Kaden Fowler Vandergriff, the boy you were and the man you've become. And I can't think of anything I'd rather be more than the wife on your arm . . . and the slave in your bed."

Kade's smile lit up the darkened cabin and nearly broke her chest open. There was so much in his eyes, so much emotion he'd been keeping hidden from her, so much love. No one had ever looked at her like that—like she was the reason the sun rose each day.

Kade slid his hands up her neck and cradled her face. "I don't want to go another day without making you mine. I've waited too long already."

She nodded in his grip, excitement rather than nerves taking over at the prospect.

He reached back to press a button, calling for the flight attendant. The guy came down the aisle, not blinking an eye at the two of them kneeling between their seats. Kade barely spared him a glance. "Tell the pilot to reroute us to Las Vegas. And please close the curtain behind you and don't check on us again until I open it."

The attendant gave a brief smile. "Yes, sir. Right away."

Tess lifted her eyebrows when he looked back to her.

"Tell me," he said with a wicked tilt to his mouth. "Was membership in the mile-high club on that list of yours?"

She grinned. "It's not, but I should definitely add it."

He stood and took her hand, guiding her to her feet. But she didn't miss the little flinch he gave when he'd gotten up.

"What about your leg?"

He put his hands on her waist and quieted her with a slow, soft kiss. When he pulled back, he gave her an enigmatic smile. "I've got ways around that."

He led her down the aisle and she assumed he was taking her to the back where there was a small sleeping cabin with a twin-sized bed. But he stopped in the open area behind the seats where two couches flanked each side of the jet.

"Take off your clothes, Tess," he said, that commanding tone sending goose bumps over her skin.

She glanced at the back of the plane. "Here?"

"Yes. Here. I suggest you don't question me."

She wet her lips. "Yes, sir."

She pulled her shirt over her head and slipped out of her jeans, then tugged off her bra and underwear. The plane jolted and she grabbed for the overhead bin to keep her balance.

He gave her a long, sweeping once-over. The cabin lights had been turned down low and the starless night bled in from the windows, painting Kade in shadows and making him look ominous and intimidating and sexy. She shivered in the cool air, her nipples pebbling.

Kade opened the bin behind him and pulled out something. He turned around, holding seat belt extenders. "Wouldn't want to risk the safety of my pretty little slave."

She eyed the straps, her heartbeat hopping against her ribs.

"Turn around and face the windows. The view flying into Vegas at night is pretty breathtaking."

"Yes, sir." She turned on bare feet, facing the row of round windows, and Kade stepped behind her.

His body was hard and warm against her as he lifted one of her arms above her head. He wrapped the seat belt extender around her wrists and made a makeshift knot. Then he threaded it through the handle of the bin above her. He secured the other wrist to the other end of the strap. "Too tight?"

"No, sir, it's fine."

"Good." He caressed her sides with hot palms as he moved down her body and squatted at her feet. He wrapped the belts around her ankles and secured her, legs spread wide—one hooked to the seat to the left and one to the leg of the couch. "There, now you won't fall if the plane hits turbulence."

"Thank you, sir." Though she suspected Kade was going to provide turbulence of his own.

He trailed fingers down her spine. "Tonight I don't want anything between us. I get checked regularly and am safe. Are you on birth control?"

"I'm on the pill. And I got tested after I found out what Doug had been doing."

"Good girl," he said, kissing along her shoulder. "I need to hear you say you're okay with me fucking you bare, baby. That's not something I will order you to do."

The dirty words made her stomach clench low, her body already growing wet and hot for him. "I want it, sir. No more condoms."

He circled his arms around her and brushed his fingers over her folds. Her legs went boneless for a moment and she groaned into the touch, the pleasure so welcome after such a stressful few days. "I agree, no more condoms when it's just us."

The words took a second to register with the delicious stroking that was going on, but all her attention honed in on his words. "Won't it always be just us? We're getting married."

"I promise you there will never be another woman for me. You're all I need, and more than one woman is not my kink. But I saw how much you enjoyed that night with Colby. And I like giving you that kind of pleasure, sharing you as my slave." His fingers dipped inside her, his slow strokes matching the soft, cajoling sound of his voice. "Like I told you that first night. I'm a kinky fucker. Our love is monogamous, so I trust in that enough that if we play with someone else, you're still all mine and vice versa."

The concept was so out there, so very different from anything she'd ever known or considered. But there was something wildly enticing about that deep a level of trust. It'd be okay to explore each other's edges, together, without worrying that it would shake their foundation. She knew without a doubt that it didn't matter how many men touched her when they had a kinky night, none would tempt her away from this man. He would truly own her body, heart, and soul.

"It's always going to ultimately be your call," he said softly. "But putting a ring on your finger doesn't mean I stop pushing your boundaries. What if I want to see how loud you come when I'm deep in your ass while you fuck someone else? I know your mind went there when you saw Jace, Evan, and Andre together."

She moaned at both the fantasy he was conjuring and the way he curled his fingers inside her. "You're a filthy, filthy man, sir."

His laugh was dark and low against his ear. "And you love it."

"I do, sir. I love *you*."

"And I will wake up and thank the heavens every day for that." He kissed her neck and traced his tongue along her pulse point. "My beautiful, smart, brave girl. My future wife. And my dirty little slave."

She smiled, warmth blooming in her chest, and lowered her head. Never would she have believed that word could be an endearment. But Kade had proved it to her. She would not be his angelic, proper wife. She would not be that insecure, people-pleasing girl. She would be Tessa for him. A woman who wasn't afraid to give in to her desires. A woman who would do things with him just because they were fun, because they felt good, because she loved him and he loved her. Because the ultimate trust was there. A woman who could stand on her own two feet but who could also get on her knees at night for her man and not feel wrong about it.

Kade brought her close to orgasm with his fingers then pulled back, dragging his hand up her abdomen and painting her with her arousal. His hand cupped her breast then slid up to capture her nipple.

"Ready for a little sting?" He gave her nipple a firm pinch and tug.

She arched into the touch and moaned. Somehow just that little dart of pain made every nerve ending stand up and pay attention, her body craving that dose of sharpness mixed in with the pleasure.

"Mmm," Kade said, rolling her other nipple between his fingers and pinching it hard. She gasped and she could hear the smile in his voice when he spoke again. "I love how you respond to any hint of roughness. I think my girl craves pain more than she realizes. I can't wait to see how deep that wiring runs."

He stepped back and his hand came down on her backside with a hard slap. The sound was like a gunshot in the small airplane. But the stinging heat that raced outward made her forget to worry about all the noise they were making. His hand whacked her on the other side and then again across her thigh. She wiggled in her bindings, but he didn't pause. The spanking was harder and longer than he'd done in the past and no spot on her thighs, hips, ass, or pussy remained untouched.

Her skin burned and ached, everything was tightening. And the resulting heat curling through her was making her so wet, she could barely concentrate. But even with all that, the voice inside her was silently begging him for more of that violence. She needed to be touched, she needed to be hurt, she needed the two together. She didn't know why, and she no longer cared. Words slipped past her lips, and she couldn't decipher what she was saying anymore.

But apparently Kade did. He coasted his hands over her fiery skin. "You need more, huh? I love to hear you begging for it. I can see you sinking, baby. Your body's giving over to it. Let it take you and I'll give you what you need."

Her mind was buzzing, her vision making the windows blur together, but she sensed him moving behind her. She mourned the loss of his hands on her.

"I'm glad I travel prepared," he said from somewhere to her left. Another bin was opened and closed. Then he was touching her hip with light fingers, letting her know he was back with her. "I think it's time to punish you for leaving town without telling me and for shutting me out instead of asking for help."

Her already racing heart stuttered in her chest. "Punish?"

"You know how worried I was when I found your house empty, your car still in the driveway."

"I was—"

He pressed his hand over her mouth. "Shh, no more talking unless it's to safe out. You said you need more. You may regret what you asked for."

He lowered his hand and dragged what looked to be a thin reed of wood across her breasts. She swallowed hard. "May I ask what that is, sir?"

"You may," he said, dragging the tip of it over her shoulder and down her back. "It's a rattan cane. One of the most intensely painful tools I have."

She stiffened, fear instantly taking root.

"In the wrong hands, it can injure." He traced the notches of her spine with the end of the dreadful thing. "In the right hands, it hurts like a sonofabitch and leaves the prettiest marks."

Her breath quickened. "Sir . . ."

He stepped up behind her and dragged her backside along his erection. Her sex clenched, desperate for him. "I need to see how deep your masochism streak runs. But more than that I want to mark you, Tess. I want to wake up tomorrow with my ring on your finger and my marks on your skin."

She shivered in his hold, a combination of fear and desperate need coalescing. The idea of him marking her spoke to some part inside her she hadn't even known existed. "I'm a little scared."

"I know, baby," he said, kissing the shell of her ear. "And that's okay. I won't force this on you. In fact, I'm not going to do it until you ask for my cane."

Her throat was so dry she had trouble speaking. "What do you mean?"

His breath was hot on her skin as he lowered his hand and teased her clit again. "I won't do it until you tell me you want my marks."

"And if I say no?" she asked, breathless from what he was doing with his fingers.

"I put it away," he said simply.

She closed her eyes and took a long breath as he continued to tease her to the edge of orgasm. Intense pain didn't seem like something she would ever ask for. But the burning warmth from the spanking was starting to fade and all her senses had gone edgy, hungry for something more, something else. Like if she could just have whatever that little extra was, it would send her over into orgasm.

"I trust you," she said softly.

Kade pressed another kiss to her hair but seemed to relax behind her. "You trust me to what, baby?"

She was so close to coming it was hard to focus. "Trust that you won't give me more than you think I can handle. Give me your cane, sir. Please. I want to wear your marks."

Kade groaned, the pleased sound reward enough, and he stepped in between her and the couch. He was on his knees in a flash and spreading her open with his thumbs. His tongue and mouth enveloped her clit before she could even catch her breath.

She let out a gasp of surprise and her fists curled in her bindings.

"Come for me, Tess," he said, pulling back for a moment. "I want you flying high first."

He went back to licking her with hungry enthusiasm, and he pushed the leather-wrapped handle of the cane inside her. Her body clasped around the invasion and she made a desperate sound. *Oh, God.*

It was all too much at once. He pumped the unyielding handle inside her with slow, insanity-inducing strokes and his lips and tongue paid homage to every delicate, aching part of her. She had no hope to hold off. The orgasm steamrolled over her, crushing any last resistance and tearing a cry from her throat.

Kade lapped at her, letting her ride the wave of sensation for as long as possible, then he slid the handle from her and was climbing to his feet. Her body was still contracting, pleasure steadily pulsing through her, when he put a hand on her shoulder to steady her and flicked the cane across her ass.

*Holy. Fucking. Shit.* Pain exploded over her with breath-stealing impact. She opened her mouth to scream but nothing came out. *No, no, no*, she couldn't take this much. But before she could suck in air to call her safeword, the reverberating pain radiated outward through her body and mixed in with the tail end of her orgasm, morphing into some hybrid sensation that made her pant and on the verge of coming again.

"God, look how beautiful you are," Kade said, his voice holding awe. He pressed fingers against her clit and circled with firmer pressure than she would've guessed could feel good. "Two more, love."

He flicked the cane again, right below where the first hit had been, and she saw stars. But his fingers kept circling, and the stimulation was just what she needed. Her body was tightening all over again, preparing for another explosion.

"Last one," he whispered.

The intensity was no less than the first two, but the gasping sobs she made had nothing to do with the pain. The sensations were making her dizzy and desperate. She didn't know how to hold it all in. She felt lost. She felt found. She felt . . . high.

Kade tossed the cane onto the couch and rained praise on her as he shucked his clothes. Then he untied her from her restraints with the swiftness of a man on a mission. She couldn't keep up with his movements, her brain spinning. When he released the last belt, she sagged in his arms, unable to hold herself upright, and he walked them over to the couch. He sat down, his cock jutting proudly upward and she wanted to sink to her knees and worship it—something, anything to thank him for the way she was feeling in this moment. But Kade shook his head when she tried. He had other ideas. He guided her down to straddle his lap.

"I want to see you while I fuck you, Tess," he said, positioning himself at her entrance. "Want to watch you take me inside you and fall apart."

He pushed into her without resistance, her body so slick and ready for him that her eyes nearly rolled back when he sunk deep.

"Fuck," he groaned, grasping her hips and seating himself fully inside her. "You feel so good, baby. So damn perfect."

All she could do was murmur in response, her executive functioning shorting out and giving over to all the sensations.

"Ride me, Tess. Make me come."

Even through the haze in her mind, she knew at the very least she could accomplish that. She braced her hands on his shoulders, met his eyes, and undulated her hips, taking him almost all the way out and then plunging back down.

His eyes were pale in the near darkness but she could see him going into that place with her. That place where all that existed was the two of them and the way their bodies felt joined together. She didn't know how long she fucked him. Time slowed and stretched, but when he grabbed her head and brought her mouth down to his, she lost all sense of everything.

They kissed long and deep, their tongues intertwining, as she took him into her body over and over. Everything they'd ever wanted to say to each other poured into that kiss. Every emotion, any word left unspoken, all the love, it was all there.

Without breaking the kiss, he tilted her hips just right and rubbed his cock along that perfect spot inside her and the world went Technicolor behind her eyelids. She broke from the kiss, sucking in air and crying out. His groan joined hers and the warmth of his release spilled inside her, marking her on the inside just like she wore his marks on the outside.

And as the lights of Vegas came into view through the windows behind him, glittering in the distance like some far-off kingdom, Tessa knew she'd finally found her place in the world. This was it. The little girl who once believed in fairy tales had finally found her prince.

Her deliciously evil prince.

# EPILOGUE

*Three months later*

Kade leaned back in his chair, sipping a glass of champagne and smiling over the rim as he enjoyed the view.

"I'd hate to be that guy," Colby observed, reaching for one of the crab and avocado toasts off the platter at the center of the table.

Gibson made a grunt of agreement. "You ain't lying. Soon he'll be saying, *Yes, Mistress. May I kiss your shoes?*"

Kade chuckled. He couldn't hear what was being said, but Tessa was giving the manager of the venue quite a firm talking to—probably something to do with the fact that there were not enough chairs for everyone and the tables had been set up too far away from the stage. He wasn't worried, though. There was still an hour before the band came on and everyone was happy to be milling around and mingling. He had no doubt Tessa would have the issue fixed before anyone even noticed.

"I can't believe there are this many people here," Colby said. "This looks like a way bigger crowd than last year."

Kade nodded. "My woman's relentless. She's probably going

to pull in enough cash on her own to send all those kids at Bluebonnet to college on full scholarship. I haven't even told her yet that all the money we raised at the slave auction was real and that there's a big check to add to the pile."

"Yeah," Colby said. "She covered every angle. I saw that she even has the kids selling artwork they created to contribute to their individual college funds. One of the paintings just sold for a grand. Twelve-year-old kid was the artist. I thought his eyes were going to fall out of his head."

"Hell, at that age, I would've lost it, too," Gib said, taking a pull of his beer. "I remember saving up three hundred bucks in middle school after a summer of cutting grass. I thought I was rich."

Kade snorted. "Then you spent it all on comic books and Playboys."

"That was money well spent, my friend. I was all set for a long winter."

Colby laughed and looked to Gibson. "So where did your date go off to? She'd probably appreciate hearing your embarrassing childhood stories."

Kade set his glass down. "Rosalie dragged Sam off to the kid's area. One of the restaurants is giving a little cooking demo for the kiddos."

Gibson shrugged. "Sam's not my date. I'm just helping her out with her training, and she thought it'd be fun to come together tonight."

"I always prefer coming together," Kade said with a smirk. "Fun for all."

Gibson gave him a droll look. "Seriously, you're still fourteen under that shirt and tie."

Kade raised his glass in cheers.

"Seems very self-sacrificing of you," Colby said with mock

seriousness. "Going above and beyond and taking your trainee out for the night."

"Drop it," Gib warned.

"What? We're not ribbing you. I, for one, am happy to see you embracing your inner switch and subbing."

"I'm not subbing. I'm bottoming to train her as a domme. I'm still in control."

"Nothing to be ashamed of, dude," Colby said with a shrug. "She's taking a few classes at one of the clubs I help out at sometimes. I've seen her in her bitch boots. She wears them well. I'm sure many men wouldn't mind getting a beating and a pegging from her."

"Keep away from her, farm boy," Gib said, pointing his beer at Colby.

Colby grinned as he took another swig off his beer, obviously enjoying this way too much. "Lucky for you, she's not my type."

"What are y'all smiling about?"

Kade turned to see Tess standing there, clipboard in hand and eyebrow arched—all business and looking hotter than ever in her little blue dress. He grabbed her by the waist and pulled her into his lap, unable to resist. "Just torturing your former boss."

"I was about to use my safeword," Gibson said, leaning back in his chair and hooking his ankle over his knee. "Thanks for saving me. Hey, wait a second, what do you mean former?"

Tessa made an *uh-oh* face as she leaned into Kade. "Sorry, Gib. I was going to talk to you on Monday, but my husband has a big mouth."

"Tessa's going to take over as co-director of Bluebonnet Place," Kade said, pride swelling in him.

Gibson's disappointment quickly morphed into a broad smile. "That's fantastic. I'll be sad to lose you, but no one will run your charity better than you. Those kids will be lucky to have you at the helm."

Tessa let out a breath, her worry lifting. "Thanks, Gib. I still have a lot to learn from Iris, the current director, but I'm looking forward to it."

"You're going to do great," Kade said, giving her a quick kiss. "Did you get everything worked out with the manager over there? I saw you two talking."

"Yes, I think he's probably wishing he had a safeword, but we're good now. And Darkfall is all set to go." She nodded at the tray of appetizers. "How's the food?"

He frowned. "You haven't eaten yet?"

"Didn't have time."

He met her eyes, broadcasting exactly what he thought of that excuse. "Sit down in this chair and eat."

She waved a hand. "I will. I just need to go make rounds and thank everyone who came."

He lifted her up and deposited her in the chair next to him. "Everyone will still be here for at least two more hours. I won't have you passing out in the middle of this thing. Eat. Have a drink. I'll go shake hands and make nice."

"Kade—"

He cupped her chin and planted a kiss on her mouth. "Non-negotiable, baby. Sorry."

"You're a bossy bastard, Mr. Vandergriff," she said, but her eyes went soft in that way that made him wish he had a private room to take her to and an hour of her time.

"Always. Good thing you love that about me." He kissed her forehead and then patted Colby on the shoulder as he walked by him. "You guys make sure my girl eats. I'm going to find my other date."

---

Kade watched Rosalie from the back of the tent as she dumped a cup of flour into a bowl with such force that all of it blew back up on her, dusting her sequined purple dress in white. He chuckled when she tried to make it better and ended up adding white handprints to the mix. The instructor attempted to dust her off, but it was no use. The little girl next to her was looking at the mess with a wrinkled nose, but Rosalie just shrugged and grabbed a bowl of spices to dump in and continue mixing.

"Looks like the dress is a loss," Sam said, sidling up next to him.

Kade smiled. "She doesn't care. Onward. That was always her motto. Nothing gets in her way when she's on a mission."

"I wonder where she gets that from, Stalker Boy." Sam nudged his shoulder with hers.

"Hey, knock my method, but it worked." He held up his left hand and waggled his ring finger.

"Yes, it did. Which is why I'm attempting the same method with your brother, just so you know."

"Good. He could use someone like you around. Whip him into shape."

She smirked. "And with me that's not a figure of speech."

"Daddy!"

The shout from across the room drew their attention toward the front. Rosalie held up a cookie. "Look, we have a swap out, just like on the cooking shows."

"Excellent," he called back.

He and Sam watched Rosalie finish up with the group then his little girl came running over to him, wrapping her floured hands around him when she reached him. "Is it time for the music yet?"

"The band's not for kiddos, Spark. Plus, it's getting late. Your mom is probably waiting for you."

Her bottom lip flipped out in a full-force pout. "But daadddy, you said I was going to be able to go to your house."

He crouched down in front of her and ruffled her hair. "Next week, Spark. Your room is all ready for you, and you'll get to stay there every other weekend and spend a whole month with me and Ms. Tess in the summer."

"You *promise*?"

"Cross my heart and pie in my eye," he said solemnly, crossing his finger over his chest in an *X*.

That sent her into a grin and chased off the pout. "No, daddy, that's not how it goes."

"Cross my eyes and hope to cry?"

"No!" She fell into a fit of giggles and he lifted her into his arms.

"Come on, Spark. I promise this is the last time we'll have to end our visit early."

She hooked her little arms around his neck and gave him a tight squeeze. "Thanks, Daddy. I don't want to have to miss you all the time."

The words were bittersweet, but a lightness filled his chest as he carried her toward the parking lot. No more sad good-byes. "That makes two of us, baby girl."

Tessa caught sight of them as they walked through the party and she came over to give Rosalie a hug. Rosalie slid out of Kade's arms and gave Tess an enthusiastic squeeze. " 'Night, Ms. Tess."

"Good night, chickadee. Thanks for coming to my party."

"Welcome." Rosalie stepped back from the hug and gave Tess a serious look. "My mommy and Chris are going to have a baby."

"I heard that," Tessa said with a smile. "That's so exciting. You're going to be a big sister."

"Yeah, I guess. But mommy said it might be a boy." Rosalie made the *gag me with a spoon* face. "Are you and my daddy going to have a baby, too?"

Tessa's eyes went big and she gave Kade the oh-dear-God-please-help look. "Uh . . ."

Rosalie put her hands on her hips. "'Cause you better have a girl. No brothers, okay?"

Kade had to press his lips together to hold back the laugh. "Okay, enough questions and demands for the night, Spark. Let's get you home."

He left a speechless Tessa behind him and got Rosalie to her mom. By the time he made it back to Tessa, the band had come on stage and the party was in full swing. He let her do her thing, taking care of the guests and directing the staff. He couldn't get enough of watching her in her element—his successful, smart wife brimming with confidence and pride over a job well done. He was more than happy to stand on the sidelines and let her bask in the accolades everyone was giving her. And he almost burst with his own pride when she presented the huge check to the team from Bluebonnet Place. The charity would want for nothing for a long while.

But after the last song was played and the last guest had wandered off for the evening, he was ready to claim what was his. He stepped up behind her as she was gathering a stack of brochures from a table, and she relaxed into his hold.

"Leave everything here and come with me."

"But I have to—"

"Hush."

She turned in his arms and looked up at him, warmth brimming in her gaze. "Sorry, sir."

He grabbed her hand. "It's time to go."

Her brows pinched together, but she let him lead her forward, trusting him to guide her into whatever he had planned. That subtle submissiveness never failed to tug strings inside him. He still couldn't believe the universe had given him this gift. She was his. *His*.

"May I ask where I'm going, sir?"

"Nope."

"Are you going to be with me?"

"Yep."

She leaned into him, and he slipped his arm fully around her. "Then that's all I ever need to know."

He closed his eyes for a moment, letting the words seep into his skin, the rightness of it all soak into his bones. The world had never felt so big and bright and full. The girl he'd dreamed about, angsted over, and lost so long ago was here. Loving him.

His perfect match.

Turns out that bitch, Fate, knew what she was doing after all.

He couldn't wait to see what she had in store for them next.

Keep reading for an excerpt from the next Loving on the Edge novel by Roni Loren

# NOTHING BETWEEN US

*Coming soon from Heat*

## 12:35 A.M.

Georgia Delaune had never been particularly drawn to illegal activity. Or taking risks. Or, okay, fine—sexually deviant behavior. She was woman enough to admit what this was. So finding herself hiding in the dark, peering around the curtains of her second story window with a set of binoculars, should've tipped her off that she was officially losing her shit. But since moving into the house on Fallen Oaks Lane six months earlier, she'd known this moment was coming. Before now, she'd convinced herself that she'd just been catching inadvertent peeks and unintentional glimpses. Her neighbor would surely shut his curtains if he didn't want to risk being seen, right?

She groaned, lowered the binoculars, and pressed her forehead to the window frame. God, now she was blaming the victim. *He gets naked in the confines of his own home. A home that's on a tree-lined corner lot with tons of privacy and a six-foot-tall fence. How dare he!*

This was so screwed up. What if he saw her? He could call the cops and she'd be slapped with some Peeping Tom charge—or

Peeping Tomasina, as the case may be. That'd be an epic disaster. Especially when the cops found no information on a Georgia Delaune. Plus, afterward, she'd have to move because there'd be no facing her neighbor again. Not after he knew what she did at night. And there was no way in hell she was moving. It had taken too much time, effort, and planning to find this spot, to finally feel even a smidgen of security and safety. These walls were her only haven and she had no intention of leaving them.

But despite knowing the risks, when she saw a lamp flick on in the window of Colby Wilkes's bedroom, she found herself dragging a chair over to the window and lifting the binoculars to her eyes. It took a second to adjust the focus, but when the lenses cleared, the broad, wet shoulders of her dark-haired neighbor filled the view. Her stomach dipped in anticipation.

He wasn't alone.

She'd known he had friends over. She'd seen the group going in when she'd closed her living room blinds earlier that night. Two women and three guys, plus Colby. Later, she'd heard water splashing and the murmuring hum of voices so she'd gone into her backyard for a while to listen to the distant sounds of life and laughter. That world seemed so foreign to her now. Being surrounded by people, having friends over, relaxing by the pool. She couldn't see anything from her backyard. Colby's pool area was blocked by the house and bordered by trees. So she'd lain in her lounge chair out back, closed her eyes, and had imagined she was a guest at his party, that she was part of that laughter. And she'd also found herself wondering what would happen afterward.

Now she knew. Colby had stepped into his bedroom, obviously fresh from the pool with his dark hair wet and only a towel knotted around his waist. And he had company with him. One of Colby's friends, a tall blond guy who was also sporting a towel, had followed him in. And then there was a woman. She wore nothing at all. Georgia's lip tucked between her teeth, heat creeping into her face. She *so* shouldn't be watching this. But she couldn't turn away. She'd learned rather quickly that her dear neighbor, despite his affable grin, Southern-boy charm, and straight-laced job, was a freak in the bedroom. Threesomes were only part of it. After her last relationship, it should've turned her off, sent her running. Guys with secrets. Fuck no.

But the first time she'd caught sight of Colby bringing a flogger down on a lover's back, Georgia had been transfixed. She'd been completely stuck on her latest writing project at the time. But after watching Colby drive a woman into a writhing, begging state, Georgia had gone into her office, opened a new document, and had written until the sun had broken through the curtains the next morning. Before she knew it, her thriller-in-progress had taken a decidedly erotic turn. Thankfully, her editor had loved the new direction. So now Georgia, in her guiltiest moments, told herself these stolen moments at the window were all in the name of book research.

Yeah. Even her sleep-deprived brain didn't buy that one.

The guilt wasn't enough to make her stop, though. Especially now when Colby was grabbing for the knot on his towel. She held her breath. The terry cloth fell to the floor at Colby's feet, and everything inside Georgia went tight. *Holy heaven above.* She'd watched—oh, how she'd watched—but never before had she been able to see everything in such intimate detail. The binoculars transported her, took her by the hand and dragged her into that room with those strangers. Colby was right there in front of her—strong, beautiful, aroused. His hand wrapped around his cock and stroked ever so slowly, taunting her with unashamed confidence. No, not her. The woman. God, Georgia should look away. But need rolled through her like thunder from an oncoming storm, her fingers tightening around the binoculars.

The other man had stripped, too, and although he was gorgeous in his own right with his polished, movie-star good looks, Georgia was drawn to the rough-around-the-edges brawn of her neighbor. Every part of Colby hinted at the wildness he hid beneath his surface—dark wavy hair that was a little too long, the ever present stubble that shadowed his jaw, and a body that looked like he could bench press a Buick. He was the opposite of the pressed and creased, Armani-clad businessmen she'd been attracted to in her former life. He was the guy you'd be wary of on first glance if you ran into him in a dark alley—the cowboy whose hat-color you couldn't quite determine straightaway.

Perhaps that was why she was so fascinated with him. She'd learned that danger often hid behind the gloss of an urbane smile and perfectly executed Windsor knot. Colby had none of that. But regardless of the reason for her attraction, she couldn't stem the crackle of jealousy that went through her as the other man laced his fingers in the woman's hair and guided her to take Colby into her mouth.

The view of Colby's erection disappearing between the lips of some other woman was erotic. There was no denying that. But it also made Georgia's jaw clench a little to hard. She could tell, even from the brief moments she'd been watching, that this woman was with Colby's friend. They were a couple and Colby the third party. But it still activated Georgia's *He's mine, bitch!* reflex.

Georgia sniffed at her ridiculous, territorial reaction, and tried to loosen the tension gathering in her neck. *Sure, he's yours, girl. You can't walk down the street without swallowing a pill first, much less go on a date if he was even interested in the weird, spying chick next door.*

But she shoved the thought away. She didn't want anything tainting these few precious minutes. This wasn't about dates. Only when she stood at this window did she feel even a glimmer of her former self. This was her gossamer-thin lifeline to who she used to be, to the capable and confident woman who would've never hidden in the dark.

Before long, the blond man eased the woman away from Colby

and guided her toward himself, taking his turn. Georgia lifted the binoculars upward, finding Colby's face instead of focusing on the scene between the other man and his woman. What she found lurking in his expression wasn't what she expected. There was heat in Colby's eyes, interest for sure, but as she stared longer, she sensed a distance in those hazel depths. Like he was there with them but other . . . separate. Alone. It probably was only because the other two were a couple. Or maybe it was just Georgia's mind slapping labels on things to make herself feel better. But regardless, it made her chest constrict with recognition. She didn't know what it'd be like to be in a threesome. Or how it would feel to have a lover kneeling at her feet like he did. But she knew loneliness. And for those few seconds, she was convinced Colby did, too. She pressed her fingertip against the cool glass of the window, tracing the outline of Colby's face. Needing to touch . . . something.

The glass may as well have been made of steel, the yards between the houses made of miles.

But she couldn't walk away. The night went on and there she sat, watching the three lovers move to the bed, the woman being cuffed to the headboard. The two men lavished her with hands and mouths and tongues. It was like watching a silent symphony, the arching of the woman's back the only thing Georgia needed to see to know exactly how these men were affecting their willing captive. The melancholy feelings that had stirred earlier had quickly been surpassed by ones much more base and primal. Georgia could feel her body growing hot and restless, her panties going damp.

When Colby braced himself between the woman's thighs and entered her, Georgia trained the binoculars on his face, unable to handle the image of him having sex with another woman. Her mind was developing quite the ability to focus on the fantasy and block out the unwanted parts. She only had a view of Colby's profile, but she watched with rapt attention as his jaw worked and his skin went slick with sweat instead of pool water.

Without giving it too much thought, she braced one elbow on the window ledge to hold the binoculars steady and let her other hand drift downward. Her cotton nightgown slid up her thighs easily. Somewhere her brain protested that this was wrong—sick and sad. She had a perfectly functioning vibrator in her bedside drawer. She had an imagination strong enough to fuel an orgasm without doing this, without watching the man next door screw another woman. But her starved libido didn't seen to give a damn about morals or ethics or pride right now. There was need. And a solution. Simple as that.

As Colby's lips parted with a sound she could only imagine, Georgia's fingers found the edge of her panties and slipped beneath the material. Her body tightened at the touch and the little gasp she made reverberated in the dead silence of her bedroom. Colby's head dipped between his shoulders, and Georgia imagined it was her he was whispering passionate words to. That deep Houston drawl telling her how good it felt to be inside her, how sexy she was, how he was going to make her come. He would be a dirty talker, she had no doubt. No sweet nothings from Colby Wilkes.

She closed her eyes for a moment as she moved her fingers in the rhythm of Colby's thrust—long, languid strokes that had a fire building from her center and radiating heat outward. It wouldn't take long. Her body was already singing with sensation, release hurtling toward her. But she wouldn't go over alone. She forced her eyes open, the binoculars still in her grip, and found Colby again. His dark hair was curling against his neck, sweat glistening at his temples. And she knew he had to be close, too. Every muscle in his shoulders and back had tensed. All of her attention zeroed in on him, and in her mind, the touch of her own fingers morphed into his—his hands and body moving against her, inside her.

Every molecule in her body seemed to contract, preparing for the burst of energy to come. Her breath quickened, her heartbeat pounding in her ears. And right as she was about to close her eyes and go over, Colby jerked his head to the side toward the window. His hazel gaze collided with hers through the binoculars—a dead-on eye lock that seemed to reach inside Georgia and flip her inside out. *He knows.*

But she was too far gone for the shock to derail her. Orgasm careened through her with a force that made the chair scrape back across the wood floor. She moaned into the quiet, the binoculars slipping from her hand and jerking the strap around her neck. The part in the curtains fell shut, but she didn't notice. Everything was too bright behind her eyelids, too good, to worry about anything else but the way she felt in those long seconds. *Enjoy. Don't think. Just feel.* The words whispered through her as her fingers kept moving, her body determined to eke out every ounce of sensation she could manage.

But, of course, the blissful, mindless moments couldn't last forever. Chilly reality made a swift reappearance as her gown slipped back down her thighs and sweat cooled on her skin. She sat there, staring at the closed curtain and listening to her thumping heart. Colby *couldn't* know, right? His gaze had felt intense and knowing because the binoculars had made him seem so close. But her window was dark, her curtains darker, and the moon was throwing off enough light that it would make the glass simply reflect back the glow.

But her chest felt like a hundred hummingbirds had roosted there, beating their wings against her ribs. She wet her lips and swallowed past the constriction in her throat. She had to look. Would her neighbor be striding over here to demand what was going on? Would he be disgusted? Embarrassed? Angry?

God, she didn't even want to think about it. She wanted to turn around, get in bed, and hide under the covers. But that's all her life had turned into now—hiding. And though she couldn't fix that situation, she refused to create another one. So she forced herself to lean forward and peel the curtains back one more time, leaving the binoculars hanging around her neck.

What she saw made the hummingbirds thrash more. Colby wasn't even in the room anymore. His friend was now with the woman in the bed, and both seemed totally absorbed in each other. Did that mean that Colby had left and was heading this way to confront her? She was about to go to the front of the house to check the yard but then paused when she realized nothing had changed about the view. Nothing at all. If Colby had been concerned about a nosy neighbor, he hadn't bothered to close the curtains or warn his friends. Surely, he would've done that.

She sat there, debating and worrying, but soon Colby returned to the bedroom. The man and woman had finished. Colby had on a pair of boxers and had brought clean towels in for everyone. He didn't look concerned. He didn't glance over at the window. He seemed perfectly relaxed as he helped untie the woman's hands, kissed her forehead in a friendly gesture, and then left his friends to sleep alone.

Georgia let out a long breath, sagging in the chair.

He didn't know.

She should stop taking this risk. Throw away the binoculars, put a bookcase in front of this damn window, and stop while she was ahead.

But she knew she wouldn't. She would find herself here again.

Because if she didn't have her secret nights with Colby Wilkes, what was left?

Four walls, long days, and fear.

She needed this. She just had to make sure he never found out.

Keep reading for an excerpt from the steamy Loving on the Edge serial by Roni Loren, now in complete novel edition

# NOT UNTIL YOU

*Coming soon from Heat*

"Andre, this isn't a good time. Can I call you back?"

I did my best not to let my cell phone slip from between my ear and shoulder. *Just don't drop the tequila.* I adjusted the enormous bottle that my friend Bailey had given me as a graduation present from my right hand to beneath my left arm and tried to dig my keys out of my purse so I could open the main door to my apartment building.

"I'm so sorry I wasn't able to make it, Cela," my older brother said, his guilt obviously trumping my request to call him later. "I got caught at an investigation site this morning. I thought I'd be able to get there in time, but we had a witness wanting to talk and . . ."

I cursed silently as my keys hit the pavement. I crouched down, doing my best not to flash my underwear to anyone who may be passing by. "Really, it's fine. They called my name. I walked across the stage and got a piece of paper and a sash for being summa cum laude. Papá yelled my name like he was at a baseball game instead of a ceremony. Mamá cried. We all went to lunch at

Rosario's and then the two of them headed back to the airport. Not that interesting."

My brother's heavy sigh said everything. I almost felt guilty that *he* felt so guilty. "Before you move back home next month, we're getting together to celebrate. My baby sister, the doctor. I'm so proud I could burst."

I smiled. I did like the sound of that. Dr. Marcela Medina, Doctor of Veterinary Medicine. Seven years of exams and studying and clinics, but it was finally done. Now it was time to leave Dallas and head back home to Verde Pass and take up the slack in my dad's practice.

That last part had my smile faltering a bit. I hooked my key ring with my finger and wobbled back to a stand. "That sounds great. But I really have to get going. I have my hands full and need to get through the door."

"Cela, you know better than to carry too much. Parking lots at night are one of the most dangerous places for women. Are you holding your mace?" he asked, his voice going into that bossy cop tone I was all too familiar with.

"It's in my hand," I lied, trying to remember where I'd stowed the last little canister he'd given me—probably in my junk drawer. "But I don't have a free hand to pull the door open."

"All right," he said, placated. "Congratulations again. I love you."

"Love you, too."

The call ended but I didn't have a way to take the phone off my ear, so I just shuffled forward in a sideways hunch, trying to juggle everything I was holding to get my key into the door. After two attempts, I got the lock turned and pressed my back against the glass door to push my way into the lobby.

As soon as I'd cleared the entrance and turned toward the stairs, male voices sounded behind me. Of course someone would show up right after I didn't need help anymore. I peeked back to see who it was, Andre's danger warnings still echoing in my head, but found something more distracting than criminals—my neighbors, Foster and Pike.

Foster stepped through the main door first and glanced my way. As usual, everything went melty inside me, his smile like a zap of heat to my system. Ridiculous. "Need some help, neighbor?"

I straightened, but forgot about my phone in the process. My brand new iPhone went sliding off my shoulder.

"Crap!" I lurched forward, trying to save it from its imminent demise, and accidentally dropped my plastic bag of Chinese takeout on the way.

"Whoa, there." Pike, Foster's roommate, was at my side in a second. His hand caught my elbow, saving me from losing the ginormous bottle of liquor along with my balance. But my phone clattered to the ground, the harsh sound mixing with the *splat* of my noodles hitting tile.

I winced, anticipating a broken screen. "Dammit."

Foster bent down, his tie brushing the ground as he swept my phone off the floor. He peered at the screen, dark brows lowering over pale eyes, then he turned the phone toward me—the happy puppy screensaver staring back at me intact. "All is well. Luckily, these things are built to take a licking."

My brain got snagged on the word *lick*, and the back of my neck went hot. My lips parted, but words failed me. *Great, imitate a gaping goldfish—that's cute.*

Pike cleared his throat, easing the tequila from my arms, and then crouched down near the open bag at my feet. He grabbed a noodle from the spilled box of Chinese food, tipped his head back, and dropped the noodle into his mouth, his eyes watching mine. "The lo mein's a loss, though."

I swallowed hard, his gaze even more bad boy than the tattoos peeking out from his open collar. His pierced tongue snaked around the noodle. *Look away.* I forced my face upward, but then ended up focusing on Foster again. *Say something.* God, I was standing there like an idiot. This was why I always avoided these two like they were contagious. They made me go stupid.

Foster held out my phone, and I managed to take it, the slight brush of his fingers against mine hitting the Reset button in my brain. I managed a feeble, "Thank you."

Foster glanced at the mess on the floor. "I'm really sorry I said anything. I didn't mean to distract you from your intricate juggling act."

I shook my head. "No, it's my fault. I shouldn't have been trying to carry everything at once. It's been a long day, and I was hoping to save myself a second trip up the stairs."

"The joys of a walk-up." Pike grabbed a few napkins and started cleaning up the noodles at my feet like it was his mess to worry about.

"Oh, you don't have to do that." I lowered down to my knees. "I'll take care of it."

He grinned over at me, the mirror opposite of his roommate. Ian Foster was all suits and dark looks—a man who preferred to be called by his surname. Whereas Pike didn't seem to even have a last name. He was a drummer in some popular local band—jeans, a sex-on-the-mind smile, and spiked, bleached hair his usual uniform. Not that I had studied either of them. Or listened to their escapades through the wall I shared with them. Not at all.

*Keep telling yourself that, Cela.*

Despite my protest, Pike helped me finish picking up the mess. "So what's the big-ass bottle of tequila for? No one could've had that bad of a day."

I glanced over at the bottle I'd set on the floor, debating whether I could be trusted to have a normal conversation with these two without sounding like I had a speech impediment. "I, uh, graduated today. It was a gift."

"Oh, right on."

"Congratulations, Cela," Foster said. Just the sound of him

saying my name in that smooth, dark voice had my stomach clenching. He was all Southern refinement, but I didn't miss the glimmer of a drawl underneath it all.

*Ay dios mío.* My body clamored to attention like an eager Labrador ready to be petted. *Down, girl.* These guys were way above my pay grade. I wasn't dumb or delusional. I'd seen/spied on/secretly hated the women who'd passed through their apartment door—women who looked like they'd earned their doctorates in the art of seduction.

I hadn't even reached the kindergarten level in that particular department.

"Thank you."

"You were going to vet school at Dallas U, right?" Foster had tucked his hands in the pockets of his slacks, and though the question was casual, I had the distinct impression he was tense beneath that suit jacket.

Pike handed me a napkin for my hands and stood to toss the food into a nearby trash can.

I wiped off my hands and pushed myself to my feet, trying to do it as gracefully as possible in my restrictive skirt. "Yes, how'd you know that?"

"The scrubs you wear have the school insignia on them," Foster said, as if it was totally normal that he'd looked at me that closely.

"Observant." Especially considering I usually only managed a head-down, mumbled, hey-how-are-ya exchange when we passed each other in the hallway. Secretly listening to one of your hot neighbors having sex had a way of making eye contact a bit uncomfortable the next day—particularly if said eavesdropper had used the soundtrack to fuel her own interlude with her battery-operated boyfriend.

Not that I had. Several times. Whatever.

Pike sidled up next to Foster—a motley pair if there ever was one. "So, doc, now that you've got no dinner and clearly too much liquor on your hands, why don't you join us? We already have pizza on the way, and we can play a drinking game with the tequila. Do college kids still play Never Have I Ever? I was always good at that one."

Kid? Is that what they saw me as? Neither of them could be *that* much older than I was. Though in terms of life experience, I had no doubt they trumped me a few times over.

"Oh, no, that's okay." The refusal was automatic, long practiced. How many times had I turned down such offers—from guys, from friends? My parents had been so strict when I was younger that I almost didn't know how to say yes even after living on my own the last few years. Studies first. Fun later. Yet, there never seemed to be any time for fun after the first one was finished.

"You sure? I don't want you going to bed with no dinner because of us," Foster said, frown lines marring that perfect mouth of his.

*Going to bed* and *us* was about all I heard. My father's stern voice whispered in my ear. *You don't know these men. You'll be all alone in their apartment. Medina women have more respect for themselves than that.*

"Really, I'm fine. I had a big lunch," I said, my smile brief, plastic. "But thanks."

"Oh, come on," Pike said, his tone cajoling. "We've been neighbors for what, two years? We should at least get to know a little about each other."

Get to know each other? I knew that Foster was loud when he came—even if he was alone. Knew that Pike liked to laugh during sex. Knew the two men shared women. And the other sounds I'd heard over the last two years . . . the smacks, the commands, the erotic screams. My face went as hot as if I'd stuck my head in an oven.

"Y'all just want me for my tequila," I said, attempting to deflect my derailing thoughts.

The corner of Pike's mouth lifted. "Of course that's not all we want you for."

"Uh . . ." *Oh, hell.* Pictures flashed across my brain. Dirty, delicious pictures. I almost dropped my phone again. I had no idea what to do with my hands, my expression.

Foster put a hand on Pike's shoulder. "The lady said no. I think we should let her go celebrate her graduation however she wants."

"All right." Pike's face turned hangdog, but he handed me the tequila bottle. "If you change your mind, we've got big plans. Supreme pizza and a *Star Wars*–themed porn marathon. *The Empire Sucks C—*"

Foster smacked the back of Pike's head, and Pike ducked and laughed.

"Kidding. I mean, a Jane Austen marathon," Pike corrected, his green-gold eyes solemn. *"Pride and Pu—"*

Foster was behind Pike, his hand clamping over his friend's mouth in a flash. "I seriously can't take him out. He's like an untrained puppy. Maybe you can lend me a shock collar or something."

Pike waggled his eyebrows, all playful wickedness.

I laughed, putting my hand to my too hot forehead, and turning toward the stairs. "Yeah, so, I'm going to go now."

"Cela," Foster said as I put my foot onto the first step.

I glanced back. "Yeah?"

His ice-melt eyes flicked downward, his gaze alighting along the length of me before tracing their way upward again in a slow, unashamed perusal. "Promise you won't go to bed hungry."

I wet my lips, my skin suddenly feeling too tight to accommodate the blood pumping beneath it, and nodded.

But it was a lie.

I always went to bed hungry.

And it had nothing to do with a spilled dinner.

**Roni Loren** wrote her first romance novel at age fifteen when she discovered writing about boys was way easier than actually talking to them. Since then, her flirting skills haven't improved, but she likes to think her storytelling ability has. Though she'll forever be a New Orleans girl at heart, she now lives in Dallas with her husband and son. If she's not working on her latest sexy story, you can find her reading, watching reality television, or indulging in her unhealthy addiction to rock stars, er, rock concerts. Yeah, that's it. Visit her website: roniloren.com.